SC~~ the BILLIONAIRE~~

BILLIONAIRE
Bad Boys
BOOK THREE

max monroe

Scoring the Billionaire (Billionaire Bad Boys, #3)
Published by Max Monroe LLC © 2016, Max Monroe

ISBN-13: 978-1539492320
ISBN-10: 153949232X

All rights reserved.

Without limiting the rights under copyright reserved above, no part of this publication may be reproduced, stored in or introduced into a retrieval system, or transmitted, in any form, or by any means (electronic, mechanical, photocopying, recording, or otherwise) without the prior written permission of both the copyright owner and the above publisher of this book.

This is a work of fiction. Names, characters, places, brands, media, and incidents are either the product of the author's imagination or are used fictitiously. The author acknowledges the trademarked status and trademark owners of various products referenced in this work of fiction, which have been used without permission. The publication/use of these trademarks is not authorized, associated with, or sponsored by the trademark owners.

Editing by Silently Correcting Your Grammar and
Indie Solutions by Murphy Rae

Formatting by Champagne Formats

Cover Design by Perfect Pear Creative

Photo Credit David Vance Photographer

DEDICATION

To tears.

We cried a lot of you during the making of this book, both for personal and professional struggles and triumph.

If not for your salty hydration, we probably would have died a slow and painful death. And then we'd have to be *real* ghost writers.

So thank you.

In the future, though, we'd really appreciate if you made a bigger effort to taste like wine—or vodka.

INTRO

Wes

I'm Wes Lancaster.

The third "Billionaire Bad Boy," as it were.

I own the New York Mavericks, BAD Restaurant, am a silent investor in several start-up companies across the United States, and yeah, I'm worth three or four billion dollars.

Sounds like the same old story, right?

I'll admit, even to me—who'd rather not lump himself into the Billionaire Bad Boy heap with the likes of Thatcher Kelly—the basics are startlingly similar. But the difference between Thatch, Kline, and me is that they keep avid track of each dollar—granted, their reasons vary greatly from one another—and I've never been one to focus on the numbers. I know a ballpark figure, and I know what that ballpark figure means.

It means freedom.

Freedom to live my life as I please, spend money tastefully but often, and enjoy all the things I appreciate with abandon. Women, cars, travel, and time—each and every one can be mine on my terms.

I like the **control**. I like the **escapism**. I like being **in charge of**

my own life.

Money may not buy happiness, but it definitely buys opportunity. For me, that opportunity comes in many forms, the most notable being my ability to live the dream of owning a National Football League team. My staff knows by the level of my involvement—something they like to whisper creative epithets about—that the desire to do so has absolutely nothing to do with the money and position and everything to do with being a part of the experience. I've overheard the very technical description of "annoyingly present" more than once—and *god-fucking-dammit, he's here again; this is horseshit* even more than that.

But now my interest has grown deeper, more complexly woven into the staff—specifically Winnie Winslow, the new team physician—and not only do I not stay away; I *can't*.

She's everything I don't want.

Strong-willed. Demanding. A mother to a young child.

But as it turns out, maybe the joke is on me. My brain says she'll ruin everything, but my heart says she's *everything I can't live without.*

Normally my brain rules the day, making the important decisions and keeping me from the certain agony a romantic entanglement would bring to my life. But apparently, now, there's a new, beating, four-chambered fuck-of-a-guy in charge.

He says this is the last time this book is about me because now, thanks to Winnie and Lexi Winslow, I'm a very big *we*.

This is *us*.

CHAPTER 1

Wes

The halls were busy, staffers running from the cafeteria to meetings and players making their way from the locker room to the weight room or the field, and each person I passed acknowledged me with a nod.

I appreciated the effort, but I actually hated the attention. It meant I had to watch myself, my expressions, my reactions—be whom they expected, which sometimes wasn't who I was.

But just as I'd built the machine that was the current operations of this team, I'd constructed my reputation all on my own. Stoic. Unemotional. Unswayable, unflappable, hard-to-rile Wes Lancaster.

It scared me how often my insides were the exact opposite—rolling turmoil that kept the contents of my stomach only seconds away from making an appearance.

My relationship with God was tenuous and largely lacking in effort on my part, but I'd still lost count of how many times I'd thanked him for the power of perception and strong esophageal control.

Overhead, the lights flickered and hissed as one of the bulbs strained to avoid the end of its life. I made a mental note to notify maintenance as soon as I finished my rounds.

Much like every other team in the league, we operated on a schedule, with certain players, be it special teams, skill positions, defensive linemen, etcetera going different places at different times. When the cafeteria closed down the breakfast service in an hour, everyone on the team would be somewhere—a meeting, a final practice, at weight lifting, or getting medical advisement or attention. Wednesdays on travel weeks needed to run even more smoothly than any other day, as the whole team would need to be out and ready in a timely fashion so that they could prepare for travel tomorrow.

And this week, we were headed to Miami. Hot, sunny, skimpy-clothes-inducing Miami. *Please, fuck, let there be some sort of bikini-wearing opportunity for Winnie Winslow,* my dick chimed in with a wink and an overly enthusiastic nod before my brain could stop it.

Goddammit.

I'd hired her as the team physician, but she'd just as quickly become my obsession, my weakness, and my distraction. Witty, thrilling exchanges laced with an edge of anger I couldn't stop picturing in the bedroom took up way too much space in my mind for the amount of interaction we'd had. Thrown together in mostly professional circumstances, we hadn't so much as touched for the first few weeks of our erotic dance of torturous teasing. Even now, we were still in the infancy of intimacy, a fledgling friendship that hovered on the edge of acquaintances.

In fact, the most contact we'd had was the soft slip of her hand in mine during Thatch and Cassie's shotgun nuptials a few weeks ago. But innocent or not, ever since, I'd become irrationally fixated on the drive to once again feel her skin on mine. It was unnatural at best, but troubling was more likely as I'd involuntarily begun to completely avoid the company of other women.

I'd actually tried to force it for the first week after our return, but as that time bled into this, and the days at work got longer and longer, my body stopped being cooperative.

That's right. Without the incentive of Winnie's touch, my dick has stopped responding. And yes, my little problem did make itself known in the most embarrassing way possible, at the very worst time. The only thing I have to be thankful for is that the particular woman had made my acquaintance before and knew it was an entirely new problem. Of course, I went home to my hand and a most explicitly detailed fantasy of Winnie Winslow, and the fucker reacted to that just fine.

"Trust me," I heard Winnie say as I rounded the corner into the hall that led directly to our training room. Open call for players with injuries or medical needs opened up at six a.m., which was nearly an hour ago. An hour's worth of restraint felt like it took Herculean effort, but the camel's back had finally buckled—I'd run out of control… and metaphors.

I had to see her. *That rough but sweet voice. The fervor in her every comment.* I wanted the feeling it gave me when she directed all of it at me.

Luckily, touching base in any and all meetings and locations was normal for me, the "helicopter boss," so the only one who would know what a fool I was would be me.

Despite the internal embarrassment of losing the battle with myself to stay away, my step got decidedly peppier. If Thatch had paid witness, comments would have been made, and I would have communicated both verbally and otherwise that he should fuck right off. But he wasn't, and all that separated me from looking Winnie dead in her heated eyes was the rest of this stupid hallway.

"I know more about you than I've ever wanted to know, Martinez," Winnie went on, her commanding voice carrying easily down the empty hall. "Google is altogether way too informative."

"I think she's saying she's seen your dick, Teen. And by the sound of it, I'm thinking your nickname isn't the only thing that's teeny," a jovial, young male voice said.

Commotion rang out, hoots and hollers and overall mayhem echoing out the door and down the hall to my ears.

"Whoa," Winnie said loudly through a laugh. "Pick up your pants, Teen. I didn't see your penis, I don't want to see your penis, *goddammit*, put away your penis."

The room sounded rowdy with all the answering chuckles, and I found myself quickening my already brisk steps in order to make it to the end of the hall a little faster.

"Penis, Doc?" I heard one of the other guys ask. "That's very clinical."

I paused just outside the door as she responded. "That's right. Clinical. The only reason I'll be looking at your penis is if you break it during a game. A penis is only a dick or a cock if I'm seeing it socially."

"The way you say that makes my penis feel very sociable, Dr. Winslow," Mitchell teased, and the other guys muttered and mumbled their agreement.

"Sorry, Cam," Winnie clucked with a stern take on playful. "My calendar's all booked up."

Despite all reason, I smiled as I stepped into the room and discovered about half a dozen more players than I was expecting. Evidently, half of them knew better than to sexually goad their physician just because she was a woman. With some internal coaxing, I forced my expression to something gloomier.

With this many sets of eyes, a smile—on my normally hard face—would be way too noticeable.

Several of the guys straightened up in both stance and attitude.

I could joke and jest with the best of them in my private life, with my friends, and in the comfort of family, but they didn't know that version of me. They all knew the persona I portrayed on this side of the glass—at work, to the media, to women—and as their boss, I wouldn't necessarily think their recent conversation and behavior fell on the right side of the line between what was acceptable and what wasn't.

Quinn Bailey, the best quarterback we'd had in years and an accent-wielding Southern boy to boot, however, didn't budge, his mouth curving up into a smile as Winnie finished wrapping his wrist.

A job he, without a doubt, could have completed himself.

"Yo, Mr. L," he called, and—I couldn't help it—I smiled. The fucker was too goddamn likable. I wasn't sure if it was his shaggy but still-clean-looking hair or the genuineness of the hook at the corner of his amused mouth, but he just wasn't a guy you could stay mad at.

"Isn't it your turn in the training room?" I asked him, but his smirk only deepened. We both knew it was, and he read right into all the inappropriate things that had prompted me to ask a little too fucking well.

Winnie Winslow and her unbelievable legs. And eyes and hair and face. *Fuck*.

Every single glorious part of her and all the things I thought about each one seemed to hang between us like very delicate bombs waiting to detonate. His scrutiny had a greater effect than making the moment awkward, though—it forced me to acknowledge something I otherwise refused.

I'd been spending a whole hell of a lot more time on this side of the Hudson River, conveniently located at one beautiful female physician's place of employment, which also happened to be a workplace where I was the boss. Nearly every goddamn day for the last three weeks.

And, as I studied the line of Winnie's throat and followed the skin as far as I could into the neck of her shirt, it was abundantly clear why the stadium suddenly held so much goddamn appeal.

And if Quinn and I had noticed, as one of the very few employees in the Manhattan office with me, Georgia probably had too.

Fuck. Where one half of the Brooks power couple went, the other shortly followed.

It was only a matter of time before Kline and Thatch were kidnapping me and torturing me with pillow fights and padded bras until I confessed all of my Winnie Winslow-themed sins.

What? Is that not how female sleepovers go?

"Is there something I can help you with, Wes?" Winnie called, pulling me from both my fantasies and my nightmares and bringing the training room into stark refrain.

Several sets of eyes were on me, and more than one was curious. I was hoping it was the fluorescent lights that made Winnie's seem so challenging—unflattering lighting and all.

A smirk ghosted her pink lips, pulling them together in the softest of purses when she noticed how good a job she'd done at making me uncomfortable.

Jesus, my brain told my dick. *Do you see this? We don't need this.*

I tightened my jaw against the litany of inappropriate, telling words I wanted to spew.

"Nope," I said instead. "Just making my rounds. Heard word of you Googling pictures of players' penises, and I had to see for myself."

Okay, so maybe my jaw didn't quite contain *all* of the inappropriate words.

A couple of guys burst out laughing, but the smart ones just watched, looking between us with big, bowling-ball-round eyes.

I'd one hundred percent, unmistakably broken character. Wes Lancaster of old—the one whose blood flowed freely throughout his body rather than congregating traitorously in his dick—never would have said that to an employee. Not in private and definitely not in public.

Martinez took it as liberty to continue their rhetoric, moving to push his pants down off of his hips.

Winnie caught sight of it out of the corner of her eye—her focus was pretty plainly, angrily on me—and let out a ladylike shriek.

"Jesus, Teeny! No. I didn't Google your penis. Do *not* show it to me."

"What exactly did you Google?" I asked, unable to stop myself. And fuck, the damage was already at least partially done.

Winnie sighed heavily, leaned a hip into the exam table, and crossed her arms over her abundant chest.

Every goddamn set of eyes in the room went right to the exposed skin there.

As I used the clench of my fists as a tranquilizer, I looked around the room to see every man working to contain his ridiculously large reaction to a very simple movement. Discreet adjustments and subtle shifting of hips. If bells were attached to our arousal, we wouldn't have been able to think for all the ringing.

God, we really were animals. You'd have thought she flashed a nipple, but she was actually wearing a very business-appropriate white blouse that covered everything.

It's just that when we (men) try enough, our vision is X-ray adaptable. Shh. Don't tell anyone.

"Stats. Past injuries. Athletic history," she replied with a raise of her eyebrows and a challenge in her eyes. She wouldn't back down. I knew it as well as I knew the back of my own hand, that every hit I delivered she'd volley right back. Every demand I had, she'd assuage, and every fucking fantasy I had for the next ten years, she would play a starring role in.

I hated that I wanted her so badly.

I never want this feeling to end.

I wanted to keep prodding, to find out the whole story. But any viable excuse for being here had just about dried up, and I'd already completely spent my allotment of unprofessional behavior for the day.

"Well, I'll let you guys get back to it." I got several nods and chin jerks without pause, everything seemingly back to normal, and Winnie seemed to take a deep breath for the first time since I'd arrived.

A sign that I affected her too.

I moved to the door and turned back just before crossing the threshold, asking the room the only thing the Wes of old would care about. "Ready for Miami?"

Cheers and curses and several derogatory statements about the people in Miami and the city in general filled the room raucously.

Thank God we had an away game this weekend.

I'd be way too busy to worry about Winnie Winslow.

CHAPTER 2

Winnie

Being in Miami for two straight days had made me more than thankful I lived in New York. The humidity was thick enough to choke on, and don't even get me started on the heat. For the past forty-eight hours, I'd perspired more than the jocks I took care of. More than the geysers in our beloved Yellowstone National Park. More than one of those fake rain fountains Joey thought made a good decoration for his apartment on *Friends*.

Lord Almighty, I'd even switched my preferred Secret deodorant out for an overpriced stick of Old Spice from the hotel gift shop. Smelling like a man was far more appealing than smelling like a sweaty foot. Plus, I couldn't stand to contort myself under one more goddamn hand dryer trying to alleviate the growing wet circles rolling out from my armpits like a wave.

Luckily for me—and my clothes—and likely by very calculated design, the Mavericks had played a night game under the lights versus an afternoon game under the blazing Florida sun. Early season like this, I would have ended up looking more *roasted red pepper* than *golden goddess*.

We'd kicked some serious football ass, shutting out Miami with a score of twenty-four to nothing, and I made no qualms about claiming that victory as partially my own. I was new to the game, but I put minds at ease and provided temporary relief so minorly injured players could keep going. I was a very small cog in the Mavericks wheel, but there nonetheless.

Quinn Bailey had played an impressive game, ending the night with three touchdowns and three hundred passing yards, and our defense fought tooth and nail every single down, preventing Miami from capitalizing on even a field goal. I was proud of these guys who were quickly, and quite surprisingly, becoming some of my favorite people. Concealing my squeal of excitement on the sidelines took concerted effort all game long, but I had a reputation to uphold. One that wasn't off base in the slightest, but had become essential to my effectiveness as a leader of this team.

Surrounded by a bunch of burly, rambunctious football players, it worked best to be the take-no-shit, tough broad who could run as one of the guys—but was smarter than all of them put together. And I had a feeling growing up as the little sister to four obnoxious, older brothers had prepared me for that.

I was only six months into this role as the Mavericks' team physician, but for the most part, I loved my new job. I loved the schedule and the fact that I no longer had to deal with crazy on-call hours at the hospital, and I even enjoyed the occasional travel requirements. And most importantly, thanks to clear expectations and familiar ground, I loved that I felt at home.

In fact, the only thing that made me feel unsettled at all was a *someone*—Wes Lancaster.

I couldn't even say that the way he made me feel completely mixed up was all bad—or bad at all. God, if I was honest, the feeling was nothing short of good.

But he was my boss, and more than that, he was probably the least appropriate man on the whole entire planet to be lusting over.

Unreadable, cocky, confident to the point of goddamn annoying…and so opposed to a commitment with a woman with children, I'd paid witness to him saying it more than once.

I just wish my body could understand the motherfucking slop mix of English-Spanish my brain had adopted since landing in Miami.

No bueno, Winnie. Not this asshole. Comprende? it had asked as I'd caught myself staring at his veiny, tan, way too exposed forearms under the beating sun at the final practice.

If the self-induced, Wes Lancaster-inspired orgasm I gave myself in the quick, lukewarm shower I'd just taken was any indication…no. It did not *comprende* even a little.

Shaking off thoughts of unavailable men and all the complications of horndogging the fuck out of them, I hit Remy's number on speed dial to check on my six-year-old daughter, Lexi.

Rem was the oldest in our brood of five, and no doubt he was Lexi's favorite uncle—though, I made sure to downplay his status when I spoke directly to him.

He doted on her constantly and took every opportunity to babysit, which benefited me greatly when the Mavericks had me traveling to away games. It also helped that he was single and not keen on commitment—I seemed to be drowning in this particular subset of men—and generally worked from home as a day trader. He rivaled Cassie's husband Thatch in the whole *good with numbers and investments* department, but he lacked in enthusiasm, and as a result, his bank account didn't end in nearly as many zeroes. Then again, neither did mine—or practically anyone's.

"Hey, hey, little sister," he greeted on the second ring, outing himself spectacularly as the Billy Idol superfan he often tried to hide. "How's Miami?"

"Hot as balls." I groaned, trying to silence "White Wedding" as it droned on uninvited in my head. "The Florida heat makes me thankful for the urine-dyed snow of New York."

He chuckled. "I'm guessing you're only saying that because you've yet to step in urine-dyed snow this year."

He was probably right. I cringed as I thought about how soon that season would be upon us and added buying a new pair of snow boots for both me and Lex to my mental to-do list.

"Looks like your boys played a hell of a game," Remy remarked. "Lex nearly lost her mind when she saw Bailey hit the three-hundred mark for passing yards."

I grinned. Since I had taken the job with the Mavericks, Lex had become fixated on anything and everything NFL football. Her little brain had been relentless in its task of absorbing every single stat like a greedy sponge.

Lex wasn't your average kid—she was well above it. Diagnosed as high-functioning on the autistic spectrum, she was highly intelligent and advanced in things such as math and reading and writing. By the age of two, she had mastered the alphabet and could write out every letter. By the age of three, she had accomplished basic mathematics. By the age of four, she had been able to read. And now, at six years old, she could compute mid-level algebra better than most sophomores in high school.

She had struggles too, but her willingness to compensate in order to overcome was humbling. There was no doubt about it; my daughter's brain was an amazing thing.

"So, how late did you let my daughter stay up tonight, Rem?"

"Not too late. She was in bed by ten."

"Ten?" I questioned, knowing full well she wouldn't have seen Bailey's stats until after the game was over, which had most likely ended a little after ten.

"Okay," he answered with a smile in his voice. "Ten fifteen, tops."

I glanced at the clock on the hotel nightstand and saw 11:35. "You're so full of shit. I bet you just finished reading her a book and tucking her in fifteen minutes ago."

He chuckled again. "I'm sticking to ten fifteen."

"Whatever, asshole," I teased. "You keep letting my daughter stay up past eleven, and I'm going to have to let Ty watch her."

"Lex would never stand for it. She loves me the most."

I laughed. "Hmm…I don't know. She's been talking a lot about Jude lately."

"Shit. Maybe I should wake her up," he grumbled.

"Do that, you die," I threatened, the antics of a brother-sister relationship only maturing slightly over the years. Those two snot-nosed kids were always inside us, waiting to whine about who touched whom first.

"Did you make it back to your hotel okay?" he asked, ignoring my jab and falling straight into his role of playing the typical, overprotective big brother. Out of all four of my brothers, Rem probably tried the hardest to shelter me. With my combination of an absentee father, poor taste in men, and a special-needs child, he hadn't been entirely successful—much to his chagrin.

"Yes, Dad," I teased. "I made it back about forty minutes ago. I'm showered and ready for bed."

"Good," he responded. "I don't want to read about you out partying with a bunch of horny football players in the paper."

"Oh, get over yourself." I scoffed. "If I want to stay out all night and take body shots off our offensive line, that's my business."

"That's not fucking funny."

"Rem." I mimicked his disapproving tone. "I might be your little sister, but I'm also a grown-ass thirty-one-year-old woman. When are you ever going to realize that?"

"Never. You'll always be my little sister."

"You're worse than the rest of them."

"That's because I'm the best brother you have."

"You're the most *annoying* brother I have."

"I'm your favorite brother."

"No way. Jude's my favorite."

"Bullshit."

I laughed. "All right. I'm calling it a night. Have Lex call me in the morning, okay?"

"You got it," he agreed, and despite our teasing and my many minor complaints, I knew in the lottery of life, all four of my brothers were big ol' winning tickets. "Love you, Win."

"Love you too."

I ended the call and decided that a quick trip to the vending machine was in order. A bag of Ruffles and a bottle of Coke had never sounded so good. Since I knew most of the team and staff had gone out for dinner and drinks after the game, I figured I didn't have to worry about my appearance and lack of bra.

Because, seriously, who wore a bra to bed? Not this chick, that was for damn sure.

I tossed my still-wet locks into a messy bun, threw on a pair of sleep shorts and a tank top, slipped on my flip-flops, and headed out of my room with only my credit card—because I was notorious for never having cash in my wallet—and my room key.

God bless the person who made sure vending machines now accepted credit cards. The only downside was the evidence of my gluttony when all of the transactions read out in a list on the statement at the end of the month. Funny how Visa never denied my card on the forty vending machine swipes for suspicious activity.

"Hallelujah," I shouted as I made it to the machine. It was fully stocked with Cheddar and Sour Cream Ruffles, and my excitement was a very real, tangible thing. They were pretty much a lock, but I never confirmed the answer as final until I had all the information. Snacks late at night, to me, were just as good as a chance at a million dollars. As I softly sang "Baby Mine"—Lex's favorite lullaby—to myself, I tapped my fingers against the glass and perused my options.

Pretzels? *Nope. Not in the mood for salted cardboard.*

Skittles? *Maybe.*

Pop-Tarts? *Sounds like breakfast.*

Yeah, Cheddar and Sour Cream Ruffles it is.

Three swipes of my credit card later, I had both hands full of chips and soda and a bag of Skittles for good measure. As I turned for the hallway, my advance was abruptly stopped as I barreled into a hard chest. And I knew it was a chest…a really fucking nice one. There might have been doubt in someone else's mind, but not in the intimacy-starved recesses of mine.

My bag of Ruffles crunched loudly between our bodies, and two strong arms reached out and prevented me from tripping over my flip-flops and tumbling to the carpeted floor by gripping my shoulders and steadying me back on my feet.

My gaze moved *up, up, up* until it met an intense yet very familiar set of hazel eyes.

Wes Lancaster.

"You okay?" he asked, searching my face with concern. The veil he wore nearly constantly was gone, and his expression was at ease in a way I'd never witnessed. No ticking muscle in his jaw, no furrowed brow, just a man in his sleepwear out for a late-night trip to the vending machine.

How…human of him.

He didn't seem nearly as intimidating like this—but his presence was still undeniably imposing. When Wes Lancaster was in a room, he was *in* it.

"Yeah." I nodded, making my lips move around the numb shock. "Sorry about that. I didn't realize anyone was behind me."

How long had he been standing there?

Hopefully, not long enough to hear my off-key singing.

I watched him as he took inventory of my body, slowly moving *down, down, down* until he had pretty much full-on checked me out without shame.

And with that simple action, all the unusual calm of our interaction was gone.

God, he pissed me off. *And* turned me on.

I wanted to smack him. I wanted to kiss him.

I wanted to climb his body like my own personal pole. I was

certain no man had ever evoked this type of bipolar reaction from within me.

When his eyes met mine again, I raised a defiant eyebrow. "All set? Or do you need me to give you a little twirl just to be sure?"

His mouth—his perfect, lush, obscenely kissable mouth—crested into a suggestively wry grin. "Do you want *me* to give a little twirl?" he asked and crossed his thick, muscular arms over his chest. "I wouldn't mind."

I couldn't stop myself—the exact opposite of *out of sight, out of mind,* thanks to his provocation—glancing down at his body and homing in on every perfect inch of his fit form, clad in a simple white cotton T-shirt and black knit shorts. *Christ.* And I'd thought Wes Lancaster made a suit and tie look explicit in the hottest possible way.

Were those perfect forearm veins really necessary?

They'd already gotten me once this weekend, and now again. *Give me a chance here, Universe.*

Between his penetrating yet oddly seductive hazel eyes and his mind-blowing body, I wasn't sure which part of him I enjoyed ogling the most.

My brain practically slapped me.

His ass, Winnie, it chided. *Definitely his ass.*

I couldn't deny his ass was downright bitable, and it wasn't like I had a fetish for sinking my teeth into men's glutes. But for Wes? I could easily make an exception—and maybe end up spiraling into the life of one of those people on *My Strange Addiction.*

"I guess I should turn around?" His question pulled my eyes back to his face. "I know how much you love staring at my ass," he added cockily with a knowing—and *anger-inducing*—wink.

Fucking shit. What, was it written on my forehead? *Jesus, Winnie. Pull it together.*

I rolled my eyes and kept all of my hysteria where it belonged—inside where it could eat at me slowly until I lost my mind one marble at a time. "I do not love staring at your ass."

Obviously, I did. I totally did. But I wasn't going to let him know that shit. When I thought about his ass, it'd be on my own, with a finger to my clit and teeth marks across the entire... *Shit.*

I know. Believe me, I know.
I sound like the horniest chick on the planet, but should I mention that it had been over a year since I'd had sex?
Yeah. One year. It's depressing.

Cassie would've probably used the term "thirsty" to describe my current lack of sex. And God, I was thirsty. Thirsty for the tall drink of water that was Wes Lancaster. Hell, I wouldn't have even used a straw. I'd have guzzled that fucker.

Guzzle? Really? Could I be any cruder?
Note to self: stop spending time with Cassie.

He leaned toward me, and his lips barely brushed my ear. "Tell me, Win. Are you cold, or are you turned on right now?"

"Excuse me?" I asked as I pulled away abruptly, confused and shocked and wondering what that had to do with drinking him up.

His gaze made the slow circuit from my lips to my neck to my chest until it paused, *right there*, directly on the cotton material covering my bra-less breasts.

Jerk. I didn't even have to look to know what he was insinuating. Just because fantasies weren't real didn't mean hormones knew the difference. But for fuck's sake, he could have ignored it. It was common decency.

"Cold," I answered, refusing to give him an inch or show him any inkling of embarrassment by hiding my now very obvious nipples behind my arms.

His eyes met mine again, and I held his stare.

"Are you sure, sweetheart?" He lowered his voice. "Because I think you're turned on. I think you're just as turned on as I am right now."

My mind whispered *asshole, asshole, asshole*, even though my body all but screamed, *touch me, kiss me, fuck me*. My eyes were busy fighting the urge to look down.

"You want me to be turned on," I corrected harshly. "There's a difference between reality and fantasy, *sweetheart*."

"You want me. That's the reality," he responded without shame. His voice was all cocky confidence and self-assurance, and his eyes, well, they blazed. He looked like he'd taken a bite out of the sun.

I thought Miami was hot, but his fucking rays were making me go crazy. With want. With need. With an embarrassing amount of desperation.

We had been walking this line of give-and-take and push-pull for far too long. I felt like I had reached the precipice, and I couldn't stand fighting this—*whatever the hell it was*—any longer. I just wanted him to put his hands on me. I wanted him to touch me. I wanted him to tear my clothes off and mark my body with his lips, his tongue, his cock. I was undeniably attracted to him to the point of being primal. Instinctual. And it had reached the point of irresistible.

"You want me, too," I murmured.

Our eyes danced their familiar game and refused to let go.

His whispered, *Come on. Give in. Do what you want, Win.*

Mine responded, *Just one night. What could go wrong?*

Within seconds, the soda and chips in my hands had hit the floor, and we were kissing, my hands in his hair, him pulling me closer. Our mouths were entangled in a tug-of-war, each of us trying to overpower the other. I bit into his bottom lip as his strong hands gripped my ass and lifted me up, wrapping my legs around his waist.

He pushed my back into the vending machine, grinding himself against me, proving irrefutably that I wasn't the only one turned on right now. My hard nipples brushed against his chest, and the heat of his body scorched through both layers of measly cotton that separated us.

He groaned. "You drive me fucking crazy."

"Yes," I agreed on a moan. I did, and he did the same right back. I had a feeling it was something neither one of us had been able to stop.

His mouth moved down to my neck, sucking and licking the sensitive skin until my legs gripped his waist tighter. Fuck, I wanted to feel him. Skin on skin. I wanted him inside me.

And then, he was kissing me again. Or maybe I was kissing him again. All I knew was that we were kissing; *fuck*, were we kissing. We were a thunderstorm of pent-up emotion, and our lips and tongues and teeth were lightning bolts shocking each other into the passionate depths neither of us could refute.

"Room key," his persistent lips whispered against my equally determined mouth.

Room key? Holy hell. What is happening?

How did we even get here? And more importantly, who started this?

Does it really matter?

No. It didn't fucking matter. Because there was no way in hell I was stopping this. It felt too good. *He* felt too good. I wanted this. *Him.*

Which was why, with one last conscious choice, I willingly slipped the room key into his hand and whispered, "Hurry."

CHAPTER 3

Wes

"**H**urry," she'd said.

And fuck if I'd have guessed, but it turned out I was really good at following orders when it truly mattered. I hurried and then some, the round swells of her ass in my hands acting like the boost start in Mario Kart.

Imaginary sparks shooting out behind me in a swath of brilliance, I was in motion in a flash, pulling her back off the glass of the vending machine easily and carrying her down the hall while she sucked at my neck. Little biting kisses and deep, healthy pulls, she mixed it up constantly, keeping me under the spell of her drug and nearly rolling my eyes into the back of my head.

Eager to have my mouth on her too, I moved at a brisk pace, glancing around only briefly to see if we were the only ones in the hall. There'd have to be some kind of apocalyptic fallout to keep me from sinking myself between Winnie Winslow's legs tonight, and even then, I'd probably still do it—I'd just make sure I was also armed with a gun.

Realization and a small drop of embarrassment burned down my spine as I arrived at her room, the fact that I hadn't needed to be directed blindingly apparent, but as quickly as it rolled in, it left. We'd both been dancing around this for months, and as much as I told myself it wasn't going to happen, my body spent most of its time preparing for the exact opposite. I may not have been expecting this when I'd dragged myself out to the vending machine to buy a bevy of snacks I wasn't actually hungry for, but it was really no wonder I'd managed to take detailed note of her room number and location.

Pressing the key to the lock with a complete lack of grace, I cleared the way to get us out of the very public hall and into her very private room where I could do all the things I'd spent several hours too long dreaming about.

I pushed the heavy door open with the soft weight of her body and then swung her out of the way to let it close. The sound of it slamming shut might as well have been the ring of a gunshot from a starter's pistol. We both bolted enthusiastically off the line.

She grabbed at my shoulders and let her head fall back, and I didn't waste the opportunity. Her skin smelled like the perfect mix of peaches and sunshine, and goddamn, I ate at her like a man starved. Every inch of skin, each sweet sigh and moan, I swallowed it all and kept it for myself, selfish and demanding and always greedy for more.

My tongue swirled a line up the column of her throat, and then my teeth closed around it in a nibble as she flexed her hips forward in a gentle urge to move toward the bed. She didn't need to prompt me twice.

Two quick steps took me the distance before I laid her down, the soft heat of her body under mine making me feel lightheaded.

Too busy to worry about Winnie Winslow. That was what I'd thought.

Yeah, I am definitely too busy with Winnie Winslow to worry now, my mind manipulated easily, turning down the volume on any and every voice with complaint or objection and cranking up the Marvin Gaye.

Imaginary candles sparked and flamed, and rose petals fluttered through the black of my closed eyes. An innocent trip to the vending machine for M&Ms had turned into NC-17 entertainment at its finest, and I was making my way from half-cocked to fully loaded in a hurry.

And now *I'm thinking about video evidence of tonight playing in my apartment late at night two weeks from now. Holy fuck. Focus. Winnie Winslow would literally carve a biohazard symbol or profanity directly into the skin of your balls as a warning to all future women,* I coached myself.

I might have held the power to control the direction of everything that happened here—I was bigger, stronger, faster. I could physically best her attempts to lead me through the evening. But I wasn't smarter, and she held the power to say no—to tell me it wasn't going to happen, not now, not ever—and really, when all I could think was "yes," that trumped every other goddamn thing.

I moved my hands down her body slowly, completely in opposition of my chaotic mind, and snagged at the soft cotton of her thin tank top. It was so trivial a barrier that it shouldn't have mattered, but all I could think was that it wasn't skin.

Hers under mine, the soft hum and heat of it mixing with the buzz of aroused electricity shooting off of me. I wanted it. I wanted to touch and taste and feel the exact essence of her until I was lost in it, mired so deep I couldn't remember what it was like to feel anything else.

She pushed her breasts toward me in invitation, so I took my RSVP a step further and ripped her top open, starting at the bottom hem.

She gasped, and I swallowed it aggressively, pushing my mouth to hers with months' worth of pent-up longing.

There was expectation in her stormy eyes—a comfort level in what she thought I would say—but I had no intention of ever apologizing for taking any piece of clothing off of her, whether I destroyed it or not.

Her breathing stuttered, and she lifted her hips as I closed my lips around one nipple and pulled roughly on the other. She was perfect in every sense of what I'd pictured and fantasized, and it wasn't because of a shape or size or the color of her skin. It was because she came alive at my touch, at my aggression—my undisputable want for her and this moment and everything that was to come.

"Wes," she moaned, and my veins pulsed as if I'd taken a hit of a drug. The high was incomparable, like nothing I'd ever felt before, and with everything I was, I prayed the effect would last for hours.

"You're even better than I imagined," I told her, knowing that women not only needed a verbal affirmation of desire but deserved it. Verbal, visual, sensation, and everything in between—when I was done with Winnie Winslow, she'd have no doubt that she had all the tools to lure and keep any man or object she ever desired.

"Wes," she said again, but I didn't let it go further.

"I can smell how much you want us." And she did. The connection we would make, the magic of me between her legs, her body sought it, was preparing for it physically, and goddamn, this hound had been born to track her pussy.

I tugged at the elastic of her sleep shorts and pulled it away from her smooth skin before looking down the line of her belly.

Bare of underwear, *bare of fucking anything*, I lost my mind and shoved my hand right in before forcing the flimsy fabric off her hips and down. Pushing my weight off of her, I pulled them free of her feet and squatted at the edge of the bed, my face barely a couple of inches from the heaven between her legs and my hand bridging the insignificant distance of that.

"Jesus Christ, Win," I breathed as my fingers slid easily along silken wet skin, pulling more moisture from her opening and spreading it up to coat her clit completely.

"What?"

"I didn't expect you to be completely bare."

"Why?" she asked obstinately, propping herself up and onto her elbows. "Mothers can't get Brazilian waxes?"

Mothers? She thought I was thinking about her being a mother right now? My brain could barely function enough to think *Holy shit.*

I almost laughed, the ridiculousness of her focused thinking and the picture she made lying there glaring at me but naked from the waist down seriously comical, but some self-preserving part of me knew that wouldn't be a good idea. And that was an ideal that bridged any kind of gender gap or stereotype. One-sided laughter and nudity did *not* go together.

"No," I assured her. "I wasn't thinking anything other than 'you're hot as fuck.'"

"Wes," she challenged, unconvinced, her voice decidedly less consumed by sex than I wanted it to be.

One sharp slap to the center of her pussy rang throughout the quiet room—and got her attention. Her squeal of surprise was the only sound I let her make.

"Quiet," I ordered. "If you want to talk, it better be to beg me to put my cock in your cunt."

My palm caught her rush of excitement, and I used it to ease the pressure of the heel of my hand on her clit.

"What do you want, Winnie?" I asked, purposely using her name to remind her I knew exactly who she was, where we were—what we were doing.

"I thought you didn't want me to talk," she said sharply, and for the second time, I had to quell my laughter. She was right, and I was, obviously, a little off my game thanks to months of anticipation.

"Answer me," I commanded instead of giving her the admission. I had to get things back on track here.

"I want you to lick me," she answered immediately, no shame, no hesitation, nearly annihilating my control.

Goddamn, her aggression was a welcome change from most of the women I slept with. *All the more fun to dominate.*

"Say please," I told her, wrapping the length of her hair around my fist and giving it a little tug.

She shook her head and bit her lip in refusal, and my dick jerked. I flipped her easily to her stomach and smacked my palm across her perfectly round ass.

Both cheeks were just a little bigger than I could fit in my hands, and as the burn of my slap rolled through the flesh, I paused it with a clench of my fingertips and leaned deeper into her body.

"Mm," I groaned against the warm, sweet skin at the back of her neck. "I was hoping you'd be a bad girl."

She gasped as my fingertips dug into her hips, and I lifted the weight of my body off hers. I shoved a knee between hers and spread her legs wide, until her chest was in the bed and her knees were at the edge, her ass high and spread.

The air conditioning in the room kicked on, and her skin pebbled almost immediately.

"Hmm," I hummed roughly. "So many choices."

Her hips flexed slightly, opening her legs farther and spreading the lips of her pussy—silently casting her vote.

"Oh, Win," I taunted. "I'm going to make you feel so good."

"Then do it," she demanded, turning her head to the side so I could understand her words without them being muffled.

Many a man would have made her wait, withheld her pleasure and built the anticipation. But I wasn't one for following, and I had a different way of doing things.

Down to my knees, I dropped between her spread legs and pinched the apex of her clit right between my teeth. She screamed, but it quickly bled into a moan as her excitement ran out of her in a rush.

I lapped at it and swirled, drinking and sucking and burying my face as positively deep into her pussy as I could manage until she cried out in climax and yanked at the comforter at the sides of her head.

Her hips undulated, pushing at my face, begging me to stop, but

I wouldn't, shoving my tongue deep and putting the pussy-soaked tip of my finger right into her ass.

Her legs quivered and buckled, but I held her up with my hands at the very top of her inner thigh, the skin of it absolutely soaked with everything her perfect cunt had to offer.

"Enough?" I asked there, sucking and biting and eating at her for several seconds before she found the breath to answer.

"No," she whispered with a shake of her head, the strength in her voice easing out of her body right along with the will to do anything with herself other than what I wanted.

"Fuck yeah," I agreed, knowing it wasn't enough and mentally fucking strutting at the fact that she agreed.

Fitting my back to hers, I pushed my shorts from my hips until they hit the floor and stepped out of them, rubbing my dick into her ass and fucking reveling in the feel of being coated in her juices.

"You feel good?" I asked softly, and she nodded. "It's only going to get better."

God, I could not wait to get my dick in her.

Pulling back and picturing my come mixed with everything already coating the inside of her legs, I positioned myself and pushed just the tip inside before realizing something important.

Pain bled behind my eyes as I shut them tight against the fact that it felt almost too late.

"Fuck," I snapped. "I don't have a condom," I told her bluntly.

"What?" she cried, clearly distressed, and that made thrice tonight I'd almost laughed.

"I guess that means you don't either?"

"How can you not have a condom?" she nearly yelled, and after all the holding back, I finally couldn't help but laugh. It was either that or cry.

"I didn't know this was going to happen," I told her honestly, and she laughed too. Hers was far more sardonic.

"Please. We've both known this was going to happen for a long fucking time."

And then I laughed again at the truth in her words and the fact that she was saying them with her ass in the air, face in the bed, and my dick partially inside of her.

Fuck.

"I have one in my room," I said, knowing putting on clothes and trudging all the way to my room was the very last thing on the planet I wanted to do right then. Hell, my dick might have actually goddamn revolted. The fucker was inching slowly deeper into her heat by the second, and I was mindless to stop him.

"Just do it," she demanded, and I tucked my chin into my chest and pushed at her hips nearly violently to stop myself from thrusting on body command.

"This is not the kind of thing you just do, Win. It's just not."

She lifted her head then, turning to look at me over her shoulder and pushing up to her hands in the bed. Her tits swung out in front of her, and I nearly fucking died.

"I'm on birth control. I'm not a total idiot."

"Okay," I rationalized, categorizing the lovers I'd had recently and their respective timing to my last STI test. "I haven't had sex without a condom since I was seventeen." She narrowed her eyes, and I laughed. "I know. I was a fucking idiot. I think I've slept with one woman since my last test, and…Jesus, Win. This is the last goddamn conversation I want to have to have with you right now."

At once, she reared back, my naked hips meeting hers as my cock touched the very end of her. Her eyes never left mine, and it was over.

The thinking. The analyzing. The thought of anything other than us and how we felt connected in the most intimate way possible.

Goddamn, it was like nothing I'd ever felt in my entire life.

Endless women, revolving nights, everything I'd ever wanted at my fingertips—none of it had felt as good as this.

And because of that…I felt ruined.

One thrust, two, on through dozens and dozens until sweat ran off of my chest and pooled on the soft curve of her naked back, I moved inside her, our sounds mingling with each other's in what sounded like a rehearsal of music—a little off, but mostly in sync, the rhythm and magic of the combination completely undeniable.

We played for hours, trying different songs and getting sweatier and closer with every note.

I went until I couldn't anymore, unwilling to stop until the very last moment.

I didn't even think I pulled out of her before falling asleep, but I couldn't be sure, because when I woke up in the morning, she, and every single piece of her luggage, was gone.

CHAPTER 4

Winnie

Sayonara, Miami.

The water of the ocean glittered and glistened, and palms swayed in the wind as I looked out the window to the shrinking world below.

I'd gone to Miami expecting heat—Florida sun, choking humidity, hell, even *boob sweat*—but I'd had no idea it would turn into one of the hottest, most erotic, roughest—in the best kind of way—sexual experiences I had ever had in my life.

Sex with Wes had been…well, there were no words to really describe it. A shiver racked my body at just the thought of it.

I'd woken up this morning deliciously sore, every inch of my body remembering where he had touched me, kissed me, turned me inside out.

Everything about it had been good—otherworldly good.

And then I'd panicked.

Because it was bad.

Cataclysmically.

We'd crossed a line that I wasn't sure we could navigate back from. We were better at being angry than awkward, and I was afraid, now that the initial tension was gone, we'd be stuck floundering in the latter. We couldn't go back, I didn't like it here, and going forward seemed horrendously ominous.

Rationally, I knew it was for the best if we never treaded toward those dangerous territories that led to us naked and doing things to one another that no one within the Mavericks organization should ever find out about. He was a player, a many-woman man, and about the least likely candidate for a ready-made family I could think of. So I got myself out of bed, packed my suitcases, and headed for the lobby to find another room or a taxi or anything that took me away from facing the consequences of my actions.

Unfortunately, irrationally, my body craved him. I wanted a repeat. And a three-peat. *And* a four-peat. My mind had already forayed into the future, organizing each and every encounter with a whole laundry list of please-do-to-me scenarios. And the stubborn part of me contemplated how fucking stupid it was to go crawling into the night.

So, instead of leaving, I'd sat down on a couch in the lobby and waited. Waited for the first staffer or team member to make their way down with the intent to head for the airport. And when Frankie Hart had done just that, I'd grabbed a ride with him, climbed the stairs to the team plane, and waited to face my fate.

The private jet full of Mavericks and managers *and Wes* climbed higher and higher, nose to the sky and ass trying like hell to catch it. The pilot announced over the intercom that we'd be at altitude within the next five minutes, and too embarrassed by the fact that I'd up and disappeared to look into Wes's eyes, I chose that moment to bury my face in my laptop and try to focus on everything but him—Mitchell's recent PT evaluation, Bailey's monthly physical, Franklin's post-op report after undergoing an ACL repair.

But my mind wouldn't stop making illegal U-turns back to the man sitting across the aisle. I could hear the goddamn GPS now, each time my eyes cut to the side, screaming to *turn around when possible*.

I'm fucking trying here, lady.

From my periphery, I could see Wes's knee bounce in rhythmic movements, and every time his fingertips swiped the page of the newspaper in his lap, my toes curled over the memory of what those fingertips felt like caressing my skin.

Rough but tender—carefully concise. The man had obviously used all of his promiscuous years wisely.

Like an uncontrollable wildfire, a flash of heat consumed my body from head to toe, and my cheeks flushed as more memories flooded my brain…

His lips placing openmouthed kisses down my chest. His hands gripping my breasts. His husky voice whispering wicked things into my ear. His mouth moving down my belly until it reached the apex of my thighs. The way I couldn't hold back any moan, any whimper as his lips and tongue consumed me into an orgasm…

Oh, my God. Get it together, Win. Now is not the time for erotic daydreams.

And seriously, why was it so hot on this goddamn plane?

I fiddled with the air nozzle above me until it was blasting on high, directly at my face. I had to cool down. I had to focus on anything but last night. I looked out the window and realized we were already miles and miles away from Miami. Water and beaches had turned into the mindless monotony of swamp and urban wilderness. I was losing it, truly losing it—so lost in my own dirty mind that I hadn't even registered the last few dozen minutes.

Holy moly, did anyone else notice how distracted I was?

I moved my gaze back to the cabin, surreptitiously glancing around to see what everyone else was doing. Most of the guys already had earbuds in and were preparing to sleep during the flight, while some chatted quietly with one another. My eyes continued to move across the numerous heads filling the spacious cabin, until they were looking directly across the aisle and into a set of emerald-gold eyes I knew on a biblical level.

Wes's gaze locked with mine, and I couldn't stop myself from wondering if he was thinking all the things I was thinking. Did he regret last night, or did he want a repeat? Was he as consumed with the wicked memories of us in my hotel room as I was? Did he hate me for leaving, or was he grateful?

God, we had been so reckless, so uninhibited, and I had never experienced anything like that in my entire life. I had never needed to feel someone so much that I found myself savoring every bite, every moan, every single deep, penetrating thrust forward. It was like I had been an entirely different person last night, like someone else had taken control and allowed me to feel all of the things I had always wanted to feel during sex.

Wordlessly, we stared at one another, searching for answers in each other that we'd yet to be able to find within ourselves. It was the first moment of eye contact we'd had since he'd fallen asleep inside of me last night, and I wasn't really sure what either one of us was saying.

And then, he averted his eyes and pulled out his cell phone. Thinking that was all the indication of his feelings I wanted to witness, I turned back to my computer as he tapped across the screen. I couldn't stop the roiling sour mass in my gut until my phone vibrated with a notification on my Outlook Messenger app.

He's messaging me.

Wes: Are you okay?

Was I okay? Fuck if I knew. But it was a little late to change anything about it if I wasn't.

Still.

This was still a game to him. It had to be. If it weren't, he would have said something about me leaving. He would have said something else, anything else, before asking if *I* was okay.

It's a game, I assured myself.

And there was no way I'd even consider letting him win.

Me: Yeah. I'm okay. Are you okay?

Wes: I'm okay.

See? My brain taunted. *He's fine.*

Me: Okay. Good.

Nice, intelligent response, Win. It was like our attraction to one another made us stupid.

Wes: Do you regret last night?

Seriously buried in the land of everything's-fine-this-was-a-game and headed straight for I'm-cool-as-a-fucking-cucumber, his question took me by surprise. Unintentionally, I looked across the aisle and met his curious yet irritatingly neutral eyes. I wanted to know his answer to that question before I gave him my own—a smart woman's form of self-preservation—but I also didn't want to be a coward. If I wanted someone to be open and honest with me, I had to do the same for them.

Without giving myself any more time to think about it, I shook my head, just once, and a soft, knowing smile graced his perfectly kissable mouth.

His eyes left mine, and his head bent to his phone. A few seconds later, my phone vibrated with another message from him.

Wes: Me neither. I can't stop thinking about it.

Me: Same. But I can't stop thinking about the fact that it probably wasn't a good idea.

I held his eyes for a few more seconds before tipping my head to my phone and typing out another message.

Me: Was it a bad idea, Wes?

Wes: Yes.

His response was immediate—and annoyingly deflating—but another message came hot on its heels.

Wes: But I wouldn't take it back for anything.

In an effort to ignore just how powerful the surge of relief his words provided felt, I defaulted to the best emotional defense mechanism four brothers had ever taught me—humor. Physically, my best defense mechanism was a left hook.

Me: Not even for a first-round draft pick and Green Bay's quarterback?

He met my eyes and shook his head.

Wes: New England's quarterback…maybe? But definitely not Green Bay's.

Me: Asshole.

Wes: I'm kidding. I doubt he smells so much like peaches.

Peaches. God. One simple sign of perception should not have made my heart beat faster.

Wes: Would you take it back if you could?

Me: No.

Me: Well...maybe for a job offer with New England. I've always wanted to meet their quarterback.

Wes: Cheeky, Win.

Me: ;)

"Are you guys texting each other while you're sitting right next to each other?" Quinn Bailey asked as his eyes moved between Wes and me.

I froze, but Wes responded with an easy grin. "Yep."

Quinn smirked. "What are you talking about?"

My eyes widened slightly of their own accord, but once again, Wes stayed composed, answering with a smooth tone. I almost got upset by his ability to keep his cool, but I quickly reminded myself that he no doubt had more experience.

"I was telling Winnie that I'm tempted to take this trade with New England for a new quarterback."

Quinn's content face creased with annoyance.

"Yeah," I chimed in, finally finding my stride. "I think it might actually be good for the team, Wes."

Wes smirked and nodded his head. "You might be right."

"What the fuck Dr. Double U?" Bailey questioned with a furrowed brow, aghast at my betrayal.

I laughed and shrugged my shoulders. "It's nothing personal, Bailey."

"Three touchdowns and three hundred yards isn't enough for you guys?"

I shrugged. "I heard Smith threw three hundred and fifty yards last night against Buffalo."

"Smith is a fucking pansy. He never leaves the pocket and had two interceptions last night."

Wes laughed, and I grinned in response.

Quinn searched our expressions. "You guys were just fucking with me, weren't you?"

I shrugged. "Maybe you'll think twice the next time you think doing a synchronized towel dropping when I walk into the locker room is a good idea."

Wes furrowed his brow. "Synchronized towel dropping?"

"Man, I'm beat." Quinn faked a yawn. "I should probably settle back into my seat and take a nap. Good talk, guys," he said before turning back around and strategically putting his earbuds in.

Wes: Next time they pull that kind of bullshit, tell me.

Me: If my memory serves me right, you pulled the same kind of bullshit on me last night after we showered.

Wes: If MY memory serves me right, you thoroughly enjoyed what happened after.

Yeah, I definitely did.

Me: It was okay.

Wes: Liar.

Me: Stop bothering me, Lancaster. I have work emails to catch up on.

Wes: Subtle subject change, Win.

Me: ;)

I made a show of acting like I was working, tapping dramatically on my laptop keyboard as I sent Georgia a quick response to her email about Mitchell's PT schedule and when he could fit in a quick interview with ESPN this week.

I heard Wes chuckle softly beside me, melodically accompanying the ping of my phone—another message from him.

Wes: *Emails to Georgia and Cassie about pregnancy-approved foods do not count as work emails.*

Me: *I'll have you know that my email to Georgia was about Mitchell's PT schedule.*

Wes: *Uh-huh. Whatever you say.*

Me: *You calling me a liar?*

Wes: *Pretty sure I already called you a liar...*

Me: *Fine. It wasn't just okay. It was mind-blowing. How's that for stroking your ego?*

Wes: *Oh, sweetheart, you can stroke me anytime you like. You should know that much by now.*

Me: *I'm rolling my eyes at you.*

Wes: *No you're not. I can see you and you're smiling.*

Me: *Don't you have work to do???*

Wes: *;)*

Lord Almighty, he wasn't making this easy.

Quiet, reserved Wes Lancaster was showing me a different side of himself. A side that was charming and playful and so goddamn endearing. And it was that side of him I found myself wanting more of. Which I feared was bad. Very, very bad.

Jesus. I had to focus on something else.

I tapped the trackpad and opened up an email from Cassie.

To: Winnie Winslow
From: Cassie Kelly
Subject: You can thank me later…

Don't worry, Win. I've got you covered for Brooks Media's big Halloween bash this weekend. Your costume has been ordered, and you're going to look fuck-hot as Harley Quinn.

<3 Cass

I sighed and rested my head against the seat. I had a feeling I probably needed to get my ass into the gym a few times this week before I felt confident enough to strut around in whatever costume—*or lack thereof*—Cassie had bought me.

I've got forty bucks on the fact that there are probably booty shorts and a crop top in my future.
Any takers?
Yeah, I wouldn't have thought I was a sucker either, but look at me now.

CHAPTER 5

Wes

"The restaurant called," my assistant, Ainsley, said into the empty space of my car—through Bluetooth as opposed to magic—as I took the exit for the stadium. It was first thing in the morning, pre-six a.m., in fact, so I knew she had to mean the call from the restaurant came in last night.

She'd probably sent an email that had gone unanswered thanks to the fog I'd been in since we'd gotten back from Miami two days ago.

Miami. Yeah, I'll talk about that in a minute.

Leaving emails unanswered wasn't at all like me, but she didn't mention it. Ainsley knew she wasn't my mother or my lover, and demanding to know why I'd done something differently or out of the ordinary wouldn't be welcome.

I know. I can hear Thatch's voice calling me a prick right along with you, but it's not some sexist, macho, authoritative agenda. I'm a private person, and my track record for decision-making is mostly blemish-free. I feel like both earn me the right to keep my reasoning to myself.

"Vandals broke the sign out front again, and it's already being replaced, a critic and an inspector came within thirty minutes of one another so Marco had a meltdown after they left, and Amanda's concerned that the turnover is statistically higher than it should be," she said, listing off the problems one by one so that I could address them individually.

I rubbed at the skin between my eyes and waited for the light in front of me to turn green as I considered everything she'd said.

"As long as the sign is getting fixed right now, I consider that a nonissue," I said. That's what I got for naming a restaurant BAD anyway. Thatch and Kline were constantly mocking the choice, but I couldn't deny that it brought the place attention. It was different, unique, and even though it had a somewhat negative connotation, I'd found people were willing to overlook the negative if it came with shock value.

"Marco has meltdowns every time something goes awry, but he always has them after he's already solved the problem," I went on, moving on to the delicate sensibilities of my staff. "Send him one of those Edible Arrangement baskets. He loves the fucking things."

Marco was one of the best chefs in New York—arguably, in the entire country—and the key to mending his finicky soul was chocolate-covered fruit from a chain company. Go figure. It'd taken me a while to figure it out, but once I had, the knowledge felt like gold.

"Okay," she answered efficiently, waiting for me to go on instead of clogging the line with mindless chatter. Yet another reason I appreciated having her as my assistant.

"And the turnover is ridiculous because we're five blocks from Broadway. Every Barbara Streisand, Taye Diggs, and Hugh Jackman wannabe in the tri-state area is or has been employed by us."

She was quiet, quieter than I expected, so I asked, "What?"

"Sorry," she said, quickly composing herself.

Still, I wanted to know. "Ains, what?"

She sighed. "I just had no idea you had such extensive knowledge of the history of Broadway cast members."

I rolled my eyes as the light finally turned, and I accelerated toward the stadium, stark and statuesque in the open in front of me.

Roughly twenty million people in the tri-state area, and my stadium sat in the middle of a field. The irony was astonishing.

"Yeah, well. You learn something new every day." I was certainly learning all sorts of unexpected things about myself these days.

"Indeed."

"I'm working from the stadium today," I told her, trying to sound casual when I didn't feel that way at all.

She didn't so much as blink. Well, verbally. I couldn't actually see her eyes. At this point, though, my working from New Jersey had to be transforming into my new normal. She'd probably have questioned me if I'd said I wasn't coming here.

"Got it."

"Bye," I dismissed her succinctly.

"Bye, Mr. Lancaster."

Mr. Lancaster. *God, I really am a prick.* As the line went dead, it hit me. Four years she'd been working for me, and I'd never told her to call me by my first name. Why the fuck was that?

The answer didn't come readily, and yet another knot of uncertainty tightened at the base of my stomach.

In need of distraction, I pulled into my spot in the underground staff garage, put the car in park, and pulled out my phone to scroll through my messages.

That and email were about the only two things I knew how to do on the stupid-smart thing. Apps, shortcuts, and special functions—I didn't know any of them.

You'd think I'd be better at technology, but you'd be wrong. It was one thing I'd never dedicated any time to learning. In fact, after a few awkward text exchanges where I tried to find my get-to-know-you footing, Winnie and I had stumbled on to the topic last night after I'd confessed to never before using Netflix.

Winnie: Oh my God, you're a dinosaur.

Me: What kind? And you have to give me a little credit. I know all about the chill part.

Winnie: A T-Rex. And I'll give you credit…right as I roll my eyes.

Me: Oh, a T-Rex! Because I'm so powerful? Dominant? That kind of thing?

Winnie: Because your arms are too short for your body. I noticed on the plane on our way back from Miami.

Me: They are not!

Winnie: They are. Don't feel bad, though. You could be lacking length in a different, more profound area.

Me: So you ARE thinking about me and beds and sex.

I smiled at the memory of her response—a picture of her bare legs, the bottom of her bed, and Netflix, bright on the screen of her TV on the opposite wall—and scrolled to the bottom of our thread to type in a new message.

Me: Just pulled in at the stadium. Can you hear me roaring from the parking lot? Shaking the earth perhaps? I was thinking about touching you when something occurred to me. If my arms are a little short, maybe you should sit on my chest, make sure everything is really easy to reach?

When she didn't say anything back for five minutes, I knew I couldn't sit in my car anymore and wait. Things needed doing, and I was the man to do them. That's what I told myself, anyway, as the longing built to a completely uncomfortable level. When I'd woken up to an empty bed, I'd thought it was over. The sex, the employment—fucking everything. It all seemed inevitable after making someone uncomfortable enough to flee their *own* room.

But then I'd climbed the steps to the plane, and she'd been there. Keeping mostly to herself, but not making any noise about never seeing my face again or suing the company or anything like that.

It was ridiculous, but it'd felt like a win. But now, thoughts of her and that night and everything it meant for me and us cluttered my mind.

Shaking off my thoughts, I kicked open the door to my car and climbed to my feet. I wouldn't really know anything until I saw her face again, looked into her eyes, and none of that would happen until I got my ass inside.

Plus, I had a meeting in five minutes that started ten minutes ago, and I didn't want to be late.

Taunting. Teasing. Fucking flirting.

I'd spent basically every second since I'd left Winnie Winslow's bed falling more and more interested in her. The sex had been explosive and unexpectedly good, but more than that, the playful innuendo and teasing had become a form of verbal foreplay in the last couple of days.

But this morning, when I'd texted her and not gotten anything back—and had several hours of tortured silence for the feeling to linger—I'd realized something that scared me.

I was getting attached.

Not just to the sweet silk between her legs, but to her. Her laugh. Her jokes. Her goddamn salty attitude.

And I didn't have time for a relationship. Not a real one anyway. I was horrendously selfish, completely unreliable, and one hundred percent happy that way. I didn't want to change. Not for her or her kid or for any-fucking-one.

That's why I liked easy relationships of companionship and sex—exchanges that ended in my mind the minute the actual exchange ended.

I didn't want to be followed everywhere by the ghost of wanting a woman, of needing to see her, breathe her, talk to her—fuck her.

And sitting here right now, thinking all these things, was exactly what I was trying to avoid.

Work never turned off for me, never shut down, and one round-the-clock job for my brain was enough. I didn't need more.

I didn't want it.

You don't fucking want it, I ordered myself.

A knock on the door woke me up, startled me even, and I looked down to see that my fists were clenched.

Slowly, I unfurled them from around themselves and steadied the anger right out of my voice.

"Come in."

The door opened instantly, and I knew who it was before the frame revealed her. The memory of her smell mixed with mine formed a phantom cloud between us and slightly modified the peaches and coconut of her perfume or lotion or whatever the fuck made her smell that way.

"Win," I greeted, determined to keep my mind focused on work. That had to be the reason she was here anyway. Winnie Winslow wasn't the kind of woman to come knocking on my office door with the intent to sink to her knees behind my desk and suck me off.

Oh, fuck.

You really are an idiot, my hardening dick chided. *You've done this to yourself.*

Her eyes searched mine briefly, and I raised an eyebrow as though my mind wasn't racing around unwanted arousal, spanking, and the very powerful image of her mouth around my dick.

I wasn't about to talk first. She'd been the one to approach, and if I opened my mouth now, no doubt I'd say something stupid as fuck.

Something Thatch would be able to mock me over for years to come. Something like, *Lie back on the desk and spread your pretty puss—*

"I think we should fuck again," she blurted.

My blink was languid, sluggish even, as it forced its way through the air, thick with disbelief. I knew I wasn't dreaming, the piercing tension headache in the base of my skull a better reminder of reality than any pinch to my skin would ever be. But fuck me every Friday, this was some serious yank-my-dick-and-slap-me-upside-the-head unbelievable shit.

Her spine got straighter as she surveyed the absolute mindfuck disaster that had to be written all over my face.

"Right now."

The perfect, wet silk of her pussy and the openly honest look in her eyes when my cock had been inside her flashed violently into my mind.

She'd been magnificent. Responsive and aggressive, completely turned on by every nuance of my answering control—and altogether too real.

One night I'd had her, and she was already like a highly addictive drug, calling to me with such intensity that it seemed like a good idea—genius, even—to let my entire life implode if only for the chance to start and end my days between her toned legs.

But we would be a train wreck. I knew it with absolute certainty. I would hurt her beyond repair, and when I got done doing that, she'd mutilate me.

Forcing my face to stay carefully blank, I spoke slowly to ensure my voice didn't betray me. It'd gone full Judas, holding the knife to my back and pushing it farther into my skin with every passing second.

"I don't actually think that's a good idea."

You are a fucking idiot, my throbbing dick protested.

Do you ever shut up? I asked him back.

Winnie's eyes lit with something I knew I wasn't ready for—roguish determination. I actually held my fucking breath as she spoke.

"Oh, I get it. You're afraid you won't be able to make me climax again."

My eyes narrowed, and the sudden rush of my blood made all sound seem muffled—and all the air I'd been holding rushed out like steam from a pot. But as much as I wanted to prove her wrong, in several, excruciatingly complicated positions, I knew enough about reading a woman to know that was exactly what she was after.

The inner rims of her irises darkened to midnight in frustration that I hadn't taken the bait.

I shook my head but said nothing, afraid—*knowing*—my mouth would betray my carefully crafted calm. Every inch of me wanted to bend her over my desk, hike her skirt up around her ribcage, and tear her panties in half, but that was just the hormones talking. The sane, adult, controlled part of me knew it wasn't a good idea. Not in general, and especially not here at work.

Two days ago, you thought it was the best idea on the goddamn planet, my subconscious reminded me. With every flirtation, I'd pictured all the perfect secret rendezvous locations throughout the stadium in explicit detail. All it took was one day of not hearing from her to point out the error of my ways. *Yeah, but that was before I realized how addicted I am to her already,* I said back.

It didn't listen.

That was the fuck of it with stupid inner monologues—they

always had all kinds of fucking shit to say but never listened when you wanted to say something back.

CHAPTER 6

Winnie

I had agreed with Wes one hundred percent when he'd said we shouldn't let sex happen between us again. I knew he was right. I knew it would only complicate things, and it was vital that we maintained a professional working relationship.

Sex wasn't something that allowed for healthy boundaries.

Sex made things messy.

It convoluted everything.

But good Lord, I shouldn't have watched him working out with the guys during practice. I shouldn't have watched the way his biceps flexed as he tossed the ball back and forth with Bailey. I shouldn't have watched the way sweat dripped between his pecs and down his defined abs until it got lost in the faint happy trail that led to the one place I shouldn't have been thinking about.

I'd spent several hours this morning talking myself out of answering his suggestive text message, telling myself that we were going way too fast down a dangerous, curvy as fuck road, and then thrown it all away in the blink of an eye because of one sexy display of athleticism.

Shit. Shit. Shit.

I shouldn't have been thinking about any of those things. And I sure as shit shouldn't have been in his office after hours with the intention of seducing him into another amazing round of hot and sweaty and delicious—fucking incredible—sex.

But I was only human.

And horny, obviously.

I was a woman who spent most of her days prioritizing work and home life, always putting my daughter first, and very rarely doing anything for myself.

I was a woman who hadn't had sex for an entire year before Wes, and I had given in to marathon sex in my hotel room in Miami.

Hell, up to that point, I had never *had* marathon sex.

There was a lot to be said for marathon sex, by the way.

But mostly, right now, what I had to say about it was that I wanted it. Again. And I wanted it from Wes Lancaster. He made me feel good without instruction or guidance, and I desperately wanted the freedom from being in charge. I wanted to not think. To just *feel*.

And if I was honest, it hadn't been some instant craving spurred by watching him at practice today. I'd come to work prepared— dressed like a high-priced hooker underneath my simple, knee-length black pencil skirt and white silk blouse. Said premeditation also probably explained the fuck-hot stilettos I decided to toddle around the field in. I mean, no one in their right mind wore stilettos to a job that was spent on the football field or in a locker room ninety percent of the time unless she was trying to impress someone into screwing her brains out again.

Before I go any further, just remember the whole no-sex-for-a-year thing.
Also, don't judge me by my hormones.

And, now, after all that effort, he didn't think it was a good idea? Well, he could join the fucking club. But if I didn't have control, he wasn't going to have it either.

"Fine," I ground out, trying to sound flippant and failing miserably.

"I'm sorry." His hazel eyes softened around the edges.

Oh, gross. He was sorry. Fuck that.

"Let's just forget it, okay?" I offered, and this time, I managed to sound unfazed. His eyebrows pulled together at the sudden change.

"Winnie—"

"We have different things to discuss anyway."

"We do?" he asked, sitting up a little straighter in his chair. "Work?"

"Yes," I confirmed.

"Okay, what's going on?" he asked, shedding his shield and settling into the work with a tug of his tie. I almost smiled at how easily I'd managed to lower his defenses.

"I think Mitchell should sit out the next game," I lied. "He looked like shit in practice."

"You have got to be fucking shitting me," he said on a near shout. Calm—gone.

Okay, so I was partially right on the fact that Mitchell hadn't looked fantastic in practice, but he also didn't look like his hamstring was bothering him one bit. And even though he was just coming off his second hamstring pull, I knew he didn't need to sit out any more games. He had rehabbed his leg through aggressive PT, and his last MRI had shown a remarkable improvement.

So why was I acting like he needed to sit out again?

Strategy.

And downright nymphomania.

I hadn't been diagnosed, but I was a medical professional. I was calling it.

Wes riled up generally led to an argument between us, and an argument between us generally led to some insane sexual tension.

My vagina was really hoping this time wouldn't be any different.

I wanted him angry. Preferably in his office. On his desk. Against the wall. Basically, anywhere. I wasn't picky.

He furrowed his brow when memories of conversations past overruled irrational panic. "Wait a second. You said he was doing well. Actually, I recall you saying his last MRI looked great and we didn't have anything to worry about."

I shrugged and slowly walked toward him. "I just don't want to take any chances," I said as I stopped right beside his chair and rested my ass against the edge of his desk.

Wes slid his chair back a few inches and turned in my direction, his jaw hard and his voice unyielding. "Cut the conservative crap, Win. He's playing."

Temperament manipulation—achieved.

Way to go, Win, my vagina cheered.

Let's not get ahead of ourselves, I answered back.

Hopping up onto his desk, I spread my legs just enough that my skirt slid up my knees, revealing a few inches of my upper thighs. My pulse thrummed at double the speed of normal.

I'd never in my life done something like this. I waited for men to make their moves, took what I wanted when they offered it. But this was a demand—backhanded and manipulative, sure, but that was just the most effective form of negotiation when it came to Wes Lancaster.

Right?

His gaze followed the line of my legs, moving down until he took in the black stilettos covering my feet, and then it moved back up again, pausing on the few inches of skin revealed by the hem of my skirt for longer than an unaffected man would have.

I smiled internally and released my hair from my bun, the strands falling softly against my shoulders.

"What are you doing, Winnie?"

"I'm talking to you about Mitchell's hamstring."

"No. That's not what you're doing," he argued, pushing his chair back from his desk and several inches away from me.

I let a tiny smirk curve just the corner of my mouth. "What do you think I'm doing?"

He considered me for just a moment before answering. "I think you're trying to seduce me."

"Well, that would be quite bold of me, wouldn't it?"

"We're in my office. At work."

"Everyone has left for the day."

"The cleaning staff is here."

"The door is locked."

"This isn't a good idea," he told me what I already knew.

"I know," I said and unbuttoned my blouse until the lacy white bra underneath was revealed for his eyes.

His eyes homed in on my breasts. "This probably shouldn't happen."

Probably. His protests were weakening.

"I know," I agreed again, even though I was hell-bent on seeing that it did, in fact, occur. Scooting my ass across his desk until I could rest my heels on the armrests of his chair, I caged him in. My skirt slid up even farther, revealing the white garters connected to my thigh highs.

"Fuck," he muttered and couldn't stop his hand from trailing up my leg. "This is such a bad idea."

"Uh-huh." I nodded and removed my blouse, peeling it back slowly, inch by inch, and then my bra, leaving my breasts bared for his now heated gaze.

His gaze caressed every inch of my skin until he was sliding both hands up my thighs and pushing my skirt up with their momentum.

"Fuck, Win. You wear shit like this to work all the time?"

I shrugged. "Sometimes."

Never. *But I'll wear shit like this to work every day if it leads to you and me fucking on your desk.*

I lifted my hips so he could move my skirt out of the way, until it was around my waist and my bare ass met the cool surface of his desk.

"Garters and a fucking thong?"

"Uh-huh."

He groaned long and low. "You're trying to kill me."

I shook my head. "No. I'm trying to fuck you again," I admitted frankly.

His eyes never left mine as he scooted his chair even closer, so close that his mouth was mere inches from where I throbbed and ached for him.

"Fuck, you're wet. I can tell you're soaked through your panties," he whispered, the heat of his breath on my thighs making me shiver.

"Uh-huh." I spread my legs even wider and kept them firmly placed on his chair.

"You want my mouth, sweetheart?"

"God, yes."

"Show me."

"Huh?"

He slid my thong to the side with his fingertips and stared up at me. "Touch yourself. Show me what you want me to do with my tongue."

I moaned in response to his words.

"Don't get shy now," he commanded. *You wouldn't take no for an answer, so now, neither will I.* He didn't say the words, but with the way he was looking at me, he didn't have to. "Rub your clit. Slip a finger inside your pussy. Show me what you need."

Holy fuck.

"Do it, Win. Now."

God, he was demanding. And hot. So fucking hot.

I slowly moved my hand to my pussy. He watched as I rubbed soft circles against my clit. And he kept on watching until I slipped a finger inside myself, feeling just how wet and hot and fucking needy I was for him—not that I needed the proof. That memo was notarized before any clothing had come off.

"You're dripping," he whispered, reaching up to smear my excitement onto my thighs. "I can't wait to lick every fucking drop of sweetness coming from that perfect cunt," he told me. His eyes were hungrier than any big bad wolf.

"Please," I begged.

"Two fingers, Win."

I obeyed, but it still wasn't enough. My two fingers pumping in and out of my pussy made me feel empty in comparison to the way I knew his dick felt inside me.

He forced my hand to a stop with a grip of my wrist and brought my wet fingers up to my nipple.

"Play with your tits, sweetheart," he instructed.

Without any delay, he gripped my ass with his big hands and buried his face between my legs.

A guttural moan slipped past my lips as he devoured me with his lips and tongue. And my hips came off the desk when he slipped a finger inside me and massaged that perfect spot.

"You taste so fucking good," he groaned against my skin.

"Fuck. Shit."

"Don't come," he demanded, but then he sucked my clit into his mouth and flicked along the sensitive bud with his tongue.

"What?" I tried to retort, but it mostly just came out as an incoherent moan.

"Don't come until my cock is inside you."

"Then get inside me."

He stood, unzipped his pants, and pulled out his thick, hard cock. He looked obscene like that, still dressed in his suit and tie, while he stroked his dick up and down, up and down. My gaze stayed locked on his movement, damn near hypnotized by the erotic scene before me. I watched as a drop of pre-come slipped down his shaft, and I couldn't stop myself from hopping off the desk and getting to my knees.

I had to taste him. I had to feel him hard and ready and inside my mouth.

I sucked him into my mouth, and he groaned.

When I licked along the head, he punched his hips forward, and the roots of my hair stung my scalp as he buried a hand and tugged.

I flicked my tongue against his shaft as I sucked him deep, and he cursed and lifted me off my knees. His strong hands turned me toward his desk and directed me to lean forward until my bare breasts were pressed up against the mahogany wood.

"God, you're so fucking bad." He growled and spanked my ass.

It only made me hotter for him. I'd never done the spanking thing before, but apparently, it worked for me in a big way.

"You want my cock?"

"Yes." I moaned.

I heard him open his desk drawer and the familiar sound of a condom wrapper being torn open.

"How hard do you want it?"

I steeled my voice and forced myself to be brazen. "Make my fucking teeth rattle."

"Grip the desk and hold on tight," he gritted out so roughly it sounded like he was barely hanging on. It made me feel heady, powerful. I couldn't believe *I'd* made him that way.

I reached my arms across the top of his desk until my fingers could grip the edge.

He nudged my legs wider with his knees, and I reveled in the vulnerability of my position. I was spread across his desk like his own personal buffet while my pussy dripped with arousal.

The second he slid his cock inside me, I cried out.

"Yes," he moaned and gripped my hips. "Fuck. Yes. Just inside you, and your pussy is already milking me for more."

"Fuck me. Please, fuck me."

He didn't hold back after that, pounding into me in a hard and steady rhythm.

"God, you look so fucking perfect right now."

"Harder. Please, harder."

He groaned and turned me around, lifting me up until I was sitting on his desk again. I wrapped my legs around his waist, and he slammed back into me. I cried out, and my head fell back. His lips were on my neck, sucking at the skin in rhythm with his cock as he fucked me hard and fast and so goddamn deep.

It was a punishing rhythm, but it didn't feel like mistreatment at all. Each stroke hit me with more intensity than the last, and I had to physically work to keep my pleasure from peaking too soon. It was the kind of sex that felt so good, I was content never to let it end.

I dug my nails into the cotton material covering his back as stars danced behind my eyes.

"Fuuuck. You better come, Win," Wes gritted out as he worked to fight off his own orgasm. "Please come. *Oh, Jesus.*"

And as much as I tried to disobey, I couldn't. I came on an incoherent moan, and he followed my lead, pushing himself deep on a groan and leaning his head forward and sucking a hard nipple into his mouth as he came inside me.

Yes. Yes. Yes.

The only "no" in my mind was in protest that it had come to an end. We hadn't even come down when I whispered in his ear, "Let's go again." Wes laughed into my neck and flexed his arms around me tighter.

"You're insatiable."

"You're a fantastic fuck."

"That's all I am to you?" he asked in a teasing tone. "A fantastic fuck?"

"You're really pretty to look at, too."

He looked contemplative, so much so, it made me pause.

"What? You still think it's a bad idea?" I asked.

Next thing I knew, he lifted me off the desk, turned me around, and spanked my ass. I squealed in response.

"Yes," he whispered as he caressed my breasts with his hands and kissed and licked and sucked at the sensitive skin of my neck. "But the box is already open now."

"The box?" I asked as he pushed his body into mine.

"Pandora."

The age-old story played behind my eyelids, and a tremor slid down my body at what stood out. Hope was the only thing left to hold on to now that the evils were gone.

I'm not sure if that's better or worse.

CHAPTER 7

Wes

The air felt like it was full of needles, prickly and harsh and altogether uncomfortable, and my breath misted the air in front of me every time I exhaled.

Ah, fuck. It's going to be winter soon.

I wasn't ever on time, but as I jogged up to the team huddle at rugby practice this evening, I'd never been more appreciative of my penchant for tardiness. It wasn't exactly inviting outdoor weather. Plus, if the way my face felt to me, from the inside out, was any indication, other people were going to be able to read all of my thoughts as if they were scrawled neatly in an open and available book.

And most of them were completely NSFW.

Winnie had kept me…occupied…in my office for longer than I'd planned. Unlike now, I'd been warm—to the point of steamy—and I owed it all to one of the best activities on the planet.

You'd planned on saying no, my brain said.

Yeah, fuck you, I said back.

God, the way she'd just taken her clothes off without looking back, one tantalizing piece at a time until all I could see was skin…

Christ. There'd been no saying no. The word had fucking disappeared from the English language as far as I was concerned.

So, thanks to two very rigorous rounds of horizontal exercise, instead of fifteen minutes behind schedule, I was thirty—and thankfully, there would be blessedly less time for gossip.

In addition to the ball-shriveling cold, there was another discomfort lurking about thirty yards away. All of the big guys with muscles and mud stains on their clothes were good camouflage, but I wasn't fooled—I was approaching a coffee klatch, a gossip hour, a psychoanalysis so thorough you'd think they all had PhDs.

"Come on, Whitney," Thatch called as my advance finally got his attention. "We don't have time to wait for your pedicure to dry."

"Thursday is pedicure day," I replied easily while scratching the side of my face with my middle finger and coming to a stop in the only open spot in the huddle. "Today was facial day."

Smiles graced the faces of each and every player in the circle, surprised at my easygoing attitude—except for those of my friends. They knew me better, had the map to get inside the façade, but I'd never really needed the defense before. So they knew what I was really thinking: *no big deal*.

Now I had secrets—big ones—things I swore up and down I wouldn't feel despite their prodding. Affection, longing—a general need to be with or talking to a certain woman at any free moment.

Thatch's eyes narrowed, and Kline's shrewd gaze zeroed in on my eyes.

Fuck. I'd hoped to be able to get my footing on this uneven ground, this newfound territory, before they caught wind of it.

Unfortunately, despite all my efforts, with the taste of Winnie's sweet pussy still on my tongue, I found it completely impossible to deaden the excitement from my eyes.

Emotionless, flat Wes had fled the motherfucking building. And Manhattan. And the surrounding four boroughs.

Kline elbowed Thatch just as he opened his mouth to speak and jerked his chin toward the rest of our company. With Tommy, Johnny, Sawyer, and Jensen looking on, even Thatch wasn't dumb enough to engage in personal talk about a woman who was friends with his wife.

That's right, wife.

Just a few weeks ago, after a bout of questionably illegal activity, Thatch had pulled out all the stops, demanded favors from everyone he knew—including me—and dropped Cassie right into the middle of a wedding she couldn't escape. Not that she'd tried. The two of them were so happy it was almost sickening. *Almost.*

It was also the first time I'd touched Winnie Winslow, her small hand tight in mine and her heart in her eyes. God, keeping my eyes off of her and on the wedding had been…challenging. Just short of impossible, really.

"You're late, but least you're here," Tommy teased. "Thatch is a beast, but Kline's skills are fading now that he's blissfully chained."

"Your skin looks fabulous," Jensen mocked, and I cranked my middle finger up like a jack-in-the-box at the same time Kline reacted to his own dig.

"Fuck you," Kline said playfully, no sting in his tone and a grin lifting the corners of his mouth. He was never one to get upset, and now that Georgia occupied his bed morning and night, he was practically unflappable.

The bastard.

"Hey, I'm married too," Thatch protested irrationally, practically begging the guys to razz on him about being tied to Crazy Cassie. He fed on the energy, built on it until the only one left floundering was the person who'd set him up. Unfortunately for me and entertainment value, Thatch was too big and the guys were too smart to say anything really biting.

"Congratulations," Sawyer offered as Johnny plucked out, "Poor woman."

Thatch was speechless, wanting them to poke at him so he could shove back, but at a current loss as to how to make that happen.

"It's okay, big guy," I teased, slapping him on the back roughly. "I'm sure Cassie will torture you for your newfound status enough for the rest of us."

"Cassie isn't torture."

Subtle smiles were exchanged before everyone started to back away. The bomb was primed, the gun was loaded, and the whole damn place was just ticking away on its little timer.

If we let it, our entire practice could easily be spent here, shooting the shit and razzing the fuck out of whatever wounded animal found its way into the circle. It was the nature of men. Torment or be tormented. One or the other.

I raised my brows as the other guys dispersed, and Kline jogged over to his bag to look at his phone one more time. Jensen called out from the pitch about how good Georgia must have looked when she sexted. Kline threw up a middle finger over his shoulder and kept his head to his phone.

"Okay, but it's the good kind," Thatch admitted, bringing my attention back to him. "Like a little spank with a riding crop or a flogger."

I smiled at the memory of slapping Winnie's pussy and ass and the fucking delightful way she reacted to both.

Thatch didn't know how to interpret it, and unknowingly granted me an innocence of which I wasn't even remotely worthy. "Are your ears burning? Was that too scary for you?"

I just laughed and turned away, taking my position and stretching my hamstrings as the scrimmage got underway. *He has no fucking clue.*

A lot of guys shared all the stories of their sexcapades, but I'd never been one to give more than a couple cursory details—and it'd never been like it was with Winnie. So he really didn't have any idea. About my proclivity or past or present.

Even the things he thought he knew were just that—thoughts.

Part of that was because even I didn't have any hard and fast rules or expectations—I liked what I liked in the moment and went with whatever made my companion the wettest. The difference now was that what got Winnie drenched, concurrently got me hard—like two halves of a sexually deviant whole, everything that made her tick made me tock, and when I came the hardest I'd ever come, she came harder.

We were a match in a way I hadn't been expecting.

And, evidently, unforeseen circumstances were the theme of the day. Like a goddamn iron fist, with speed and an arch created by a powerful kick by Tommy, the ball hit me right square in the nuts.

Pain erupted like a million firecrackers exploding in my pants, and I closed my eyes against the onslaught.

Thatch yelled, "Oh, shit!" from across the pitch, but the tremor of laughter in his voice made me take out a mental sticky note and write an IOU in the junk-punch department.

"Okay," I breathed out as I crumpled, hands to junk and knees buckling before the stabbing knife of pain consumed me to the point that I couldn't fake it anymore. "Fuck." I huffed as I dropped my knees and forehead to the ground and prayed to the Goddess of Mercy to grant me some.

I guess I won't be using my nuts within the next twenty-four hours, I thought sardonically. Distracted by Winnie, not paying any attention to the game, I'd been thinking with nothing but my dick, and now he was going to pay the goddamn price.

My mental pen and paper were busy as I wrote another note to ask Winnie if she'd be willing to kiss it better—and then added an addendum to make sure I could get it up first, in a jerk-off session test, to make sure I didn't goddamn embarrass myself.

"Come on, man," Kline called from above me. His voice was reassuring but fucking annoying all the same. "Get up."

"You get up, cocksucker," I insulted him nonsensically.

"What?" Thatch asked. "You pussying out? One little tap to the junk and you're done for the day?"

"Go fuck yourself," I told him around a moan as I writhed on the ground like a fucking child with appendicitis. "I'm a grown man with nothing to prove. I'm not looking to out-fucking-rugby anybody, so today, yes, I'm done." I'd already burned all the calories necessary for the day in much more pleasurable activities.

Thatch laughed and turned to the team waiting on the field. "Whitney's got her period. Time to call it, boys."

I heard a few groans, a couple of jabs, but mostly, everyone seemed thankful. None of us were striving for the Olympics at this point, and we'd all been at work all day. There were drinks and sex to be had, and no one minded when they weren't the excuse. "Just give me a reason!" their eyes screamed. My battered and bruised nuts answered. Decision—final.

Slowly, I climbed to my feet and walked toward the bleachers gingerly, wincing with each step and thanking Jesus I'd had Winnie so many times today in my office.

Thank fuck she wasn't willing to take no for an answer.

As the crowd thinned and everyone moved out of earshot, Thatch's eager bob became a bounce.

"Can I talk now?" Thatch asked Kline like a little boy asking his father for permission.

With an incline of his chin and sweep of his arm, Kline granted it regally.

"You fucked her. More than once."

I sat silent as they stared at me.

"Well?" Thatch prompted after several seconds of waiting to no avail.

"Well, what?" I asked innocently. "You made a statement. I didn't hear a question."

Thatch looked to Kline with a smile, and Kline leaned into the bleachers and settled a hip. "When's the wedding?"

I shook my head as I pulled myself to standing and made my way toward my bag.

"Silence," Thatch commentated with a chuckle.

"You know what that means," Kline continued as I pretended to ignore them both.

But my mind was all too aware of the veracity of their words when Thatch said, "Just like the wickedest of witches, with the right weapon, our own little Wes is melting."

And that's actually exactly how it felt—like I was slipping away, fading into a new normal.

How long will it take me to slip past the point of no return? I asked myself. *Until there's no evidence left of all that I am other than the puddle of memories past on the floor?*

And will Winnie Winslow be strong enough to save herself?

CHAPTER 8

Winnie

"What in the hell is this?"

"That's your Harley Quinn costume, Win."

"Are you serious?" I asked Cassie as I stared down at the clothes laid out across the bed in her guest room. Though, describing this amount of material as clothes was being pretty fucking generous.

Good God, it's fabric swatches at best.

I'd hauled ass over to her and Thatch's apartment after the Mavericks' practice had ended—three trains and a four-block power walk—just so that I could get ready for the Brooks Media big Halloween bash with her, at her ridiculous pregnant request, and this was the thanks I got?

She grinned and nodded her head. "I'm very serious."

"Fishnets? Booty shorts?" I muttered mostly to myself. My voice was high-pitched—how it gets when it's bordering on hysteria. "Will I also be selling blow jobs for twenty dollars?"

She scoffed. "Have some self-respect, Win."

I started to laugh, but she interrupted. "That price is ridiculously low."

"Cassie!" I snapped, and she laughed then.

"Haven't you see *Suicide Squad*? This is *exactly* what Harley Quinn wears." She moved across the room and pulled out two bottles with pink and blue caps. "And don't worry. I even got temporary hair color! Your hair is going to look fluffing amazing in pigtails!"

"Don't worry? You're coloring my hair shades of the rainbow, and my ass cheeks are going to be hanging out all night!"

She winked. "Good thing you've got a hot ass. And don't worry because everyone is going to know exactly who you're going for. No mistaking you for a call girl. Swear."

I shook my head as I looked back to the bed and mumbled to myself, "Georgia was right."

I clearly didn't mumble incoherently enough. "What was Georgia right about?" She put a hand to her hip as she stared back at me with annoyance.

Facing her head on, I raised my voice and skewered her with the truth. "She warned me that I shouldn't let you pick out my Halloween costume. She pretty much predicted something like this would happen."

She smirked and started to head for the hallway, unfazed by me and my declarations. "Georgia is just pissed that I won't tell her what my costume is. She's been berating me about it for the past month."

I still wasn't completely used to these people, to how wild at heart they were—how unafraid they were of living. I wanted to be, though. *I want it for myself.*

"What is your costume?" I called behind her, shaking off my thoughts and dreams and steeling myself for the things to come.

"You'll see," she responded on a nearly evil laugh, shutting the bedroom door on her way out. I stared down at my attire for the next few hours and tried to prepare myself to face it. To *own* it. I had a feeling confidence was the only thing that would ensure my survival, and I had to survive. I had a daughter to go home to.

"Get your hot little ass ready, Win!" Cassie shrieked through the door, startling me into motion. I snatched the fabric and hugged it to my chest while I took one last breath. "Thatch says we need to leave here in about a thirty minutes!"

This is it, I told myself. *Chest out, head up, be the woman...Ah, fuck.*

I boosted my brain with a little dose of reality, and my vagina rejoiced. *Hopefully, this gets me laid.*

About an hour later, with strobe lights twirling and an eclectic mix of psychopaths and sexy animals gyrating on the dance floor in front of me, I came to a stop just inside the entrance of one of the giant ballrooms of The Metro beside a pregnant nun and Mr. Rogers.

I honestly had no idea what in the hell Cassie's and Thatch's costumes were supposed to mean, but it didn't matter—because I looked more ridiculous than both of them combined. Covered by nothing more than fishnet stockings, booty shorts, a tight half-shirt that said *Daddy's Little Slugger* across my boobs, knee-high black stiletto boots, and pink and blue pigtails accentuated with glitter eye shadow, I was a few beats away from a mental breakdown. If I was honest, I'd been this way for a while. From the moment I put the whole ensemble on, my little bedroom pep talk had been nothing but a memory.

Thatch and Cassie had tried to assure me that I didn't look like a complete disaster, but with the way those two liked to express things... let's just say it fell on some pretty deaf ears.

And yet, here I was—some awful part of me hoping Wes would find the ridiculous getup irresistible.

Is this what you were going for with that whole living wild thing? my subconscious mocked.

Shut up, I told it.

As Thatch and Cassie started to move, I walked with them and tried to get myself out of my head. It wasn't going all that well.

Mildly disgusted with myself, I was happy we were headed toward the bar. Kline and Georgia were standing off to the side, sharing a private smile and laugh, and all I could think was, *Where's Wes?*

Kline put his arm around his wife's shoulder and tucked her into his side, kissing her forehead softly, and smiling like he knew he was the luckiest man in the world. Jealousy pounded like a hammer in my gut. I hated that something so vile was one of the most powerful emotions I'd ever experienced. I wanted to give that influence to positivity and good thoughts, but I wasn't in charge.

But all that jealousy slid away, morphing in midair to hilarity when their costumes finally hit me. I glanced at Cassie and Thatch, and then back at Georgia and Kline, and then burst out into laughter.

"What in the fudging heck are you guys?" Cassie questioned once we reached them, the haze of pregnancy slowing her normally acute detective skills.

Georgia giggled for a moment until her eyes moved up and down Cassie's naughty nun costume, and then over to Thatch's cardigan sweater, nerd glasses, khakis, and loafers.

"What the fuck are *you guys*?" Georgia asked back as she slid out from under Kline's arm and moved closer to Cassie.

"We're Kline and Georgia," Thatch chimed in, a smug smile etched across his mouth.

A slow rumble of laughter rolled from Kline at that, and I joined him, trying to at least keep the volume low enough that I wouldn't anger the beast…cough…pregnant woman.

"Who the hell are you guys supposed to be?" Thatch asked.

"We're *you guys*," Georgia explained, and it wasn't without exasperation. She'd had the winning idea in her fucking grasp, but Thatch and Cassie, having done the exact same thing, snatched it away.

Thatch's face morphed into confusion as he surveyed their costumes with new insight. "Why the fuck are your pants too short?" he asked Kline. "And why do you look like you're ready to Hulk right the fuck out of your clothes?"

Kline didn't respond to that, merely smirking at his much larger best friend.

Thatch bristled immediately. "Dude, that's not how I wear my clothes."

Kline's smirk never faded, not only unfazed by Thatch's irritation, but fueled by it.

Meanwhile, the girls were seconds away from dissolving into an all-out cat fight. "You guys stole our idea!" Georgia shouted with an angry, accusatory finger in Cassie's face. "You say you're dressed like me, but all I see is a pregnant nun who's ready to give lap dances at a bachelor party!"

Cassie raised an eyebrow. "Yeah, well, you look like an actual hooker."

Georgia shrugged. "I was just trying to get the costume right, and I know how much you love Julia Roberts in *Pretty Woman*."

Cassie's eyes narrowed, and her hip cocked. "Okay…I'll give you the hooker—"

Thatch held up his hand for high fives. No one obliged.

"—but explain to me what the fluff is going on with your teeth?"

"I'm you, pre-pregnancy," Georgia retorted. "One glass of red wine and you've got immediate *True Blood* mouth."

Thatch laughed, but it didn't last long as Cassie whipped her head around to glare at him.

"What?" he questioned with both hands held out. "She's not wrong on this one, honey. One fucking sip of Merlot and you look like you just got done feeding ten seconds ago."

"I will bite your dick off."

"That's not gonna help with the *True Blood* mouth," I muttered to myself. Kline smiled.

"Later," Thatch said with a smirk and a wink. "We can't leave the party before it even starts."

"You guys' foreplay is so weird," Georgia announced.

Cassie was undeterred. "Or awesome."

"No. Weird. It's almost creepy. I feel like I'm watching the porno version of the *Saw* movies."

"Have you been peeking in our bedroom windows at night, you little freak?" Cassie asked with a grin. "Because we just did—"

Georgia interrupted, holding up one hand in Cassie's face. "Nope. Stop right there. I don't want to be disturbed by the weird shit you two get off on."

Cassie just laughed and slapped her hand away. "Like you should talk. You and Big-dick have boxes full of sex toys."

"From my mother."

"And using sex toys your mother sends you isn't weird?"

"We don't use them!"

"Uh-huh…sure you don't."

"We don't." Georgia looked at Kline. "Right, baby?"

Kline smirked. "Am I supposed to lie or tell the truth here?"

Georgia groaned, and he immediately wrapped his arm around her shoulder, pulling her in close.

"I think it's awesome Big-dick was able to open Georgia's Pandora's box of freak."

Pandora.

The memory of Wes inside me on his desk hit me so hard, I nearly took a step back. Looking around, I searched for him almost desperately while the conversation of the fierce foursome continued all around me.

"Me too," Kline agreed.

"Kline!"

He grinned down at her. "What? You know I love it when you—"

Georgia slapped her hand over his mouth. "That's enough oversharing for one evening, thank you very much."

Everyone laughed at that, even Georgia.

"What do you want to drink, Winnie?" Thatch asked, but before I could answer, Wes finally made an appearance.

Always arriving last to the party, but never failing to look like sex-on-a-stick.

He gained the attention of many a woman as he stood in the entrance of the room in a dashing black suit, crisp white shirt, no tie, and jacket open, with aviators adorning his handsome face covered in a few days' worth of lick-worthy scruff, surveying the room. And if I said I wasn't one of them, I'd be lying. He was just *so* handsome.

When his eyes found mine, a smile curved the corner of his mouth—not a little one—fucking *huge*.

One point for Cassie's costume skills.

His strides were long and smooth as he wove his way over to us, his piercing eyes shining like beacons directly at mine the whole time.

"Winnie?" Thatch called. I struggled, almost twitching with the effort, but I finally broke the connection just as Wes made it to the group.

He could tell immediately that I needed saving.

"What's going on?"

"You're late."

He smiled and shrugged, and I got lost in his eyes all over again.

"I was trying to get Winnie's drink order," Thatch clarified as he wrapped a casual arm around his wife.

"She's a big fan of expensive Pinot Noir," Wes told him casually and winked in my direction.

But when his eyes met mine, they didn't leave. Time seemed to stand still as he stood there looking at me like there was no one else around—eyes roaming up and down my body, taking in every single little inch of skin revealed—even though we were smack-dab in the middle of a whole slew of other fucking people. Our group, the room, all of it faded away as he used a tiny slip of his tongue across his bottom lip to talk to me. It was so small, an inconsequential movement to anyone else, but he might as well have taken a torch and lit my skin on fire.

Before I could give my actual drink order, Thatch started to sing softly. "I wear my suuun-glasses at night." His head bobbed back and forth, punctuating each word dramatically. I had to bite my lip to keep from laughing.

Wes reached up to the top of his head to pat the aviators that sat there.

"Seriously, Whitney, what are you?" Thatch questioned once he finished the chorus. "You know it's a Halloween party, right?" he continued, looking Wes up and down. With a snap of his fingers, he pointed at Wes. "Wait…let me guess…you're Wes Lancaster when he's out trolling for pussy, right?"

"Robin Thicke," Wes corrected, shaking his head with a grin. He was just amused by the rest of us, but I didn't miss the glance in my direction at the mention of his "trolling."

Thatch grinned. "'Blurred Lines'?"

Wes nodded, and a sly, confident smirk kissed his perfect lips. "That's exactly the look I was going for."

"I see…I see…" Thatch added with a nod. "So…you're hoping women will just rip their tops off and dance around you?"

Wes slid his hands into his pockets and shrugged. "A man can dream, right?" he responded nonchalantly, but his eyes held mine as he spoke, each word driving into me like a perfectly placed spank.

Holy hell, I needed a fan. Or maybe I was coming down with a fever.

The truth?

I didn't feel sick. But I sure as hell felt like reenacting another night of marathon sex with Wes Lancaster.

A few hours—and drinks—later I found myself in a place I never, ever thought I would be: sitting at a table with a pregnant, naughty nun and a hooker, discussing our favorite Golden Girls.

"Blanche!" Cassie exclaimed enthusiastically, her fervor entirely thanks to personality rather than alcohol. That made one of us.

Georgia and I laughed…and laughed…and laughed. Way more than was necessary or expected, but hey, that's tequila for you. We'd at least moved on to straight wine.

"What? Why is that so funny?" Cassie demanded, her amusement with the two of us running just as dry as her cups.

"It's not funny, it's fucking predictable," Georgia responded on a hiccupping giggle, snorting so hard at the end that she choked on her own spit.

Oh, yeah. We're pretty right now.

"You're drunk, you bitch!" Cassie railed until it trailed into a whine. She wanted alcohol like I wanted the D. We were both sad little sacks while we struggled through the wait.

Georgia just nodded and held up her glass of wine. "Cheers, honey."

Cassie flipped her off.

As the music switched over to Beyoncé's "Drunk in Love," I decided that Harley Quinn needed to enjoy the night. She needed to let the fuck loose and dance her little booty-short and fishnet-wearing ass off.

And that she…was me.

So, that's exactly what I did without saying another word to anyone.

Because sometimes, you just didn't need anyone else. You just needed to feel the music and let it consume you. Sometimes, you just needed to forget about what people thought and not worry about whether you looked like an idiot out on the dance floor.

Sometimes, you just had to *let go*.

As I walked toward the dance floor, I heard Cassie ask, "Win? Where are you going?" but I didn't slow down.

I just turned around and grinned at her, and then made my way to the center of the dance floor. The beat moved through me like a wave, and as I finally caught it, I shook my hips and raised my hands in the air.

I was just loose enough that I didn't need to look around the room, wasn't waiting for someone to join me—all I needed was myself and the music. Two songs in, as irony would have it, the catchy opening beat of "Blurred Lines" started to play. I laughed to myself and shook my hips even harder, the cool kiss of the air-conditioned—thanks to an early roasting room packed full of bodies—space touching skin that rarely even saw my bedroom.

But I put that out of my mind and made eye contact with an older gentleman across the dance floor, and he seemed amused by my dance moves enough to bolster my confidence. If he'd done it differently, in a creepy way, I probably would have wilted. But it wasn't like that at all. His eyes were kind, and his body language said he could tell I was having fun.

And then, as my eyes moved across the crowd, Robin Thicke himself seemed to appear from nothing.

It actually took me a minute, thanks to the impairments of alcohol, but eventually, I figured out it was really just Wes Lancaster dressed as Robin Thicke.

And that was even better.

He moved toward me slowly, with a sexy little smirk on his lips. Transported by the music and the moment, I couldn't do anything but keep dancing and watch him get closer.

It took both forever and no time at all, but as the wait burned inside me, the heated connection of our gaze became too much. I'd barely turned away before his chest was to my back and his hands were on my hips, his body following my movements, and I could feel my body moving as it sought contact with each surface inch of his.

His warm breath near my ear, I swore I heard him take a deep inhale as if he was savoring the smell of me.

I doubt he smells so much like peaches, he'd said.

On instinct, I leaned my head against his shoulder and let him take the lead. His hands skated easily down to my hips, and then back up again, skimming the sides of my belly. I sucked in a breath involuntarily.

His hands felt like heaters against the cool of my skin as his fingertips gently slipped beneath the half-shirt and caressed me. Goose bumps danced across my stomach like glitter.

His voice was rough, so close to the edge of control I had to close my eyes tight against the onslaught of arousal as he whispered in my ear, "I couldn't let sexy little Harley Quinn dance by herself."

He grabbed my hand, spinning me out away from his body and then pulling me back to him so that we were chest-to-chest, gazes locked, and hips still moving seductively together.

The corners of his lips curled so completely that they grazed the corners of his eyes. Open and free, Wes Lancaster looked at me like I was everything. Not everything he'd been looking for or known he wanted, but like I *was* everything. Happiness and pain, love and hate, all the words he'd ever spoken and all the ones he never would.

I was lost after that.

Completely consumed by him.

It was just Wes and Winnie. Robin Thicke and Harley Quinn.

There weren't any questions about what we were or recriminations from the complicated answers those questions might mean.

As we danced there, the music switched over to a sexy, electronic remix of a Disclosure song I loved, "You & Me," and everything seemed simple.

I wanted him. Now and again and over and over after that.

My hands went to his shoulders without a conscious command, my fingertips brushing at the soft hair of his neckline, and our locked gazes intensified. Heated. Moved from maybes to definites and then some—wanting. Begging. Pleading.

"I want you," I whispered when the ache in my abdomen became unbearable, and our breaths mingled so completely it felt like there was only one.

Wes sank his hands into my hair and tilted my head to the side, his soft lips brushing back and forth at the sensitive spot behind my ear. "I *need* you, Win," he said there, his ardor consuming my entire body and soul.

Moving quickly, he grabbed my hand and pulled me away from the dance floor, through the crowd, and down a darkened hallway, back into the corner where absolutely no light touched any surface. My legs churned in their effort to keep up with him, but I didn't say a word.

Hidden there, just out of plain sight, I wrapped myself around him like a second skin, and our mouths attacked one another, kissing and licking and biting and sucking frantically until nothing else mattered anymore.

CHAPTER 9

Wes

"Leave it," I whispered as her phone rang from her tiny purse that lay discarded on the floor, groaning and pushing her deeper into the wall before sucking the peak of her nipple into my mouth.

We were in the trenches of my favorite two-person activity, and I had absolutely no desire to add a third—especially knowing whoever was on the other end of her phone wasn't a model for Victoria's Secret.

Relax. I'm mostly joking.

I'd been working diligently at the removal of each and every piece of her clothing for the last five or so minutes, but we were so desperate to keep our mouths on one another, the process had been slow going and she'd yet to have the chance to reciprocate.

I couldn't help it, though, and I didn't mind that I still wore my clothes. Her skin was like a flavor, one I swore had been specifically designed for me by Baskin Robbins, and her nipples were like the cherries on top. Deep red from my attention and perfectly delicious.

But the bleating of her phone threatened to pop my flawless

pleasure bubble.

And I was in no way ready to stop.

"Wes," she whispered as it continued to ring, and I shook my head, my lips skimming the skin of her throat as I did.

"No, sweetheart. Leave it," I reiterated.

I was frantic—desperate to get inside, to go further, deeper, harder—and her skin felt electric in my hands.

"God, Win," I breathed into the space between her breasts as her thighs clenched me even tighter at the hips and she started to shake. I wasn't even inside her yet, but the friction of my body on hers and the danger of being found were enough to make anyone go crazy.

Her nails dug into the skin of my neck as she squeezed, needy and greedy and trying to figure out how to get my mouth to be everywhere at once.

That was a lot to glean from the hold of her hands on my neck, but trust me, it was all there and then some. The shift of her hips, the catch in her breath, the way her chest vibrated with the effort it was taking to control her breathing.

My ears roared the way they always did when I was trying to be quiet, so the harsh reminder of her cell phone as it rang a second time pierced painfully into my brain.

Goddammit.

I ached in other places too, but the pain was entirely different. Nagging, unsatisfied, and, if I had to assign a color to it, I'd have no other choice than a hue of very deep blue.

"Wes," she whispered urgently. I dropped her feet to the floor obediently and pulled my body back, unmolding it from hers, but not before sinking my fingers more tightly into the flesh of her bare ass one more time.

"I know," I told her. She had to answer it. *She has a kid.* "Go ahead."

She practically dove for her purse, unzipping it and wildly brushing the contents out of the way until she came to the offending device.

"Hello?" she answered, reaching down to grab the tiny shorts of her Harley Quinn costume at the same time. She didn't bother with the fishnets that lay discarded haphazardly on the floor, but the time to be naked had apparently passed.

I felt like crying.

"What?" she asked, the tone of her voice changing as she hopped on one foot, the phone between her shoulder and her cheek, and struggled to get the shorts on and pull the material of her shirt back down over her breasts at the same time.

I grabbed her hip to still her frantic movements and slid my hand down the outside of her thigh as I sank slowly to my knees and grabbed the fabric from her hands. She looked down at me, but the dark hall made it hard to see what was on her face.

All I knew was that I wanted her to feel better—to alleviate her frenzy.

Slowly, gently, I eased her shorts back into place, skimming the skin and breathing all that she was in before kissing the inside of her hip and settling the waistband there.

"How many?" she questioned sharply into the dark.

As much as I knew I should move, I couldn't. It didn't make any sense, but something about staying there in front of her, my hands at her hips and my thumbs soothing the exposed skin as she spoke, settled something inside of me.

Normally rushing from one activity to the next, I didn't spend much time like this—with nothing on my mind other than the sensation of her skin under mine and my ability to slow her breathing and quell the shake in her voice with something as simple as helping her get dressed and a gentle caress.

I'd never in my life felt like I was missing anything. Not the absence of a mother figure or the lack of a real romantic relationship or the unconditional love of a child or a pet.

But this, right now, the peace and satisfaction I felt from a simple exchange with a woman I hardly knew, felt overwhelmingly, *unmistakably*, like something I'd very much been missing.

"Okay, okay. I'm not panicking," she told the caller as I pushed to my feet. "Do I sound like I'm panicking?"

She was asking him, but when her eyes met mine, the distant light glowing off the brilliant blue of them now that I towered above her, I knew she was asking me too.

I shook my head softly.

"Exactly," she said, and this time, with the backing of my confirmation, it was more confident.

"How is she?"

Lamely and dumbly, I cringed at the fact that I honestly hadn't put anything together until that moment. *Her daughter*.

I grabbed her elbow to call her eyes back to mine and raised my brows in question. Her face melted into a small smile before she mouthed, "She's okay. Stitches."

The knot in my stomach unfurled slightly at her silent words, but another, different one formed just as quickly. One that had more to do with the insecurities of a commitment-phobic man than worry over the health and safety of a child.

"Thanks, Rem. Just tell her I'll be there as soon as I can. And get her a donut; she loves donuts. Not cake. A donut." She let her head fall back and sank into the wall, covering her eyes with the hand free of the burden of her phone. "I know you know."

Reaching out, I gathered her into my embrace, hugging tightly until I felt her relax in my hold. It took a few seconds for the tension to melt from each muscle, but when she finally did, everything felt right.

Her voice muffled in my chest, she spoke again. "I'll be there soon." She nodded there, the movement scraping the fabric of my shirt across the nerves, and I squeezed her tighter on reflex.

"Thanks, Remy." She paused. "I love you, too."

She pushed against my chest lightly, and reluctantly, I let her go and looked down into her upset-but-handling-it eyes.

"Where are we headed?" I asked. The skin of her jaw felt like butter under my thumbs.

"What?" she asked softly, and then, realizing my intention, shook her head. "You don't have to leave, Wes. She's fine. On her way home from St. Luke's now. She saw a doctor I know and trust, and my brother is with her."

"But you're leaving, right?"

She paused, confusion influencing the features of her face to pull tighter. "Well, yeah."

"Then I am too."

"Wes…" she started, but I didn't let her finish.

"I'll take you. I have my car, and it'll get you there a lot faster than the subway."

That sealed it—without even a moment of question.

"Okay."

Apparently, I wasn't above using a mother's love for her child to get my way.

The real surprise, though, was the *way* I was fighting so hard to get it.

By my own doing, I, Wes Lancaster, self-proclaimed kid-phobic and anti-family man, was about to meet her daughter.

Fuck.

Winnie had only been surprised briefly that "my car" was, in fact, a car service. I did, after all, drive myself to the stadium daily, and our timing had been such on a couple of days that she'd witnessed this for herself.

But driving around the city was a nightmare I didn't particularly like having—especially not in a recurring capacity.

Because of that, I only used my personal vehicles when I was driving outside of the city or somewhere I knew would have easily accommodated parking.

Winnie lived in a nice brownstone uptown, and thankfully, the traffic had been sparse as we'd catapulted our way there from The Metro in Midtown.

But she hadn't paused to take in the scenery upon our arrival, so I hadn't either, following her into the house and signaling my driver to wait for my call with a gesture over my shoulder. There wasn't time for anything else.

Winnie didn't even notice I'd followed her, so intent on laying eyes on her daughter that nothing else mattered in a consequential capacity. I didn't blame her for it, and more than that, I made absolutely no attempt to call attention to myself. I had the distinct feeling the only reason I was actually gaining entry into her home was because she didn't realize I'd done it.

Down a long, molding-lined hallway, we made our way to the kitchen, the bright lights of it shining like a beacon the entire way. Winnie didn't pause or falter in her quest to touch her daughter and reassure herself of her safety, moving across the room swiftly and with purpose, but she did it in a way that wouldn't rekindle the flame of her daughter's own anxiety. A soft kiss to her cheek, a sweep of her blond hair from her tiny shoulder, and a look into her daughter's eyes were all Winnie needed to know she was all right. One brief perusal of the six or so stitches on Lex's chin, and Winnie's shoulders visibly relaxed like a deflating balloon.

So entranced by the interaction, I didn't even notice there was anyone else in the room.

"Who the fuck are you?"

I couldn't say the same for the man stalking in my direction with steel in his gray eyes and menace in his posture—a man who, I presumed, was Winnie's brother Remy—because, boy, he had noticed me.

His features mirrored Winnie's, and his authoritarian presence reminded me of the drive I saw in her every day. But he was dark to her light, his nearly jet black hair and olive skin at complete odds with the blond and fair nature of everything Winnie.

And murder raged behind his eyes.

At once, a thought I'd never before popped unwittingly into my mind: thank fuck for Thatch. Years of standing unblinkingly in the face of the big, bulky giant's threats had prepared me for this moment.

The answer to Remy's question didn't come from me, though. And it didn't come from Winnie either.

"You're Wes Lancaster," Winnie's daughter stated boldly into the tense room. Remy's surprised eyes left me immediately, but I didn't take notice for long. My gaze followed his to the source, and at roughly three-and-a-half-feet tall, Winnie's daughter, Lexi, made a far more imposing sight than I would ever have expected.

With a rough swallow to suppress my nerves, I jerked my head up until my eyes found Winnie's. She smiled a little, unsure but confident all at once. "Lexi is pretty into the Mavericks," she explained, tilting her head down to look at her daughter. "Right, Lex?"

Lexi looked up to me and back to her mother quickly. I expected her to meet my eyes again, but they never quite made it back, instead focusing vaguely on the column of my throat.

God. I wonder if she noticed the nervous swallow.

"Self-made restaurateur, one of Forbes' wealthiest men under thirty-five with a net worth of four-point-six billion dollars, owner of the New York Mavericks for six years with a five-year stretch including five NFC East titles, two NFC Championships, and three trips to the Super Bowl with one Super Bowl victory," she rattled off easily, counting off each number she said with a flick of the appropriate number of nimble little fingers.

Apparently, when your eyes almost bug out of your head, it makes you stutter. "Yeah. Uh. Yeah. That's…that's me."

Remy's assessing gaze found mine again immediately. I avoided his eyes in all the ways I could think to—by looking at literally every other person in the room.

I glanced up at Winnie, but her face was hidden as she put some cookies out on a plate on the counter, so I forced my awkward attention back to her daughter. Her attention was so intimidating, I found myself considering looking back to the angry, two-hundred-or-so-pound man.

"Do you have a favorite player?" I asked, trying to be normal and thanking my lucky fucking stars I had knowledge of the subject matter.

"Quinn Bailey went for over five thousand yards in the regular season last year, fifty-five touchdowns, and only threw ten interceptions."

I looked to Win again as my eyebrows shot to my hairline. Her daughter was fucking incredible.

"Where does she go to school, Win? College?"

A blush flushed the apples of her cheeks before trailing slowly down the line of her neck. It was unbelievably fucking inappropriate, with her brother *and* her daughter in the room, but I couldn't steer my mind away from one thought.

I hope to God she's turned on.

You're such an idiot, my brain rebuked. And I knew it was right. I cleared my throat in an attempt to banish any such inappropriate thought.

Tipping my gaze back down to her daughter, I found Lex looking at me intently, her intelligent eyes like laser beams straight to my insides. I hoped like fuck she couldn't read minds.

"So…" I ventured. "Quinn Bailey is your favorite?"

She blinked, her chin tucked to her chest as she peeked up at me from below. She looked slightly evil and like she might eat my soul. Which, ironically, was exactly how I'd been picturing children for years. My illusions of them weren't nearly this smart, though. Fuck, *I* wasn't this smart.

"No."

Done with me, she turned and walked right out of the room without looking back. I half expected her to give me the old middle finger salute over her shoulder as she left.

I wasn't really sure what was going on, but I thought, maybe, just maybe, Winnie's six-year-old daughter had just schooled me. Hard.

It took me a minute to turn around as I stood there staring after her retreating form.

Winnie spoke hesitantly from behind me. "I'm sorry. She's…well, Lex is different."

Her voice sounded funny, and not the kind that made me laugh. I turned to face her in the hopes that visual cues would provide some kind of clue as to the reason.

A line pinched the skin between her brows, and the corners of her lips turned up. It was a self-conscious mix of embarrassment and pride. And for the life of me, I couldn't understand the first.

"Don't apologize to this guy," Remy told her caustically.

Unflaggingly, I agreed with his message, but unlike Remy, I had no plans to address it directly, and I sure as fuck wouldn't have used that tone.

Working hard to turn my glare down to a simmer, I looked from Remy to Winnie and softened everything about myself when I saw the insecurity on her face.

Winnie was a brilliant woman—one who didn't need me or her brother or any-fucking-body telling her anything about the way she raised her daughter or didn't. She could draw her own conclusions from the awe in my voice.

"She's awesome. I can't believe she knows all that shit," I told her, confessing, "I don't even know all that shit."

Remy nodded, seemingly satisfied with my response, and turned back to his sister, his hands going accusingly to his hips when he noticed something other than his night of crisis and the "stupid fuck" her sister had brought home for the first time. At least, that's what I figured he thought of me.

"What in the fuck are you wearing?"

She rolled her eyes and waved him off. "It's a long story."

When he raised his eyebrows like he was waiting for her to tell it, she went on, "One I'm too tired to tell."

I watched like a ping-pong ball, oscillating back and forth from one to the other as they exchanged an entire additional conversation with just their eyes.

"Thanks for everything." Her eyes flicked from him to me and back again. "You can go now."

"Him or me?" her brother asked, outraged, and fuck if he was the only one wondering. Still, I said nothing. I figured silence was my best bet.

She seemed to make a decision then, and I didn't even have to guess if I was going to like the answer—I wasn't.

"Both of you, actually. It's been a long night. I just want to get Lex to bed and me to bed, and I'd really like to do it not in this costume."

It was on the tip of my tongue to tell her I'd be happy to assist in ridding her of any and all apparel when her brother's knowing eyes jerked to me.

I kept my face carefully blank.

"I'll talk to you tomorrow," she told us, ushering us toward the door. "And before you ask, I mean both of you."

As we stood shoulder to shoulder on her porch, Winnie shut the door with a smile and a wave. Neither her brother nor I moved an inch for several, long seconds.

Remy's body seemed to hum with what was coming, the very energy of his words reaching out in warning before he uttered even the first syllable.

"I own a shotgun, a shovel, and have three very eager helpers for the disposal of your body."

My eyes closed in a mix of everything at once—humor, surprise that the first threat of this kind was coming to me at such a late age, and uncertainty about whether or not I could be the man who didn't deserve a body bag.

"Noted," I replied finally, but he was already on his way down the steps and he didn't look back.

Way to go, Wes, I told myself as I descended the stairs slowly. *Years of sleeping with anything that moves, and you've chosen to become obsessed with a woman with a child and four brothers.*

Goddammit.

CHAPTER 10

Winnie

"Here, Lex," I said as I handed her a calculator from my desk to fool around with. "Work some numbers while I finish up a little paperwork, okay? And then we can go grab something to eat."

Her blond hair shifted off of her shoulders as she moved across the room and snatched the calculator out of my hands with excitement. My little Lexi was a numbers girl through and through. Hell, she could probably teach mathematics to high schoolers at this point. Which was why a calculator came in handy when I was in the process of trying to occupy her and finish up some work.

I rarely considered bringing my kid to work, but this actually made the second time in a week. Her nanny, Melinda, who attended NYU, had fall break last week and a huge economics exam to study for this week, and I tried not to rule her like a fucking dictator. She was a young girl, working her way through school and doing her best to straddle the line of adolescence and adulthood. I could see her clear as day, her struggles and determination, and when I looked *really* closely, I saw a younger version of myself rather than Melinda.

My mom had worked like a dog to support the five of us after my dad left, but there were only twenty-four hours in a day, seven days in a week, and fifty-two weeks in a year—and a very finite amount of money to be made.

So I'd been that girl, working my way through college and medical school with two jobs, fighting to find the light at the end of the tunnel that would afford me the ability to juggle one life instead of three.

When Nick Raines had shown up with his quick smiles, easy attitude, and life-lightening humor, I'd grabbed on as tight as I could and ridden the ride as long as he'd let me.

Of course, as all roller coasters do, the one with Nick had come to an abrupt end, and when the high wore off—and the pregnancy test read positive—I'd added responsibility to my life rather than absolved it.

Because being a single mother was a job, probably the hardest one I'd ever had, and by far the least predictable. I didn't go in at nine or leave at five, and the expectations of the job were never—not once—the same.

But if there was one thing that was a constant with my daughter, it was her inquisitive nature and the questions it produced.

Constant, curious, intelligent questions about anything and everything.

That was all well and good on a normal day, but when you were in college and trying to cram for an exam that would equal fifty percent of your grade, the questions were a little hard to manage.

As the person trying to work and pass her test simultaneously currently, I knew. I really knew.

Lexi moved over to the small leather chair in front of my desk and plopped her little butt down, her legs swinging back and forth underneath it. She scrunched her nose up as she focused, and her fingertips tip-tapped across the keys.

Silence—thank God. I loved the sound of her voice, had waited tirelessly to hear the words every mother dreams of when Lexi was struggling the most with her speech delay, but concentration and chatter, no matter how adorable, didn't go hand in hand.

Focused again, I carefully described every detail on the report for Harrison's torn ligament and moved on to the broken vertebrae DeMarcus Bassy had suffered in practice.

I still marveled at the injuries a sport could produce, the overall very real physical roughness of football, and the absolute grit most players displayed when you told them they couldn't play. There was never relief in their eyes or fear in their hearts—they lived and breathed football, and being told they couldn't be out there felt like a death of a part of them.

Five minutes later, the words, "Pen and paper, Mommy?" pulled my attention from my laptop and back to my daughter, but five minutes were better than none. Plus, her sweet face was a happy distraction from all of the gruesome details of the end of a man's dreams—at least for the season. Bassy's ass would be riding the bench for a good long time.

"Sure, honey." I grabbed a small notepad and pen from my desk drawer and set them on the edge of my desk.

Her Mary Jane-covered feet ran across the hardwood floor, and she stopped in front my desk, hand already gripping the pen and scribbling something down on the notepad.

As much as I wanted to savor my time with her, drink in her knowledge and learn all the things she surely had it in her to teach me, I didn't have the luxury. Instead, my eyes went straight back to my laptop, closed out the reports as I typed the final details, and hurriedly tried to finish a few more emails before the six-year-old standing across from me would cause any more distractions.

Mom life, right?

Sometimes, it was real fucking tough to get anything done.

And on top of the obvious time constraints, we were constantly fighting the guilt of feeling bad that we weren't giving our children all of our time, yet still trying to find the balance of not losing ourselves in just being Mom all day, every day.

It was a struggle every single day.

"Knock knock."

I glanced up to find Wes standing in the doorway of my office with a soft smile on his face. Everything inside of me woke up at once.

It'd been just over a week since the Halloween party at Brooks Media, and everything about that stretch of time said Wes and I were *something*.

Not defined in the slightest, but well above nothing, we'd managed to sneak away during work hours for sex four times in the last eight days. And as much as I expected my desire to die, after we were done, the flame always burned that much brighter.

His smiles came more easily and with much higher frequency, and after the first time I'd had to bring Lex to work, he'd even seemed to warm up to her. I'd noticed his discomfort at first, at not knowing how to interact with her without the manipulation he used on so many adults, but it hadn't taken him long to find a way to talk to her that seemed to put them both at ease.

"Are you stopping by the practice tonight before you head out?" he asked, both hands on the top frame of the door with his body leaning forward.

Good God.

"Probably not." I motioned toward Lexi and shook my head. "I've got a lot of work to finish up and, well, let's just say some things are very *distracting*." And two of my medical aides were on the field. I'd get a phone call if anyone seriously needed me.

Wes chuckled softly and walked toward my desk to stand behind my daughter, peeking over her shoulder. She was still too enthralled in whatever had her mind busy for the moment and hadn't even noticed his arrival.

His eyebrows rose dramatically at whatever he saw on her notepad. If I had a different kid, I might have feared a dirty drawing or limerick with the way his forehead seemed to disappear, but I didn't, so instead, I prepared myself to be floored. He must have jerked his head from the paper to me and back again a full three times before finally settling his surprised eyes on mine.

I tilted my head to the side with an indulgent smile and asked the question that was almost always relevant. "What am I missing?"

"Do you see what she's doing?"

I bit my lip in an effort not to laugh, as the answer, thanks to a good six feet of space and a lack of superhuman eyesight, was blindingly obvious. Still, I pictured her usual work and ventured a guess. "Writing numbers?"

"I'd say it's a little more complex than that," he responded, an actual bounce in his demeanor as he smiled bigger than I'd ever seen before. He may have been smiling more frequently, but right then, I realized I hadn't seen anything yet.

Lexi, as though she could feel the happiness radiating off of him, finally left her little bubble and glanced up at his face. "Wes! Now we're three."

"Hi, Lexi." And the smile deepened even further.

Good Lord, I'm in real trouble here.

"We're three?" he asked me curiously.

"There are three of us," I explained.

"Ah," he breathed, looking back down to Lex just as she moved her eyes to his throat and smiled. She was getting used to him, genuinely happy to see him, but still too overwhelmed by the complexities of his unfamiliar face to look him in the eye.

You're not alone, sister.

He pointed toward her notepad. "What are you doing there?"

"A linear equation. Each term is either a constant or the product of a constant and a single variable. Example: linear equation with only one variable. Ax plus B equals zero. A and B are the constants, and A does not equal zero."

Wes's smile, having barely faded at all, went back to full wattage.

"Mommy, linear equations."

"Wow, baby."

Seriously. Wow.

"I wish I could do them with you—"

Not a fucking chance I could do them *with* her. Watch her maybe.

"But I need to finish up a few things. Maybe we can do some when we get home."

Disappointment clouded her face instantly, and an arrow of guilt, sharp and unrelenting, stabbed me over and over again in the gut.

"Do you want to come down to the field with me?" Wes asked Lex, squatting down to get on her level, and I could feel my whole face freeze in shock. The skin felt tight, and my eyes rivaled fucking saucers.

"You don't have to do that—"

He waved me off and pushed to standing.

"No, this is perfect. She can come hang out with me on the field, and if I forget any of my players' stats, her brilliant little mind will come in handy."

I stared at him for a long moment, taken aback by the much-needed offer. I was starting to wonder if all of my assumptions about him were true. I felt like maybe there was a whole other side to Wes Lancaster, but trusting it as real seemed like a venture into idiocy.

Lex jumped up from her seat and put her hand in Wes's, his offer to take her with him as good as an order to her. Her mind worked in absolutes, and it really had never even occurred to her that I might say no.

Wes's surprised eyes still met mine in question, though.

"Sure. Why not." I shrugged my shoulders and smiled. "Be on your best behavior for Wes, and I'll come down to the field and get you in a little bit."

"How many minutes, Mommy?"

My daughter. The time stickler. The mere idea of her need for structure made me smile.

I glanced at the clock and calculated the time as quickly as I could in my head.

"Forty-nine minutes, baby."

Lex looked to the clock to do some math of her own. "It's 5:11 p.m. You'll come get me at six o'clock."

I smiled. "That's right, sweetheart."

And with that, Wes looked to Lexi's little hand in his as she led him out of the office, glancing back to me just once before they completely disappeared from sight.

In his eyes? Wonder.

Holy moly, if you're not careful, you're going to want a lot more from Wes Lancaster than just hot sex…

At exactly 5:55 p.m., I stood on the field, watching Wes kneel in front of my daughter, holding a football in the kicking position as Lexi stared down at him in absolute fascination.

Even crouched down below her, he looked like a giant compared to my little girl.

A surprisingly gentle giant.

And as I saw the adoration on her face as she continued to listen intently to whatever he was saying, I couldn't deny that my heart skipped more than a few beats.

I was five minutes early on purpose, knowing that Lex watched the clock like a hawk, and the strike of six would mean she was ready to pack it in—and I wanted to sneak a few peeks at the action before that.

The team was finishing up for the night, on the opposite end of the field, huddled together and deep in game plan conversation, leaving Lexi and Wes in a huddle of their very own.

I moved closer, carefully, so I could hear their conversation without either of them realizing I was there.

With the skill of a man used to children, he gently held her ankle as he showed her the correct way to kick the football. From the look on his face, I didn't think either of us expected it to come so naturally.

"You're going to come at the ball in a three-quarters type of position, Lex. And then keep your ankle locked and drive your foot all the way through the ball. Locked knee. Locked ankle."

He demonstrated the motion with her leg, rather than showing her with his own, and my chest squeezed. The fact that he'd so quickly figured out how to best help her learn proved how closely he paid attention, and having failed to master my poker face, I wasn't sure I was ready for him to pay that close attention to me.

"Why?"

He grinned up at her. "Because your body will generate a little skip, and that's where the power is going to come from. And just remember, the ball always needs to be lined up with the laces pointed toward the field goal," he explained as he ran his fingers down the white laces of the football.

"Why?"

"Because it will make the ball go farther."

"Why?"

He paused for a brief moment, and then his grin grew wider. "When you kick the ball from the back seams, that's the spot that creates maximum compression."

She nodded in understanding. "Compression makes the football travel farther and higher."

"That's right."

"Where do I stand? I'm predominantly right-footed. But sometimes, ambidextrous."

Geez. If Wes smiles any harder, his lips are going to tear right off his face.

"Since you're right-footed, for most people they need to stand about three large paces back and two paces to the left of the ball. But it will take a little practice before you find what's comfortable for you."

"I'm going to practice every single day for exactly sixty minutes."

Wes chuckled softly. "Well, then I think it's safe to say, in about fifteen years, I'll be offering you a spot on the Mavericks."

Lexi's smile was brighter than the sun. My eyes stung. All kinds of emotions were bubbling somewhere deep inside me, and I wasn't ready. Not to face it, not to question it, and not to fucking find out it wasn't real. I pictured a fist and mentally tamped it down so hard I almost choked.

"Now, when you make contact with the ball, aim for the 'sweet spot,' which is about four inches above the bottom tip of the football. Where you make contact with the ball is very important because it allows you to manipulate the distance and height that the football will travel."

"Ten point two centimeters from the bottom tip of the football."

"Exactly." Wes smirked. "Do you want to give it a try?"

Lexi nodded enthusiastically and did exactly what he'd instructed, taking three steps back and then two steps to the left of the ball. Her little legs moved quickly toward the ball as she tried her first attempt at kicking a field goal.

I watched on with amusement and pride as the football flew through the air higher and faster than I honestly thought my pint-sized daughter would've been capable of.

She immediately started jumping up and down in excitement.

Wes stood up and grinned down at her in a way a proud father would, and I couldn't help but wonder if he even knew that was the look he was giving my daughter. "Holy sh—hel—heck!" he cheered. "You nailed it!" He picked her up, spun her around, and then set her back down on her little feet.

Her eyebrows pulled together at the impossibilities. "I don't have a hammer."

Wes laughed and shook his head at himself, putting a hand to her shoulder and giving it a very brief squeeze. "You're right. I'm sorry."

Figuring it was time to make my presence known, I cupped two hands around my mouth and shouted, "Way to go, Lexi!"

She turned around and, at the sight of me, immediately started sprinting in my direction. It didn't take her long to make it to me.

"I was so accurate!" she yelled as she threw herself into my arms.

I hugged her tightly to my chest, breathed in her shampoo and soap and everything that was my daughter, and laughed. "You were! You did amazing!"

"I want to play football again!"

Wes's soft laugh filled my ears as he came to a slow stop in front of us. "I think you should get her on a team, Win. She has a natural talent for it."

"How many minutes until I play football again?"

"Honey—"

"How many hours?" she adjusted.

"Lex—"

She breathed a deep sigh, her face sinking desperately. "Days?"

I looked down at her and then back at Wes. "Can she do that? I mean…I don't know of any football teams with little girls on them, and the season already started." I gestured around the field as if to say, "Obviously."

"You let me handle it. I've got some contacts. I'll find her a good team with nice boys, and I'll even help her practice."

Lexi's little hands covered both of my cheeks and forced my eyes to hers. "I can play in one day?"

I shrugged. "I might have to wrap bubble wrap around you like a mummy, but sure, why not."

"Ayeeee!" she screeched. "Football in one day, one day, one day," she sang.

Wes smiled down at my daughter. "Don't worry, Win. I'll make sure she has all of the right equipment. I'll even take her to practice if you're too busy."

It took a lot of willpower to keep my face in an easy smile versus the what-in-the-hell-is-happening look that I really wanted to give.

Because, seriously? What was happening?

Wes teaching my daughter football. Wes saying he would take care of everything—team, equipment, even driving her to and from practice…

Who was this man?

And the real question…was he planning on sticking around?

CHAPTER 11

Wes

The halls were quiet, the hustle and bustle of players and coaches fading into the night just like the last splinters of sunlight.

I'd been getting lost in Winnie and her daughter when Coach Bennett came over and pulled me away for a last-minute briefing—something I'd specifically requested he do in the past—and I had immediately gotten annoyed. I'd been trying to make sense of *why* ever since.

Why would a guy who'd all but tattooed the fact that he wasn't into women with kids or kids in general on himself suddenly feel bereft after being taken away from…a kid?

It was a serious mental conundrum, and I hadn't come up with much, but there were two things I'd managed to walk away sure of.

One: I owned a goddamn football team, but the time I'd spent on the field with Lexi Winslow a couple of hours ago had been the most fun I'd had with the sport in years. Maybe it was because I was stressed, or maybe it was because Lexi had real, untainted, unmarred by years of disillusion passion for it, but either way, the result was the same.

The career you have because you love it can so easily turn into something you have to work to love. I wouldn't have ever thought that would be me, but it was. I'd let it become a job—and I hated myself for it.

And two: Lexi Winslow might have been six years old, but in practice, she was more of an adult than Thatch. So, really, it was basic science that she'd annoy me less than him.

Right?
I'm still not sure, but it seems plausible.

I wanted more time to test the theory.
Which brought me to now.
The hours got long during the season for people like Winnie and me, people who had decisions to make and staff to organize past the point when the last player's cleat left the field. I'd been doing this—putting in hours and hours after the sun went down—since I could remember, and I knew Winnie hadn't exactly been relaxing in the tropics for weeks at a time.

So, tonight I hoped to find her before the hours bled into nothing and the time to do something other than work completely escaped. I wanted to change, and the first step toward that was to spend time with her—get to know her.

We hadn't had time for much other than foreplay, fucking, and football, and my brain was finally starting to wonder what it was about her personality that kept me coming back for more. I knew why I craved her body, but I didn't have the answers for the rest of my yearning. Prolonged attraction and downright affection for a specific woman *and* some newfound tolerance for kids? Honestly, I was really nothing more than a big ol' bag of *what the fuck* these days.

As I neared the end of the hall, moments away from turning the corner into the one that led to her office, a buzzing started to build in my blood.

Anticipation or some form of psychosomatic indication that Winnie Winslow was near—it could really have been either one. Her back to me, she moved with grace, but not the kind that lacked a spark. She swayed and swooped like she had something hidden in each step. With the way I felt when I watched, I was starting to think it might be magic.

Her hair fell down her back like a sheet, covering a large portion of the plum color of her shirt, and a barely there wave had set in thanks to hard work and a little sweat.

I wonder if her skin tastes salty…if her pulse will thrum slow and steady or erratic like the buzz of a hummingbird's wing while I suck softly on the vein in her throat.

"Winnie," I called, eager to see her reaction to me and calm the one in my pants. We'd left on pretty good terms, and I felt pretty confident that I'd scored some points with the whole aiding-in-distracting-her-kid thing.

When Winnie turned and her nostrils flared more than her eyes, I decided maybe I shouldn't have been so eager. And yet, even in the face of her distaste or disinterest or uncertainty—or whatever it was making the whites of her eyes get bigger and the plump of her cheeks hollow out—the scales tipped so far toward needing more time with her, with them, confusion felt like a distant memory. The Winslows were apparently like chips, as I was left completely unsatisfied with just a little of them.

"Busy?" I asked. She reached up to fidget with the ends of her hair, pulling a nonexistent piece out of her face—it was clipped back at the top—and shifting her gaze to the beyond boring pattern of tile on the ground.

It took a few seconds, but eventually, her shoulders relaxed and her eyes met mine again. "Just finishing up, actually."

Fantastic.

"Come out to dinner with me," I told her. I figured I had a better chance that way than if I asked her. It was one of those rarely practiced truths; people said no a hell of a lot less if you didn't present them with an easy opportunity.

She looked down the hall to her closed office door, a door I knew concealed her daughter, who waited on her mom to be done. She was probably curing cancer or answering several unsolved meteorological quandaries, but no matter the math or science, she was, indeed, waiting for her mom to finish up.

She's just doing it with style. I smiled at the thought.

Winnie's eyes softened slightly at the change in my face, but they didn't lose their edge completely.

Her expressions walked such a thin line, every smile only a heartbeat away from a frown, and every glare just moments away from ecstasy. So easily manipulated, I loved to see the way her face changed, and I often found myself playing with her just to get the chance.

Knowing exactly where the conversation was about to go and wanting her company badly enough not to care, I beat her to the punch.

"Lex too. I want to take you both." I smiled and reached out to put my hand to her jaw, but I stopped when she looked hesitant. I tugged at the very end of a clump of hair instead. "Hell, I owe her dinner after how smart she made me look today. Players and coaches, everybody thought *I* taught her all that information."

Laughter creased the very corners of her eyes, and she bit her lip, shrugging one sweater-covered shoulder. It was practically a turtleneck, the cowl covering nearly every inch of skin at her throat, but my mind wandered to the skin underneath as it moved and pulled, and suddenly, it seemed like the sexiest clothing ever made. Her wardrobe had been transitioning slowly along with the turn in the temperature, and I found there wasn't ever something Winnie used to cover her body I didn't like—except for the very obvious obstacle it presented when I tried to catch a glimpse of a whole lot of skin.

"She taught herself all that."

"I know."

"On a Wednesday."

I smiled deeper.

"In an hour."

I thought of the way Lexi constantly dug for information and imagined being the person who most often had to supply it. "She must keep you on your toes."

She laughed and shook her head, the tension melting right out of her shoulders as we talked about her biggest accomplishment. "She's easy. Far more mature than most kids, and looks the other way when I have to cheat and look up the answers to her questions on Google."

I could picture it happening: Winnie, acclaimed doctor and brilliant mind, sneaking away to find the answers to questions posed by her six-year-old.

"That's how I learned so much about Teen," she went on.

"Ah. The clinical penis," I said, remembering that day nearly two weeks ago. In some ways, it seemed longer. In others, it felt like no time had passed at all. I still wanted her with an intensity I couldn't justify, and I still knew it was a bad idea.

The only difference now was that there was no stopping, no turning back—I couldn't have if I'd tried.

"Dinner?" I prompted again. If I dropped it, so would she. I was going to have to be like a dog with a bone this time around.

"Wes…we're fuck enemies," she said, surprising me. I'd honestly thought we were coming to a blatantly opposite place. Apparently, my notions weren't anything more than romantic propaganda pushed by a misinformed heart.

"Fuck enemies?" I asked with a sardonic laugh.

"Like fuck buddies without the friendship."

Sharpness twisted my chest and squeezed at the bluntness of her words.

It took me a few seconds longer than I would have liked to calm my racing thoughts, but eventually, I focused on my most important truth: That *wasn't* how *I* felt.

"Win," I said. "Truthfully?"

She nodded tentatively, unsure of what I had to say but willing to hear it. She looked like she thought it would be callous—mean, even.

"I'd have to change a thousand things over to be your enemy." Her breath left her in a surprised whoosh. "You and I are friends."

"Wes..." She shifted on her feet, as though maybe she weren't so sure.

"Maybe you could hate me," I conceded. "But I could never not like you."

"I don't hate you," she said with her mouth. *Not even a little*, she added with her big, honest eyes, and I finally relaxed. Her talk of being enemies was just that—talk. A mechanism to distance herself from a man whose every move screamed he needed it.

But my needs currently worked in opposition to my wants, and I'd never been that good at denying myself instant and frequent gratification.

"Good," I told her, prompting again, "Dinner?"

Uncertainty haunted the dark depths at the centers of her eyes, but the pull she felt toward me, the same magnetism that made me ask, kept her from saying no.

"Okay. But it's a school night, and Lex—"

"We'll go to my restaurant," I interrupted, too busy celebrating my victory to give any consideration to the fact that it was already eight o'clock—not that it would have changed anything if I had. I *had* to have their company. "In and out in record time, and if she's a picky eater, the chef will make her anything, whether it's on the menu or not."

"You don't have to worry about Lex and food. She eats just about anything. I'm the pickier one between the two of us."

Something, some feeling deep in the pit of my stomach, told me she wasn't just talking about food. Life and experience and a hell of a long time raising her daughter alone had taught her to be selective about everyone they welcomed into their lives. And she wasn't sure I was worthy of it yet.

Neither am I.

But I wasn't ready to say good-bye, so I used a word I couldn't remember consciously using in years. "Please?"

She looked surprised at the word, and though she looked beautiful, I couldn't feel anything other than disappointment. My mother had died giving birth to me, but I still suspected she'd have been disappointed in the way I'd treated people for the last several years—and I knew my father would have.

Even though I greatly respected nearly everyone, their backgrounds and unique outlook and successes, I hardly ever showed it.

And when I had demands, I usually *demanded* them. Maybe I needed to stock up on honey and give up a little bit of my vinegar.

"Okay. I'll get Lexi."

I smiled widely. "Good."

"But you're buying my dessert too."

"Hey," I teased. "I own the place. Something tells me I can make it happen."

Winnie and Lex had been grateful for my help in avoiding taking the labyrinth of trains they would have normally taken to get home, and I was happy to have company on a journey I normally made all on my own. Just three weeks ago, I had been convinced I was most content with the opposite.

Like I said…big ol' bag of *what the fuck.*

I drove nearly silently while they chatted, Winnie mostly asking specific questions in order to get Lexi talking a little more. It'd been a busy day, and according to what I had witnessed, that was one of the times she felt the least like talking.

And I couldn't say I blamed her. I usually didn't feel like it either. Why everyone thought every silence needed to be filled with chatter all the goddamn time was beyond me. Some of us were content to be quiet.

Still, this was a little different.

Winnie had finally shared with me that Lex had been diagnosed as high-functioning on the autistic spectrum—through an entirely unplanned conversation during postcoital supply-closet talk. I couldn't be sure, but it kind of seemed like she'd just needed to get it out, and I'd been happy to listen. Granted, I'd still had my hand on her breast and probably would have been content to do just about anything. But in hindsight, I really was glad I'd listened—and that she'd trusted me enough to share it with me.

Apparently, an important part of Lex's therapy was pushing her out of her comfort zone a little at a time. Kind of like stretching a muscle—if you worked her into it slowly, eventually all of the things that would be socially expected of her would come easily.

I was all for the success of the kid, I was by no means an expert on a child I'd spent time with three times at most, and I knew what they were doing was one of the reasons Lexi was able to talk to me as much as she was now, but I had a secret—I liked her like she was.

I like a kid. Huh. I'm just as shocked as you are.

After dropping my car off at my apartment garage, we walked the few blocks to BAD and occupied a table in the back.

It was pretty busy—good for business, so I couldn't complain—but I could tell the noise and overall activity was starting to become a little too much for Lex. She was agitated and antsy, and both of those made Winnie more and more uncomfortable by the minute.

I frowned as I realized that she wasn't reacting solely to Lexi's discomfort, but also to the threat of mine.

She was obviously afraid I'd be bothered, and—shamefully—under any other circumstances, she probably would have been right.

I simply hadn't had the experience with this kid or any other to understand. But everything I knew about Lex only made me want to know more—and I knew enough to know that anything seen as negative by someone else when it came to this kid, was something far deeper, and way further beyond her control than any of us could possibly understand.

An idea struck me.

I squeezed Winnie's leg under the table—to touch her, to get her attention, and to fly under the young genius's radar.

"I'll be right back, okay?"

Winnie's eyebrows drew together slightly, but she nodded, her cute black-frame reading glasses bobbing slightly on the bridge of her nose—apparently, she needed them to see the menu. "Okay."

I scooted out of the booth and headed for my office here at the restaurant. Thatch liked to joke that I sure had a lot of offices for someone who never fucking worked—which was not true, of course. But according to Thatch, his version of the truth was always better.

I flipped on the switch and blinked at the bright light before rounding my desk and opening and slamming drawers quickly.

My manager, Amanda, a cute woman in her midtwenties with rainbow-colored hair, apparently noticed, peeking her head in with a knock on the metal doorframe. "What's the commotion, boss man?"

I rolled my eyes and shook my head, opening the last drawer and shouting a little in victory when I saw the old scientific calculator right on top.

Amanda raised her eyebrows and stepped back at the unexpected show of emotion.

"Don't mind me," I said as I waved her off.

She looked at me as though I were a mythical creature, the discrepancies born of my own habits, but I didn't have the time or patience to address it.

Brushing past her, I gave a little wave and moved back toward the table where Winnie had Lex pulled close to her side and was speaking softly in her ear.

I slowed my step until it seemed like their moment was over and then sped back up to my normal pace.

"Hey, Lex," I said. "Look what I found. I used this thing in college, but even then, I didn't have half the brains you do."

"What did you major in in college?" Winnie asked as Lex reached out to take the calculator and quickly occupied herself.

I settled back into my seat and smiled at having done something right. Lex was content, and now that she was, maybe Winnie would be at ease too.

When I glanced back to Winnie, she was looking at me with something else in her eye again, but I couldn't quite place it.

"Electrical engineering. I've used it well, huh?"

Life was weird. I wouldn't have predicted anything about my career—other than the restaurant. I'd known from a very young age that I wanted this, but it wasn't about me. It was all about my mother.

Winnie laughed but shrugged. Made a show of looking around the packed restaurant. "You look like you're doing all right to me."

My gaze flicked between her and Lex. They put more questions in my mind than answers, but I knew one thing that was definite. I felt happier than I had in a long time.

When I met her eyes one last time, I added a wink.

Goddamn, Thatch would be proud.

"Right now, it looks that way to me too."

CHAPTER 12

Winnie

"You need a fucking doula, Cass," Georgia repeated for the fourth time since we'd sat down for lunch at a bistro not too far from the Mavericks' stadium.

Every table that lined the exposed brick wall was filled with couples and families and people taking a midday break from work, but in our party, I was the only one who hadn't taken the entire day.

Georgia claimed to be working from home, and Cassie made her own schedule. But Dean had flown the Brooks Media coop and trekked all the way from Manhattan just for this lunch date in New Jersey. Apparently, he was filing it as an expense, citing sanity and happiness in the workplace.

I'd questioned if he thought that was a good idea, but he'd pretty much waved it off. *"Kline Brooks isn't going to say jack shit about a day date with his wife,"* he'd said. I wasn't quite so sure, but I wasn't an expert by any means.

"For fluffernutter sake's, Wheorgie!" Cassie screeched and slammed her palms down onto the table, a wild woman finally pushed over the edge. It took quick hands and reflexes on everyone's part to prevent our water glasses from tipping over, but other than that, none of us batted an eye.

This had become the norm: Georgia constantly worrying about Cassie and the baby and fixating her neuroses on anything and everything pregnancy-related. I was concerned for everyone's well-being when Georgia and Kline decided to start a family.

Seriously.

With the way she acted toward Cass's pregnancy, you'd think Cass was actually her surrogate.

"I honestly don't think Cass needs a doula," I offered in hopes I could play Switzerland and stop a full-on catfight from breaking out. "She's planning on having the baby in the hospital and—"

But Cassie had other plans, chiming in before I could finish my attempt to keep the peace.

"And I'm getting all the fudging drugs they will allow me to have. *All* of them. I want them to numb me from the neck down. I have *no* desire to feel this child shoot out of my vagina. I mean, have you seen the size of my husband? He's huge. And I'm not just talking about his giant schlong. I mean, big hands, big feet, big fluffing head." She pointed to her belly as evidence. "Look at me! No one should be this big at twenty-some-odd weeks pregnant *with their first baby*. If the size of my belly is any indication, the fudging doctor is going to need bridge cables to suture up the hole."

Dean and I couldn't *not* laugh at that, but Georgia stayed steadfast in her doula views.

"A doula can still help you even if you get an epidural." She pleaded her case. "They'll just be there to guide you through the rough parts, before you're able to get an epidural."

I shrank back at the look on Cassie's face. Dean pretended to scratch the air like an angry cat, and I had to bite my lip to hold in my laugh. "What do you mean *before* I'm able to get an epidural?"

"Some doctors make first-time mothers wait until they have dilated to four centimeters before they can get their epidural," Georgia explained.

"What! Four centimeters!" Cass shouted in response, and people inside the bistro started to give us the side-eyed glances that said, *What the hell is going on over there?* I wasn't sure whether I should scoot closer and try to defuse the bomb or run while I still could. In the end, the horribly morbid part of me couldn't stand to miss the carnage.

Georgia, the pregnancy expert, nodded while a slightly smug smile consumed her pretty pink lips. "Yeah, four centimeters."

Cassie looked at me for help.

It's your own fault for not leaving.

I shrugged and contorted my face apologetically. "She's right. Some doctors *do* make first-time moms wait until they're past that four-centimeter mark."

"Oh. Hell. No." She shook her head maniacally. "Hell fucking no," she muttered and then placed both hands over her belly and stared down at it. "Sorry, baby, but Mommy is not going to wait until she's almost halfway to complete and ready to push before she gets some goddamn relief from you trying to claw your way out of my uterus. I love you, but yeah, not happening, little man."

"And the cursing is back," Georgia muttered, in my opinion, unwisely.

"You can shut the fuck up!" Cassie snapped back.

Dean's face scrunched up in disgust. "Can we not talk about pregnancy and uteruses and vaginas? I came here to eat, not vomit."

"Oh, shut up, drama queen." Georgia glared at Dean. "This is important stuff. She needs to be prepared." And then her eyes moved back toward Cass. "And you need to read those pregnancy books I bought you. And ask your doctor questions about delivery. And honestly, you need to really consider getting a—"

Cass pointed at her. "Do. Not. Say. That. Word. Again."

"*Doula.*"

"Fine!" Cassie shouted, and her hands went up in the air. "Dean's my doula. Congrats, Dean. You've got the job."

Dean's face morphed into absolute panic. "Oh no, honey. *Hell no*, actually." He held up both of his hands and wiggled his fingers. "These are not the hands of a man who touches pussycats. Especially ones that are crowning and ready to deliver." He grimaced as the words left his lips.

"Actually," I pointed out with the raise of one finger. "It's the baby that crowns. Not the pussycat."

Dean leaned forward and pretended to retch. Needless to say, that got us more attention from the surrounding patrons.

And I couldn't stop myself from bursting into laughter.

Georgia and Cassie stared at me in confusion.

"What? I'm sorry, but the mere idea of Dean being in the delivery room while you're screaming your head off is beyond comical. It is fucking gold."

Dean grinned, and Cassie started to laugh.

But Georgia had not a single change in her serious, steadfast facial expression.

I pointed toward her as my laughter slowed. "Look, I get it, you're worried about Cassie and the baby. And I think it's really adorable you care about her so much." I glanced at Cass. "Seriously, she's only doing this out of love, so cut her some slack."

My eyes met Georgia's again. "But come on, Georgia. You need to cool it on the crazy. Cassie is taking care of herself. She's taking care of the baby. And both mom and baby are healthy and happy. I mean, look at her. Only a healthy pregnant mom could walk around with that gorgeous glow. Plus, if the size of her boobs is any indication, her baby will be well fed and taken care of, always."

"Okay. Okay." A soft smile crested Georgia's mouth, and she held up both hands. "I get it. I'm a little bit crazy, but it's only because I love you," she declared as she winked at Cass. "I promise, I'll do my best to try not to be so overprotective and worried about my best friend and godson. But just cut me some slack, all right? Some days, I just worry about you. I just want you and little man to be healthy."

"Those are literally all the exact things you just said," Dean whispered to me under his breath. I giggled a little but shushed him so that the ladies could finish their moment.

"Stop stealing my husband's moves." Cassie winked back at her. "And I promise I will try to be more understanding. Love you, Wheorgie."

"Love you too, Casshead."

"Awwwwww...." Dean said with a big smile. "You two are the fucking cutest."

"Hey! Watch your language around my kid!" Cassie exclaimed as she held both hands over her belly. "He can hear you. And I'd really love it if he doesn't have a fucking mouth full of curse words the second he comes out of my vagina."

"But, honey, *you* just said fucking," Dean admonished.

She rolled her eyes. "I'm covering his ears."

We all laughed at that.

Dean smirked and stared at Cassie's chest in disgust. "You're right," he told me. "They are literally bigger than my head." He waved his hand over them and looked Cassie in the eye. "Do you mind covering those up a little more when we meet for lunch? I mean, they are starting to scare me. I honestly think I'm going to start having nightmares."

Cassie tugged down the neck of her shirt even farther. "Yeah, well, my husband thinks otherwise. And I prefer him to walk around with a constant boner, so consider your suggestion declined."

Dean put on some imaginary *Fuck you* lipstick with his middle finger, and then checked it in his real-life compact that he pulled from God knows where.

"Speaking of Thatch, have you guys decided on any names yet?" I asked, genuinely curious and trying to move the conversation along. I knew it had been an ongoing debate between the two of them. So many of the names Cassie suggested were ridiculous, I had started to wonder if she was just pranking him.

Oddly enough, pranks had been the foundation of their relationship. I'd missed the details, but every once in a while, the group liked to take a trip down memory lane.

Her lips curved like a cat with its cream. "You have no idea how much fun I'm having with this." Jumping into action, she pulled her phone out of her purse and set it down on the table, tapping the screen a few times and pulling up a text conversation between her and Thatch. "Read these."

I foolishly took the phone from where it sat and started scrolling.

Cassie: Naked Dinner tonight? I'm horny and need to be stuffed full of your giant cock. Pretty please? With cherries and whipped cream and a naked Cass spread across the kitchen table?

Thatch: Fuck, Cass. That got my cock hard, instantly.

Cassie: So, that's a yes?

Thatch: That's a FUCK YES. GET NAKED. I'M LEAVING WORK NOW.

Cassie: But…it's only noon, honey.

Thatch: I DON'T GIVE A FUCK. NAKED LUNCH. GET NAKED, CRAZY. DADDY'S COMING HOME.

Cassie: I have the best Daddy in the whole wide world.

So horrified I didn't think I could speak, I shoved the phone at Georgia.

"Uhhh…" Georgia muttered once she read through the same conversation I'd just choked back down in the form of vomit. "I really could've gone my whole life without knowing you call Thatch 'Daddy.'"

"That big tall drink of motherfucking water could be my daddy any day of the week." Dean sighed and then pointed at Cassie. "You are one lucky bitch. Don't ever forget that."

I laughed. "So…is naked lunch code for a brainstorming session for baby names?"

Cassie smirked. "Nah. Naked lunch is code for *Fuck my brains out, Daddy.*"

"Why did you make me read that?" Georgia asked, but the smile on her face contradicted the admonishment in her voice. "Now I've got all kinds of weird shit floating around in my head."

Cassie cackled. "God, I love you, Wheorgie. You always make my day." She swiped the screen a few more times and pulled up a different section of the conversation.

"Here. This is what I meant for you to read."

None of us reached for the phone.

"Oh, for fuck's sake. Stop being little bitches." Cassie shoved it toward me.

Georgia and Dean scooted around and leaned over my shoulders so we could read at the same time.

Thatch: What do you think about Liam?

Cassie: That reminds me of this model I photographed about four years ago.

Thatch: *growls* Never mind.

Cassie: What? It was just some random model I took photos of.

Thatch: Did you fuck him?

Cassie: Yeah…we probably shouldn't use that name.

Thatch: Benjamin, but Benny for short.

"Benny?" Georgia shrieked. "Are you fucking kidding me right now? That's practically my name."

"Relax. That was Thatch's idea, not mine," Cassie comforted.

When Georgia's eyes went back to the phone, Cassie mouthed, "Front-runner."

I shook my head, and Dean chortled into his mimosa.

Cassie: *singing* She's got electric boobs and a Mohawk too… Buh-Buh-Buh-Bennie and the Jets….

Thatch: "She's got electric boots a mohair suit."

Cassie: Those are not the lyrics.

Thatch: Yes. They. Are. Google it. And Benjamin is out now. You just ruined it.

Thatch: What about Max?

Cassie: When I was in fifth grade, I had a gym teacher named Max. He must've had 100 moles on his body, and his chest hair always peeked above the neckline of his shirt. God, I'm getting nauseated just thinking about it.

Thatch: Fuck. Never mind. What about Declan?

Cassie: Awwwww, I'm picturing this little leprechaun with a pot of gold now!

Thatch: Jesus, Cass.

Cassie: We could dress little Declan up in a green suit and green hat!!!

Thatch: NO.

Cassie: Thatcher…

Thatch: No. Give me some name ideas since you just ruined all of mine.

Cassie: My top three: Walter. Kanye. Channing.

Thatch: Are you high off pickle juice again? I mean, seriously, Kanye?

Cassie: I thought Kanye Kelly was a kick-ass name.

Thatch: Yeah. No way, Crazy. No fucking way.

Thatch: I love you, honey. I really do. But I'm getting worried our child will be nameless.

Cassie: What about Seaman?

Thatch: Pretty sure that's what got us here trying to pick out baby names.

Cassie: Not SEMEN, but Seaman. Little Seaman Kelly…I think it's got a certain quality to it, honey.

Thatch: Yeah. A spooge-like quality. I can't continue this conversation with you right now or else I'm just going to start beating my head against my desk.

Cassie: Naked Dinner tonight?

Thatch: I'll bring the SEMEN.

Georgia's nose scrunched up. "Seaman? Really, Cass?"

Cassie grinned. "Hilarious, right?"

I nodded. "Not gonna lie, I thought it was brilliant."

Dean grimaced. "If you name your child Kanye Kelly, I will scratch your eyes out like a feral cat."

Cassie laughed. "Fierce words, diva."

He nodded with raised eyebrows.

"Well, will you promise to take care of little Kanye Kelly because his mother won't be able to see worth a sneakers without her eyeballs?"

Dean's head tilted to the side. "Huh? Sneakers?"

"It's her replacement word for s-h-i-t," Georgia explained on a whisper.

"You realize the baby can't spell yet, right?" I asked with amusement.

"Considering your kid is doing advanced calculus at the age of six, I think you might be wrong. My baby could be figuring out a way to cure cancer inside the womb right now for all we know."

Georgia burst into laughter. "Yeah. That's not what a baby made by Cassie and Thatcher is doing right now, I know that with certainty."

Cassie glared, but Georgia held up a finger and went on. "Scheming? For sure. Plotting? Yep. But finding a cure for cancer? Nope. Not happening."

Cassie's ice-cold stare melted into a grin.

Dean downed the rest of his drink in one swig and signaled for the waitress to bring another.

"What's your deal?" Georgia asked, twirling a finger in the direction of his glass.

"I'm in fucking New Jersey," he whispered like the words tasted foul.

"Oh, come on!" Georgia said with a laugh. "You took the day off. My husband is essentially paying you to be here."

"Well, of course, you like it," he dismissed. "You live here now. You didn't have to sit next to a shirtless man on the train who smelled like a decaying rabbit."

Cassie covered her mouth, mumbling from behind her hand, "Well, that's graphic."

"Trust me," Dean said with a sigh. "The commute is *that awful.*"

Cassie must have noticed the look on my face. "You do it every day. Is it really as bad as the drama queen says, Win?"

I looked from her face to the others' and back again, admitting, "I don't know about the dead rabbit, but it's not great."

Georgia's eyes softened sympathetically.

"I'm actually thinking about moving over here."

"Oh my God!" Georgia bounced in her seat as Dean made a face of disgust. "You could get a house close to Kline and me! We'd be able to help out with Lex if you needed too!"

Cassie rolled her eyes at Georgia's enthusiasm.

I reached for Georgia's hand and gave it a squeeze. "Thanks. I'm not sure if I could afford a house near you guys, though."

"It's not—"

"It's a fudging mansion," Cassie cut her off.

I started to go on, but I stopped talking when the waitress set down our plates. Before I could manage the first bite of my chicken salad, my phone pinged on the table with a text notification. Wes's name flashing across the screen with the words, **Wanna do a late night in the office tonight?**

Cassie snatched the phone from the table before I could stop her.

"'Do a late night in the office'?" she asked with a sly grin. "Hmm... A late night... in the office... with Wes? What does that mean exactly? I'm probably going out on a limb here, but is *do a late night* code for getting fucked on Wes's desk?"

I rolled my eyes and grabbed my phone from her.

"Holy s-h-i-t!" Georgia exclaimed. "Are you and Wes having s-e-x?"

I took the largest bite of my chicken salad that I could manage and then proceeded to gesture toward my mouth and shrugged.

"You have got to be kidding me," Dean announced. "You are boning the delicious, mysterious, hotter-than-the-sun Wes Lancaster? I'm literally eating lunch with the three biggest bitches in the tri-state area right now."

We all three giggled at that.

"Seriously. Why are you taking all of the hot ones off the market?"

"Kline, Thatch, and Wes like pussy," Cassie teased. "You like cock, remember?"

Dean grinned. "I do like cock. Love it, actually."

The woman at the table across from us put her hands over her daughter's ears. I tried my best to give a nonverbal apology, but she was probably going to want to keep them covered.

Cassie pointed toward me. "So, how is Wes's cock?"

The burn of the hot seat upon me, I forgot all about that lady and her daughter and engaged in cock talk of my own. Though, to be fair, I was using it to say I *wouldn't* talk about the cock. "I'm not talking about Wes's cock over lunch."

"But you've seen it?" Georgia continued the interrogation.

I just stared back at her as I took a sip of my water.

Cassie's smile nearly consumed her face. "And you've licked it? Sucked it? Fucked it? Rode that—"

"Yeah. Okay," Georgia said with a hand in Cassie's face. "The baby doesn't need to hear these kinds of things."

I blushed. Neither did I.

Cassie slapped her hand away. "But I do. Tell me. Are you having sex with Wes?"

I shrugged and did my best to square my shoulders. "Maybe. A little bit."

"I knew it!" Cassie exclaimed. "I fluffing knew it!"

"Are you guys dating?" Georgia asked.

I shrugged again. "Uhh…well…no. I don't know… We're just sort of…."

"So, you're fuck buddies," Cassie answered for me. "That's fantastic. Good for you, Win. Good. For. You."

"Do you want to date him?" Georgia questioned. "Like, do you want a relationship with him, or is it just about the sex?"

I honestly didn't know the answer to that.

"What's he think about your downgrade to Jersey?" Dean asked with a raise of his perfectly coiffed brow.

"He doesn't think anything," I countered. "We're not in a relationship."

Eyes turned wild and suspicious all around, and I couldn't really blame them. There was a certain amount of want in my voice despite my efforts to conceal it.

Do I really want a relationship with Wes?

That seemed like a huge risk with a man like him. A man who had a mile-long history of never settling down and always perusing the pussy buffet.

I honestly wasn't sure he was capable of a relationship, especially with a woman who had a child.

But he's different with Lex…

Which was true. But that was right now. What would happen six months down the road? Would he still enjoy being in a relationship with a woman who would always make her daughter top priority?

"Winnie?" Georgia called softly with a gently knowing look in her eyes.

With a quick shake to clear my head, I pointed to Dean and decided the only thing I could at that moment.

"When the waitress comes back to bring you another round, I'm going to need one too."

CHAPTER 13

Wes

Another week and a couple of degrees Fahrenheit gone, November was officially in full swing. I glanced at the date on the lock screen of my phone and cringed.

The 20th. *Jesus. November is almost* over. *Where the hell is the time going?*

We were headed straight toward the fucking awful part of living in New York with below-zero wind tunnels thanks to tall buildings and physics, and old, garbage-contaminated snow, but, thankfully, other things were heating up.

Our season was on fire with a nine and zero record, and Winnie and I burned even hotter than the team. With sex and banter whenever we could manage, I was the happiest I'd been in…as long as I could remember. And when I thought about all the friction we used to build the flames—against walls, bent over desks, in the fucking locker room showers—the need to complain about winter in New York just up and disappeared.

I glanced up from fiddling on my phone straight into the clear blue eyes of Winnie Winslow herself. With her hair pulled back from her face and a lavender sweater covering some of the sweetest inc of her skin, she looked beautiful. Confident and poised and so goddamn irresistible I had to force my eyes away from her when another person spoke.

"You need to up your social media game, sir," Sean Phillips said with an easy, slightly antagonistic smile. His eyes popped against his darker skin, mischief flickering in the light green depths. It was times like these that I could see his relation to Cassie so clearly it was startling.

"I don't need to have any social media game," I told him, Winnie, and the three other players crowding the not-all-that-small space of the training room with their sheer size and bulk.

Professional football players had a way of looking small on the field, but they dwarfed any normal-sized man. I was comfortable with my height at six foot two, but according to Thatch, being six two in a room full of football players was like being five foot seven on *America's Next Top Model*—you were the runt of the professional litter.

Plus, I wasn't carrying seventy extra pounds of muscle like these guys.

"He's right," Jeremy Rollins, one of our star wide receivers, agreed. He had a vertical jump fucking cats would envy, but right then, as he agreed with Sean and started an epidemic of pushing me into the social media foray that I knew wouldn't end with him, I considered taking out both of his kneecaps. "I saw the Bruins owner tweeting all kinds of updates and shit. Really got the fans into it."

Winnie's eyes flared with her agreement.

Fuck. Maybe I could make Georgia do it.

Winnie laughed like she knew what I was thinking, and with the amount of time we'd been spending together, she probably did. "Not someone else. You. *You* should tweet," she asserted.

"I don't *tweet*," I said with a curl of my lip.

"Not yet, you don't," Quinn Bailey agreed with a wink. "But we're going to teach you."

"No."

"Yes!" Winnie said, excited and nodding.

Fuck.

"Fine."

All of them just stood there and stared. Winnie with happiness, Quinn with way too much knowledge, and the others waiting for Twitter to grow roots and spring from the ground right in front of me, apparently.

"Well?" I prompted. "Do I just email it?"

Earnie Fletcher, one of the best tailbacks in the league and all-around monster runner, choked on a laugh before straightening himself up when my face didn't change. "Oh. You're serious."

My eyes burned with the effort I put into telepathically saying, *Fuck all of you.*

"Okay, so you're going to need to go to the App Store. Do you know what the App Store is?" Quinn asked with a tremor of humor in his voice, jerking his head to my phone.

I honestly wasn't sure I did, but fuck if I was going to let them know that.

"Yes," I sneered with a tilt of my head. "I know what the App Store is."

Winnie smiled, all the way from her mouth to her eyes, and touched her nose. She knew I was lying.

Holding up her phone from behind the crowd while the guys looked at me, she pointed to a blue button on the screen. I searched for the same icon on my phone and pushed it.

"Now, just search for Twitter," Sean instructed.

I did that and pushed the little box that said "Get." I didn't know anything about this shit, but I also wasn't an idiot.

"Now what?" I asked when it loaded.

It only took them five minutes and a heated discussion over what my "handle" should be to get me in the position to actually tweet something.

It was @NYMavsTopGun, by the way—a cute play on the movie *Top Gun* and being the guy in charge. I was both disgusted and impressed by the argument those four men had while strategizing my name. It was a lot like any exchange between Kline, Thatch, and me. Apparently, almost all grown men are children.

"All right. What do I say?" I asked testily, growing a little frustrated with the whole thing. I wasn't really great at being the guy who didn't know what was going on.

From a very young age, and likely because of the lack of my mother's influence, my father had raised me to be independent and in charge. Honestly, I think he just needed me to help him raise me by raising myself. He hadn't planned on having to teach me all of life's lessons on his own. But men like him never did. They walked into the hospital with a smile on their face and excitement in their hearts—and they left, brand-new baby bundle in their arms, heartbroken and without a wife.

"Anything you want," Fletcher offered. I had to focus in order to remember what I had even asked.

Winnie's eyes shot to mine, and she almost shouted. "Not anything! Jesus. Don't get him into trouble, guys."

Quinn rolled his eyes with a smile. "It's just Twitter."

Oh, yeah. Twitter.

"And how many followers do you have on Twitter, Quinn?" Winnie fired back pointedly.

God, I loved when she got heated. I had to look down in order to conceal my smile, but I peeked up from underneath my lashes so I could watch Quinn's reaction.

He didn't even have to think about it. I was guessing, by the line of his jaw, Southern charm, and cut body, he had a lot. "Point taken."

"He could just say something about practice," Rollins suggested.

"He should say something funny," Sean insisted as he jumped up onto Winnie's table and leaned back on his elbows, feet dangling.

"How about he doesn't say anything?" I grumbled.

Winnie laughed. "Relax."

I thought about it, and out of nowhere, something came to me. I moved my fingers over the keyboard and then showed it to the room. "How's this?"

They passed the phone around, starting with Winnie, and I thanked fuck I had my messages set to show the notification without the message. I didn't need something popping up on there while any of them had their hands on it. Especially because, when you were friends with someone like Thatcher Kelly, you never knew what was going to show up at any given moment.

Winnie's eyes grew moist, just barely—but enough that I noticed—and I knew no matter what any of the other fucks said, I was posting it.

"It's perfect," Quinn thankfully agreed.

"He just needs a hashtag," Sean said as he passed the phone back to Rollins.

"A hashtag?" I asked. Fletcher smiled when he read the words on the screen and lifted his eyes to mine. There was noticeably more warmth within them—as though I'd finally proven myself as human.

"Usually something ironic, funny, and common-ground building," Quinn explained.

"You put this little thing—"

"The pound sign?" I asked.

Sean bit his lip and bugged out his eyes, muttering under his breath, "Hashtag: signs you're old."

I was pretty sure the little asshole was mocking me, but as he typed away in order to give me whatever the fuck the all-important hashtag was about, I realized I couldn't kill him until he was done.

Winnie, as though reading the murder in my eyes, stepped forward and took the phone from Sean to pass it to me herself. I looked down to read what he'd added.

@NYMavsTopGun: Season rush yards: 5468. Pass yards: 4367.

Lessons from a six-year-old. #areyousmarterthana1stgrader #no

It looked good to me. "What do I do now?"

"Push tweet," Sean said with a roll of his eyes.

God, this was ridiculous. My thumb hovered for the barest of seconds before making contact with the screen.

"Okay, done."

"Congratulations," Winnie offered enthusiastically, and the guys laughed.

"Why does this feel like the beginning of the end?" I asked with a groan.

"Because it is," Quinn said with a wink.

Another fucking winker.

I shook my head.

Struggling to take my eyes off Winnie and her warmth, and completely done with the other bozos in the room, I forced myself to focus on the phone in my hands and use it for something other than tweeting and chirping and shit.

Me: Meet me in the storage room?

Winnie's phone pinged, and her cheeks got rosier the instant she read the message. The blush overwhelmed the peach of her skin even further when the guys noticed her reaction.

"What's up, Dr. Double U?" Quinn asked with a good-ol'-boy smirk and far more knowing eyes than Winnie or I would have liked.

"'Who is it, Pooh?' asked Tigger," Sean Phillips teased. He was smart and had a good head on his shoulders—despite being related to Cassie.

In fact, all four of these young men were smart, and they'd pretty quickly become some of my favorite picks. Picks I'd make again, repeatedly, if fate saw fit to give me a Groundhog Day scenario.

Rollins and Fletcher were quieter. Reserved. Watchful.

But what they lacked in exuberance, they more than made up for with intelligence.

Win squatted down and reached for something from her supplies so she wouldn't have to meet any of our eyes.

I kept my phone up, my fingers typing, and my face neutral—what Thatch often referred to as my "natural state."

Me: Tell them to go fuck themselves. It's none of their business.

She read again, and the very corner of one end of her mouth curved up. I could actually feel her fighting the pull to meet my eyes. And it wouldn't be the players she'd be telling to go fuck themselves if and when she gave in.

I typed again.

Me: Tell them it's Coach Bennett. They're all late.

Her face after I said that was my favorite, the horror and realization of a prospective assumed affair between her and the head coach making that excuse a definite no.

I was seconds away from sending another suggestion when she killed my fun but put a whole other kind into motion.

"It's my babysitter," she announced to the room. That seemed to calm the inquisitive young minds around us. "I have to make a call."

As she approached the door, and me, her eyes finally, briefly, caught mine. They said soon I would pay.

I just hoped it was in all the ways I liked best.

Unfortunately for me, when I escaped the guys and followed her to our supersecret location—the storage room—there weren't actually pleasurable things waiting for me.

A lecture. But no pleasure.

Though, really, I had to admit, I really liked when Winnie shoved my shit right back at me. So maybe there was a little pleasure.

"You can't text me like that in front of people," she commanded, backing me into the door with a finger in my face, and I did my best not to smile. Smiling right now would lead to nothing but trouble. Not one goddamn good thing. And I was really trying to be on Santa's Nice List at the end of this exchange so I'd get the orgasm I'd spent so much time writing the letter asking for.

"What am I supposed to do?" I asked as innocently as I could manage. "Spell things out?"

"No!" She swatted at me. I watched her hand move and then looked back to her face and pretended to think about it.

"You're right. Not only would the guys know, but Lex would too. No way spelling will work. She knows more words than I do. So hand signals it is."

A startled laugh sounded surprisingly like a bark as it left her throat. *Woof, woof, baby.* "Hand signals? What?" She parted her lips and pinched her eyes slightly.

"We're going to need a highly coded but easily articulated set of hand gestures for communication. If technology is off-limits, this is the only other way."

"Are you sure we shouldn't just use carrier pigeons?" she asked sarcastically, and she gave me a little shove so that my back tapped the door.

"Of course," I deadpanned. "They're completely unreliable."

She relaxed her face, and just the hint of a smile curved her lips, but she didn't step back. *Thank God.*

"Plus," I added dramatically. I put one hand to her hip and pulled her even more tightly against me. "There's also the whole bird flu thing."

"Wes—"

I held up my free hand and showed her the inside of my fist. I held it like I was a fifth grader, determined and ready to master all the facets of a real kiss.

You know you did it too.

"What's that mean?" she asked with frustration, a grown woman stuck playing children's games thanks to an aggravating man, but it didn't last long.

I'd never liked the tell part of show-and-tell in class, and this was no different.

As my lips met hers, I didn't think there'd ever be any doubt what this hand signal meant—to either of us.

CHAPTER 14

Winnie

"Oh! Go, baby, go!" Georgia shouted across the field, clapping her hands and jumping up and down on her high-heeled boots like a giddy-chic teenage girl, as the rugby match started. Her eyes were on her husband, and she looked like today—and every day—she wanted to swallow him up whole. And by the tender yet fierce intensity of the return smile he gave her, it was safe to say, he only had eyes for his wife.

Georgia and Kline were quite literally beautiful together—she was his world, and she didn't know one existed outside of him.

I want that.

God, I want that so bad.

I wanted to be loved in a deep, all-consuming way. The kind of love that made you feel invincible and special and like the huge expanse of the world had somehow, some way found time for the tiny speck that was you—because the two of you together was *that* important. So important that it did things for people other than the two of you. Kline and Georgia and Thatch and Cassie had those kinds of relationships. They gave the people around them energy and hope.

And most of the time, when I wasn't having a pity party for one, that was a good thing—the best.

Wes could be that man for you, my heart told me. *Sure he's headstrong and stubborn, but he respects you and...*

Whoa. Whoa. Whoa.

Where had that even come from?

I glanced around the bleachers to see if anyone else had noticed my moment of temporary insanity, if I'd somehow mistakenly mumbled all the crazy things aloud. Because that's what it had to be, thinking a man like Wes—a man who didn't even acknowledge me as anything more than a fucking friend in mixed company—could possibly be the other half of my whole. Temporary insanity.

I looked to the field just as Wes ran by and shot one of the sexiest fucking smiles to which I had ever paid witness over his shoulder.

God.

It'd been aimed at the other guys on his team, but sweet Jesus, it slayed me all the same.

Shit. Could Wes be that guy? *My* guy?

He *had* been spending a lot of time with my daughter, teaching her football, occasionally taking her to practice, and going out of his way to do little things for her that only a child like Lexi would understand and cherish.

And the flirting and teasing and fucking with him was... *incredible.*

No man—*no man*—had ever touched me, pleasured me, understood what I needed like he did.

My mind recognized all the red flags, but my heart was doing a bang-up job of ignoring all the fucking evidence. My heart and my goddamn horny vagina—both of them, mutinous.

And that scared the shit out of me.

I forced my attention out of my head and onto the field, where the guys played on, mostly oblivious to the ludicrous happenings on the sideline. My personal treadmill, Cassie's angry cankles, and Georgia's completely misdirected enthusiasm.

But once my eyes caught sight of Wes, serious and determined and looking like the sexiest motherfucker I had ever seen, I could do nothing but ogle him.

His biceps rippled and stretched as he sprinted smoothly toward a player on the opposite team, the thick muscles in his thighs demanding attention with each powerful step.

Jesus. Did he really have to be that perfect? It was cold out, for fuck's sake. I was wrapped in a *blanket,* and he was in *shorts.* They all were. What was wrong with him? What was wrong with all of them? Those hot, stupid, ridiculously muscled men.

Christ, I needed to go to more sporting events if this was what they were like.

As crazy as it sounded, it made sense that my physical attraction to Wes was so horrendously out of control. I'd known what kind of man he was—spotted it from the very first second—and still, under the spell of his swoony hazel eyes and chiseled jaw, I'd completely abandoned my six-year run as a smart woman.

Of course, then, I'd gotten to know him, and I'd based my hiatus from sanity on his serene yet quiet confidence. The way he carried himself and the way he handled himself in all things, business and personal.

And, well, as it does, all those stupid choices had led to the ultimate stupid move—I had sex with him.

He was an intuitive lover. Always knowing what I needed without me even having to tell him. Wes had a power that no one else had ever had. He could take me out of my own head to the point where I would just feel.

Feel *everything.* Every touch like it was a soft caress across my skin and each touch seeped into my pores until it became a part of me and I couldn't be anything but in the moment and *feeling.* Just feeling.

Put simply, it had been off the charts—and still was.

Great...now I'm picturing him naked. This can't be good in public...

As surreptitiously as possible, I glanced down at my chest to make sure I wasn't visibly showing off my arousal to the world. All clear. If it weren't for the little bit of padding in this bra, I might as well have had a giant neon arrow over my head letting everyone know, "This woman has sex on the brain. Wes-sex brain."

"Kick his fluffing ass, Thatch!" Cassie shouted with both hands cupped around her mouth. Her feet were propped on the cooler in front of her—an empty cooler carted there by her husband for just this very purpose—and her skin flushed red as the bitter wind whipped around it.

"I can't believe you're wearing a tank top right now," I muttered, even though I knew better than anyone that the hormones of a pregnant woman were an unpredictable thing.

Confirming that very observation, Cassie's eyes cut to me threateningly.

Eek. "Sorry," I muttered when the power of her stare started to feel like actual knives. Georgia bugged out her eyes at me from over Cassie's head, and I decided it was best to metaphorically take a careful step back.

Turning back to the field and its roguishly handsome inhabitants, I watched as Thatch ran at full speed toward the opponent's end of the pitch. He was seriously athletic, they all were, but it didn't seem natural for a man that size to be so agile.

"Bumrush him, Thatcher! Bumbazzle him!" Georgia screamed in excitement.

As if propped on top of screws, my and Cassie's heads turned to the right in perfect synchronization. I had to put a hand to my mouth to stop myself from completely losing it.

"What?" Georgia asked as she surveyed our wildly tickled faces.

"I think you mean *bamboozle* him," I explained through my amusement. "Or break through the defenses. That would work, too."

"Whatever," she said with a scoff and turned her gaze back to the field. Thatch had the ball and was dodging defenders left and right.

Georgia surged to her feet and hopped comically from one foot to the other like she was doing some kind of rugby-rain-dance. "We need our team to score a fry! Go, Thatch! Go, Thatch! Get the fry! Get the fry!"

Cassie and I looked at each other behind Georgia's back, and when the dam finally broke, Cassie sounded like a wounded animal being attacked by a hyena, her hysteria was so powerful—which, in turn, made me laugh harder. She held her rounded belly with both hands as it shook violently up and down, and I watched through wet eyes, wiping vigorously at the tears streaming down my cheeks.

Georgia was undeterred by our humor-induced meltdown, but Thatch looked over just as he crossed the try line, the sound of Cassie's laugh like a primal call into the wild for her mate.

"Wooohooooooooooo!" Georgia clapped and screamed. "We just got the fry! Wooohoooooooo!"

"*Try!*" I exclaimed through choking breaths. "They got a try, Georgia. Not a *fry*."

She turned toward me and tilted her head to the side in confusion.

Cassie struggled to speak through her wheezing. "We're not at McDonald's, Wheorgie. No one's ordering Happy Meals. We're at a rugby game. French fries *do not* come on the side."

"It's called a try? When they score the goal?"

I grinned. "It's just a try, honey. Not a goal or a fry. *A try.*"

"You suck at sports, G," Cassie added. "I mean, are you trying to suck this bad at sports? I'm honestly starting to wonder."

"I do not suck at sports!"

Yeah. She really did. Her sports knowledge was so bad it couldn't even be scored.

Cassie nodded, sweeping a hand out toward the field. "Um… yeah…you do."

One stubborn hand went straight to Georgia's hip. The real attitude had arrived. "I work for the Mavericks, you know. I work for them, and I know a lot about football."

I nodded thoughtfully and pursed my lips before asking, "What's the quarterback's name?"

"Quinn."

"What's his last name?" Cassie pushed.

She stared Cassie down for a second, and it was obvious she was racking her brain for the answer. Her mouth formed silent words, but they were easily read.

QB Pie…Q…B…Quinn…B…Quinn…

Her eyes lit up. "Bailey! Ha-ha! His name is Quinn Bailey! Suck on that, cupcake!"

Cassie smirked. "That's so cute, Wheorgie. That you call the quarterback of a professional football team, *QB Pie*."

Georgia's jaw dropped, and then her nose scrunched up in frustration when she realized she had laid her cards right on the table without saying a single word.

"You are literally the most adorable human being I've ever met," Cass added with a wink.

"She's right," I agreed. "You're fucking adorable."

"Goddammit," Georgia muttered. "I will know sports someday. I will."

I reached around Cassie and patted Georgia's shoulder. "I have full faith in you."

Cassie coughed to hide her words. "Gnome, you don't." And then she coughed again. "I gnome I don't."

Georgia shoved her, and I laughed.

"I hope you shit yourself when you deliver the baby," Georgia mumbled, but she said it loud enough for us to hear.

"Excuse me?" Cassie asked and squinted both her eyes in irritation.

"I said," Georgia enunciated dramatically, *"I hope you shit yourself when you deliver the baby."*

"That's ridiculous," Cassie scoffed. "No one does that."

Oh, Jesus. *Here we go.*

Georgia's smile was full-megawatt, *I motherfucking told you so.*

Cassie's head swung back and forth like a flag in the wind, and then she paused—the calm before the storm.

"WHAT!" she screamed as she jumped to her feet, and the people sitting in the bleachers in front of us turned to look. "I'M GOING TO SHIT MYSELF WHEN I HAVE THIS BABY?"

I honestly thought time had stopped in that moment.

Just stopped.

And the entire universe was focused on the three of us.

Cassie held her hand above her eyes to shield the sun, and she stared out onto the field in search of her husband. "THATCHER!" Her voice was a fucking bellow, possessed by the evilest of spirits. "YO! SUPERCOCK!"

Thatch, noting the severity of the situation, stopped midrun and turned to look at his crazy wife.

"Cass? Honey? I'm kind of in the middle of something here," he yelled back to her.

"THATCHER! DID YOU KNOW THAT I'M GOING—"

I hopped to my feet and slapped my hand across her mouth before she could take this situation from ridiculous to downright insane.

"It's fine!" I called out to Thatcher. "She's just having a moment!"

He smirked and shook his head. "Tame the crazy until after the game, honey, okay?"

Cassie tried to yell something back to him, but I held steadfast in my silencing ways.

No one at this game, no one in this city, no one on planet Earth needed to have those kinds of visuals put inside their heads. If anything, I was doing this as a civic duty to protect humanity.

Even Wes had taken notice of the situation and looked up toward the bleachers where we sat. His concerned gaze met mine, and he mouthed, "Are you okay?"

I just nodded and offered a reassuring smile. He turned to go back to play, but he paused and looked up at me once more.

"Are you sure?" he mouthed.

I nodded again.

And then a sly, slow smirk crested his perfect lips, and he did the one thing that I didn't expect.

He held up his hand and showed me the inside of his fist with a wink.

Our signal. In front of everyone there, Wes Lancaster had unmistakably declared him and I as a unit in that moment.

To say I swooned would've been an understatement.

Sure, the parameters were still hazy as fuck, but the evidence of the lines were there.

"What was that?" Cassie asked when I finally pulled myself together and removed my hand from her mouth.

"What was what?"

"That little thing Wes just did. With his hand. What was that?"

I shrugged. "I have no idea what you're talking about."

Great, Winnie, my hearted chided. *The hot sex-god finally makes a declaration, and you do everything you can to avoid admitting to it?*

We sat back down on the bleachers, and while I forced my focus toward the field, I could feel her staring holes through the side of my face.

I ignored her intensity for a while, but eventually, it felt impossible. When I turned toward her, her smile got bigger than her face. It was creepy, to be honest.

"That was a thing, wasn't it? A sex thing."

I shook my head and added the wag of a finger for good measure. "It was not."

"I think it was a thing," Georgia stated, jumping into our tête-à-tête without hesitation. "A kinky sex thing."

Cassie nodded in agreement. "I think you're right, Wheorgie. I think Winnie is falling head over heels in fluff-drunk love with Wes, and I think that was the symbol for butt stuff. You're a little freak, huh?"

I rolled my eyes. "You guys are ridiculous."

But they ignored me. And started talking about wedding plans.

My wedding plans.

Mine and *Wes's*.

"Someone save me, please," I muttered to myself just as Wes met my eyes as he ran and slid his tongue along his bottom lip.

Sweet Jesus.

You don't want to be saved. You want to be swept off your feet by Wes Lancaster.

Was everyone crazy here? Even me?

I was honestly starting to wonder.

CHAPTER 15

Wes

"Please! Holy hell, Kline, I can't believe you're spewing this crap to me," Thatch boomed as I approached the round corner booth they'd somehow managed to snag. McCallan's Pub was packed, jammed with people looking to ease the stress of work and commune with friends and foes alike—and, probably, escape from the ball-shriveling cold.

And yes, I'm the type of person who constantly whines about how cold it is, only to bitch about the heat when the weather turns. You're better off accepting it now.

Something about the mix of alcohol and food always made McCallan's seem like the perfect place to sit down for a laugh with your mortal enemy—if ever there was a place.

If I'd been here on time, I probably would have paid someone for the best booth in the place, but there was no way Kline had stooped to my level. I'm sure he'd somehow managed to rationalize to the manager he or she should set it aside for us.

Shaking my head at the mental picture of him doing just that, I didn't notice Winnie looking at me until I was right there, too close to escape the effect she had on me and far too distracted to conceal my reaction.

She seemed surprised as my face lit up openly, but shock quickly morphed into elation.

Happiness sure looked good on her.

Christ, the truth was, everything looked good on her. I'd been half a nut for the entire game as I tried to keep one eye on the ball and the other on her. She'd been laughing and smiling and looking at me like I could walk on fucking water—and yeah, I'd seriously wanted to take her home with me and fuck her.

I'd planned to do just that, but she'd been gone before the game was over, and I hadn't had the chance to ask. Something about running home before dinner to do…something. Fuck if I really knew, I just knew she was gone.

But she was here now.

"All I'm saying is that you can't blame Jacob. She cried to him and counted on him, and fuck, the kid is jacked. It's no wonder he thought maybe he had a chance at being more than friends with her," Kline explained to Thatch passionately, talking with his hands and gesturing to Georgie in an effort to get her to back him up.

"What are you guys talking about?" I asked, taking a seat next to Winnie, running my arm along the back of the booth and making sure my thigh pressed tight to the warmth of hers. One glance down had me wishing I hadn't been so hasty to put my arm up near her shoulders.

A sliver of her long, tan legs peeked out from the hem of a shorter than normal office skirt before being concealed again by thigh-high black suede boots. Clearly, one of the things she'd done at home was change clothes.

Goddamn, I'm in trouble tonight.

Winnie noticed the direction of my gaze, but she didn't mention it. Instead, she rubbed her thighs together teasingly and bit into the flesh of her bottom lip.

I had to drag my eyes away with virtual sled dogs as Georgie provided an answer to my question.

Her face was bright, on the edge of manic, as she shared, "They're having a *Twilight* argument."

"Twilight?" I asked before it clicked. Because, really, there was no reason for it to make sense that quickly.

"You know, *Twilight*," Cassie explained. "Favorite movie to teenage girls all over the world and the catalyst to several thousand vampire fetishes. Thatch is wisely Team Edward. Kline, here, is trying to make a case for Jacob." She scoffed.

I laughed once, almost harshly, before both Kline's and Thatch's eyes shot to me. They didn't look happy.

Looking from face to face, I met each of our party's eyes with disbelief before my gaze landed back on my best friends. My adult, male best friends. "You're serious?"

"Fuck yeah," Thatch boomed before turning back to Kline. "Bella and Edward were fucking destined for each other. Jacob was only there because he was pining for the combination of their sperm and egg. You can't fight lifemates, Klinehole. You just can't."

"Jesus," I said to myself, but all three women laughed. The sound of one caught my attention in particular. Rough but sweet, Winnie lost herself in that moment with her friends, and I hated myself thoroughly for denying myself the opportunity to watch. But I was getting in deep, so much so that I was starting to worry I might never be able to pull myself free. Winnie Winslow's quicksand was strong, and it was only wise to hold myself safe from that. Right?

"I think I need a drink," I muttered to Cassie, my eyes meeting hers as she put a hand to her stomach and smiled.

"Me too," she agreed, and I frowned.

"I said I needed it, not that I was going to do it," she protested easily. "But you have to live it for me. I'll order shots."

Fuck. I hadn't done shots since college. "I don't know about—"

Tears pooled at the corners of her unique eyes immediately. "No shots?" she asked, sounding like I'd told her her baby had no toes.

I buckled more spectacularly than a Pilgrim.

"Okay, shots. I'll do shots."

Winnie reached over and squeezed my knee as immediately as Cassie's tears dried right up. Satisfied, she turned back toward Thatch and leaned around him to get the attention of the waitress. I wasn't even sure what her gesturing was supposed to mean. To me, it looked like she was milking several extremely large cows, but the waitress seemed to understand.

I'd been played like fuck, but the feel of Winnie Winslow's hand on my leg without persuasion or invitation mended my ego immensely. "Don't feel bad," Winnie whispered, pressing the tips of her fingers into the meat of my thigh. "She's really good at hormonal manipulation."

I glanced down to catch sight of her hand on me, and, embarrassed, she moved to pull it back. I moved faster, though, pressing the palm of my hand into the back of hers and sealing it tight to the denim fabric at my thigh.

Leaning over slightly, I whispered directly into her ear. "Uh-uh, Win. If I'm going to spend my night at the sleepover from hell, discussing chick flicks and doing brightly colored shots, the least you can do is put your hands on me."

She blushed, and the color on her cheeks looked so good, I decided to push it even further. "Though, if I had my way, you'd move that hand about five inches to the right."

Truth be told, I'd have been even more thrilled if we'd moved both of our hands about eight or so inches to the left—to the inviting space right between her legs.

As her throat worked to control her reaction to my last comment, I gave her more, groaning roughly before stating, "That inch of skin is sexier than anything I've ever seen." Easing my hand off of hers, I ran just the tip of my pinkie finger from the outside of her thigh in, right along the top of her boot. "God, Win, it makes me want to do things to the skin I can't see."

"Wes," she murmured softly, her breathing completely unsteady.

"Touch it, eat it…fuck it. I'm gonna make you feel so good."

The whole not-sleeping-together-because-it's-not-a-good-idea thing was a distant, fleeting memory. When it came to Winnie Winslow, I had none of my normal self-control—and I'd finally realized it wasn't worth the wasted minutes I spent fighting it.

I could use that time to fight *with* her, tease her, touch her…taste her.

She was my new oral fixation, and it'd been entirely too long since my last hit. I'd deal with the consequences of the end of it when they came. And there would be emotional consequences—for both of us. Of that much, I was sure.

"Is that what I looked like?" Thatch asked Kline, and the way he said it pulled my hazy attention from Winnie.

"Like you were high, drunk, stupid, and seconds away from lifting a leg?" Kline replied conversationally.

Thatch nodded. "Yeah."

"Then, yeah."

I wasn't sure I completely understood their conversation, but I knew it was about me, so I rubbed on some middle-finger ChapStick and then watched as my finger bird flew away in their direction. They just smiled and chuckled to themselves like a couple of clucking goddamn hens.

"Oh, yay!" Cassie squealed as the waitress leaned over to set a full tray of neon shots in the center of the table.

"Fuck, Cass. What level of unconscious are you trying to make me achieve? Almost dead or completely there?"

"They're not just for you. They're for everyone."

"Um, no," Georgie denied immediately. "I'm ridiculous when I'm drunk."

Every single head at the table started shaking.

Kline laughed. "You drunk is probably one of the best things ever invented, Ben."

Every single head at the table changed direction and nodded enthusiastically.

"Come on," I urged her with a smirk. "You can't let me do this alone."

She wrinkled her nose. "You're my boss!"

"Oh, okay," I teased, raising my hands in mock surrender. "Drinking with the boss is bad, but sleeping with him is all good."

"I'm not sleeping with you!" she nearly yelled, and we all laughed as Kline pulled her closer with an arm around her shoulders. Realization dawned as she tipped her head back to look at his face.

Not this boss. *That* boss.

"Ah, fuck," she breathed in defeat.

Winnie laughed loudly, and I couldn't help but watch again. Her face was open, amused, and relaxed, and I felt satisfaction from the knowledge that she hadn't had this not too long ago, before taking the job with the Mavericks. She'd been working eighty-hour weeks with no downtime whatsoever and taking care of a young daughter on her own.

She'd been a doctor and a mom, but tonight, she was free to be just a woman.

An unbelievably sexy woman.

"Take the shots already!" Cassie complained.

"All right, all right," Georgie grumbled. "Calm your spawn, for fuck's sake." She reached forward and handed us each a shot. I honestly didn't even know what I was getting ready to swallow, but I was too ready to get it over with to care. "Bottoms up, kids."

"To the baby," Winnie toasted cheekily, and I laughed. Only a Kelly baby would have a toast before shots dedicated to it in utero.

"To the baby," we all recited dutifully, and then tipped our rainbow-colored glasses back as one. The green, apple-flavored liquid burned a little as it slid down my throat, but it went easily otherwise.

Winnie coughed and sputtered a little around her yellow one, choking out, "Lemon," as I rubbed a hand across her back soothingly.

Just as I started to relax, the waitress returned with a second tray.

"What the fuck?" Kline asked Cassie.

She shrugged shamelessly. "Four more rounds coming, Big-dick. Saddle up."

"Smooth Criminal" played over the speakers of the pub's sound system as I danced and pulled Winnie deeper into my arms. After five rounds of shots, we were all feeling pretty relaxed, me more so than the rest. Winnie hadn't been able to handle past number three, and thanks to tears and a tantrum from a pregnant woman, I added her two to my five.

Considering how drunk I was, math wasn't exactly my specialty at the moment, but I knew that made way more alcohol than I'd consumed at one time in over a decade.

"Winnie, are you okay? Are you okay? Are you okay, Winnie?" I sang, slightly altering the song as I swayed our hips back and forth together. She laughed and held on as I spun us around and made the room blur. I'd been singing along to every song that came on, and I was probably having more fun than I'd ever had before.

Her skirt seemed to be getting shorter by the second, a helpful trick of my unbelievably turned-on imagination, and her hair fell around her face in loose waves. Her lips were bare and her eyes were open, and I only wished I'd been sober enough to understand what I was seeing inside them.

As Paula Abdul started to warn of a coldhearted snake, I glanced to the jukebox to see Kline and Thatch hovering near it in a nearly hysterical fit of glee. But I was feeling too good, and Winnie was feeling even better in my arms, so instead of retreating into my shell, I sang to Winnie and told her to look into his eyes as I held hers with my own, and then ordered her not to play the fool.

When I asked if she thought he thought about her while he was out, I knew everything in my body said I thought about her all the goddamn time.

"Win," I groaned into the skin of her neck, touching just the tip of my tongue to the salt of her dewy-from-dancing skin.

She pulled away just enough to look me right in the eye and promise everything I was too stupid to ask for.

"Come on, Paula," she said with a smile that made my knees feel weak. "We'll go to my place. It's a very short walk from here."

My head spun as I thought of all the things her house meant. Good things like beds and sex and the smell of her fucking everywhere, and bad things like having way less control than I was used to and innocent ears and the distinct possibility that I was going to be spending more than a small portion of my morning with my head close to a bowl of water no head should ever be close to.

"We can't go back to your house!" I said loudly. I might not have noticed had she not shushed me with a small giggle and light, unburdened eyes, but that look wasn't something any sane male would miss—drunk or not.

"Little Lexi will sniff me out in a second." Realization of how my conversations with Winnie's daughter normally went sent me into near panic. "I'll never be able to pass her tests drunk! I can barely pass when I'm sober," I admitted.

Winnie looked like she was trying not to laugh, but even more than that, she looked like she already was. Apparently, I'd become endlessly amusing.

"She's not there," she assured me.

And, thanks to my sluggish, impaired state of my mind, I only wondered why I was disappointed for a second.

CHAPTER 16

Winnie

It was a little after one in the morning when I unlocked my front door and gestured for Wes to follow me inside. After a long day of rugby and drinking—and a full week of work before that—I should have been exhausted.

The funny thing about football with a professional team was that it was both a marathon and a sprint, and this was the first Saturday I'd had off since I started. The rest of the schedule was pretty much the same, but when it came to the weekend of a bye week, apparently, it was time to let your hair down and relax. Because, come Monday, it would be time to make a mad dash to the end. Especially since we had a Thanksgiving game this Thursday.

I set my purse and keys on the table in the foyer and watched Wes walk through the small entryway and toward the living room. His eyes roamed my home, not judging or assessing, just taking in all of the details that made up my space. I wasn't much of a decorator, furnishing with a simple sectional sofa and pictures of Lex and me and my family. I'd never had time to acquire a whole bunch of knickknacks. I hadn't worked less than a sixty-hour week in my entire career.

Wes walked the line of my couch and over to the mantle, touching a sweet picture of Lexi's face turned up into the sun with one tentative finger.

"So, this is it," I said with a shrug, a little uncomfortable with his quiet observation.

He hummed thoughtfully. "More than a drive-by this time," he added, and I tilted my head in confusion.

"My last visit was quick, remember?"

"Yeah," I said with a small, slightly embarrassed smirk, thinking about how I'd kicked him and Remy out before they could fully engage in a modern-day battle of wills…or fight to the death. The latter had probably been the most accurate.

"It's great, Win. And, quick visit or not, I noticed the first time." His voice was soft and measured, and I tried to live comfortably in the compliment rather than analyzing it.

"Thanks." He nodded and turned back to the mantel, the cotton of his shirt stretching along the hard lines of each muscle. He found a picture of my mother and me, wrapped up in each other and smiling like nothing in the world could touch us at my college graduation. For her, she'd succeeded in raising me all the way into womanhood on her own, and for me, I had the whole world laid out thoughtfully in front of me. I still felt that way about life, but I'd also learned a few things along the way. Plans shift and your definition of happiness *will* change; you just have to go with it.

"You look just like your mother," he whispered, and a part of me tingled at how intimate this whole discussion felt. These pictures—and the people in them—were the foundation of who I was.

"Thank you," I said again—and I meant it. My mother was a stunning woman, inside and out. I couldn't think of anything more flattering than being likened to her. "But you don't need to whisper, remember? Lexi isn't here."

He nodded, but the volume of his voice barely changed at all. I wondered if he felt as vulnerable as I did or if it was something else. "Where is she tonight?"

"She's staying at Remy's for the night."

His mouth tipped into a slightly tipsy grin. "So, it's just us."

He'd been so careful with his words and manner before, I'd actually almost forgotten just how much alcohol we'd consumed. But the effects were starting to dull as time bled the buzz from our systems, and all that was left was freedom from inhibition. For me, it meant a looser tongue and an unlocked door on my carefully crafted cage, and for Wes, it meant a playdate with his lighthearted side.

And God, playful Wes was so endearing. I wanted to eat him with a spoon.

I smirked. "It's just us."

"What are we going to do with all this alone time, Win?" he asked cheekily, a glint of mischief in his eye. I felt a shiver run down my spine. His eyes were like a fucking arousal superpower. *Pussy Power, activate!*

Desperate to get my bearings, I looked down at my feet for a brief moment. Of course, with the hum of his powers *and* the alcohol freely flowing through my bloodstream, all that did was give me time to imagine how nice it would be to see what Wes's hard, sexy body looked like wet. "Want to get in the hot tub?"

"You have a hot tub?" The corner of his mouth curved into a naughty smile.

"Yeah." I nodded. "It's on the back deck."

He immediately started slipping off his shoes and unbuckling his belt...*in the middle of my living room*. I watched, transfixed on his every move and frozen in place, as he reached behind his neck to pull his shirt over his head and yanked his belt from its loops. The metal buckle clanked as it landed on the wood of my floor, but I couldn't look down. A firm stomach and golden skin and the slight hint of a happy trail made my swallow rough with anticipation.

It was a slow climb to the top, but when I finally made it back up, his eyes held mine shamelessly. The button of his jeans pulled free with a pop, and I finally found my voice.

"So…I take it your vote is yes?" I asked on a laugh.

Forgoing words, he answered with a wink and a nod and continued to disrobe. I watched in fascination as he pulled his keys and wallet and cell phone out of his pockets and set them on an end table and pushed his jeans to the floor. One foot and then the next, he stepped out of the pooled fabric and kicked it gently to the side.

And then he was standing in nothing but his boxer briefs.

Just his boxer briefs.

Holy hell.

I could see the outline of his cock through the black cotton material, and to put it simply, he looked *obscene*. Sweet Christ, I had the urge to cover my eyes with my hand, but it would have been fruitless—I could already imagine myself peeking through my fingers.

I wasn't sure how much time had passed as I sat there, ogling the fuck out of him, mentally tracing the veins and licking my lips, but he had to clear his throat to bring my attention back to his face. "Win? Hot tub?"

I nodded but didn't move. Somebody needed to call the fucking police because this asshole was concealing a goddamn billy club in his pants. I hated to be this predictable, but…how in the motherfuck had that thing fit inside of me so many times?

"Are you going to change?"

"Change?"

No. No. No. Let's not change anything. I was just spit-balling. I'm sure I can make you fit. Fucking double sure.

"Your clothes, sweetheart. Are you going to change your clothes?" he asked with an amused grin. "I'm crazy about those boots, but I have a feeling they might not be so great in the water."

I glanced down at my clothes dumbly, almost as if I was floating outside of myself, and realization finally sunk in. "Oh," I muttered, and if my cheeks hadn't already been rosy from the numerous shots Cassie had pushed on me, they sure as hell would've been then. "Right. Just give me a second to change into a bathing suit."

His lips crested into a devilish smile. "You know I won't mind if you go without…"

Jesus. Playful Wes was going to be the death of me. I was sure of it.

I shook my head on a laugh and turned to head to my bedroom. "I have neighbors. I'm putting on a bikini."

He grabbed my hand as I passed him and tugged me back until my body hit his, his chest pressed against my back. "I'm really good with bikinis," he whispered into my ear, and I giggled at that. He nuzzled my neck and pressed his mouth softly to a sensitive spot that he *knew* would spur goose bumps. I spent a lot of time pretending everything was casual, but Wes Lancaster *knew* my body. I could feel his lips move up into a satisfied grin against my skin.

"I think it's safe to say you're good at taking them off, not putting them on," I whispered.

"I promise," he said with a seductive hum into my skin. "If you go change right now, I'll be good at *a lot* of things."

I rolled my eyes and pushed away so that I could look him in the eye.

"Give me five minutes. I'll meet you outside."

Clad in my skimpiest pink bikini and fake confidence, I walked outside onto my deck, my bare feet carefully tiptoeing across the wood, and found Wes lounging comfortably in my hot tub, his arms stretched across the edges. Droplets of water shimmered in the moonlight as they slid down his firm chest and back into the water.

Oblivious to my approach, his head back and his eyes closed, he looked like a Greek god.

I honestly wasn't sure if this was the best idea I'd ever had—or the worst. Tonight, right now, I knew it would feel good. But what had started under the assumption that a few romps would be the perfect solution for getting him out of my system had turned into an obsession. I was starting to crave him like a drug, spending all my time from one fix to the next trying to figure out how to make it happen again.

According to just about anyone who had the power of speech, Wes was not the kind of man who settled down, especially with a woman who already had a child—wasn't even really a monogamous kind of guy. But it didn't *feel* like that anymore. It felt real and deep and a little bit like I was going to feel like such a goddamn fool when it turned out a man didn't up and change everything about himself for a woman. Because as much as I tried to warn myself of that very thing, my naïve, romantic epicenter in my chest wouldn't stop whispering that maybe it could be that way for me.

I took a deep breath and finally started to walk again.

All things in moderation. That was the advice I had given thousands of patients, and I should have been able to follow it myself.

His eyes opened and turned to me. It was sheer absurdity how quickly I got lost in him.

Fucking shit, moderation sucked balls. I didn't want bits and pieces of him here and there. I wanted all of him—all of the tiny details that made him the man I was so obviously falling for.

Shit, Winnie, my brain whined. *This quickly? I thought you were smarter than this.*

His eyes turned hooded and heated, watching closely as I climbed in and slid into the water across from him. My skin prickled from the sharp change in temperature. I'd spent entirely too long outside the water doing the mental hokey-pokey.

"Come here, Win," Wes whispered and held out his hand.

I took it without a second thought, and with a gentle tug, I was sitting in his lap, his strong arms wrapped around me and his hands softly caressing the exposed skin of my belly.

His nose brushed down my skin as he nuzzled my neck. "You always smell so fucking good," he whispered, and my nipples immediately hardened beneath my bikini top. The tip of his tongue made a seductive path from my neck to my jaw and back to my neck again.

I moaned, any chance of holding out nullified by the direction of his hand.

It moved up my stomach, between my breasts, and kept going until his fingers cupped my chin and moved my lips toward his. He sucked at my bottom one before slipping his tongue inside to dance gently with mine.

Gentle, exploring, we were unhurried for a long time. But, eventually, the heat of his skin burned hotter than the steamy water, and the ache between my legs forced a keening cry from my desperate throat. Frantic, our tongues tangling deeper, our mouths sharing quiet moans and panting breaths, he gripped my hips and turned me around until my legs straddled his hips.

I gasped loudly as he attacked my mouth again, hunger and fire leaking from his mouth right down my throat and straight into the space between my legs. I pushed myself against him in earnest, desperate to get some relief. He broke the kiss with a groan, licking and sucking at my neck and then my chest, before his fingers slid the triangles of my bikini top to the sides and bared my breasts to the frigid air and his seductive gaze. Both made my nipples peak to a point just shy of pain.

I ground my hips into his as I pushed my breasts toward his mouth. "Please," I begged.

He sucked a hardened nipple into his mouth and flicked at the sensitive bud with the tip of his tongue, and it only encouraged my hips to push harder against his thick, rigid cock.

"Please," I begged again.

"Patience, baby," he coached seductively, and I groaned.

I just wanted him to *move*. To make the decisions for me and make me let go. Make me *feel*.

His hands slid down my sides while his eyes gazed up into mine. He pulled my hips tighter to his, and the water sloshed around us. I moved my fingers through his wet hair as his large hands gripped my ass.

Our mouths touched again, but we weren't kissing, just breathing each other in.

He was taking charge, just as I'd wanted, but instead of diving right in, he was teaching me to wait. Showing me how good it could feel not to rush this part.

I pressed my mouth to his, greedy and begging.

"God, Win," he groaned when he pulled away, allowing both of us to catch our breath. He gripped my throat briefly, gently, as he gazed into my eyes, and then his thumb slid down my neck, between my breasts, until his finger easily slid across my skin and into my bikini bottoms.

"You make it hard to go slow."

I nodded, my forehead against his. "So do you."

"Tell me what you want," he said, and his voice was quiet yet demanding. He was an aphrodisiac, and I couldn't do anything but speak the truth. There was only one *specific* thing I knew I wanted.

"You. I want you."

His hot mouth latched on to my pebbled nipple again as his hand slid into my hair and tugged my head back. I moaned, and he didn't stop, his perfect mouth sucking and licking and flicking across my breast until he moved to the other one to give it the same mind-blowing treatment.

His lips moved back up my body, placing openmouthed kisses upon my chest, my neck, my jaw, until his lips were on mine again, devouring me like I was his favorite meal.

"Please. Now," I begged, and I didn't wait for him to stop me. I pulled his cock out of his boxer briefs and slid my bikini bottoms to the side. The instant the tip of him pressed against my clit, I whimpered. "Please. I need to feel you inside me."

I was beyond shame or embarrassment. I just needed him. Skin on skin. Inside me.

I needed to feel him.

And I didn't care that we were on my back deck. I didn't care that anyone could've seen us if they had wanted to. I didn't care about any of it.

I just wanted. Needed. *Desired.*

"Make me feel, Wes. Make me feel everything."

His hands were in my hair again, and his lips were on mine. His tongue slipped inside my mouth at the exact same moment he pushed his cock inside me. Our breaths mingled and danced as our lips and tongue did the same.

And he pushed deeper and deeper and *deeper* until I couldn't stop shaking.

God, the sounds I made. They were greedy and frantic, and I couldn't stop my nails from practically clawing at his skin. His unusually expressive eyes never left mine, staring past my heart and into my soul. This wasn't just fucking. This wasn't just sex.

This was something else entirely.

Something I'd never in my life felt before. I understood what people meant by *you'll know when you fall. You'll know when your heart tethers itself to someone else's heart.*

Because, in that moment, it happened to me—my heartstrings pulled straight out of my chest and knotted themselves with Wes's.

I loved him. I was *in love* with him.

I felt like I was outside of myself, watching from a bubble that very well might burst.

But I didn't care. For now, I was floating in a dream, and I had no immediate plans to wake up.

CHAPTER 17

Wes

For the first time since my friends had fallen, I understood why they were so happy in their emotional jail cells.

Because, metaphorically, the accommodations were much nicer than they were on the outside, the linens finer, the satisfaction abundant, and the happiness overflowing. I felt content to live my life in those eight-by-ten feet, trapped in the spell of Winnie and everything she had to offer, and I couldn't place a reason for it.

Instead, it was all the reasons, all the little things that made her up, the soft looks and exasperated eye rolls, and the constant fight to earn both.

I wanted to live every emotion she had to offer, see the way it changed her face to make it even more beautiful than before, and work out any of the lingering aggression in the most pleasurable of ways.

As I stood at the side of the field, listening to Coach Bennett wrap up the last practice before tomorrow's game, my phone buzzed in my pocket.

I would have let it go, certain it was Thatch, contacting me to paint his nursery or go pick up a breast pump, but lately, someone else had been sending me messages with some frequency—someone I was much more eager to hear from. Someone who'd been so goddamn hot, so overwhelming, in her hot tub four days ago, I'd temporarily lost my mind. I'd been *this close* to telling her I loved her.

Fucking LOVE, people.

Even now, I wasn't sure what had actually stopped me. Common sense, premonition…a carefully exercised intervention by God, perhaps. It was just too soon. That kind of declaration wasn't something I needed to take lightly. This was more than some simple purchase that you take back to the store when you're dissatisfied or a hole wears through the sole—or *soul*, in this case—too soon. This was a real, live woman with feelings, a career carefully interwoven with mine, and a *daughter*.

It was good I'd waited.

It is, I assured myself.

Looking down to the phone I'd already mindlessly pulled out, I focused on the words on the screen.

Winnie: What expression are you going for right now?

I fought the urge to look up, knowing she was somewhere nearby, watching me. I wanted to watch her too, but several players and coaches had their eyes on me in my spot next to Coach Bennett. The phone would be nothing new, a busy man with frequent interruptions something they were used to.

The smile that would surely overwhelm my face at the sight of Winnie Winslow, however, would be highly out of the ordinary.

Me: What, are you taking a page out of Thatch's book now? Stalking? Seems pretty low class for a doctor.

Winnie: More watching than stalking. Don't avoid the question.

I swallowed a laugh and ventured a guess at all the things my face said. It was the last team meeting before our Thanksgiving game tomorrow, the guys had been on a killer season, and not one of them knew anything real about me. All of that added up to one thing, something I recognized best as my default expression.

Still, I wasn't quite sure how she would see it.

Me: Confidently pissed off?

Winnie: You look constipated.

I nearly choked trying to contain my laugh. I tried to turn it into a discreet cough, but fuck, she'd caught me off guard. There was only so much I could do to "Photoshop" my natural reaction. Coach Bennett even paused and looked over to see if he needed to do the Heimlich Maneuver.

Shit.

With an apologetic raise of my brows, I pulled myself together and looked back to my phone without looking into the eyes of anyone else. Part of it was that I didn't want to know how many of them noticed the chinks in my armor. And the other part was that, to my own complete and utter surprise, I just didn't care.

Not how I looked or if someone would figure out what was going on.

I just wanted more of Winnie.

Me: LOL. Fuck.

Winnie: I like this expression better.

Me: Oh, yeah? What's it called?

Winnie: *Genuinely happy.*

She had no idea how right she was.

Me: *You just like it because it makes you feel powerful.*

Winnie: *Making you smile in public? Yeah, you're right. I do feel powerful.*

I had to see her.

Me: *Training room. Now.*

Maybe everything was going to be okay. Maybe I wasn't the only one thinking this was more than some repeated, emotionless fuck.

"Gentlemen," I said with a nod, stepping away and heading straight for the tunnel that led to the inner workings of the stadium. I hoped she'd follow from wherever she was, because I had no plans to pause to look or find out.

I walked straight to the end of the hall and around the corner and into the training room, turning my back to a table and leaning into it to wait for her arrival.

We were finally going to have an honest talk.

But with the way I was feeling, I had to be honest. It was probably going to be right after we had an even more sincere fuck.

A breeze blew in just as she did, a frantic kind of worry in her eyes. I didn't know if she was worried she'd stepped over some boundary or what, but I hoped it was anything but that. Winnie wasn't the type of woman to worry what anyone thought, let alone some stupid fuck of a guy, and the thought that maybe I was turning her into that kind of person, bled a small amount of doubt into my abdomen.

"Is everything all right?" she asked. But the way she asked it, comforting like a bandage to a bleeding wound, actually made it so it was.

She wasn't worried she was stepping over some boundary. For maybe the first time since I was a kid, someone was worried about *me*. It was confounding. Eye-opening. Goddamn beautiful.

Unable to wait any longer, I moved toward her swiftly, backing her wide-eyed wonder straight into the door until it closed, and locking it with a hand between her hip and her arm.

I moved my hands up to cup her jaw, ran the pad of my thumb along her soft bottom lip until it caught, and rubbed the tip of my nose along the side of hers. Everything inside of me came alive as a shiver tore through her body and vibrated into mine.

"It's never been better," I told her and myself.

It had never been fucking better.

The sex, the company, the way I felt.

Her eyes eased closed, the flutter of her eyelashes just kissing the apple of my cheek as I stood there and breathed her in. She didn't just smell like peaches and coconut anymore—now she smelled like *mine*.

"Take your panties off, Winnie," I whispered, and her hips flexed softly into mine.

She shook her head just slightly, and I nipped at her throat.

"Take them off, baby," I coaxed again, moving one hand down to rub a soft circle into the front of her hip.

She kissed her way to my ear, slowly, tenderly, tugging at the lobe there, and ended the trail with a whisper. "I can't."

Sensation skated from her breath on my neck to the rapidly beating heart. Pounding and pumping, it nearly jumped out of my chest.

I moved back just enough to meet her eyes, hard dick throbbing restlessly against my abdomen, and asked roughly, "You're not wearing any?"

She shrugged then, a cute mix of helpless damsel and flirty minx. "Laundry day."

Both my laughter and my tongue flirted with her throat as I lost all control, reached down, found the hem of her sensible skirt, and yanked it up to the very tops of her hips. I skimmed my hands along the perfect skin of her ass and down, lifting up when I met the place where ass met thigh and forcing her smaller hips to meet mine.

She didn't need an invitation, reaching down between us and taking charge all on her own. The buckle of my belt and the top of my pants were undone so quickly, I barely had to pause before I was inside of her.

"Wes," she whispered, and with her voice so rough and vulnerable all at once, I pushed more, trying to get deeper.

My lips to hers, I nibbled and sucked and licked my way around them until the only place unexplored was inside. Parting her lips with the tip of my tongue, I started to move, in and out with my hips and my tongue, making love to her mouth and pussy at once and getting equally lost in both.

Her breath hitched with every inward stroke, and the way she clung to my shoulders, the very edges of each nail carving their way into my skin and my soul at once, had me working not to come before she did.

I didn't need to think anymore, didn't need the dominance or the play on control between us. All I needed was more, deeper, further inside the woman who was burrowing her way inside me more and more each day.

She wasn't even trying, pulling away just as much as she pushed inside, trying to keep herself and her family safe from the unrequited love of a needy but unavailable man.

But it was that strength, that resilience and complete grasp on her own self-worth that drew me to her with an unfrayable, unbreakable rope.

"Yes, Wes," she breathed, and—thank God—I knew she was getting close.

I pushed our torsos closer, moving them up and down together as I moved in and out of her, striving for the place that made her moan every time.

There was no skin slapping, no fast strokes of a frenzied man.

Instead, this was the slow and not-so-patient trial of a man physically showing a woman that the meaning of her to him was so much more than physical.

It was visceral, spiritual, and poignant in a way I'd never known was possible. Maybe it was the lack of example at home—maybe it was just the way I was made—or maybe it was the lack of the right woman, the one who made me want to be anything she wanted me to be because all of those things made me a better version of myself, but I felt like I'd been emotionally born all over again.

"Fuck," I grunted as a jolt of pleasure gripped the base of my balls and squeezed so hard there was no way I'd avoid coming now. Thankfully, she screamed too, abandoned and completely unconcerned with who could be on the other side of that training room door.

No doubt she'd have felt less complacent about it in just a few short moments, but for now, she was fully invested in me, the moment, and our connection.

Still inside her, come barely done shooting from me into her, and breathing so harsh I sounded ragged, the words rushed out in a geyser of honesty.

"I know you were thinking about moving to New Jersey, but I hope you don't. I hope you'll stay in Manhattan with your brothers."

"With my brothers," she whispered, tucking her chin to my chest and huffing a small, thoughtful puff of air.

Okay. Half honesty.

"And me," I admitted, lifting her eyes to mine with a thumb and finger on her chin. "I hope you'll stay with me."

"Wes…"

"I know the commute isn't ideal logistically or financially, but I'm willing to work with you on that. Whether it's a commuting stipend or hiring a car…or if you're vehemently opposed to those things, you could ride with me."

"Wes—"

"Just don't say no," I babbled on. "I know I'm asking a lot, and I'm being honest here when I say I'm asking for myself. I don't know the particulars of how anything is going to work between us, or even what I'm after, but I know I want to try."

"Why?"

"Because every time I see you, I expect the excitement to lessen or the universe to finally turn back to right-side up, but it doesn't. I miss you the minute you leave until the moment you arrive, and daydream constantly about you all the time in between."

"We're new and—"

"Win," I interrupted, and she leaned it to listen. "I knew you might say no, but I had to ask anyway."

"Why?"

I shrugged helplessly. "How else are you supposed to say yes?"

She smiled then. Raised a hand to cup my jaw.

"Wes."

"Yeah?"

"I wasn't going to say no. I was going to ask if we could maybe have the conversation when your come wasn't running down my leg, but I wasn't going to say no."

"So, yes?" I asked hopefully, and she laughed.

"Maybe. The answer is maybe."

"Okay, Fred. Maybe it is."

"Fred?"

"Short for Winifred," I explained with a smirk. "That is your name, isn't it?"

"Who told you?"

I shook my head; she poked me in the chest. "You better tell me. I've got a stake all carved for their heart."

She wheezed as I laughed and tightened my arms around her.

"Sorry, Fred. Not gonna happen."

"God." She cringed and shook her head in distaste. "At least use the whole thing if you have to use it at all."

"No," I disagreed and touched my lips to hers. "I'm saving the 'Win' for the day your maybe becomes a yes."

CHAPTER 18

Winnie

New York was freakishly warm for the day after Thanksgiving, and as a result, I'd decided to turn the heat off and open the windows.

Lounging on the couch, me watching *Golden Girls* and Lexi nose-deep in her iPad, watching videos about dominos and then running to play with her own set, we were enjoying the soft sun and warm breeze flitting through the house and some quiet time together when my phone rang.

Incoming Call Wes…

Since the Mavericks had played their game yesterday, and I'd spent the day working instead of having Thanksgiving dinner with my family, Lex and I had decided to make today all about each other. This was the easy part, lazing my way through mindless TV, one show at a time, while Lex did her own thing close by. But tonight, I'd planned to make the big, special dinner. And I wasn't sure I had the time to open my mind up to all the things going on with Wes.

The lovemaking. The feelings. The offer to chain ourselves together every morning and every night for the commute to and from the stadium. I hadn't even had to ask to know who told him I was thinking about moving. Fuck, with Georgia and her meddling, Cassie and her lack of filter, and Dean with his boner for all things Billionaire Bad Boys, I figured it had been all three.

Still, I picked up pretty eagerly on the second ring.

"Fred," he greeted. I scowled and did my best to make my voice sound cool.

"Wes."

The sound of his chuckle was coarse against my ear.

"What are you up to?"

I sighed and dropped the attitude. His laughter made it really fucking hard to maintain anyway. "Oh, not much, just sitting here and enjoying not having to be anywhere," I answered, and Lexi snuggled closer to me, nuzzling her head against my shoulder. I glanced down at her and smiled and started to run my fingers softly through her hair.

"Sounds perfect. Mind if I join you?"

Before I could even respond to his question, I noticed something in her hair.

Something *moving* in her hair.

What in the ever-loving hell is that?

The tail end of Wes's question almost registered. "—you still there?"

"Uh-huh…" I replied, but everything in me was focused on Lexi's scalp.

And that's when I figured it out. Three tiny little bugs scattering across her scalp every time I ran my fingers through her hair.

Oh. My. God.

Lice.

My daughter had lice.

The fight-or-flight instinct was strong, and an honest to God twitch took up residence in my upper thigh as I struggled to decide. Physician or not, the flight side wanted to hop off the couch and run the fuck out of my house. And the fighter…well, she wanted to burn my entire motherfucking house down.

Holy. Fucking. Shit.

"Oh, no," I muttered and scooted almost violently away from my own daughter.

I was really trying to pull myself together and be a good mom who didn't have the urge to shave her daughter's head and then set fire to all bedding, linens, pillows, and clothing, in the front yard, but the human survival instinct was tugging pretty fiercely on the other end of my rope.

Lexi's eyes moved off her iPad and met mine, and I tried to turn my *oh-holy-shit* face into a smile. "Mommy?"

"Fred?" Wes demanded into my ear. "Are you okay?"

I shut my eyes and tried to take deep breaths. I was Dr. Winslow. I had handled some of the worst trauma injuries ever to walk through St. Luke's ED doors. I could do this. I could handle these little lice fuckers without losing my cool.

I could.

I could do it.

Before I tell you the next events, just remember, lice.
LICE. In my daughter's hair.
If you've never had to experience lice in your lifetime,
get on your hands and knees now and tell God you love him.

When I opened my eyes, I glanced down at my shirt and that was when everything took a turn from internally freaking out to externally losing my ever-loving shit—a little bug crawling around the sleeve of my T-shirt, mere millimeters from my skin.

"Holy fucking shit!" I shouted, too freaked out to think about the age-inappropriate words coming out of my mouth and my daughter's propensity for repeating things, and jumped off the couch so high, if my living room had been a sanctioned venue, I could have qualified for the Olympics. Catapulting myself over the coffee table, I hopped around maniacally from foot to foot and smacked my hand against my shirt to rid myself of the demonic, disgusting parasite.

I honestly had no idea where the phone went at that point, and I didn't fucking care. All I wanted was the ability to set myself on fire without suffering life-threatening burns.

"Mommy?" Lexi repeated with her little head tilted to the side. "Mommy, what's wrong?"

The worry in her voice was the only thing powerful enough to pull me out of my plans for self-detonation. When I looked down at her, her bottom lip was pushed out and slightly quivering.

Shit. Shit. Shit.

If that wasn't a mom fail, I didn't know what was.

I scurried back over toward her and kneeled at her feet, both hands gently gripping her cheeks. "It's okay, baby. Everything is okay. I promise."

"But why was Mommy shouting?" she asked as her little hand reached up to scratch at her scalp.

Because you have an infestation of lice on your head and now I probably have lice and we're going to have to shave both of our heads and I haven't studied up on how to get away with arson...

I fought the urge to grimace and tried to ignore how incessantly my scalp—my whole body—was now starting to itch. I felt like I had bugs crawling all over me.

"Mommy was just playing around a little. Just dancing," I bullshitted, hoping she'd buy it.

Her nose scrunched up, and she squinted one eye. "Scared dancing?"

God, I felt like the worst mom ever. I would've thought my years in the medical industry would have prepared me for handling a mild case of lice, but obviously, they didn't.

But the time to freak out was over. Now I had to deal with it.

"Hey, I need to run to the store real quick. If you promise to be a good girl, I'll let you pick out a toy. Sound good?"

"A calculator?"

"You want another calculator?"

She grinned and nodded her head.

I shrugged. At this point, I didn't care if we were a forty-calculator household if it kept her happy and agreeable. "If you're good, sweetie, you can pick out anything you want."

Lexi's grin turned wide and excited as she jumped into my arms and buried her face between my neck and shoulder.

I wish I could say I wasn't internally cringing, but when I felt her hair brush across my arm, I very nearly lost my shit all over again.

Somehow, the mom inside me won out over the lunatic this time around, though. I stood up and set her on her feet. "I've got an idea. Let's see who can get their shoes on and be at the front door the fastest. Sound good?"

She nodded again. "Twelve…nine…six…three…zero… Go! Go! Go!" And then she sprinted toward her room as fast as her little feet could take her.

Only my daughter would count down in multiples of three.

Twenty minutes later, we were walking—more like *speed* walking—back to our home, lice talk with Lexi officially complete, my wallet one hundred dollars lighter, and a bag full of every lice treatment known to man. Apparently, facing my one true weakness, I still wasn't over the lice. Constantly glancing down at my shirt or Lexi's hair and mentally freaking the fuck out, this was, quite literally, hell.

Again, I considered the consequences of setting my home on fire with all of the things we loved inside it, or you know, moving out until the infestation died, but that still left me fucked. The lice were on Lexi, and she was the one thing I couldn't stomach burning to the ground.

As we rounded the last corner and solidly set foot on our block, Wes appeared, pacing in front of my front door, phone pressed to his ear and face set with worry and concern. He glanced up from watching his angry feet grind each step into the sidewalk and, when his eyes met mine, relief consumed his face.

"She's here. I found her…and they're both okay. Yeah." He smiled sardonically and ran his tongue along the front of his bottom teeth inside his lip. "I love you, too."

I love you too? Who the fuck is he talking to?

He quickly hung up the call and shoved the phone into his back pocket.

"Wes!" Lexi shouted and sprinted toward him before I could stop her.

"Wait—" I started to say, but it was too late. He picked her up and held her close to his chest. The last of his lingering worry receded.

His hazel eyes met mine. "What the hel—heck happened? You screamed, and then you were just gone." At the memory, his face went straight to ravaged again.

Jesus. I obviously wasn't handling this well at all.

I should apologize.

"Who was on the phone?"

Whoops.

He shook his head and looked to the sky before looking back at me. "Your brother."

"Remy?"

He nodded. "I haven't met the rest of them, have I?"

It still didn't make any sense. "You love him?"

Understanding lifted the corners of his mouth as he rolled his eyes. "His sentiment was a far sight less flowery."

Shit. "Sorry."

He shrugged. "I was worried about you two."

Lexi leaned back and looked him in the eyes. "Head lice are scientifically known as *Pediculus humanus capitis*, and an infestation with head lice is medically known as *pediculosis capitis*. They are obligate parasites. They cannot survive without a human host."

He studied her closely before moving on to the clear, plastic shopping bag in my hand.

"She has lice?" he asked, having Sherlock Holmes-ed the situation quite skillfully.

"So…about the whole lice thing…" I jerked my chin toward Lex's head where it rested on his shoulder. "You probably have it now too."

He remained completely neutral for a second before he burst into laughter.

His mouth turned into a knowing smirk. "The screams? They were because of lice?"

I nodded, a little bit ashamed.

> *But, in my defense, we are talking about lice here.*
> *LICE.*
> *They are up there with bed bugs.*

"I can't believe Dr. Winslow can't handle lice."

"They creep me out, okay?" I protested.

He held me captive in his stare, everything in his eyes screaming the most flattering things I'd ever been told. He didn't mind that the lice were on him, and more than that, he didn't mind that I did. I wasn't going to have to handle everything alone—not this time. He winked and then looked back at Lexi. "What do you say we get you inside and take care of the *pediculosis capitis*?"

She grinned and nodded.

Fifteen minutes later, Wes, Lexi and I crammed into the tiny space of my bathroom, Wes was in full kill-the-lice-fuckers mode. He had read all of the instructions on the treatment and was busy applying it to my daughter's head.

"You're next," he told me, and I melted even deeper into the wall.

Lexi sat comfortably on the closed toilet seat, her little legs swinging back and forth as she stared down at Wes's phone and tapped random math problems into the calculator app, and all I had to do was stand back and watch.

I was in complete awe of him.

His tall, muscular frame standing in my small, en suite bathroom looked equal parts right and wrong, and he made my little girl look so tiny. But God, the look in his eyes melted my heart, the hazel irises soft and warm and filled with nothing but care and tenderness. It was truly apparent he cared about Lexi just as he cared about me.

It was awesome, but holy God, did it scare me.

Lexi adored Wes. Looked at him like he could do nearly anything. And I didn't want her to have another father figure in her life, only for him to leave her behind.

The mere idea of that broke my heart. She had already been through so much with her own father. Nick rarely made a point to keep contact, let alone make her feel special. Sure, he lived in a completely different city, but he could at least pick up the phone. My daughter didn't say all that much, but she had everything to say. Nick never listened.

Lexi did not deserve to go through something like that again.

"Almost done, sweetie," Wes said as he squirted a little more of the treatment into his hand and kneaded it into her hair and scalp.

"How many minutes?" she questioned predictably. Those little pieces of her—the quirks I could always count on—felt like home.

"Three more minutes until I'm done," he answered patiently, eyes focused on the task at hand. "And then we wait for twenty minutes until we can wash it out."

She looked at the time on his phone. "3:04pm and 3:24pm."

"That's right, Lexi girl. And then, you'll be all done," he said with a proud smile on his face.

But God, the way he was with her, so intuitive to her little, unique mind. It made it really hard for me to know what was right for her, for me, for both of us.

"And then, it's mommy's turn to get treated."

My nose scrunched up in annoyance. "But I don't want to have lice," I whined.

Wes's smile was both condescending and comforting. "But you *do*. And the last thing I need is for you to give lice to an entire professional football team."

I groaned, and he just laughed, visibly amused by my discomfort.

"Plus, we can't," he added, and then his lips made a little high-pitched, sexy whistle, "if you don't let me get the disgusting parasites out of your hair." He winked at me. "Which, I gotta say, is an even higher priority than the team."

I rolled my eyes but still couldn't stop myself from laughing.

"I can't whistle until the lice is out of my hair?" Lexi asked.

"Yep," he answered with a giant, roguish grin. "We can't whistle until the lice is gone."

I pointed at Wes, still giggling quietly. "There is something seriously wrong with you, you know that?"

His smile never faltered. Sweet, sexy bastard.

What was he trying to do to me?

CHAPTER 19

Wes

The only thing worse than winter in New York is *really fucking winter* in Wisconsin.

It's the kind of cold that gels your insides and eats away at the will you have to do basically anything—other than drink.

Which is essentially what people do in Wisconsin. I'm pretty sure that's why my dad moved there, relocating from the Pacific Northwest after I flew the nest. That and his love for summers on Lake Michigan. And even I had to admit I understood that one.

There was something about it that felt like magic.

But it wasn't summer, and I wasn't here to visit with my dad—though he always made the effort to see me when the team was here. The Mavericks and I were here to secure our spot in the play-offs and maintain our undefeated streak. We hadn't had a season this good since I'd taken ownership—actually, well before then—and I knew it had a lot to do with the recruiting we'd done. Sean Phillips was a maniac, a complete dual threat, and Quinn Bailey had the kind of poise you rarely saw in anyone. And now that Mitchell was back on the field after a long but necessary recuperation, we were starting to feel unstoppable.

Meanwhile, things with Winnie felt stuck in cement no matter how hard I tried to go. What we now referred to as the *Thanksgiving Lice* had come and gone, along with a couple of weeks, and Christmas would be here in almost the same time. I felt good for a few days after the lice thing, having stepped in and handled the situation so that Winnie could have the freedom to freak out for once. I still fucking itched from time to time, but after years and years of practice, my ability to fake calm while a storm raged inside had actually come in handy. But what I hadn't noted in that moment was that Winnie didn't come to me for help, wouldn't have had I not intervened, and if I hadn't been on the phone with her the moment it happened, I might not ever have known.

Because I was just there; I wasn't the guy she called in a pinch. I tried not to take it too personally, seeing as Winnie Winslow didn't turn to anyone in a pinch, but I was genuinely trying to build something with her at this point. I pushed and she pulled, and the more time that passed, the more I started to wonder if she'd ever take anything about me seriously, other than my cock.

But here she came now, strutting down the hall with her irresistible confidence and a down comforter for a coat as I pulled away from a back-pounding hello hug with my father. I smiled at her getup, a defense from the cruel wind on the field, and her face softened at the unexpected affection from me. Though, at this point, I wasn't sure there was ever a time I greeted her with anything less than the full strength of my most genuine smile.

She gave me a wink, finger flutter, and a circling finger—our symbol for "Later, I'll be around"—intent on moving right past us, when I reached out and grabbed her elbow to pull her to a stop.

She stuttered in surprise as I pulled her to my side. Granted, she didn't have any clue who the man standing with me was and might have been expecting me to keep my normal game-day distance, but I was tired of it. I wanted to be able to pull her into my arms no matter where we were.

My dad looked on with the knowing smile of a man who loved women and interacted with them on the regular—big and bright and a little inappropriate. He hadn't been with anyone seriously since my mother passed, but he'd been with many someones, and at my age now, he no longer tried to shelter it.

Kyle Lancaster had always been an attractive man—and still was—with the world at his feet. What people never recognized, thanks to the never-graying hair, hard jaw, and well-muscled physique, was that when I said he had the world at his feet, I meant literally. Buried six feet down, in the casket he picked out with a newborn in his arms.

His example had always made sense to me—never settling down again after my mother passed. In the early years, he had me to worry about, a crying, puking, screaming baby with all the stubbornness I had now and then some. But his routine in loneliness never waned, and I figured it was a move of a man who *knew* he'd had the right fit from the puzzle of life, and the rest of the pile was just pieces. Maybe, if you pushed really hard, they'd bend into place, but as far as being made for that spot, cut specifically by their maker to fit with him, he'd never find a duplicate. It was ironic, but lately, it felt remarkably like I was living his life in reverse. My mother had died during my birth. Up until then, my dad had had it all, and after, for the entirety of my life, he'd been living with just a mound of pieces—and so had I. But I was snapping in with my one fitting piece now. At least, I was trying my goddamn hardest to.

"Dad, this is—" I started to introduce then. Winnie's eyes flared noticeably on the word "Dad."

"Dr. Winslow," she interrupted. "Winnie to you," she added with a wink.

I smiled at the melodic confidence in her voice. "She's—"

"The team physician," she broke in again. "New to the team, but I really love it."

"I like her," my dad remarked with a batty old smile—the only part of him that hinted at his age. "Knows enough not to wait around for you. Gets right to the point herself."

I wasn't thinking that myself, though.

It felt to me like she was beating me to the punch to prove a point—to draw a line between us. A line that defined personal and business and meant a very specific thing about a meeting with my father. A goddamn line I didn't want drawn because it was ugly and dark and reeked of permanent marker, the words "fuck buddy" illustrated perfectly in shaded bubble letters.

It conceded the point, finally, that we were friends, but it didn't budge an inch on the possibility we might be more.

I wasn't yet sure exactly what I wanted, but I didn't want that.

"Actually, Dad, Winnie and I are dating."

Winnie sputtered and choked on nothing more than her tied tongue and a mouthful of saliva. I pulled her tight body close and peered down into the distressed and murky pools of her too-pretty eyes.

"Okay, Fred?"

The use of her ridiculous nickname only agitated her more. The seas of her blue eyes raged, and her plump lips thinned into a tight line. In some twisted way, it felt fucking satisfying to make her feel the same way I'd felt only moments before by stating one simple fact.

"Uh-huh," my dad hummed knowingly. "The sex between the two of you must be dynamite."

Jesus. I jerked my head. My dad never said shit like that. Acted it out, implied it, sure. But said it outright? *No.* That was really more Dr. Cummings's—Georgia's mother—style. She was a sex therapist, and her knack for getting straight to the weird and dirty was quite impressive.

"What?" Winnie asked through a startled laugh, sure she'd heard him wrong, but I could guarantee she hadn't. Each horrifying word was burned in my brain forever, a souvenir to take forward into each and every one of my nightmares.

I probably owe Georgia an apology because this is embarrassing as fuck.

My dad didn't seem even a little ashamed, though—even when I dragged a very threatening finger across the line of my throat. In fact, if I wasn't mistaken, I saw a goddamn twinkle of enjoyment in his eye.

"All that passion." He smirked and looked directly at Winnie. "You went willingly into his arms, doll. That means the heart knows. All that fire in your eyes means your brain is the only part strong enough to fight."

"Dad—"

"That's how it was for Wes's mother and me."

My throat clogged at the unexpected mention of my mother. He spoke of her fondly always, but he never spoke about them as a couple. I always got the feeling that it hurt too much—that years and years did nothing to make it easier to talk about. Everything I knew about them together up until this point had been pure assumption.

But he looked at ease now.

I felt Winnie's entire body shift with the force of her swallow.

"The fight is fun," he told Winnie on a whisper, and then shook his head. "But not even half as much as giving in."

Her body relaxed into mine minutely, as if commanded by his words, and I took the opportunity to plaster her side to mine even tighter.

Unfortunately, her phone rang almost instantaneously, shocking her out of the trance and robbing me of my enjoyment. Part of me felt like it was an emergency call that she'd planned in advance to bail her out of this completely unpredictable situation—the timing was just that perfect.

She put the phone to her ear and listened for three or four beats in time, and I knew what the words out of her mouth would be even before she spoke them. "On my way."

Still, it *was* game day, and I *did* have a vested interest in any of the potential things that could have been happening on the other end of that phone call. When I raised my brows, she put my mind at ease. "Nothing big. No worries."

Turning to my father, she took his hand in hers. "It was so nice to meet you, Mr. Lancaster."

"Kyle, doll, and the pleasure is all mine."

She smiled genuinely, the beam most women gave to flirtatious old men with something extra, and took off down the hall at a speed-walk.

She didn't look back—and I hated it.

"I should have talked more about your mother," my father whispered as soon as Winnie was out of earshot. I closed my eyes tight and shook my head.

I was too mentally wrecked to have the big talk now. I just *couldn't* do it.

So, without acknowledging his admission, I started to usher my dad in the opposite direction. "Better get you to your seat, Pop."

He pulled me to a stop and barked a harsh, "Bullshit."

"Dad," I warned and started to walk again.

"I'm not going to say much of anything," he protested, pulling me to a stop a second time like an anchor would a boat. I could float all I wanted until the slack ran out, but until I let him say what he had to say, he'd just keep yanking me right back. "Just one, tiny little nugget from one man to another."

I took a deep breath and nodded.

"She's right to be wary of you."

I tried not to let his words hurt because I knew they were true. Still, I expected a tiny bit more coddling from my father. Unbidden and unwelcome, an ache took shape under the left side of my rib cage.

"Thanks," I said bitingly, reaching up to rub the tension in my forehead.

"Son," he called, and I lifted my head to look him in the eyes—eyes that looked just like mine.

"You're right to fight to prove her wrong."

CHAPTER 20

Winnie

"Are we really doing this?" I asked Wes as I cut a fresh loaf of bread into slices.

He dropped the pasta into boiling water and hitched his hip against the counter. "Doing what?"

"The whole meet-the-parents thing?"

Wes had decided that he would like to join my family and me for our weekly Thursday dinners, and he then hadn't given me a chance to say no. But he hadn't given me a chance to say yes either, and I honestly wasn't sure which answer I would have given.

Time with him, in general, felt like home. When we weren't having ah-may-zing sex, we were flirting and teasing and being playful, and he genuinely made me happy.

But there was so much I didn't know, couldn't predict, about our future, and the more I inserted him into my life, Lex's life—my family's life—the more it would hurt if and when he decided not to be in them anymore.

"And meet the three remaining brothers, too," he added with a smirk.

I laughed. "Yeah. That."

He came up behind me as I stirred the pasta sauce and patted my ass. "You've got nothing to fear, Fred. I've got this," he whispered into my ear and then placed a soft kiss to my neck. If I hadn't been feeling anxiety about Wes spending an entire meal with my mother and four older brothers, my mind probably would've taken a detour from Serious Business Avenue straight to Pervy Road.

"I don't think you know my brothers."

"I know one of your brothers. And he's really warming up to me."

I turned in his arms, rife with skepticism.

"Remy's warming up to you? How do you figure that?"

"Just a few weeks ago, he was telling me to go fuck myself every time he saw me. Now, he just glares. That seems like progress to me."

I shook my head.

"A Christmas miracle, perhaps."

"It's not Christmas," I said, and he pushed his lips to mine and spoke there.

"Almost."

He was being lighthearted, my very favorite version of him, and my entire body started to throb as my heart rate sped up.

God. *I'm falling for him.*

"What are we?" I blurted out, sliding my hands from his shoulders to his forearms and pushing him away slightly.

His eyebrows pulled together at both the question and the distance. "What do you mean?"

Uncomfortable with my own goddamn question, I turned back to the stove and started stirring the pasta vigorously.

He grabbed my chin in one hand and froze my frantic wrist with the other, pulling my gaze back toward him. "What do you mean, sweetheart?" he whispered seriously, everything about him soft and open.

"Are we..." I started and then paused to lick my lips. His pupils dilated as he watched. "Are we together?"

He tilted his head to the side in serious contemplation, and my lunch started to crawl up my throat with unease.

"Do you *want* to be together?" he asked. His gaze held mine and pled. I just couldn't tell for what.

"Do *you* want to be together?" I tried.

He smirked. "I asked you first."

We stood there for what seemed like forever, lost in each other as I tried to find the courage to tell him how I felt.

Why is it so fucking hard?

"Knock knock! Yo! Winnie girl! Where are you?" a loud, booming voice called from the foyer. I jumped, but Wes never moved an inch.

We stayed there, staring at each other until the moment was completely ruined by my oldest brother Remy bounding into my kitchen. "There you are!" he said with a grin, pulling me into a tight hug and away from Wes.

When Remy finally let me go, Wes stuck out his hand to shake hello. "Remy."

Remy took his hand and squeezed. Hard. "Go fuck yourself, Lancaster."

"Jesus, Rem," I griped. "What is wrong with you?"

Wes smiled, though, and it wasn't long before it spread from his face to my own.

"Progress, huh?" I teased.

Wes winked. "Minor snag."

"Uh oh…Uncle Remy said a bad word," Lexi singsonged as she entered the kitchen with my mother and several bags full of dessert. They'd gone on a run to the three of the best bakeries in a five-block radius just so Lexi could have her donuts, Jude could have his cannoli, and Ty could have fresh chocolate chip and almond cookies. I wasn't spoiled enough to ask for something specific like my stupid brothers, but, if things kept going as they were, I'd probably take a healthy sample of all three.

"Remington Winslow, where are your manners!" my mother chastised as she set the bags on the counter. Her light blond, conservatively cut hair sat perfectly on her shoulders, but her eyes said, *"I will fuck you up if you keep acting like an idiot."*

Momma Winslow had that look down pat. It was the only way for a mother of four sons to keep her wild boys in line.

The whole group of us stared at Remy, but he just shrugged, not the least bit concerned about the fact that he looked like a complete dick. That wasn't anything new, though. He'd never, but never, given that first fuck about proper conduct.

"Come here, Lexi Lou!" He stretched out both arms.

But before she could sprint into his embrace, Ty barged in. "No way, I get first dibs on hugs from my favorite little niece," he said as he snatched Lexi into his arms. I hadn't even heard the door open with his arrival, but the more people who arrived, the less aware I would be. With a family our size, all of our weekly dinners shared one common theme: chaos.

Flynn and Jude arrived shortly after and crowded into the shrinking kitchen. Each and every brother made a show over picking Lexi up and fawning over her, and my heart grew two sizes bigger in my chest like it always did. My daughter hadn't had the easiest road when it came to father figures in her life, but my brothers had all stepped up.

Her father, Nick, was about as absent as one could get. His appearances in her life were few and far between and almost always self-serving. He wasn't a *bad* guy. Intrinsically selfish, he just wasn't father material.

In the beginning, it had been very hard, being a single mom who could not rely on the father of her child for anything besides finances. It had been a long, tough road. If I hadn't been nearly done with medical school when I got pregnant, I don't know that I would have finished.

But I had, starting my career as a physician with a brand-new baby in tow, and thanks to my strong support system, I'd managed to do just fine.

My brothers were a huge part of that.

"Are you going to introduce us, Winnie?" Ty asked.

"Yeah," Jude agreed. "I thought that's what this whole shindig was about…parading the new sacrifice, that kind of thing."

My mother smacked the back of his head, and I smiled. *I win.*

Jude gave me the finger behind his back, but I backhanded it with an imaginary tennis racket.

Flynn laughed and reached across the space to give me five.

"This is Wes!" Lexi shouted and ran over to slide her little hand into his. She tugged him toward her uncles with a giant grin on her face. Wes's eyes sought mine. The wonder in them when he made contact? Blinding.

Everyone else was busy trying to mask their surprise. Lex was a different kind of kid, and sometimes, it took a lot of effort for her to really show affection toward someone who wasn't her family.

It had taken her nanny, Melinda, a solid year to get on Lex's good side.

But somehow, Wes Lancaster had managed to become one of my daughter's favorite people in a mind-blowingly short amount of time. She was so inherently comfortable around him, and he her, it was like he understood her little soul on a higher level than most people could. And more than that, he made a real effort to learn the things about her that weren't as obvious.

"Mom, this is Wes Lancaster." I started introductions with the most innocuous of all the guests.

"Hi, Mrs. Winslow," he greeted and pulled her into a quick, thoughtful hug. "I'm Winnie's boyfriend. It's nice to finally meet you."

Boyfriend? Did he just say boyfriend?

Wes's eyes met mine for a brief moment, purpose and intent in them. I was surprised by the declaration, but he sure as shit wasn't.

My mother giggled a little, and a bright smile lit up her face. "It is wonderful to meet you, Wes. Please, call me Wendy."

"Boyfriend?" Remy asked.

Yeah, news to me, too, I thought to myself, but I somehow managed to school my facial expression into an amused grin rather than the deer-in-headlights, downright shock that consumed me.

Ignoring Remy and my panic, I finished up introductions. "Wes. Flynn, Jude, Ty, and you know Remy," I said as I pointed to each of them.

Ty shook his hand with a pathetic attempt of a friendly smile. It looked more like, *"Sleep with one eye open, buddy, because I will cut you."*

Jude shrugged.

Flynn offered a halfhearted wave.

And Remy just stared Wes down.

Wow. This was going to be interesting, for sure. My mother breathed the deep, beleaguered sigh of a woman who'd been dealing with this group of obstinate, aggravating humans for the vast majority of her adult life.

But Wes handled it all in stride, moving to each of my brothers, save Remy, and offering a friendly handshake and a smile in the face of each murderous glare flashed in his direction.

"Honey, would you like me to help you with anything?" my mother offered while Wes and my brothers started to chat about the Mavericks' upcoming game against Philly.

"Uh, yeah, sure," I answered and turned back to the stove where pasta was boiling and meatballs and garlic bread needed tending to.

When I looked up again, Wes, my brothers, and Lexi were all gone.

Shit.

"Where'd they go?" I asked my mother frenziedly. She had the audacity to *laugh*.

"Nothing is funny about this!"

"Oh, relax. He'll be fine," she assured with a pat to my back. "He went willingly into the living room with them. Either that or your brothers have gotten really good at concealing their techniques."

"Mom!" I whined.

"He's handled everything just fine so far. You don't have anything to worry about. Plus, he's got his fan club with him."

Lexi.

"You noticed that, huh?"

"I've never seen her take to someone like that," she murmured quietly, all traces of humor gone, and I had to fight the sting in my eyes.

"Do you love him?" she asked a few quiet moments later as she stirred the pasta sauce.

"Mom."

"What?" she protested. "It's a valid question. He's here in your house, and very obviously in your life, if Lexi's attachment is any indication."

I sighed and ventured honestly, "Should I know the answer to that?"

She tilted her head to the side as her motherly gaze assessed my face. It was a look only a mother could pull off, her honey brown eyes reaching into my soul and listening intently to all of my secrets. "Our hearts always know the answer to that question, but sometimes, our minds put up walls to prevent us from really seeing the situation for what it is."

"And you think I love him?"

"Oh, honey. I don't think anything. I'm just asking what you think."

"I hate it when you do that," I complained. "I just want my mom to give me the freaking answer. Is that too much to ask?"

She smiled again, and a small, quiet laugh escaped her lips. Her gaze went back to the pasta sauce while I just stood there, feet frozen to the floor and mind racing a mile a minute. *Leave it to my mother to push me into the wilds of a reflective state—and then leave me there to fend for myself.*

"It's complicated," I said, voice quiet and vulnerable. "I'm honestly afraid of what might happen if I let myself love him."

Laughter rang out from the living room, and my head jerked in that direction. My mother looked at me.

"What are you afraid of?"

I scoffed. "Uh…everything?"

"Winnie."

I blew out my breath in a huff. "He has absolutely no history of settling down."

My mom chuckled. "Why would he have settled down before now if *you* are the right woman?"

Well…I guess she was right.

Fine. Next.

"He's completely married to his job. He's so busy, has a hand in so many things, and it's literally his whole life."

My mom raised her eyebrows. "Sounds like you."

"I have Lexi," I countered, and she smiled a gentle smile.

"And what does he have, dear?"

I'd just met his dad that previous weekend. One of the *two or three times a year* he saw him. Other than that and his friends, I was guessing the answer was "not fucking much." *Goddammit.*

"Matters of the heart are never easy," my mom educated gently. "But sometimes you just have to take the risk. It's the only way you'll find out."

"How can you say that so easily after everything you went through with Dad?"

She shrugged, but a light of understanding flared in her eyes. "I don't regret taking that risk with your father. That risk gave me five beautiful, intelligent, and kind children. And one of those kids gave me a gorgeous, brilliant, and gifted granddaughter. No amount of heartbreak from him could rob me of that."

"Why do you think he did that?"

"Some men just aren't meant to be fathers. Some men just aren't meant to be husbands. Sometimes, they try. Sometimes, they think they can handle a wife and kids. But sometimes, they find out it's just not where they are supposed to be. And really, it's not my duty or burden to know why. It's *his*. I still have all of the gifts we created together, and he does not."

My mother was a remarkable woman—with a pure, kind heart. I wasn't sure I'd be able to only say nice words about a man who literally up and left me to fend for myself and my children. Sometimes, I wondered if she was actually an angel sent from heaven.

"You're too forgiving," I complained.

She shook her head. "So are you," she pointed out kindly.

Nick.

"That's what all your hesitance is really about, isn't it? By your description, Wes is a selfish, career-driven, good-time man. That sounds familiar, huh?"

"Exactly like Nick." She nodded.

I pulled up short and forgot the dinner, so that I could turn to face her directly. "Except..."

"Except?" she asked when I didn't go on.

"Except, Wes isn't the good-time guy. His friends are. They're the ultimate good-time people. But Wes isn't."

His laughter rang out from the living room again, and my mom's eyebrows lifted suspiciously.

"God, Mom, I think I make him like that." I pointed to the living room. "He's only like that with me."

She seemed to make a decision then, and she reached out to brush some hair off of my shoulder and then settled her hands on my upper arms.

"After it was all said and done, do you regret the risk you took with Nick?"

I shook my head instantly, without any second thoughts or doubts. "No. I don't regret it. That relationship gave me the best gift I've ever been given."

"Most times, even if giving your heart away ends in heartbreak, the risk was still worth it. Sometimes, that risk gives you little miracles. And sometimes, that risk gives you life lessons that allow you to grow and learn more about yourself. With your father, I learned that even though I'd love to find someone to share my life with, I'm a very strong woman," she explained with a soft smile.

"I can always take care of myself and my kids. I didn't know I was that strong until after your father. I learned a lot from that relationship and walked away with many gains. Sure, when your dad decided to leave us, it was the hardest thing I'd ever been through in my entire life, but it also made me the woman and mother and grandmother and friend that I am today."

"So you think I should take the risk with Wes?"

"I think you should really listen to your heart. I think you shouldn't let fear prevent you from taking the risk, if that's what your heart is telling you."

I sighed, and she chuckled quietly.

"You're an intelligent woman, Winnie. And I have no doubts that you will always do what is best for your daughter. She is learning from you, you know. She sees how confident and independent and strong her mother is. She sees it every day."

"I'm just scared, you know? I'm scared of letting another man step in with Lexi and…" I didn't need to say the rest. I didn't want him to leave.

My mother glanced out into the living room where Wes had Lexi sitting on his shoulders. They were both smiling and laughing as he spun her around in a perfect three-hundred-and-sixty-degree circle per her request.

"He might make mistakes along the way—we're only human—but I honestly think a man like that wouldn't do anything to hurt you or my granddaughter intentionally."

I watched Wes and Lexi continue to horse around in the living room while my mother pulled the garlic bread out of the oven.

"Dinner's ready!" she shouted loud enough for everyone to hear, and just like that, our heart-to-heart was over. It was time for me to listen to myself and give it my best effort to follow through. If I ended up wrong…well, I was allowed to make mistakes, too.

"Thank God!" Remy shouted. "I've been here for at least thirty minutes!"

Everyone headed into the kitchen and started to take their seats at the table. Wes helped Lexi into her chair and scooted it in. She sat there, outwardly showing a patient little girl waiting on her meal, but the slight bounce in her legs as she fidgeted them back and forth told me she was feeling a little anxious.

But before I could offer some sort of distraction, Wes had already grabbed her iPad off the kitchen counter and set it in front of her.

She grinned up at him and then buried her nose into the screen.

As my mother walked to the table with the plate of garlic bread in one hand and the serving platter of spaghetti and meatballs in the other, Wes's eyes met mine. He offered a soft, reassuring smile and I couldn't stop myself from returning it.

"All right! Let's eat!" Ty cheered.

And that was that.

When the Winslow brothers said it was time to chow down, it was motherfucking time to chow down.

I sat in the chair right beside Lexi and directly across from Wes at the kitchen table and started getting her plate together while she kept busy with a game on her tablet.

Once I had gotten both of our plates filled, my phone buzzed in my back pocket.

I pulled it out and saw a text from Wes.

Wes: Your brothers already have my gravesite purchased. I thought that was very reassuring.

I all but choked on my own saliva.

Me: Well, you're the one who called yourself my boyfriend.

Wes: I did, didn't I…

Me: Yeah. You did.

Wes: I'm actually taking the whole gravesite thing to mean I've passed their test.

I shook my head. This guy and his misguided ideas about "progress."

Me: How do you figure that?

Wes: Come on. You only purchase a plot for your family. They've obviously welcomed me into the fold.

Winnie: Oh yeah, you're in the fold, all right.

Wes: I think I can be in a lot of things later tonight. Once Lex is in bed and everyone has gone home. My mouth is craving that sweet, greedy little cunt of yours.

Me: You're evil.

Wes: You're mine, sweetheart. And tonight, you really will be.

I should've been pissed at him for several reasons. For one, he had completely avoided the boyfriend question. And two, he was texting the word *cunt* to me while my entire family was sitting at the table with us.

But was I pissed? Nope.

Turned the fuck on and emotionally content? Yes.

I knew my mother had given me her wise advice of following my heart, but holy hell, it was hard to distinguish which was loudest right now: my heart or my vagina.

These were not the thoughts I wanted to be having while sitting at the table with my four overbearing and way too protective older brothers.

Me: All right. Cut it out, Casanova. Unless you want an early view of your gravesite.

He flashed a knowing smirk, and I almost got lost in it. But Jude's question brought me right back from the brink.

"How the fuck does a guy with an electrical engineering degree from Harvard end up with a football team and a restaurant and who fucking knows what else?"

There'd obviously been an interrogation going on in the living room, but hell, I wanted to know the answer too.

"Hard work and luck mostly," Wes said around a sip of his water.

"I get the football team," Ty interjected. "That's cool as fuck. But I still don't understand the restaurant."

And then, with one simple statement, all my doubts about Wes moved right out of the way as he shoved me off the cliff.

"The restaurant wasn't my dream, but I owed it to the woman who wanted it more than almost anything."

"The woman?" Remy barked.

Wes's eyes never left mine. "My mother."

"What did she want more than the restaurant?" I asked, my voice echo-y to my own ears as if I was floating outside of my body.

"Me."

I knew the feeling.

I want him more than anything else too.

CHAPTER 21

Wes

Horns honked and taxis swerved in front of our car as we rode through Midtown Manhattan on a Saturday night, a swirling mix of snow flurries filling the late December sky. Nearly an entire month had passed, and yet, almost everything had stayed the same.

Winnie and I were still in this limbo-like place, searching our souls—separately, rather than together—for all the answers to our relationship. And it was only that defined because I'd made it so, declaring her my girlfriend at her family dinner. I wondered at this point if there'd ever be any definitive answers or set boundaries or ironclad roles, or if it would be this way until we slowly petered into the ultimate brink—death.

After the come to Jesus moment with my dad, I'd known I was going to have to fight, but I didn't have the experience to know how to go about it. I'd done what I could, giving our relationship a parameter that should have facilitated a roadmap for expected behavior, but we still weren't there.

There wasn't much of a time when I wasn't around anymore, taking Lexi to football practice and games, having dinner at their house, and sharing all of my commuting space with Winnie, morning and night.

Yep. She buckled on the commute. I have a feeling it had more to do with trains that smell like feet than me, however.

But if I didn't ask to come over, Winnie didn't protest or offer. It was like she *expected* me to flake out. And the energy it took to prove her wrong was wearing us both out.

I honestly had no idea what Winnie and I were at that point.

And I had a feeling she didn't know either.

The one thing I was certain of was that I wanted more of her.

I wanted *all* of her.

An old Metallica song, "Fade to Black," played in my head in time with the swerving traffic and gawking pedestrians at the mental image of our slow descent into nothingness.

I hoped we found a way to accept and appreciate each other before that actually happened.

People posed for pictures and laughed as the bright lights of forty-foot blinking billboards highlighted the contours of their faces, and some even stuck their tongues out to catch the falling frozen water.

It was chaos out there—the worst kind for actual Manhattanites—clogging the streets and making it hard for us to be cynical to the same degree we normally were. The week between Christmas and New Year's was never less than insanity in New York. And these thousands of people, some of them seeing Times Square in all of its brilliance for the first time in their lives, were the epitome of happy.

The reason I was here, subjecting myself to their ecstasy, however, was so that I could make Lexi Winslow feel the same thing.

It was the worst possible time to be traveling to this part of town—the tourist sector, if you will—but when Lexi had started spouting facts about award nominations and work history of each and every member of the cast of *Wicked*, I knew I'd be spending a night like this.

I knew I'd do it without comment or complaint and that, if it turned out as well as I hoped, I'd do it a hundred times over.

With Winnie on one side of the car, me on the other, and a sweet, quiet little girl in between us, I looked out the window and blurred out the mass of people until all that stood out were the landmarks. The TKTS booth, the towering billboards, and the New Year's ball just waiting to be dropped. Just a few nights from now, approximately one million people would cram themselves into this tiny space just to get a chance to witness its trip down.

Lights danced through the window as we crossed over Broadway and came to a stop about a block away from the Gershwin Theater, and my heart doubled its pace.

Wanting so badly to give Lexi something from me, something I'd noticed and noted through our time together, I'd unconsciously put more pressure on this one night than I was comfortable with. Somehow, in my mind, the success of tonight—or lack thereof—would be some sort of indication of whether or not I could handle this kind of life—stepfather and family man, someone who put other people's needs before his own.

Knowing there was a lot more to a Broadway show than met the eye, I'd purchased tickets with Lexi in mind, toward the front for the ultimate experience, but over to the side in case it became too much to handle at any point.

I didn't want her to feel embarrassment or shame, and as her mother, I didn't want Winnie to feel it either.

The whispers happened whether they were deserved or not: "What a shame she can't control her child" or "That little girl has no manners." In reality, this mother and little girl were the cream of the crop, but they'd been dealt a different set of cards in the game of life.

As the car finally crawled to a stop, a mob of people quickly surrounding it in the crosswalk and the rest of the street alike, I climbed out first, holding the door for both of them and pulling Lexi into my side as Winnie climbed to her feet. She looked gorgeous in a knee-length merlot-colored dress, and my eyes flared as she bent forward and her breasts filled the V-neck of the top even further.

She noticed and smiled, throwing me a wink and squeezing my hand as she stood beside me. It did things to me, things I wasn't sure what to make of, the hormonal man and the people-pleasing child inside me at war with one another. I decided to split my focus as best as I could.

With one girl on each arm, my hand warmly around the skin at the back of Lexi's neck, I escorted them down the sidewalk and across the street, under the marquee and into the entrance of the theater. I half expected Winnie to chatter, but she didn't, staying so silent at my side that I found myself glancing over at her face every few seconds just to assure myself she was all right.

Fortunately, a soft smile had pulled up a figurative stool and taken up residence there, greeting me pleasantly every time my gaze met hers.

As we pushed through the far left set of glass doors, the weight of solid construction and years of history flexing the muscles in my arm, I noticed a woman perk up at the sight of us.

Her steps were hurried as she rushed forward to cut us off at the pass.

"Mr. Lancaster," she greeted as she reached out to shake my hand. "I'm Emily, the theater manager," she introduced herself.

Either she was some kind of medium or fantastically prepared for her job, having recognized my face the second we walked through the door, but regardless, I took her hand in mine, shaking twice and offering a polite smile.

I still didn't smile often, but thanks to Winnie, I was trying to add it to my everyday repertoire. "Hello, Emily."

I squeezed the hand at Lexi's neck and pulled her slightly toward me. Her eyes came up quickly, but after a very brief encounter with a woman she didn't know, met the swirled pattern in the carpet just as fast.

"This is Lexi, *Wicked* fanatic and the reason we're here." I turned to Winnie and pulled her closer with a hand at the small of her back. "And this is her beautiful and brilliant mother, Winnie."

Emily correctly read Lexi enough to know not to attempt to touch her, but she reached forward and took Winnie's hand as she said hello to both of them. "Hello, ladies. We're so thrilled to have you here tonight," she went on before turning toward the theater and sweeping out an arm. "Shall we?"

With the affirmation of my nod, she turned and led the way, escorting us through a side door and around the back to our seats. It was weird, having people thankful for your presence just because you had more money than the other people who had paid the same amount of money for their tickets—and it wasn't something I'd noticed until now. Regretfully, shamefully even, I'd somehow thought I deserved special treatment.

Now, wanting so badly to earn positive attention from a woman and child who would not give it to me if I didn't earn it—that kind of notion just seemed stupid.

Still, for tonight, I'd take it, for special treatment of me meant special treatment of *we*.

With a wave of her hand, a man appeared at Emily's side with a cushion for Lex's chair, intended to make her the height of everyone around her so she wouldn't miss a beat, and I breathed a small sigh of relief.

I hadn't thought of that, so I was thankful the theater had—though I would have propped her up on my knee if I'd needed to.

"How many minutes until it starts?" Lexi asked as I took the cushion from the guy and moved to sit down.

The theater manager, still within earshot, smiled and looked to her watch before the rest of us could.

"Looks like thirteen minutes on the dot."

Lexi smiled at the direct answer and happily climbed into her seat, and my own face lit up at her contentment.

I'd learned pretty quickly that she worked better in absolutes, with concise and clear instructions or warnings about what to expect. She didn't need pattern or routine—just a warning. If she knew what lay ahead, she was ready and excited. I didn't know if it soothed something in her or if it allowed her to better prepare for the extra stimulation, but I loved that it was something I could give her easily.

"She's been listening to the soundtrack," Winnie whispered into my ear, pulling my attention back to her for the first time in several minutes.

Guilt flashed, hot and uneasy in my gut, as I realized I didn't really know how to balance the time between mother and daughter. Frankly, I felt a little like a fish out of water. Entertaining one woman for a night was easy—trying to meet the needs of two very different, drastically oppositely aged women at once was another thing altogether.

But Winnie didn't let it linger, leaning over to speak softly again. "Watching you with her…" She paused, but the silence was substantial—purposeful.

Tonight, she saw me—saw *us*—for what we really were. Meaningful, romantic, enduring kismet. Weight lifted off of my chest, and warmth quickly replaced it. "Thank you for tonight."

"No," I refuted with a shake of my head and a small kiss to her lips. "Thank *you*."

Lex's eyes were wide and watchful as a swath of green light cast a glow on her sweet face.

Her focus, as always with something she was truly interested in, was avid, and each word Elphaba spoke seemed to soak right in through her skin. Like it was becoming a part of her, I knew Lexi would carry every bit of dialogue, every moment created by the lighting and cast and heart-freezing music, through the entirety of her life.

Right then, as her little but meaningful hand reached out to rest on the fabric at my arm, it felt like I would carry it through mine too.

Elphaba's otherworldly voice made the tiny hairs on the back of my neck stand up as she sang about her differences and her peers' refusal to accept them. Her life had been horrible, outcast, and burdened with the weight of her father's jealousy thanks to the color of her skin.

It was so relatable, the story they'd created here, and eye-opening to the power of perspective. Two tales of the Wicked and Good, so powerfully interwoven that it was hard to tell what was true and what wasn't. But the truth of tonight was that Elphaba, no matter her supposed dissimilarities, wanted the things all people wanted: love, tolerance, and understanding. Lexi had never truly felt those things outside of her family, but she had mastered the art of disregard for such trivialities.

Or so I'd thought.

Now I could see I was wrong to assume that the hurt didn't penetrate, that the whispers weren't heard as the set of her shoulders so clearly indicated her burden and the weight.

I shook my head and clenched my jaw against the overwhelming surge of raw emotion.

My little Lex heard everything and remembered it even more, and all the intelligence in the world couldn't keep her pale white skin from sometimes seeming painfully green.

I'd never shed a tear in my life, but right then, when all the special, amazing things Lexi Winslow was intersected with all the stupid, expected things she would never be, I couldn't have stopped the tiny trickle of emotion if I'd tried.

As she watched them on stage, I watched her. Winnie sat silently on my other side, the small catches in her breath exactly what I needed to watch her too—without having to take my eyes off of Lex.

Because I'd spent months falling into the trap of Lexi Winslow's mother, but right then, with some of the most powerful voices on the planet ringing out in front of us, I fell deep into her warm little well.

She was everything I'd never expected from a child—both easier and more difficult, affectionless in a lot of the ways I expected, but much, much better in all the others I could not have predicted if I'd had a crystal ball.

When the final notes of the final song echoed in the auditorium, Lexi looked up to me. I held her eyes through the applause that so often made her uncomfortable, and I pictured it in her eyes. The pounding in your chest and the assault on your ears—everything that would be way too much if I'd had the intellectual capacity to notice each individual sound and action as a separate entity—the way her brain saw the world.

The song had moved her. The fact that she viewed me as a venue of safety and acceptance impassioned me.

And, after months of getting here, I was officially in love—with our newly formed "we."

CHAPTER 22

Winnie

Wes: *What field are you at?*

Me: *#4*

Wes: *On my way. How's Lex? Is she nervous?*

Me: *I think I'm nervous and she's excited. :/*

Wes: *She's going to do great. Tell her I'm 3 minutes away.*

Me: *Is that an exact time estimation?*

Wes: *What do you take me for? A novice? This is Lexi Winslow we're talking about here, sweetheart, and I know my girl.*

My girl. Jesus. He'd pulled the pin, and my ovaries were just about ready to blow.

Me: lol…Right.

I slid my phone into my pocket and felt a little hand tug at the bottom of my sweater. Lexi stared up at me with the calm of a girl who loved pattern and knew this one well. We'd been here before, several times, in fact, since she took up playing football midseason. But as much as she loved routine, I loved her *more*, and it was never quite so easy for a mother to let go.

"Wes, Mommy?"

"He will be here in three minutes, sweetie."

"Time, Mommy?"

I glanced at my watch. "Five fifty-seven."

She nodded. "Six o'clock."

"That's right, baby," I said, and my hand instinctively went to run through her blond locks, but stopped when it met the cold, hard material of her football helmet.

God, she always looked adorable all suited up and ready to play football.

My little kicker.

It took all of my strength not to burst into tears on the spot.

Motherhood changed you from the second you looked into the big, innocent eyes of your child. Within an instant, you had an unlimited supply of love for that precious, tiny being. They would forever be yours, and you would forever be the one person who would always love them, protect them, cherish them, worry about them, and fight for them.

Everything else felt minor in comparison.

It was a different kind of love. The kind of love that had me bursting into tears over something as simple as my daughter in a football uniform.

I was just so proud of her. So unbelievably proud of her. She'd overcome *so* much. We both had.

"Wes!" she exclaimed. My gaze followed hers, locking in on the man who'd helped both of us get to this point. I'd never, in my wildest dreams, expected it to last. But it had—and it seemed like it might go on forever.

New Year's had been quiet. Just the three of us in my house with a fire and movies and laughter.

And then, once Lex had gone to bed, some of the best sex I'd ever had. His back to the headboard while I straddled him, breaths mingling and thighs shaking with the effort to keep moving, we'd rung in the new year completely connected, in both mind and body.

He'd traced the line of my lips with the tip of his tongue before sinking it deep into my mouth for as long as we could stand without coming up for air, and then, both of our orgasms receding slowly into the night, he'd looked me in the eye and told me he'd never been happier in his life. Me and Lex and everything we gave him, he couldn't wait to give it back for the next year and then some.

I could still taste the tears that I'd choked down the back of my throat at the sentimentality in his words.

And, unfortunately, I could also feel a sour roil in my gut because not one of them had been "I love you."

"Lexi girl. Looking fierce!" he responded just as enthusiastically, a giant, proud grin etched across his handsome face, and I felt instantly guilty about having even an ounce of lingering doubt. I had *this*, and I wanted to lament over three stupid words? It was goddamn ridiculous.

The second he reached us, he lifted her up into the air so that she was eye-level with him. Her little cleats dangled off the ground, and she giggled.

"You ready to show these boys how you really kick a field goal?"

She nodded and her uninhibited laughter rang out into the open space again.

I felt a tingle all the way down to my toes.

He set her back down and came over to stand beside me, wrapping his arm around my waist and tucking me into his side. He kissed the side of my forehead and whispered into my ear, "Don't worry, Mommy. She's got all of the proper protective equipment. She won't get hurt, and she's done this before.

"In fact, she freaking crushed the Brooklyn Boys last week." He glanced down to Lex's upturned face and gave her the sweetest tap on the shoulder. "Didn't you, Lexinator?"

She nodded enthusiastically and danced from one foot to the other. When the five-minute warning whistle blew on the field and Lexi turned to look, I lowered my voice and asked out of the side of my mouth, "Am I that obvious?"

Wes glanced down at me and grinned.

"Man, I thought I was really doing a good job holding it together. Five games deep, I thought I'd have it in check by now."

He laughed and shook me lovingly side to side before stepping away to look me in the eye. "To the untrained eye, you're holding your shi—stuff together perfectly. It's just me who can tell, and ironically, that's because of *your* tell."

I raised my eyebrows. "A tell?"

He nodded. "You bite your lip when you're uncertain or worried about something."

I shoved his shoulder. "I do not!"

"Oh, yeah. Yeah, you do," he answered far too quickly, smug smirk in place. "You also do that little lip-biting thing when you're begging me to," he added, and a low, sexy whistle followed suit.

"Begging? Why's Mommy begging?" Lexi chimed in.

I rolled my eyes at Wes and little ears, but he just laughed it off, far too amused with himself. "Mommy is *begging* for me to take you guys to get hot chocolate at Serendipity 3 after the game."

Her eyes lit up like Christmas lights. "With marshmallows?"

"I don't know..." he replied with a gentle smirk. "Let's make a deal. If Mommy promises to *whistle* with me later, we'll do hot chocolate, marshmallows, *and* donuts."

Lexi's eyes moved straight to me. "Promise Wes you'll whistle with him, Mommy! Pretty please! Promise, Mommy! Promise!"

I elbowed Wes in the stomach and felt a little satisfaction when I heard a tiny whoosh of air leave his lips.

Of course, three seconds later, he was back to laughing. And I'd tried so hard for lasting damage.

Coach Sanderson blew his whistle from the center of the field and motioned for the team to head toward him. "Let's get ready to have some fun!" he exclaimed with a hearty laugh and smile.

Within seconds, a pack of tiny football players ran out toward him excitedly.

To my surprise, Wes took Lexi by the hand and walked out with her. I stood back and watched in awe as he kneeled beside her in the team huddle. One last talk between the two of them, and she was ready to play. Her football helmet shielded her expression from my view, but I couldn't miss the huge, proud smile on Wes's face.

He came back to my side and linked his fingers with mine, but his eyes never, not once, left her, even when she was doing nothing more than standing patiently on the sideline.

I knew exactly what Wes was to me—to us. And there was no doubt that it scared the fucking shit out of me.

We hadn't ever fallen for someone so hard.

Two hours and several frozen appendages later, we were sitting at a small, bistro-sized table inside of a very crowded Serendipity 3. Winters in New York often brought tourists from all over the place to the iconic restaurant, and today was no different. But I didn't give a flying flip. It was warm, and I had a fucking huge mug of their famous frozen hot chocolate in front of me. Chocolatey goodness in every gulp, I alternated sucking it through a straw and scooping out big, heaping portions by the spoonful.

"She was so awesome out there today," Wes mooned, looking

across the table at Lex. Her nose was buried in his phone, watching some type of YouTube video on advanced algebra problems, but he didn't need her return attention. Much like me, he'd become completely content just to look at each other.

I'm sure it's nauseating for outsiders.

"A lot of that was thanks to you," I said. "You've made things so much easier for her by helping her through every step of the season."

A soft smile lifted the corners of his mouth, and his eyes lit up like he was a little boy himself. "I'm having the time of my life, Win. This is what it's about, you know? This is the reason I love football."

I nodded.

"She's done such a good job of adjusting too. It's not easy being the only little girl on a team filled with rowdy boys."

I laughed and nodded. "Truer words have never been spoken."

His voice turned giddy. "She's on a team full of little warriors. I can't wait to see her play in the championship game. That team from the Bronx is no joke."

"What, have you been scouting the Pop Warner teams?" I asked incredulously.

He scoffed and tipped his head to Lexi. "Come on. You had to know we were going to do our research."

"And your research says the Bronx kids are bruisers?"

He nodded excitedly, and I groaned. "Okay, maybe I'm not as okay with it as I thought I was."

He chuckled softly. "Don't worry, Fred. She'll do just fine."

I rolled my eyes at the nickname. *Stupid nickname.* It probably shouldn't have made my heart beat speed up at the mere mention of it. I had to take a sip of my frozen hot chocolate just to distract myself from the frantic pace.

"Have you told her dad about football yet?"

I shook my head. "No. I haven't talked to him since she started."

He didn't exactly look surprised because it wasn't like Nick had been around in all the time that Wes had, but he still asked, "Is that normal?"

I nodded and rolled my eyes before lowering my voice to a nearly silent volume. Lexi was preoccupied, but she still heard *everything*. "Nick is very much an absent father."

"Has it always been that way?"

"Yes," I admitted. "From the very start, it's always been that way. He didn't try for a while and then figure out he couldn't do it. He knew from the moment I told him the news, he wasn't ready to try."

He stretched his mouth into a tight line. "So, you've been doing this on your own from the very start?"

"Well…yeah," I answered with a shrug. It was all I knew as normal. That's why I had such a hard time accepting this version of Wes as real. "I've always had my family, though. There is no way in hell I could've finished med school and residency without my mom or crazy brothers. Remy, especially."

His face hardened at the mention of Remy, and I laughed. "I know, hard to believe with his offensive demeanor and all. But Lex is probably the only person who knows how many licks it takes to get to the center of his lollipop heart."

He stared at me in awe. "You're really something, you know? Kind of like a real-life superhero. Maybe it's weird to be proud of you," he said with a cringe. "But I am. I'm proud of everything you've accomplished and everything you've done and do for your daughter. She's lucky to have you as her mother."

"Thank you." I couldn't not blush at his sincere, sweet words. I felt like every day I was seeing a new side of Wes. And every day, I fell for each of those sides. God, I had to concentrate on talking again, thinking about each goddamn word individually, so powerful was his ability to consume me. "But I should say that I learned from the best."

He tilted his head to the side in confusion.

"I used to date Clark Kent. Well, Henry Cavill, but I figured that's the next best thing. It's a shame I just couldn't find the time to return his phone calls. He's very needy."

Wes smirked. "Poor Cavill."

"I know, right?" I laughed. "I actually meant my mother. My dad just up and left one day. It came out of nowhere, and all of a sudden, he just didn't want to be a part of our family anymore. And somehow, despite the pain and heartbreak she went through, she managed to pick up the pieces and give all five of her children a good life."

"Wendy Winslow is a saint."

"Yeah, she really is. If you think I'm strong, she's even stronger than me."

"I know how strong both of you are," he said with obvious pride in his voice. "I've seen you in action. Busting balls and taking names with a bunch of overgrown kids dressed in professional football uniforms. No other woman on earth could've walked into that locker room and handled those cocky sons of bitches as well as you did from the start—except maybe your mother. She's basically commanding a locker room every time your brothers get together."

"All four miscreants were good training, that's for sure."

He grinned. "I'm sure it was a little of that, but it was also just because you're fearless Winnie Winslow. The take-charge woman who attacked me near a vending machine in a hotel in Miami."

I rolled my eyes. "Oh, get over yourself. That was all *you*. You started it."

Wes laughed. "I'm pretty sure you started it, sweetheart. I've got detailed mental notes."

No way…he started it.

Oh, who was I kidding? We both started it. For months, everything we apparently biologically knew was right for us in the other had nagged and poked and pushed until the tension was so high we'd all but attacked one another in front of a vending machine in Miami. And…it seemed we hadn't really stopped.

Only now, we'd developed hand signals and whistles to discuss our pervy desires in front of my daughter.

I just had to hope Wes wouldn't grow tired of that. He'd lived fast and loud, but people *did* change. They could grow. They just had to have a reason.

But could Lex and I really be the reason for Wes?

CHAPTER 23

Wes

"How was Lex at practice?" I asked Winnie as I unbuttoned my suit jacket and sank into the car to go to dinner with the enemy.

Jerry Townsend owned the Baltimore Bengals, and we were one hundred percent not each other's favorite people. But he had something—*someone*—I wanted, and the chance of getting Andre Bodville, one of the best, yet underrated, left tackles in the league, was worth the gamble—and the torture of our meeting. Nothing would be effective until postseason was over, but other than pretty much every regular facet of my life, I couldn't deny my belief in the early bird getting the worm. And I wanted this fucking worm really badly.

But Lexi's championship football game was tomorrow, and my gut already churned that I'd put business before her last practice—especially since the timing of this meeting was born of nothing other than Jerry Townsend's convenience.

After joining the team midseason, Lex had really taken to it—at least, as far as enjoyment was concerned. She wasn't the most athletic kid on the field, but she put in more than full effort and always listened when the coaches gave her guidance. She smiled in my direction on the sidelines often, but today, when she'd looked for me, I hadn't been there.

Nausea swirled yet again in my stomach.

You're not cut out to be this girl's father figure, a hidden foe in my mind taunted. I'd had a good example of what a father should be, and a tiny fleck of doubt concealed permanently in the depths of my brain didn't think I was that kind of guy.

But any kind of reflection on the taunts always ended the same: what the hell kind of guy is that anyway? I wanted Winnie, and I wanted Lex, and I wanted them both to have everything they deserved out of life. I wasn't perfect, but other than striving to maintain those basic principles, what else was there?

Exactly. You don't know.

Chaos erupted behind my eyelids as the two arguments clashed and warred as if perched on opposing shoulders like the devil and God himself.

"She was fine," Winnie answered finally, blissfully silencing my thoughts with the rough hum that connected her words. They ran together like a melody rather than punching the air individually, and it made it so easy to get lost in them. I wasn't sure if it was new, if she'd softened over time from the once intimidating woman of the Mavericks locker room, or if perspective and time had brought clarity to my awareness. "Pretty good. Well, at kicking. You know the whole actual-contact-with-the-ball-while-running-or-catching-or-throwing thing is not her strong suit."

"Why was she working on anything else anyway? She's the kicker."

"Wes…" she said gently. "They're six. It's for fun, so they give all the kids a chance to do everything."

"When I'm there, all Lex does is kick."

She laughed a little then. "I think your Irritated Owl—"

I rolled my eyes at the name she'd made up for one of my expressions.

"Intimidates Coach Sanderson," she finished.

"It should. I should rip out his throat for making Lex do the other stuff."

She laughed, and I felt each and every low note in my dick. "She enjoyed it. She wasn't good at it, but she enjoyed it."

Lex's smile flashed in my mind. It killed the hormonal walk down Fantasy Lane, but really, since I was in a car, hundreds of miles away from the woman I'd like to have help me do something with it all, it was a good thing. "I'll practice with her," I said immediately.

"Mmhmm," she hummed, and the throaty sound of it had me feeling like a dirty old man again. *Jesus*. Filling these particular shoes was exhausting. Was this how every married father felt? Lost in the murky sea between paternity and passion?

Putting it all out of my mind, I focused on the things I could gain satisfaction from now. "And how was practice for you, Fred?"

"Better than you calling me Fred."

She still *hated* when I called her Fred. I loved all of it—the nickname and the loathing.

"That good, huh?"

"I might have liked a sport with less contact better."

I laughed then. "The kicker is pretty much as no-contact as football gets. And it's flag. There's no tackling."

"There's no tackling when the kids don't trip and fall into one another," she corrected.

I shook my head with a smile into the starkly empty car.

I miss blond heads and pop quizzes.

Disappointment set in when the restaurant came into view, and I knew I had to hang up soon. Silence stretched on the line between us as I steeled myself to say the words. I'd never ever felt this much regret over hanging up a fucking phone.

"I've got to go, Win."

"Okay."

"I'm pulling up to the meeting," I added, so she'd know I

wasn't hanging up because I wanted to—like a love-sick, desperate psychopath.

I really needed to get my shit together.

"Okay, Wes," she repeated, this time with a smile in her voice.

"I'll be home in the morning, and I'll call you tonight," I went on, saying basically every goddamn thing in the universe other than the thing I should have said.

I love you. You and Lex. And I'm scared that if you guys ever realize I'm not good enough for you, I'll turn into a goddamn awful shell of a man. Or you know…maybe something slightly less melodramatic.

"Actually, as much as I'd love that, could you just call in the morning? Maybe text when you get back to your room so I know. I'm exhausted."

"Okay," I agreed, thinking if she was awake when I texted, I'd call then—and hating the possibility that she might not be.

God. Maybe I should just tell her how I feel.

"Win—"

"Hold on a sec, Wes," she said before muffling the sound slightly as she probably turned away from the phone. "Yeah, baby?" A laugh. "No. Geez. Yeah, I don't know, honey. I'm gonna have to look that one up."

Lex murmured something in the background, but as hard as I tried to listen, I couldn't make it out.

"Wes?" Winnie called, turning her attention back to the phone and me.

"Yeah," I said around a swallow.

"I've gotta go, okay?"

I nodded even though she couldn't see me and closed my eyes. "Yeah."

She laughed again. "Lex, wait. Stop. Don't do that without help." Back to me. "I gotta go."

"Okay, sweetheart."

"Bye!" she chirped, and before I could say another word—not

that I would have, such the coward I was—she was gone.

"Wes," Amelia Townsend, Jerry Townsend's daughter called as I moved down the sidewalk to the waiting car outside of Bovu Restaurant.

The whole night had been a waste, hours of negotiating and bargaining only to learn Jerry didn't intend to give me anything I wanted—no matter how much it could benefit him.

Frustrated and cold, having chosen to forgo an overcoat despite the nasty weather, I turned around with a snap.

I wanted to go back to my hotel room, sleep for some ridiculously small number of hours, and then fly the hell home so I could see Winnie and Lexi. I wasn't in the mood to have any late-night sidewalk chats with scheming, conniving women, but something about the look in her eyes made me pause long enough to give her the chance to elucidate.

Rubbing her hands up and down her bare arms, Amelia shivered and stepped out of the doorway toward me. Her red hair blew across her face as the wind kicked up relentlessly.

"Yes?" I asked as she stopped in front of me.

"I'm sorry for the way my father was in there."

I shrugged and turned to look longingly at my waiting car before turning back to her.

"I know what you're proposing really is what's best for everyone. Let me talk to him about it without you there."

I started to shake my head, more than done with the whole thing, but she went on before I could fully execute the maneuver. "You know he's got this *thing* with you. Ever since last year's draft."

"Every player we recruited came to us fair and square," I snapped unfairly. None of this was her fault. Not her father, or the meeting, or the fact that I wanted desperately to be 200 miles northeast of here.

She held her hands up conciliatorily. "I know. Just let me talk to him."

"Fine," I offered. It's not like it would hurt anything—our relationship really couldn't swirl any lower around the bowl of the toilet, and after how fucking awful I'd acted just now, I felt like I owed it to Amelia.

"Where are you staying?" she asked. "I'll come find you after I talk to him."

Alarms started blaring all over the place, and my head shook without even consciously telling it to. "It's late," I said, rather than having to go into any other, uglier version of the truth.

"You're right," she agreed easily, and I relaxed a little. "Coffee, in the morning before your flight, then."

"Amelia—"

"It's just coffee, Lancaster."

For some reason, the use of my last name put me at ease. It felt more like comradery than seduction.

"All right," I agreed. Still, I didn't really want her knowing where my hotel was, so I kept the meeting details vague and unrelated. "Nine. Coffee. The Starbucks on Seventeenth."

"Perfect," she agreed. "See you then."

She reached out to take my hand, and I shook it.

And then I told myself she didn't hold it a little too long before turning to head back inside, leaving nothing behind but the uneasy pit in my stomach.

CHAPTER 24

Winnie

"Wes, Mommy?" Lexi asked, bouncing around in the kitchen on the tiptoes of her cleats. She was all suited up for her last football game of the season, the championship, for fuck's sake. When Wes had volunteered to find her a team, I'd wrongly assumed he didn't mean in the NFL.

Okay, so they weren't that good, but for a bunch of six-year-olds, it sure seemed like they were. And for Lexi, I didn't even think it mattered if they were good or not. She was just happy to be playing, with a whole slew of other kids who treated her like an equal. And because of that, every game day had started exactly like this one, with her bouncing around the house in excitement, her uniform on and at the ready *three hours* before kickoff.

Hell, she'd tried to put the damn thing on the second she'd gotten out of bed this morning.

I glanced at the time on my phone and frowned. I still hadn't heard from Wes this morning, and I was starting to wonder if everything was okay. It wasn't like him not to call. It wasn't like him not to *be here*. But as much as I wanted us to, we didn't live in a bubble, and Wes was a busy fucking guy. This meeting was important for the Mavericks, and the Mavericks had become important to me.

So I was trying really hard to be all *casual chic* about it in a mature, calm, cool, collected way. All I'd really succeeded in doing was containing the hysteria to the inside of my body.

"I'm sure he's busy flying back from his meeting, sweetheart," I tried to reassure her and myself.

The Winnie of four weeks ago would have assumed the worst *of* him—that he'd forgotten or didn't care.

But the Winnie of today knew better. Wes was nothing but loving and patient and kind with my daughter and me, and he looked forward to her games more than she did. No, this Winnie was worried *for* him. Scared something had happened to him that would be far worse than him choosing to walk away—a tragedy that robbed everyone of the luxury of choice.

Shit. My thinking in doomsday scenarios wasn't doing any of us any good.

I set my phone down on the counter and rummaged through the fridge to see what was available for lunch. "What sounds good, Lex? Turkey sandwich? Grilled cheese?"

"Text him, Mommy."

"Text who, baby?"

"Wes."

I shut my eyes for a moment and thanked God that my facial reaction was hidden behind the fridge door.

"Text Wes, Mommy," she repeated. "Ask him how many minutes."

I felt something tap against my back and turned to find my little footballer nudging my phone into my T-shirt.

"Text Wes, Mommy."

"Okay, sweetheart." I took the phone from her little hands. "I'll text him and see what time he'll be at your game."

"Ask him how many minutes."

I nodded my head and turned toward the large kitchen window over the sink. "Do me a favor, baby. Go get my empty coffee mug from the living room, okay?"

"Okay! One minute, Mommy!" she exclaimed, and I heard her cleats tip-tap across the hardwood floor and out of the room.

"Shit," I muttered to myself. "Shit. Shit. Shit."

I had a really bad feeling about today, and I had no concrete reason to back it up. At least, I hadn't. Not until my highly intuitive daughter had shown quite clearly that something felt completely off to her too.

I reasoned that she'd just come to expect him here, or that she was picking up all the anxious vibes I had to be putting off.

But Wes and I had both put my daughter in a position where she expected *everything* from him. And as guilty as that made me feel, I wasn't willing to compromise on it because of some stupid sense of pride.

If we were ever really going to work, I had to find a way to accept our relationship as safe. I needed the freedom to be fearful. I needed to feel confident in my expectation.

Wes wants to be here, I assured myself. *Find out what's going on.*

Me: Still going to the game?

Delete.

Me: Lexi wants to know how many minutes until you'll be at her game. :)

Delete.

Me: I miss you. Lexi misses you. I really hope you're going to make it to her game.

Delete.

Christ. I couldn't even come up with the right approach. Finally, I settled on the most honest of all my thoughts. It let go of the fear and shame and focused on fact.

Me: *We can't wait to see you.*

When Lexi barreled back into the room, she set my coffee mug down on the kitchen counter and asked again, "Wes, Mommy? How many minutes?"

And for some unknown reason, I found myself saying something very similar to what I would have said about her father, Nick.

"I'm not sure, baby. He didn't answer me yet."

She pushed her little lip out into a pout.

God, this was exactly why relationships were so hard when you were a single mom. It wasn't just about you. It was about them too.

"Don't worry!" I encouraged. "You know Wes. He's going to try his very hardest to be there. He will *not* miss it unless he absolutely has to."

She still looked completely let down. Just the saddest little girl in the whole world.

God, my heart ached. I was feeling a lot like a sad little girl myself.

"But guess what?" I said before thinking it through. I just wanted her to feel better, but I wasn't even sure I had anything to back up the change in conversational pace.

"What?" she muttered suspiciously.

Shit...Uh...Think quickly.

"Uncle Remy is going to be there, and he said he's so excited to watch you play and..."

I paused, and she noticed. *Goddamn tiny detective.*

"And what, Mommy?"

"And he said he's going to take you out for ice cream after the game."

Her eyes lit up ever so slightly. "Vanilla with rainbow sprinkles, Mommy?"

"Uncle Remy said you can pick out whatever kind of ice cream you want," I fibbed.

She grinned. Crisis averted. I internally sighed a breath of relief.

"Grilled cheese sound good for lunch?"

She shook her head. "Peanut butter and jelly. And yogurt. And an apple. And chips. And a cookie."

"Oh my, someone is hungry. Are you trying to get big and strong for your game today?" I asked and reached out and tickled her belly.

She giggled. "Stop, Mommy!"

I did, and it didn't take her long to change her tune. "Do it again!"

I tickled her again, and eventually, she ran out of the room, her giggles echoing down the hall as she made a beeline for her bedroom.

Once I knew she was no longer in sight, I picked my phone back up and texted Remy—after checking twice to make sure there wasn't anything back from Wes.

There wasn't.

Me: Oh, hey, by the way, you have to buy Lexi ice cream after her game.

Remy: I love how you use me to get yourself out of situations with my favorite niece.

Me: But isn't that what big brothers are for?

Remy: You're buying your own damn ice cream.

Me: Cheap bastard. Won't even buy his adorable baby sister an ice cream cone?

***Remy:** Nope. She might be cute, but she's a total pain in my ass.*

Me: :D

CHAPTER 25

Wes

My watch said 9:40, and I was seconds away from walking out of Starbucks on Seventeenth Street in Baltimore when the bell over the door chimed with Amelia's arrival. Granted, I'd only arrived twenty minutes ago, a good twenty minutes late myself, but I was antsy this morning. So much so, I was surprised I'd managed to wait it out as long as I had.

She was dressed in a long wool overcoat and dark brown leather gloves, and her makeup looked as if she'd never removed it the night before. Thick and meticulously applied, I knew that wasn't the case. She wasn't the type of woman to sleep in her makeup, and she wasn't the kind of woman to go without. She wanted to paint the illusion that she was born with this beauty just as competently as she worked the canvas of her face.

Winnie had this subtle glow about her—I wasn't sure if she even wore any makeup at all. But whatever she was doing worked in a big way.

God, I miss her. I hadn't texted her last night, too caught up in my own thoughts and fears and bullshit to man up and tell her how I felt.

I'd unsuccessfully tried to convince myself this morning that it was better talked about in person anyway.

"Wes!" Amelia called when she spotted me, a huge smile on her face as she tossed her auburn-red hair off of her shoulder and shrugged her way out of her coat.

A low-cut top nearly smacked me in the face immediately. I was human, male, and straight, and they were breasts, so I'd be lying if I didn't admit that it took some effort to look away.

But what struck me as different was the urge to do so—look away, that is.

Outside of biologically, I didn't have any desire to ogle anyone's breasts other than Winnie's. Imagine that.

I smiled at the thought, and unfortunately, the wattage of Amelia's grew brighter.

"I'm sorry I'm so late. Everyone is freaking out about the weather. Apparently, it's supposed to be a bad one."

Shit. "The weather?" I asked like an idiot, sitting up straighter.

"Yeah," she nodded. "Snow, I guess. It might sit here, right on top of us for a while."

Fucking fucking *shit.*

I needed to hurry this along. "So, did he change his mind after I left last night?" I asked.

She blushed slightly before shaking her head. "Unfortunately, no."

Okay...what the fuck were we doing here, then?

When I struggled to figure out how to ask that without cursing all over the goddamn place, she waded in. "But we're friends, right? I figured we could use the time to catch up."

Be polite, be polite, be polite.

I forced a smile, and it made me think of what Winnie would say I looked like. Probably something horrible like a doe in heat with six bucks chasing her little white tail intent on a gang bang. In other words, wild-eyed. Panicked. Intent on escape at all costs.

Ridiculous, I know. But these descriptions often got lengthy.

"That's nice."

It's so not fucking nice.

"But I've really got somewhere to be. I've got to go if we don't have any real business to discuss."

Well, that was blunt. But fuck, I was having a really hard time finding my finesse as I looked out the window to see fucking *flurries* falling.

Shit.

"I appreciate the effort," I added, trying to make one of my own. "Really. But I'm sorry you came all the way out here."

Disappointment suffused her features, but she managed to maintain her dignity. "I was actually hoping we could spend some time together—"

I stopped her before she went on with a raise of my hand and an apologetic smile. "Amelia."

"Yeah?"

"I'm sorry. I'm seeing someone."

She nodded and wrapped her hands around her gloves. "It had to happen eventually, right?"

I tilted my head in question.

"I always knew you'd settle down eventually." She shrugged. "You're a nice guy. And the nice guys almost always do."

I reached out and squeezed her shoulder awkwardly.

I meant to stand up immediately, but for some god-awful reason—I was blaming this on Thatch and Kline—I started to talk.

"She's amazing." Amelia smiled as much as she could manage on the very cusp of rejection, so I went on. Babbling like a buffoon.

"She's actually the new team physician for the Mavericks." I blushed. "I didn't think it was going to go anywhere—she fought me tooth and fucking nail, but yeah."

"Wes," Amelia said with a sweet smile. "It's okay. I'm happy for you."

"Thank you."

I wanted to stop, really, I knew I was just using her for her ear at this point, but it felt so good to talk about all the things I'd been keeping bottled up for months.

"Good luck in the Divisional on Saturday. You guys have looked so strong all year."

At the reminder of football, I finally stood up and threw on my own coat. "That's where I'm headed now…a football game."

Her eyebrows shot together, so I laughed and clarified. "Pop Warner. She, Winnie, my girlfriend," I stuttered, "has a six-year-old daughter. They made it all the way to the championship game. She's the kicker."

Her eyes widened. "Wow. A six-year-old."

I nodded and smiled just thinking about Lexi.

"How long have you guys been together?"

"Since October."

"Jesus."

I narrowed my eyes, and she covered her mouth before reaching toward me in apology. "No. God, I'm sorry. It's just fast. Good, I'm sure it's great, Wes. I…well, I was just thinking about myself. I don't think I could know that quickly. Not with the added responsibility of a kid."

My mind reeled. Sure, it'd been fast, but Lexi didn't feel even remotely like a responsibility. And Winnie sure as fuck didn't. "I really am sorry," I offered again, and she nodded.

"I am too," she murmured. "Especially if I held you up."

I nodded.

"I'm sure they're great, Wes," she semi-repeated, apology in her eyes.

"They are," I confirmed. *Too good for me*, that little voice of doubt whispered in my ear.

Goddamn, I hope she didn't hold me up.

Winnie: We can't wait to see you.

"I'm sorry, Mr. Lancaster," my pilot said as he walked down the aisle of my plane toward me. "We're going to be delayed. They've called a ground stop on all outgoing flights. Incoming planes are being diverted to Charlotte."

I looked first out the window to the ominous dark clouds and blanket-like snow and then to my watch as sleet started to pelt the frame of the plane.

"How long?"

I knew the answer before I even asked. When the pilot came out of the cockpit to talk to me, no urgency in his manner, it wasn't good news.

His face was apologetic. "At least a couple of hours." He paused before admitting, "Probably more."

I knew my face fell. I could feel it in every cell of my body.

Lex's championship football game was supposed to kick off in an hour and a half, and I'd *promised* her I'd be there.

Fuck. I knew I shouldn't have taken that extra meeting, not for the chance at the trade, not for Amelia, not for fucking anything—especially not without looking at the weather first.

"We can wait here, though. As soon as they lift the ground stop, we're ready to fly."

"Thanks, Josh."

I backed out of Winnie's message and pulled up the weather app on my phone, something she'd jokingly shown me how to do, and nearly wept when I saw the clear skies over New York and endless cover over Baltimore.

Lexi's game was going to happen.

And I was going to be here.

As I dialed Winnie's number and got no answer, a headache took root in the very base of my skull.

The two of them had never had a man to call their own that they could count on without question. We'd all foolishly trusted it to be me.

I hated myself—and they were going to hate me too.

It took twenty hours for the snow to clear enough that we could take off.

I'd considered renting a car, but with reports of dozens and dozens of wrecks and abandoned cars all along the interstate, Winnie had requested I not.

I'd finally gotten in touch with her—after the game—and the disappointment at my absence was stark in her voice. She'd tried to hide it, especially at the seemingly no-fault situation of a weather delay. But I'd yet to tell her all the details. That'd I'd put business before them, that I'd thought I could have everything, and that I was self-fucking-important enough to think the world would wait for me.

The whole situation literally felt toxic inside me, eating away at not only the organs, but all of the carefully cultivated happiness Winnie and Lex had planted there over the last several months.

I thought about the hours and hours they'd spent without me, waiting for my return, and the thought that I'd made a promise I hadn't tried my absolute hardest to keep to a little girl with too few normalcies in her life plagued me.

It chewed and gnawed, and by the time I knocked on the door to Winnie's house, I didn't think there was anything left behind.

No certainty. No contentment. And absolutely no worthiness when it came to the love of these two women.

I'd finally decided I wanted it all, and I'd still blown it.

And now…I felt numb.

Winnie opened the door with a small smile, and I couldn't match it.

I waited for her to usher me inside the door, then I pulled her into my arms and inhaled her smell one more time.

I had so many things I wanted to say, all of them coming together in my brain at once, but in the end, all I could say was one colossally stupid goddamn thing.

"I can't do this."

CHAPTER 26

Winnie

"I can't do this."

Those words hit me like a bullet to the heart, and thanks to our proximity on the porch and a day and a half of convincing myself all would be well, it was at point-blank range. The pain was damn near unbearable. My knees shook and knocked together, making it an impossibility to stand on my own, and I reached a shaky hand out and gripped the doorframe for support.

I blinked several times as I processed his words.

He can't do this?

Over seven long years ago, I'd heard those same words from a different man as a tiny combination of the two of us grew inside of me. I could still picture Nick's face, wide-eyed and apologetic—almost—as he told the woman to whom he'd pledged his eternal love, that a baby, a family, wasn't in his five-year plan to dominate neurosurgery. That if I wanted to keep the life I harbored a few inches under the warm flesh of my rounding abdomen, I'd be going it on my own.

The wound felt nearly as fresh as I looked into Wes's beautiful, wild, hazel eyes.

With a rough mental slap to bring myself back from the brink, I concentrated on the simple combination of words. So basic in their structure and vague in description, Wes could have been talking about anything. Overreaction and transference abounded in déjà vu scenarios like this.

Right?

Relax, Winnie, I told myself. *Don't dramatize his statement until you know the facts.*

What...*this*...could he not do?

"You can't do this?" I finally found the strength to repeat his words for confirmation, calming my voice and waiting for the relief to rush through my veins.

"I can't," he semi-repeated, nearly choking on the words as he pushed them out.

Programmed after months together, I reached forward and tried to pull him into my arms. Just for a minute. Just to make it stop hurting so much—for both of us.

But he stopped my progress with a tight grip on my upper arms, the prints of his fingers mottling the cold, flushed skin white.

"*Winnie.*"

"What *this*, Wes? What *exactly* can you not do?" I asked, the tether to my control fraying one tiny piece of rope at a time.

An unsinkable ship, they'd said about *Titanic*, and after the last couple of months, I would have thought the same for Wes and me. But just like on that cold night in April of 1912, the words stood out like stars in an unobstructed sky. *This ship* will *sink*.

And in the context of Wes's deceivingly simple phrasing, I was now a *this*. A sad, four-letter word backed by zero emotion or meaning.

Me *and Lex* were just a this. A small little blip in Wes's relationship history, and now, he had decided he was done with us. We were disposable. Sure, we'd lasted the longest of anyone he'd ever made a go of it with, but what the fuck good did that do us?

We were more attached, more hopeful, and in the end, still all alone.

All alone.

I wasn't sure which was harder, letting those words sink all the way in, or forcing my lungs to breathe air in and out.

He only gave the slightest of nods. He could tell by the look on my face, I already knew what this was about. "This. Me and you. I *can't* do it."

All of this time, I had been feeling so much guilt and shame over the little voice in my head warning me of Wes's past. I'd felt fucking awful, actually nauseated I was so disgusted with myself, that I was even contemplating thinking the worst of him, and now…he was proving all that goddamn ugliness inside me right.

I was very likely going to be cynical and alone for the rest of my life. Too jaded by the jilting of two goddamn men, and I fucking *hated* them for it.

Wes, as he stood staring holes into my head, most of all, because he'd shown me what it was like to have everything and had *then* taken it away. At least Nick had never bothered.

I couldn't find the strength to search his eyes. Honestly, I didn't want to see what was in them. I feared it would only cause me more pain, and maybe even worse, more hope for him to crush. Because he'd looked like he was hurting just as much as I was, not like a smug playboy who'd gotten his fill, and as he'd already taught me, kindness before torture was worse than torture all the way through.

I looked out toward the street and focused my gaze on the streetlight illuminating half the block as my mind spun in erratic circles.

This man, with whom I knew I was without a doubt in love, was telling me he couldn't do it. This man, whom I'd let fully into my life, into my world, into my daughter's heart, was turning his back on not only me, but her, too.

I clutched at my chest with both hands in a pathetic attempt to ease the discomfort. Or maybe I was just trying to prevent myself from bleeding out from the wounds his words had caused because any good doctor knew they needed pressure to stanch the flow.

Eventually, the effort to look away seemed to be greater than looking at him. I couldn't *not* look at him anymore. Because, as much as I theorized in my head, I didn't have any *real* answers. And that left me baffled and confused and so fucking hurt. *God, I hurt.*

I glanced down at my skin, my clothing, convinced the evidence of my agony was splattered across my hands, my shirt, in bright, red, dripping splotches.

But no, it would've been too easy to see exactly where Wes had cut me. Because then, I could've fixed it. Sewn myself back together.

This was internal. *My heart.*

Thoughts spiraling, I fell into a nose dive again, picturing the certain death of any chance of a romantic future.

How in the hell could I let any man into my life after this?

Not only was he hurting me, he was hurting that adorable little six-year-old inside my house. And two cycles of paternal pain for her made two times too many.

***Love** goes both ways, but in this moment, **Love** is a one-way street, headed in the opposite direction of me.*

Now, I had to try to find a way to live with the consequences. I had to try to find a way to pick up the pieces for both Lex and me and move the fuck on.

God, the urge to break down in sobbing, uncontrollable tears was so strong—I actually could feel the hiccupping breaths waiting to escape my lungs. But I refused to let him see me lose control like that. It wouldn't be easy to come by, but in the end, I'd still have a little dignity left.

Fuck Wes Lancaster. Fuck him for treating me like a piece of trash. Fuck him for worming his way into mine and my daughter's hearts and then changing his goddamn mind.

My pain mutated to anger as I stood there and watched Wes stare back at me, his eyes locked with mine and bloodshot.

I hope a goddamn vessel bursts and ruins all that interesting fucking color. I mentally spat on him. *Asshole.*

I felt like such a fucking fool.

"Well, I can't say that I'm all that surprised," I retorted. "I mean, this is what you're known for, right? Fucking and forgetting?" I fought the urge to cringe at my words.

They were awful, awful words, and I wasn't even sure why I'd said them, but they were out there, hovering between us, and I saw the exact moment those words, my horrible words, slipped into his ears. His eyes creased down at the corners, and the air pushed out of his lungs in a quick, shocked breath.

My heart interrupted my brain and forced it to order me to raise my arms and put them around him, but still in charge, my anger refused. This was *not* my fault.

He had chosen to call it quits. *He'd been the one* to back out of this relationship like a fucking coward.

Despite the pain pinching his eyes nearly closed, I shrugged, refusing to show any more weakness in front of him. When he was gone, I'd drown the fire of my pride in a sloppy, tear-filled mess. But *not* now.

"It's not a big deal, Wes. I mean, I should've expected it, you know? What real relationship starts with an angry fuck?"

"Win—"

I held my hand up and stopped him before he could continue. If he wanted to play games with my heart, then I sure as shit wasn't going to sit around and take it without putting up a fight.

"It doesn't. We were doomed from the start."

Sure, I would most likely regret these vile words later, but in that moment, all I saw was bright, flaming, motherfucking red. I felt the urge to scream at him, shove him off the porch, pound my fists into his chest. Anything to let this pulsating rage out of my body.

All the while, he just stood there. Not saying anything. Not defending himself or making his own accusations at me. Where passion should have lived, instead sat *nothing*.

Fuck this. I don't have to stand out here and look at him. I don't have to do anything, besides walk the fuck away.

"Well, have a good night, Wes. I'll see you at work Monday morning."

This fucking *prick*. He had the audacity to appear speechless.

"I'm going to go back inside now," I said, and I couldn't stop the resentment from leaking into my voice. I had the door halfway closed when he stuck his hand in the jamb to stop it. Two point five seconds of visualizing the carnage I could create by crushing them later, I opened the door wide again.

"What?"

"I just...I'm sorry—"

Never mind. "You know what? I don't want to hear it."

"Winnie, please."

I ignored the pleading, desperate timbre of his voice and took a stab at inflicting some wounds of my own. "They won, by the way."

His swallow was rough as he tilted his head to the side in confusion.

"Lexi's team," I explained. "They won. She even got to kick a field goal. She was really excited to tell you about it."

At the mention of Lexi, affection, love, pain, and regret warred for supremacy on his face more than even before, and the dam on his words finally broke. "Is she still awake?"

My jaw dropped to the cement. *Is she still awake?* What in the hell was he trying to do here? He just said he can't do this. Now, he wanted to see Lexi? Seriously, was I in the Twilight Zone?

"No," I lied. "She's already in bed."

He looked away for a brief moment and stared out toward the street. A shaking hand ran through his hair until his eyes eventually met mine again. "Will you tell her I stopped by and that I'm really proud of her?" he asked, voice quiet. He didn't need a decoder to crack the mystery of my face. Anything he wanted to say to my daughter could die a painful death in hell. "Please, Winnie."

Before I could muster the strength to form a response—even "fuck you" took energy—he turned on his heel, jogged down the stairs, and away from my life. He didn't go to the car and driver that he always kept on staff to get him around the city, and he didn't look back. I was powerless, standing there in the bitter wind and watching until he reached the end of the block and turned the corner—for good.

I had no idea how long I stood out there on my porch, staring in the direction that Wes had gone. I knew his driver had long since vanished, and I knew the cold burned all the way into my bones. But I honestly couldn't find the brainpower to get myself to move.

As the icy air numbed my anger, inquisitiveness tingled along my skin.

What in the hell just happened?

It was like Wes Lancaster had just broken up with me even though he didn't want to break up with me.

If that wasn't the biggest mindfuck I'd ever been dealt, I didn't know what was.

CHAPTER 27

Wes

Five...Four...Three...

The last seconds on the clock ran down as New England's quarterback took a knee on the forty-yard line. I stared at the scoreboard and watched with a heavy heart and regret gnawing at my chest. It felt like so much more than a shitty end to an otherwise spectacular season as I watched Winnie on the sideline from above. She was still beautiful, but all the light was gone from her eyes. Instead, anger lived there, laced toxically with the memories of us in every inch of stadiums across the country.

Two...One...

I watched from the Owner's Box as our opponent ran out onto the field in celebration, rowdy and taunting, their chants nearly audible despite the distance and thick glass, and the Jumbotron blinded my eyes with confetti and congrats to New England.

Our season had officially come to a close, the evidence of a seventeen to thirteen loss in the divisional round play-offs stamped out on the scoreboard. Our guys had played good for the first two quarters, great even, but shit had sprayed violently from the churning fan after halftime. Three minutes into the third quarter, we'd been up by thirteen when Bailey had thrown an interception that led to a defensive touchdown for the opposition.

And unfortunately for us, that set the pace for the rest of the game.

One mistake trickled into another, penalties and turnovers and too many goddamn third and outs to count. We'd become our own worst enemy, playing head games with ourselves, and eventually, loss by self-detonation occurred.

Our guys walked slowly off the field with their heads down and their helmets hanging limply from their hands, disappointment visible in every step they took toward the tunnel, but my focus wasn't on them.

I only had eyes for the victim of my own self-destruction, her blond hair and white shirt shining startlingly bright through the crowd of blue.

I had let my own demons fuck with my head. I'd been scared of the commitment and the speed with which I'd decided on it, Amelia's words ringing soundly in my ears.

For the first few days this week, I'd done my best to blame it on Amelia, like she held responsibility for my downward spiral by simply voicing her own fears.

It was cowardly and petty and nothing more than an attempt to avoid the facts: the tragic end to my relationship with Winnie Winslow rested solely on my shoulders.

When she disappeared into the shadowy recesses of the tunnel, my mind and focus finally came back to the room around me.

The chatter was dismal, as expected, but I just didn't have it in me to make small talk or to relive the mistakes of this horrible game. I needed to get the fuck out of there. I picked my jacket up from one of the black leather sofas resting against the wall of the suite and put it on, zipping it up to my chin. Halfway into January, the frigid temperatures had set in. A true fair-weather dweller, I always hated this time of year, but now, after everything I'd done to destroy my own life, the real cold lived inside of me. Deep in the depths of my empty soul, and I didn't know how to vent it out.

I missed both of my girls more than I had ever missed anything in my life.

I missed Winnie's texts. I missed her smile, her laugh, our inside jokes. I missed having her in my arms, both platonically and laid out beneath me as I made love to her. I missed everything about her—everything about *us*.

And I missed Lexi. Her football season was over just like this one, and after all the work we'd put in together, I had nothing to show for it. I didn't get to see her smile at me at first sight, and I'd never hear her sweet voice as she scoured the world and people around her for knowledge.

And now, with the Mavericks' season officially over, my opportunities to see Winnie at work would be few and far between until the summer months.

I had absolutely nothing tying me to them anymore.

I can't do this.

Four bullshit words had ruined everything.

My office was drab and dreary for a Friday morning and smelled nothing like peaches and goddamn sunshine.

In fact, it smelled so bad in comparison, I'd almost gone out to get an air freshener. But I didn't want to go out into the bustling crowd of Manhattan. There were too many people in a really small proximity to hate. I'd have wound up getting arrested or stabbed or worse.

I wasn't really sure what was worse than a stabbing, but I was pretty sure it lived in Manhattan and it definitely resided post Winnie-breakup.

My office was eerily quiet, none of the hustle and bustle of the stadium, and notably less to look forward to. But as much as this place blew, the stadium wouldn't have been any better.

After last week's upset in the divisional game, most of the employees had crawled away to get in vacations and family time before serious preparation for next year began.

I had no family to have time with. I'd considered going to see my dad, but January in Wisconsin seemed even worse than heartbreak in New York.

So I was here. In my office. Doing a whole lot of nothing disguised as something.

I'd just finished reading an article in the *New York Post* about a blind hoarder in Brooklyn who'd been unknowingly living with the skeletal remains of her daughter for nearly *thirty years*. Apparently, she'd thought her daughter had simply moved out.

And still, when I thought of all the people who were the most unbelievably fucking ridiculously dumb in the world, my name came up number one on the list. Losing Winnie and Lexi was proof of that.

A knock on the door barely preceded its opening, and Kline and Thatch stepped in without invitation.

"Ah, see," Thatch told Kline after nothing more than a quick glance in my direction. "The little bird's nest has come back to Manhattan."

"Shh," Kline shushed him before stepping forward into the office and taking a seat in front of my desk. He rubbed at the leather of the armrests as he made himself disgustingly comfortable.

His hair was messy as though he'd visited his wife first.

I hated him for it.

"She's busy working, you know," I said in an effort to lash out, picking up a random stack of papers on my desk and slamming the stapler down on them.

"She wasn't five minutes ago," he countered without shame and no more than a glance in the direction of the angry stapler.

"Fucker," I insulted.

"Nah," Thatch said with a laugh. "Just a little foreplay."

Kline laughed at that, but all I could do was glare.

We stared at each other, letting the testosterone fill the space until any movement from the outside world would make it explode.

"So?" Thatch questioned like an impatient bastard.

"So…what?" I asked, snatching the football-shaped stress ball off my desk and squeezing it to the point that the fake laces threatened to pop.

"How are you going to win Winnie back?" Kline asked, cutting right to the chase. I both loved and hated that he was so straightforward. Hated it because it was annoying, but faced with it or Thatch, I unabashedly loved Kline's ability to cut to the chase.

"Win Winnie," Thatch murmured. "I like that."

I shook my head before I even started to speak. My mind was made up. "I'm not."

Kline blinked and turned to Thatch, who reacted altogether less calmly.

"What the fuck does that mean?" he asked with both freakishly long arms held out in exasperation.

"They're better off without me," I told them, and they were. I was completely messed up and mixed up and just…fucked up. I was a fuck-up, that was for sure.

I'd gone over everything again and again in my mind, from the meeting to the way I'd handled everything afterward, and it all reeked of immaturity. Thirty-five goddamn years old and immature. But, out of everything, I hadn't been able to forgive myself for not being man enough to ever tell her how I really felt. She deserved that—someone who not only loved her but told her he did. Repeatedly. They both fucking did.

"How the fucking fuck do you figure that?" Thatch yelled. Kline put a hand to his elbow and subtly shook his head.

All of Thatch's anger had already snapped something inside of me, though, and I started to talk.

"I'm fucking unreliable, busy, always goddamn late. I'm not any of the things Win and Lex need."

Thatch opened his mouth, but Kline again stopped him from speaking, and I gladly filled the silence.

"Lex is so fucking special. Smart and unique and goddamn perfect. Society doesn't think so, but they're wrong. But she doesn't need me out there getting into fistfights with every fucking person who looks at her wrong, and Win doesn't need that either. She works so hard and, God, she's brilliant too, so it's no wonder Lex is as smart as she is. Win needs to be able to come to work without dealing with some Neanderthal asshole. She needs to be able to relax for once in her goddamn life and know everything is taken care of."

By the time I was done, I was breathing heavily, and Thing 1 and Thing 2 had smiles on their faces that would rival a lottery winner.

"What?" I asked with irritation highlighting my voice.

"Okay," Kline said simply, and I blinked.

"No argument?"

He shook his head and shrugged. "You're right."

"I'm *right*?"

"Yep."

What the fuck did he mean I was right? They weren't going to try to convince me otherwise? I was *that* wrong for Winnie and Lex? So much so that my own friends weren't even going to try to tell me I wasn't.

Jesus. I wasn't Satan, for fuck's sake.

And I loved them. Both of them. They could do worse than me.

Angry, I told Kline and Thatch that. "I'm not that bad, you know. I love them. Christ, I could be fucking no-good-Nick, having it all, and throwing it all away, even though they constantly gave me chances."

Kline bit his lip and then shook his head. "No, you're right. You're too busy for them. You can't be there the way they need you to be."

"I can be there," I protested.

"You missed that game," Thatch pointed out, and I faltered. I had. I'd missed it, and goddamn, the disappointment in their voices and in

Winnie's disgusted eyes still made me feel sick when I thought about it.

But I could do better. I had the money to slow down. I didn't have to be here every second of every day.

"I could take a step back from stuff."

Kline looked skeptical.

"I could," I affirmed.

"Well, I mean, if you think you could," he said in half-assed agreement.

"I could. And anytime I couldn't be there, I could send one of you guys. I could make sure they always had someone."

"You're right," Kline agreed, and I paused.

Jesus. Reverse-psychology-wielding motherfucker.

"Stop being so goddamn clever," I demanded.

"He's good, huh?" Thatch said with a chuckle.

Fuck. Two minutes with this guy and he'd managed to rework my entire line of thinking. But he was *so* good, he didn't tell me the way it was; he made me figure it out all on my goddamn own.

"You know, I'm pretty sure I actually helped you fuckers when you needed it instead of putting you through this fucking bullshit."

"But I thought you didn't want a relationship like we have?" Thatch teased.

"Fuck you guys."

"We love you too," Thatch said mock-sweetly.

Even though Kline had helped guide me to realization, I still wasn't sure how I could right the awful wrong. How could I get Winnie to forgive after I had done what every other man had done in her and Lex's life?

It truly was the fuck-up of all fuck-ups in the history of fuck-ups.

I'd hurt her—them—in the absolute worst way.

And honestly, I wasn't sure how in the hell I could fix that…

CHAPTER 28

Winnie

January had bled into February, and now March was in full swing. Remnants of dirt-covered snow—*probably piss-covered, too*—rested against the edges of the streets, and it took a whole lot of effort to get my favorite black suede pumps into the building without a tragedy of epic stiletto proportions.

Tonight, I was attending a Children's Hospital charity function at Apella. The sleek and modern reception venue was decked out in a kids'-style circus theme. Tables were covered in bright cloths, mimicking the appearance of a clown's costume, and the spacious room was encased in a gorgeous red tent that hung from the ceiling. The ambiance all but screamed, *I'm whimsical and entertaining.*

If only I felt as upbeat. For two straight months, my insides had been feeling like perpetual night. I waited and waited for time to heal my Wes-inflicted wounds, but the goddamn sun never rose.

Attendees littered the room, chatting animatedly with one another as I headed in the direction of our assigned table with Scott Shepard, my date for the evening. I'd known Scott for years, having attended med school together at Yale, done the same surgical rotation at Mount Sinai, and even worked together at St. Luke's for about three years before I had left to work for the Mavericks.

He was an all-around good guy. Super sweet, charming, and handsome in a slightly rugged way, and his dark hair, even darker eyes, and jawline covered in five days' worth of scruff had a lot of female staff members at St. Luke's begging for his attention.

But I'd never really seen him that way. We had more of a brother-sister kind of relationship, which probably had a lot to do with the fact that he reminded me of my brother Jude.

But Scott was a good friend. He had always been a good friend. And even though we didn't speak often, I knew he was someone I could always count on. Which was why he was doing me a huge favor by being my date for the evening.

Although I'd never specialized in pediatrics, I still donated my time and money to help the Children's Hospital raise funds and awareness for various causes, and tonight's focus was on autism research. Obviously, it hit very close to home. I knew firsthand what it was like to have an autistic child, and I knew how much specialized programs and therapies could help families raising children on the spectrum.

"You look gorgeous tonight, Win," Scott complimented as he pulled out my chair and helped me into my seat.

Gorgeous? I hadn't felt gorgeous in what felt like forever.

Broken? Yes.

Sad? Of course.

But gorgeous? Maybe I was in a tragic way, I guess. But it was safe to say, ever since Wes had broken my heart, it took a lot of effort to have an outward appearance of put together and okay. I was still so far from okay that no high-tech navigation system or Siri herself could help guide me back at this stage in the heartbreak game.

I smoothed my hands down my simple yet classic black silk gown and forced a grin in his direction as he sat beside me. "You're not looking so bad yourself, Dr. Shepard," I said with a wink.

"Oh, c'mon, Winnie. We know I *always* look good."

I laughed. "Are you trying to tell me I don't always look good?"

"Well...I've seen you at three a.m., half asleep and busting ass out of the call room..."

"Whatever," I scoffed. "Just so you know, your three a.m. bedhead look isn't exactly cover-worthy either."

"That's not what the nurses say," he teased, and I rolled my eyes.

"Tell me, Scott, how do you find the time to brainwash all those girls?"

A server stopped by our table and took our drink order—wine for me and a beer for Scott—and made quick work of getting our drinks while we chatted politely with the other guests at our table. A few were also physicians we had met through various hospital and charity functions, like nearly every gathering of certified med-heads, the conversation pretty quickly dissolved into a gore-fest recounting of our most cringeworthy cases. An orthopedic attending surgeon at Mt. Sinai had just finished regaling us with tales of amputation when the waiter brought us our second round of drinks.

"I thought Lexi was coming with us?" Scott asked after taking a drink of his beer.

"I figured it'd be best if Melinda didn't bring her by until after dinner. That way, she can enjoy the kids' fair without having to sit through boring adult conversation."

Scott grinned. "You calling me boring, Win?"

I laughed and shrugged. "Maybe."

"I've been told I'm quite the conversationalist."

I nudged his shoulder playfully. "Yeah. I'm sure Tammy, Sandie, Fiona and... Which charge nurse always works the night shift?"

"Samantha," he responded immediately.

I grinned. "Oh, how could I forget Samantha? You two used to date, didn't you?"

"If by date, you mean sneaking quickies in the call room, then sure, we used to date," he clarified with a sly smile. If it wasn't already apparent, Scott was a great guy but also a huge flirt. He pretty much made a show of "dating" anything with big boobs and long legs. He wasn't the type of guy who settled down. He was still enjoying being single and having zero responsibilities related to relationships.

"Do you guys still *date*?"

"Occasionally." He winked.

"Who else are you *dating* at St. Luke's now?" I probed further with a teasing smile.

He waggled his brows. "Mandy."

"I don't remember a Mandy…"

"She's a new physician they just hired. She's a lot like you, actually. Mean. Demanding. A total ballbuster."

"I'm not mean," I said in feigned irritation, and he just chuckled softly in response.

"When shit isn't going smoothly, you can get a little mean, Win. Especially if you haven't had a chance to caffeinate."

"Well, someone had to take charge. St Luke's gets too many traumas to let chaos rule the flow."

"That's why I miss having you there." He tapped my hand that rested on the table with his fingers. "You ran a tight ship without pissing everyone off. A lot of people miss you, by the way. You sure you like this whole football gig?"

"I'm sure." I grinned and then thought more into his question. "Wait…is that why you agreed to come with me tonight? To try and lure me back to the ED."

He shrugged. "It was part of it."

I tilted my head to the side in curiosity. "What was the other part?"

"I was hoping you'd reward me with some Mavericks tickets."

I laughed. "You're a dick."

"Hey, stop thinking about my dick, Win," he joked playfully. "You're like a little sister to me."

"Gross." I scrunched my nose up in disgust. "Don't make me lose my appetite before they serve dinner."

He just laughed it off and wrapped his arm around my shoulder, pulling me close and kissing my temple chastely. "I've missed you, Win. Even though you're kind of annoying, I've still missed you."

I patted his chest. "I've missed you, too. Even though you're a total pain in my ass most of the time."

He chuckled. "Let's keep in touch more. Okay? We can't go months again without talking or hanging out."

"You're ridiculous. I just talked to you last week when you called me about that aortic aneurysm." I shrugged him off and took another sip of my wine.

"Medical shit doesn't count."

"What happened with that anyway?"

"I was able to repair it, but Cummings had to do an emergency C-section before I could get her off my OR table. It was touch and go for a little bit, but mom and baby are doing well. Still admitted, but they're recovering without any major complications."

"Nice work, Shepard," I said and truly meant it. I knew when he had called me about that case, the odds of both mom and baby surviving a surgery like that weren't good. It had to take some serious surgical skills and practically a miracle to get that mother off the OR table without something tragic happening. "Wait…So Will finally decided to commit to obstetrics?" I asked, curious to know how my buddy, and Georgia's brother, Will Cummings was doing.

He nodded and then shot me a quick wink. "Yep. Cummings found his calling being elbow-deep in vagina."

I laughed. "Good for him. I think he'll make a fantastic high-risk OB."

"Meh. He'll be all right," he responded with an amused smirk.

"You're such an ass." I laughed again and took a sip of wine.

Scott's phone vibrated along the table, and he sighed, long and deep. "I better get this. Give me a minute?"

"Of course," I said with a wave, and he got up from his seat and headed toward the terrace doors of the venue.

"Can I get you another glass, miss?" the waiter asked, gesturing toward the bottle of wine in the ice bucket.

I shook my head, and as he headed toward another table, my gaze followed his movement across the room, until it locked with someone else's. I stilled in my seat when I realized the hazel eyes staring back at me were familiar. Very, very familiar.

Wes sat at a different table across the room with an attractive blond woman mooning over his every word. I couldn't stop myself from sizing her up, my eyes taking in her pretty face, her attractive figure. She ran her fingers across the top of her wineglass and smiled up at him.

But his eyes weren't on her; they were locked on me. His fucking eyes were trained on me while he was on a date with another woman.

Why couldn't he just leave me be?

He haunted my thoughts every goddamn day, and now I had to see him here? With her? I felt overcome with the urge to burst into tears or scream or storm out of the restaurant. But none of those reactions would have been appropriate. Wes wasn't mine. We weren't together. And we never would be.

But God, it hurt. It hurt to see him with someone else. Someone I didn't know, but I could tell she wasn't a mere acquaintance or long-lost cousin. The flutter of her eyelashes, the flirtatious smiles, the perfectly revealed cleavage—those were the trademarks of a woman on a date. A woman whose intentions didn't end at friendly.

U2's "With or Without You" started to play softly in the background, and it couldn't have been a more apt song choice for this moment. I felt every single lyric pass through the speakers of the venue and into my soul.

Those lyrics, that song, it hit home. It caressed my battered heart.

I couldn't live without playful, loving, and caring Wes.

But I couldn't live with the man who'd let the words *I can't do this* leave his lips when I was so close to letting go of all the things that worried and imprisoned me.

Wes's gaze searched mine, and somehow, I found the strength to avert my eyes before I showed him just how painful this situation was for me. I took another sip of wine and swallowed the much-needed alcohol down along with the irrational tears clogging my throat.

I was determined to end this evening with my pride still intact. I would not be anything less than strong and composed. I could let my guard down and freak the fuck out when I was home, alone in my bedroom with another bottle of wine to keep me company.

I needed to get myself together. I refused to let Wes witness that seeing him with someone else was hurting me. I had been through too much with him, and I could not stomach the idea that he had as much power over me as he did.

You can lick your wounds at home, I told myself again.

I'd be damned if I showed any signs of weakness in front of Wes Lancaster.

CHAPTER 29

Wes

She smiled and laughed, and my lungs felt like I had dunked them in ice. It was the burning, barely-holding-on-to-life kind of cold that you'd get from falling in a frozen lake or taking a Titanic-like dip in the North Atlantic. In other words, it was agony.

Winnie Winslow was on a date.

With a man who was distinctly, noticeably, heartbreakingly…*not* me.

He was good looking and genuinely pleased to be in her company and so wrong for her I could barely stomach it. He laughed at the wrong time and talked over her when she was speaking, and to make matters worse, Winnie looked like she didn't motherfucking loathe the space he took up.

She looked like he was interesting and charming and way better than I ever was. And, goddamn, I wanted to clasp my hands around his neck and squeeze.

"Wes?" an annoying voice called from across the table.

With work, I pulled my eyes from Win and her smarmy date and looked into the brown eyes of my own—date, that is.

I know. I hate me too. But I just wanted something to make the pain go away.

It should be noted that I'd previously had my assistant RSVP for me plus one for this charity function several months back with the mind-set that I'd get Win to go with me, as *my* date. Obviously, thanks to me, things had changed, and now, because I was an idiot and didn't realize Winnie would obviously be here too, I got the excruciating opportunity to witness what my Winnie looked like in the company of another man.

I guess she could probably say the same for me, though.

I wasn't here alone. That's not to say I was actually enjoying my company like she seemed to be enjoying hers.

There wasn't anything wrong with my date. Felicity was good-looking, nice, and on any other night, I'm sure she would have been interesting. Tonight, I wasn't sure anything could help me stop wanting to stab *everyone*.

And no, she doesn't look anything like Keri Russell.

But who was I kidding? This wasn't just about tonight. This had been every night since I fucked everything up and would continue on for what felt like eternity.

In my eyes, no woman could or would ever match up to Winnie Winslow.

And, as a kicker, a little bonus to my already fucking awful mood, I actually felt bad that I was doing this to Felicity because I was doing exactly what I hated—promising attention and not following through.

Women deserved honesty always.

And I wasn't giving that to this most-likely-perfectly-fine woman because all my honesty, all my energy, all of me, was focused across the room—on the woman, I realized, I *needed* to be mine.

My family, my honesty, my energy. Her and Lex.

My effort and affection and anything else they could ever want from me.

And I wanted everything with them.

I'd known it when I had talked to Kline and Thatch, but I still didn't know how to put it into practice. I'd been scared to make the changes, scared to take the leap and not have Win want me back.

But that was stupid, and tonight proved it. You can't choose what you're destined for. That's the whole fucking point. But you can choose how you handle it, how you live it, and up until now, I'd been doing a really shitty job of understanding that.

Finally, I looked my date in the eye and smiled—and then internally cringed as she smiled back.

"I'm really sorry, Felicity. This is probably the very worst thing a guy could do to you on a date, but…" I shrugged. "I'm in love with another woman. Two, actually."

Her eyes got round as I muttered on to myself.

"One of them is six, so there's that."

"Oh, my God," she gasped, and I realized what it sounded like.

Oh, holy fuck, I'm an idiot.

"Oh, God. *Jesus.* No, no. It's her daughter. She has a six-year-old daughter who I love like a daughter. No sicko, pedophilia stuff here. I swear."

I could hear the dirt hitting the ground as I kept on scooping it out with my shovel. Felicity covered her mouth with her napkin, and if my current luck was any indication, she was probably going to hurl.

"I just wasn't sure I was ready to be a dad," I hurried on to explain.

Some of the crazy finally left her eyes, and I took a deep gulp of vomit-scent-less air. Gauging the current status of a date on lack of puke wasn't perfect, but fuck, breaking it off by telling her I loved someone else wasn't going to be.

Now I needed an opening.

When I looked up, Winnie was alone.

I stood to move, only to have Mr. Fuckface slide back into his seat right at that moment.

Goddammit.

Note to self: next time, be faster at explaining opposition to pedophilia.

CHAPTER 30

Winnie

"Sorry about that," Scott apologized as he slid back into his seat beside me.

I waved him off with a nonchalant hand. "No worries. It's not like I haven't been there before."

He grinned. "Mind talking over a case with me?"

"Dr. Scott Shepard wants my medical opinion on something?" I teased.

"Hey, I might be a prideful son of a bitch, but I'm smart enough to know when I could use a little guidance."

I laughed. "Let me step outside and call Melinda to find out what time she's dropping Lexi off, and then I'm all ears."

"You're the best, Winnie Winslow."

"Geez, I already said I would. No additional buttering up is necessary." I nudged his shoulder with my hand as I stood up, and he responded with a chuckle.

"I'll be right back." I grabbed my purse and strode toward the lobby, using all of my strength to not glance in Wes *and his date's* direction. Once I cleared the entrance, I walked toward the side of the modern building and leaned my body against the brick wall.

My phone pinged with a notification, and it startled me out of my racing thoughts.

Melinda: I think Lexi might be too tired to come tonight. She nearly fell asleep in her macaroni and cheese during dinner.

Me: LOL. No worries. Just keep her at home, then.

Melinda: Okay, good. She's actually already in bed. :)

Me: I should've figured. Once she hits the wall, she's done for. Can you stay for a few more hours, or should I call Remy and see if he can hang out at the house for a little while?

Melinda: Oh, no. I'm good. Stay out as late as you want. I'm hijacking your Netflix and watching that new show, **Stranger Things.** *I'd like to get through the whole first season.*

Me: Perfect. You're the best.

Melinda: I know... :)

I slid my phone back into my clutch and sighed a breath of relief. It was for the best that Lexi didn't come out tonight, especially with Wes being here.

In the past week, she'd just finally stopped asking about him.

I had a feeling, if she would've come tonight, it would have opened a fresh can of worms that I honestly didn't know if I could face. I mean, it's not like my track record with insects in general was all that great.

I rubbed at the spot on my chest that seemed relentless with its need to ache. I couldn't deny that seeing Wes with someone who wasn't me was pretty fucking terrible.

God, I had to get it together. I just needed a few minutes to get some fresh air before I could face the very last fucking thing I wanted to see...*again*.

I knew Wes was already dating, already moving on, already finding the next woman. I knew that, and yet I'd never expected it to hurt this bad. I didn't think seeing him with someone else would've had me considering contacting Lexi's father to schedule a lobotomy.

"Win?" an all-too-familiar voice called toward me.

For the love of God, why couldn't he just leave me alone?

Sure, we worked together, but he'd been pretty much scarce from the stadium lately, and I'd gone back to taking the train. God, those train rides now were even *more* awful.

I shut my eyes, rested my head against the wall, and inhaled a deep breath.

"Win, are you okay?" Wes asked, his voice closer now. He placed his hand gently on my bare shoulder and every cell in my body lit up with the urge to react. I wanted to scream at him. I wanted to sob. I wanted to curl into the fetal position and lose myself to the pain that had slowly seeped out of my heart and consumed every nerve.

"I'm fine," I whispered and somehow found the strength to open my eyes.

His perfectly clear hazel eyes searching mine only made me feel worse.

"You can go back inside, Wes," I said. "I just came out here to make a quick phone call to Melinda." Okay, so maybe that was a teensy tiny white lie, but seriously, he just needed to leave me alone.

"Is Lexi okay?"

God, why wouldn't he just leave? Why couldn't he realize his concern was misplaced? Why couldn't he understand that he was hurting me more by never really letting me go? He wanted to keep me at arm's length, not too close, but not too far. He still wanted to be involved in Lexi's life, yet he didn't really want to be a part of our lives.

I was tired of it. So fucking exhausted.

I shrugged his arm off my shoulder and pushed off the wall. In that moment, I couldn't bear to feel the warmth of his skin on my skin. "Enough," I spat in his direction before I could stop myself. "You have to stop this."

"Stop what?" he asked and had the nerve to look baffled.

"This," I answered harshly, gesturing between us with an erratic hand. "Stop being the guy who asks me how my daughter is. Stop being the guy who acts like he cares, but in reality, he doesn't care. Stop. Being. That. Guy."

He faltered back a step like my words had been a knife to the chest. "I do fucking care. I care about you *and* Lexi."

I shut my eyes and shook my head. "You're so wrong. Because if that was the truth, you wouldn't be on a date with another woman right now." The words were out of my mouth before I could take them back.

So much for acting like you're unaffected…

His face morphed into surprise, and I watched his mouth open and close a few times before he gritted his teeth. "I'm not the only one on a date."

Yeah, big date. I might as well have brought Remy.

He stepped closer, and I moved back until the wall stopped my momentum, and that only allowed him to move in closer. "Who is he, Winnie? Is he your boyfriend?" he questioned in a harsh whisper, his mouth so close to my face that I felt the warmth of his breath brush across my nose.

"He is none of your fucking business," I retorted.

"He *is* my business."

I shoved him away with both hands. "He's not, Wes. Don't you get it? It's over between us, and that decision wasn't mine. It was yours. You *wanted* things this way."

"That's fresh, considering you were all too quick to write us off as some meaningless fuck."

"If you only knew," I muttered.

"What? If I only knew what?"

I stared at him for a long moment, taking in his clenched jaw and narrowed eyes and the way his chest moved when he inhaled a harsh breath.

There were so many things I wanted to say to him in that moment, but I knew the conversation was pointless. He had made his choice. He didn't want anything serious. I had merely given him the out he needed. I let him walk away without shouldering the guilt of the reality of our situation. He had strung me along just the right amount of time for me to fall, and then he pulled the rug out from under me without warning and walked away like it was the easiest thing he had ever done.

I had loved him.

Still love him.

But love had no point when it wasn't returned.

"I gave you the out you needed, so why can't you give me the space I need?"

He furrowed his brow in incredulity. "The out I needed?"

"Yes. The out you needed to walk away unscathed."

"*Unscathed?* You think this is easy for me?"

A humorless laugh escaped my throat. "You're here, *on a date*, Wes."

"So are you!" he shouted, and the emotion in his eyes had me so very close to telling him the truth. That I wasn't here on a date. That Scott was my friend.

But I didn't want to give him that satisfaction.

I wanted him to feel like I felt. *Gutted.*

"God!" he exclaimed, roughly dragging both hands through his hair. "I didn't want it to be like this. Can't you see? I know I set it in motion, but I *hate* it, Win," he admitted, and the pain in his voice had tears clogging my throat again.

I will not cry. I will not let him see how much this hurts.

I looked away from him until I could blink the tears away, and when my eyes met his again, I ignored the pain in his gaze. I ignored the fact that he didn't look okay. I ignored it because I *had* to ignore it. Deep down, I knew I wasn't alone in the way I felt about him. But I also knew I couldn't go down that road again.

I wouldn't survive it.

"I need to get back inside," I said, and then, knowing what my daughter's safety meant to me, took the slightest amount of pity on him. "Lexi is okay. I was just calling Melinda to see what time she was dropping her off tonight—which she isn't. Lex fell asleep. So stop worrying. Everything is okay. You can go back inside. Go enjoy the rest of the evening with your date."

"But what about you? Are *you* okay?"

Not even close.

"No, but I'm getting there." I gave him the partial truth. "Every day, it gets easier. Every day, I'm one more day closer to being okay."

"Winnie," he said and reached his arm out to stop me. "Wait."

I shook my head and stepped away from him. "Have a good night, Wes."

I kept walking forward, and I didn't look back.

That was good-bye, I told myself.

Like a bell of dismissal, my phone started to ring inside of my clutch. I dug it out as I walked, wiping away one stubborn tear as it trailed down my cheek before swiping the screen.

"Winnie!" Georgia shouted into my ear the second my finger tapped the accept button.

"Georgia?"

"Winnie! Where are you? Seriously! Where are you?" she shrieked, and I cringed at the resulting ringing in my ear.

"Why are you shouting?"

"Because Cassie is in labor! She's going to have the baby! Can you believe it?"

I stopped dead in my tracks. "Oh, shit…really?"

"REALLY!"

I yanked the phone away from my ear, but it was too late. My eardrum felt like someone had used it as a kick-drum.

"Meet us at the hospital!"

"Seriously, stop shouting," I called toward the receiver, still keeping the phone a safe distance away from my ear.

"I can't help it! I'm too excited!"

I laughed at that. "Okay. Okay. I'll be there." I looked at the time on the screen and put it back within hearing distance of my ear. "Give me thirty minutes, and I'll be there."

"Get here sooner!" she protested. "Cassie is having a baby!"

"It's her first baby, Georgia. Trust me, it's not just going to fall out."

No matter how much Cassie might want it to.

"HOLY MOTHERFUCKER FUCKING FUCK, YOU GUYS! FUCK THIS SHIT! I HATE EVERYTHING!" Cassie shouted through her last contraction.

"Honey," Thatch said with a grin. He stood right at her bedside, holding her hand and occasionally putting cool washcloths on her forehead and neck. "I thought we were trying not to cuss around the baby."

Cassie's face morphed into something I had only witnessed in horror movies. Any second, I thought her head would probably do a complete three-sixty and return with a mouthful of green vomit in her husband's face.

She gripped his hand with all of her might, and it was obvious by the grimace on Thatch's face that this pregnant chick had some serious strength with her hands. It was like she had been using Shake Weights religiously or something… Yeah, let's not go any further with that thought process.

Shake Weights and Thatch and Cassie? Yeah, definitely do not go there…

The redness in Cassie's face went down, and she took a few deep breaths as the contraction slowly disappeared. "I don't give a fucking fucking fuck fuck about cussing right now, Thatcher. Our baby should understand that he is literally crawling out of my body. A human being is going to come out of my body. So fuck anyone in this room who gets offended by the words that will be accompanying our baby's big debut and, sadly, destruction of my pussy."

"Jesus, Cass," Georgia chimed in. She stood off to the side near the big window overlooking the city with a stopwatch in hand and her pencil and paper resting on the windowsill.

She looked ready for the big game, but the game had been rained out.

Georgia was secretly trying to take on the role of doula, but Thatch was kind of doula-blocking her at the moment.

"What?" Cassie snapped, and her face turned to a grimace, indicating that another contraction was about to briefly ruin her life.

"Could you not say p-u-s-s-y? I mean, you're getting ready to deliver our beautiful baby boy into the world. Don't you think maybe you should avoid the use of foul language, especially of the p-u-s-s-y variety?"

"Do you think I care? Do you think I fucking care?" Cassie shouted through a contraction. "IF I WANT TO SCREAM THE WORD PUSSY WHILE I BRING THIS BABY INTO THE WORLD, I WILL!"

Thatch glanced at me, and we both held back the urge to laugh.

All the while, Cassie and Georgia were having a complete standoff, eye to eye, stubbornness fueling the whole thing.

"Knock knock," the nurse said as she walked into the room. "How are you feeling, sweetheart?" she asked as she moved toward Cassie and applied a blood pressure cuff to her arm.

"Like a baby is trying to crawl out of my *pussy*."

Georgia scoffed, and Thatch nearly fell over he guffawed so hard.

Cassie in labor was about the funniest thing I had seen in ages. And tonight of all nights, I desperately needed the pick-me-up.

Thatch and I grinned at one another, while Georgia and Cassie continued to flip each other the bird and toss nasty glares in each other's direction.

"Well, I'm Misty, and I'll be your nurse today," the pretty young nurse introduced herself as she proceeded to get Cassie's vitals. "Has anyone checked you yet?"

"Checked me?"

"To see how far dilated you are?"

Cassie gripped the side rails of the bed as another contraction started to peak.

"How long has she been having contractions this intense?"

Thatch's brow furrowed. "I'd say for about the past few hours."

The nurse checked the strip of paper printing from the monitor that tracked the baby's heart rhythm and uterine contractions. "Hmm," she muttered to herself.

"What was she dilated at her last doctor's appointment?"

"Not quite two centimeters," Georgia answered before anyone else could.

See what I mean? Self-appointed doula.

"And when was that?" Misty asked with a tilt of her head.

"Wednesday," Thatch answered. "So, a few days ago."

Cassie continued to keep her eyes closed as she breathed through another contraction. Once it had released its hold on her, she set her focus on the nurse. "I need all of the fucking pain medicine you can give me. I can't fucking do this. This is awful. Just call the pharmacy, and tell them to send everything up here. I want five epidurals."

Misty smiled, and a quiet laugh escaped her lungs. "Let me just check to see how far you've progressed, and then I'll contact anesthesia for an epidural. Do you want anyone to leave the room?"

"Nope," Cassie said and immediately pulled up her gown and spread her legs as wide as they would go.

"Jesus, Cass," Georgia said and covered her eyes.

I turned my head toward the window and fought the urge to burst out laughing. I couldn't blame her, though. I mean, I might not have been as open to visitors seeing my bag of goods, but it was true that all modesty flew straight out the fucking window when you were in labor.

"It's called a pussy," Cass said.

"Hell, you're crazy, Crazy," Thatch added with adoration in his voice.

From my periphery, I noted that the nurse sat on the edge of the bed beside Cass and proceeded to put a glove on. "This might be a little uncomfortable, okay? Especially since this is your first baby. A lot of times your cervix is very posterior and hard to reach."

"No worries. I'm sure it's nothing compared to these fucking contrac—" Cassie started to explain, but yet again, another contraction started to peak, and all she could do was hold on to the side rails of the bed and breathe through it.

Jesus, her contractions are really close together.

"Oh, God!" she cried. "I think I just peed!"

"No, sweetheart, you didn't pee," Misty reassured. "Your water just broke."

Cassie groaned. "Well, that's fantastic. And fucking gross."

"Are you having the urge to push?"

"I have the urge to poop, but that's about it." Blatant honesty laced with ridiculousness. That's pretty much how the rest of this labor and delivery were going to go, I was sure of it.

"Yeah, sweetheart, that's actually the urge to push that you're feeling right now." Misty glanced at Thatch. "Can you push the nurse call button for me?" she asked in a neutral tone.

Confusion and concern etched his normally relaxed face, but he did as she asked and tapped the nurse call button.

Uh oh…this did not sound good for Cassie…

"Can I help you?" a female voice said over the speaker.

"Hey, Mary Lou, I need a delivery table set up in Room 14 stat. And can you go ahead and call Dr. Sabin and tell him we're going to be ready for delivery soon? I'd like him close by."

"Huh?" Cassie asked. "Delivery soon?" She sat up on the bed, and her eyes went wide in shock. "What do you mean?" She looked at Thatch. "What does she mean?"

"Cassie, you're fully dilated, and your little baby is already at a very low station."

She scrunched up her face in confusion. "Low station? Like FM radio? I don't need music right now. I need an epidural."

"No," Misty said with a grin. "Low station as in the baby's fetal descent station. You're already at a +2 station, sweetheart. And I could tell with your contractions, that the baby is positioned perfectly for delivery. And you probably didn't realize this, but you were already pushing a little bit with your contractions."

Cassie glanced around the room frantically. And then her eyes went back to Misty.

"Okay…okay…so just get me an epidural, and then it's go time."

She looked at Thatch again, her eyes turning scared and helpless. "Right? Epidural first and then we can have this baby?"

"Cassie, I don't think we have time for an epidural," Misty explained softly.

"You don't think!" Cass shouted. "What do you mean, you don't think!"

"I know, actually," she answered and got up from the bed and proceeded to get the room ready for delivery. Another staff member wheeled in the table and began to set up the sterile instruments.

"No-no-no-no-no," Cassie chanted. "Nope. I'm not doing it. Not without an ep—"

Oh, no… Another contraction…

"Oh, holy fuck! Holy fuck! Holy fuck! I need to push! I need to push!"

Thatch didn't hesitate for a second and took each of his wife's cheeks in his hands and locked his eyes with hers, forcing Cassie's focus to him. "You got this, honey. You're the strongest woman I know. You can do it, baby. But you need to wait to push until the doctor gets in the room. Just breathe… There you go… Just breathe… You're doing so good, honey. I'm so proud of you." He coached her and encouraged her and just loved her in the softest, most tender voice and then kissed her forehead gently once the contraction had slowly past.

I walked over to a tearful Georgia and wrapped my arm around her shoulders. "Let's go wait in the waiting room. I think this needs to be their special moment."

Well, special and *very painful* for Cassie moment.

Georgia nodded and wiped a rogue tear from her cheek.

A few minutes later, we were sitting in the waiting room, watching the two smartest people in the hospital, Lexi and Kline, play a game of chess on her iPad.

They were both in deep thought regarding their next moves, and I chanced a glance at Georgia. She sat quietly, watching her husband, with nothing but pure love in her eyes. It was obvious that a Brooks baby was going to be the next step for them. They had the suburban home, the SUV, and the dog and cat. Now, they just needed to make their family official with a little baby of their own.

"What?" Georgia asked once her eyes met mine.

I grinned. "I didn't say anything."

"Yeah, but you're thinking something."

"I'm only thinking what you're thinking about, and I'm really happy for you."

She stared at me for a long moment and then smiled softly. "Thanks, Win."

"Wes!" Lexi shouted and hopped up from her seat. She skipped toward him and jumped straight into his arms.

He wrapped her up tightly and held her for a whole lot longer than someone who didn't want a kid should have. I hated that he was so blind to what he really wanted. It was so obvious in every little thing related to Wes and Lexi's close relationship.

He would lasso the moon for my daughter if she asked him.

He would quite literally do anything for her.

Maybe it's not Lexi that he doesn't want; maybe he just doesn't want me...

The mere thought of that smarted like a son of a bitch. I hated that this man had spurred insecure thoughts like that. After Nick and I had broken up, I'd promised myself I would never let a man make me feel like I wasn't good enough.

And yet, there I was, letting the insecurities permeate my soul.

Wes set Lexi back on her little feet, and his eyes immediately sought out mine. I had no idea what he was thinking, not a fucking clue, but it looked like he was trying to give me a million words with one single look.

I averted my eyes in an obvious show of refusal. I didn't want his words.

Fuck his words. His words meant shit to me.

At least, that was what I was going to keep telling myself.

If he wanted something from me, the only way he could prove it was by action. To show me that he was actually the man I had originally thought he was. Not the kind of man who ran when things got too intense, too real.

"What took you so long?" Kline asked Wes with a smirk.

"I was at a charity event, and traffic became a nightmare. You know how New York is, everyone trying to go in the same direction, yet no one really making any progress."

I winced. I'd been at the same charity event and gotten here just fine. But I had a feeling he hadn't gotten the news quite as soon as I had—and I hadn't bothered to share.

Kline chuckled. "That's exactly why I love living in the suburbs now."

"Is it why you love driving the minivan, too?" Wes teased. His words sounded good, but his tone was completely off—halfhearted if I'd ever heard it. And I had. I'd been practicing the same goddamn thing all night.

Kline grinned anyway, too high on the happenings to dirty himself with Wes's details. "Well, that, and the fact that Georgia loves how spacious the backseat is."

"Kline!" Georgia chimed in.

"What, baby? You said you loved it that night—"

"Kline!" she said again and slashed a supposed-to-be-menacing finger across her throat.

He just laughed, visibly amused by his wife's embarrassment.

The sound of the automatic doors that led to the labor and delivery ward caught our attention, and Thatch walked out with a giant grin on his face.

"Is he here?" Georgia asked excitedly.

Thatch nodded. "Ace Tobias Kelly is here."

I grinned at the mere thought that Cassie had been teasing Thatch for her entire pregnancy with the name game, constantly pranking him with ridiculous names, and in the end, she named her son the one name Thatch had truly wanted from the start.

"Mom and baby doing good?" I asked.

He smiled proudly. "Mom and baby are perfect."

"Congrats, man. I'm really happy for you." Kline stood and wrapped Thatch up in a man hug, patting his back a few times.

We all followed suit, hugging Thatch and congratulating him on the birth of his son.

"How much did he weigh?" Georgia asked.

Thatch smiled proudly. "Nine pounds, ten ounces. Twenty-two inches long."

Georgia's eyes went wide. "Holy fucking shit."

"Your wife just had a toddler," Wes added with a chuckle.

"What can I say? Kelly men are big. *Everywhere.*" He added a wink to bring his point home.

"Really?" Kline asked with a smirk. "You're really going there right now?"

"Yep," Thatch answered without hesitation. "It's the happiest fucking day of my life. My beautiful wife just gave me the best gift I've ever been given, without castrating me in the process, and my baby boy takes after his father."

CHAPTER 31

Wes

I was happy for Thatch and Cassie.

Scared to death of what the combination of the two of them would mean for the world, but happy for them. Really fucking happy for them. They were about the craziest two people ever to procreate, but seeing them with their new son put everything into perspective.

Undeniably, I wanted what they had. The easy affection and trust—the knowledge that one person would put you before nearly everything. And I wanted a family to call my own.

Of course, I'd gone and completely fucked that by thinking I wasn't worthy of putting in that kind of effort. Like it was the same fate bestowed upon me rather than a conscious choice to do right by them—and by myself.

So here I was—post birth, staring into the window of the nursery at dozens of nameless babies and hoping beyond reason Winnie would stumble over to stare through the same window.

That she would somehow find it in her heart to forgive me all of my stupid choices and let me love her and Lex.

I wanted it so fucking badly I could hardly breathe, hardly think.

The tiniest sensation flared at my hand, warm skin on mine as a delicate, feminine version of it slipped solidly into its embrace.

I looked down my arm, gray suit fabric covering it blandly until the purple polish resting at the back of my hand made it come alive.

"Lex," I said softly, and she lifted her head to look up at me.

"Babies' fingernails are formed in the womb starting at week twelve of gestation," she told me, and I smiled so big my cheeks hurt.

"Oh, yeah?" I asked, trying to steady my voice over the ache born of missing her so much.

"Yeah," she confirmed with a nod.

"I want to know how that's possible," I muttered in awe. In awe of the fact she'd shared with me, but even more in awe of her.

"Me too," she agreed, and I knew she'd find out. Through Google or an encyclopedia—if she could find one—or asking the goddamn doctor herself. Her confidence shone the brightest in her thirst for knowledge. Whatever she needed to do to gain it, she'd do. It was all the other stuff that she struggled with—the interactions and small talk and culturally deigned importance that really wasn't that important at all. Not if she didn't need them to be.

"How many babies do you think were born today?" I asked her. I'd missed her brilliance and wanted just a little taste of how superiorly her mind worked.

"There are twenty-five babies in this nursery, a variable of probably ten in their rooms, about five thousand, six hundred hospitals in the US, so given the metropolis of New York versus the populous of small-town America, probably somewhere around eleven thousand. In the US."

Hot damn. Am I right?

"I bet Thatch and Cassie's baby is going to cause more trouble than the rest of them combined," I remarked.

Her eyes held mine, a progression so significant it helped in my effort not to take offense to her looking at me like I was an absolute imbecile.

In her mind, my little statement was so statistically impossible it was laughable. That would be what embarrassed her about her parents—actual stupidity.

God, I had the urge to pick her up and hold her tightly to my chest.

I want to be one of her biggest embarrassments.

I wanted to be everything to this beautifully brilliant little girl. I wanted to be her father figure, one of the two biggest supporters in her life.

I wanted her to be mine. *My* little girl.

"Lexi bug," I heard behind us, the rough voice of her uncle Remy and the realization of what it meant making me squeeze her hand tighter.

He was here to pick her up, and I didn't know when I'd get to see her next.

The uncertainty nauseated me. I literally felt my stomach churn in discomfort over the mere idea of never getting to take her to football practice, of never getting to watch her focused little face while she worked out a complicated algebraic equation that was no doubt over my goddamn head. Birthdays, holidays, lazy Sundays at home.

I had no claim to any of it, and that was the worst kind of hell.

Lex turned immediately, a smile on her face for one of the great loves of her life, and I did my best to go with her momentum instead of fighting it. She didn't need any of my personal baggage adding to her own.

"Wes," Remy greeted coolly as my gaze met his.

I didn't blame him.

A picture of a commitment-phobic, selfish version of me had been painted, and my goddamn hand had been the one holding the brush.

"Hey, Remy," I said back, smiling and looking down into Lexi's excited eyes. I'd scale any mountain, withstand any foray into the most awkward of moments to keep that look on her innocent face.

Still, I couldn't help but poke the bear just a little.

"Spending time with your second-favorite uncle?" I asked. "Sounds like a good night to me."

"Second-favorite?" Remy muttered roughly, the outrage lashing so far out of his throat it felt like the tip of a whip—but it was of the pleasurable kind.

Lex giggled, and that was all it took to turn his scowl into a smile. She was his world.

I just hoped he'd eventually understand she was mine too.

The dingy lights of the hospital shone more powerfully as the blond of Winnie's hair came into view behind Remy.

I looked straight past him, right to her, as I offered, "I can take Lexi home if you need to stay here at the hospital for a while."

Remy's brows drew together briefly before looking over his shoulder to see his sister.

"Actually," Winnie said, "I'm meeting Nick for a late dinner."

Nick? Lexi's father? The one man who'd stupidly chosen his career over this beautiful, perfect fucking woman and the most precious, brilliant little girl in the world?

Fuck, this hurts.

Pain pierced my skin and flooded into my eyes enough that even Remy winced.

Holding out a hand to Lexi, he murmured, "Uh, Lex and I are gonna take off. You two can talk."

Translation: you need to.

We looked like mirror images of one another, both looking after their retreating forms longingly. Lex looked back and waved, and both of us smiled and waved back.

I wanted us to be doing it as a unit—but we couldn't have been further apart emotionally if the entire span of Earth had been between us.

As silence stretched on, the threat of her date with Lexi's father looming in the air, I knew it was now or never. I had to lay it on the line and tell her how I'd felt since the beginning.

"I knew it would end this way," I blurted in admission, the heady mix of thoughts and desires blurring my ability to organize any of them into a helpful order.

She tilted her head to the side, and I watched as her blond hair slid softly from her shoulder. She searched my eyes long enough that I repeated my words.

"I did. I knew it would end this way."

"You knew what would end what way?" she asked, even though I was almost positive she knew both of the answers.

"Us," I clarified anyway. I looked her directly in the eyes, and my heart seized at the truth there. Heartbreak. Longing. Unabashed disappointment.

I pushed on anyway, hoping by some miracle I'd be able to make it better.

"I knew we would end badly. From that very first moment, I knew it would be a train wreck."

She looked like I'd slapped her, the red suffusing her cheek with the same intensity as if my hand had left its actual mark.

"Then, why?" she demanded. "Why go there at all if you knew?"

"Because," I told her honestly, hoping my heart was in my eyes. Because now, unlike all the times before, I was actually trying *not* to hide it. "It was unmistakably impossible not to." My voice dropped to a whisper. "From the first moment my eyes met yours in that locker room, I knew I'd never breathe another satiated breath until I had you."

I knew it came out wrong the second I said it, the words "had you" implying something altogether uglier than the warmth and affection—fucking love—that bled and pumped through my heart. She was seeing my confession as something shallow, something I didn't want it to be, and the urge to fix it came out garbled too.

"I wanted more than just to sleep with you."

Fuck, Wes, I mentally chastised. *Enough with the goddamn past tense.*

"I have to go," she breathed, turning to leave without a second thought.

And her mind wasn't the only one thinking in half measures. I reached out and grabbed her, closing my fingers around her arm and pulling her back toward me before the action even registered in my mind.

There was no plot or plan, not even a scheme for what would happen when I got her there, plastered against me.

But my body didn't need any incentive or explanation. My lips met hers in a flash, the speed and intensity so vivid it was almost harsh, and her intake of breath provided the perfect opportunity to touch my tongue to hers.

She gave in at once, dancing a sensual dance with me for one heartbeat and the next, until almost a full five seconds had passed and my hands were holding on to her ass like a lifeline—and then sanity returned. For *her*. As her hand connected with my face on a smack, I knew mine would be gone for some time—quite possibly forever.

"Winnie," I whispered, desperation clawing from my throat and spilling past my lips.

"No," she whispered fiercely. "I deserve better. Lex deserves better. And for fuck's sake, Wes, so do you."

And then she was gone—an empty hall, the quiet cries of innocence, and a broken heart all that were left to keep me company.

Fuck, I couldn't—no, I *wouldn't* let it end like this.

Not. Like. This.

I wanted Winnie and I wanted Lexi and I wanted our family.

CHAPTER 32

Winnie

The New York wind whipped around my face as I opened the door to Gramercy Tavern. My cheeks felt like little ice cubes in response to the short walk from the cab to the restaurant, hell, my entire body felt like it had been doused in ice-cold water, but I had a feeling that had nothing to do with the chilly, early spring weather.

I couldn't shake the racing thoughts of Wes and his words and how easily I'd lost myself in that kiss. It had taken every ounce of willpower I had to dig deep enough into the recesses of my brain—that seemed far too content to feel Wes's lips against mine for the rest of forever—and find rational thought in that moment.

Maybe it was a little overkill to actually slap him across the face—*holy shit*—but I couldn't seem to stop these insane emotions when it came to him. He quite literally drove me crazy.

You wouldn't care if you weren't still in love with him, my heart rationalized.

No kidding, Captain Obvious, my brain shouted back.

I wasn't sure if I would ever *not* be in love with Wes.

But I knew that I had to find a way to move forward, versus

backward, where I let myself give in to epically stupid moments like letting Wes kiss me, and more than that, kissing him back with just as much fervor.

I made a beeline for the restroom, before heading to the table Nick had reserved. I just needed a minute. Just a fucking minute to find my sanity.

I felt like pieces of myself were scattered across the marble floor, and I couldn't pick them up fast enough. I had too many emotions, too many fucking feelings and no one to run to. No shoulder to cry on. No comforting arms to find peace in.

Wes is that person. He is that person...

Fuck. I had to pull myself together.

I switched my focus to applying an unnecessary coat of lip gloss and decided I really just needed to get this night over with so that I could get my ass home. Ugly pajamas, a pint of ice cream, endless Netflix episodes and my bed were much needed right now.

As I walked out of the bathroom and spotted Nick at a table for two, it took a lot of effort to keep my feet moving toward him, rather than turning on their heels and heading straight for the nearest exit door.

"Glad you could make, Win," he said with a soft smile, as the server pulled out my chair and helped me into my seat.

It was safe to say, I was in the very last place I wanted to be, sitting down across from Nick Raines at Gramercy Tavern to "talk." Whatever that meant. He was in town for a medical conference with NYU and decided it was vital we have an important discussion.

That was exactly how he had put it: *important discussion.*

He tended to be fairly emotionless in general, when he wasn't on one of his good-time highs, never really opening up and always guarding himself from the outside world, for whatever reason that might be. It was something I had most definitely learned to expect from him.

And honestly, I often wondered if the deep-rooted issues and insecurities within himself were the sole reason he kept his distance from his daughter.

But those weren't my demons to battle. They were his.

I had tried to battle them in the past, tried to get him to open his eyes and realize what he was missing by being absent from Lex's life, but it was impossible to convince someone of something when they weren't ready.

They had to decide those things on their own, for themselves.

"You look beautiful, Win," he said as I adjusted my seat closer to the table.

"Thanks."

"Do you need a minute to look at the menu?"

I glanced up at him, surprised by his patience. Nick was not a very patient man when it came to normal, everyday life. In his career, in medicine, he was the most patient, talented neurosurgeon you'd ever meet, but real life urged the complete opposite response from him.

He looked different. His face was softer. The usual three-week beard he generally sported had been trimmed to a handsome two- to three-day length. And his normal attire of stuffy suits and ties had been replaced by a well-fitted sport coat and a white collared shirt that had the first two buttons undone in a relaxed manner.

His brown eyes appeared tender, and the serious lines around his eyes had seemed to vanish, nowhere in sight.

I looked down at my menu and then back up at him. "No, I'll probably just get their smoked tomato soup."

He grinned. "You've always loved that soup. But I have a feeling it has more to do with the gourmet croutons than anything else."

God, he was being weird tonight. I honestly hadn't thought he'd known a single restaurant menu item that I enjoyed, much less a simple yet surprising insight like that.

I shrugged. "Well, I tend to be a pretty big fan of anything carb-related."

He laughed softly, and when the server stopped by our table, Nick ordered for both of us, even adding a glass of my favorite Riesling to the list.

Seriously, who was this man, and what had he done with Nick?

I was starting to have flashbacks of the Nick I'd first met, way back in med school. The guy who loved to have a good time, the guy who wasn't so focused and serious, the guy I had once enjoyed spending all of my time with.

That Nick had fled the scene a very long time ago. I honestly hadn't seen him since before I found out I was pregnant with Lex. Once he had decided to make neurosurgery his priority, nothing else mattered. Nothing else but Nick and his career.

A few moments of comfortable silence passed between us, and then he cleared his throat, pulling my attention from the center of the dining room back to our table.

"I'd like to discuss a few things, Winnie."

Well, that was a bit cryptic...

"Ooookay."

"I'm looking to move back to New York permanently. I'd like to be closer to our daughter. I'm tired of missing out on so many things in her life. I have a lot of regrets related to that. The way I've been as a father."

"Absent father," I added without feeling the least bit bad about it. He needed to hear those words.

He nodded sullenly. "You're right. I deserved that. But I would like to change that. I'd like to really get to know her, spend more time with her. I'd like her to be comfortable with me. I want to be a part of her life as much as I want her to be a part of mine."

I let his words sink in for a few moments, unsure of my exact emotions. I was torn between feeling relieved and feeling very skeptical. I mean, this was a man who had made a career out of avoiding his daughter. He had often made promises he couldn't keep. He had disappointed Lexi time and time again.

He had disappointed her so many times throughout her life that my little girl had just given up hope of him being there for her. Sure, I had never heard those words pass her little lips, but I knew my daughter. I knew her facial expressions, and I knew her heart.

And I just couldn't bear to let him break it again.

"Can I be honest?" I asked once I finally got my thoughts in order.

"Of course."

"I can't really believe your words, Nick," I admitted. "I think the only way I will eventually believe you really mean this is if you *show me* over and over again that you are really going to be the father that Lexi deserves."

"I understand. I really do. And I will prove it to you. I promise, I will prove it to you."

He'd used the word promise so many times in the past that it literally meant nothing to me. Nick's promises were absolute shit. They were hollowed-out words that were void of meaning or good intentions.

"Let's just give it time, Nick."

"Time?"

"Yes, time," I responded. "You need to give me time, and most importantly, you need to give Lexi time. I don't want you to hurt her again. She's been hurt too many times by you in the past. And I know it is going to take her time to be comfortable with you, to *want* to spend time with you."

"What about you?"

My brow furrowed. "What do you mean? What about me?"

"Will it take you time to give me another chance?"

I sat back in my chair, shocked by his question.

"I want another chance with you, Winnie. You are the love of my life, and I hope one day you'll give me a second chance to prove that I really do mean that."

My jaw dropped to the floor. *"The love of your life?"* I nearly choked on the words as they slid across my tongue.

"Yes, the love of my life," he repeated, and honestly, I just wanted to smack him.

Hell, I guess I just wanted to smack every-fucking-body tonight.

I really needed to get my ass home before I ended up in a New York jail cell.

"You really have an odd way of showing that I am the love of your life," I stated, my voice growing more irritated. "You left me by myself to care for a newborn baby, while I was still trying to get through my residency. For the first few months of Lexi's life, you never answered my calls. You didn't even see her for the first time until she was four months old. I honestly have a hard time believing that I am the love of your life."

"I was scared, Win. I was afraid and I was young and I didn't know what the fuck I was doing."

I shook my head. "No, you actually did know what you were doing. You wanted to focus on your career, and you didn't want any distractions that could possibly pull you away from that. You wanted your career more than you wanted a family."

Completely unexpectedly, his face melted into a smile. I pushed away from the table, apparently, even my posture had aggression, and slammed my back in the chair. "What the fuck?"

He shook his head, smile still engaged, and smacked an enthusiastic hand on the table. "Well, look at you, Winnie Winslow."

"What?" I asked. "What the fuck is going on here?"

"Relax, Win," he urged. "I'm kidding."

Kidding? What was this? Some kind of sick joke?

"Kidding? God, you are some kind of asshole. She's your *daughter*."

He turned serious then, reaching for my hand as I pushed back from the table to stand. "No, no. Jesus. I'm not kidding about Lexi. I'm moving to New York. I just accepted Head of Neuro at St. Luke's, and I really do want to get to know her. But at your pace—her pace. I know my track record is shit, but I'm not that big of an asshole."

"Then what the fuck are you kidding about?" I nearly shouted.

He smiled again. "About us. Me and you, us. I know you'd have to have a fucking tumor to consider trying anything with me more complicated than an orgasm."

I rolled my eyes.

"Though, I'm guessing those are off the table too."

"Nick!"

He held up his hands in a placating gesture. "I'm just proud of you is all."

I scoffed in response. "Proud of me? You are an *asshole*," I said a bit too loudly as I stood up from the table and tossed my napkin down.

"Seven years ago, you never would have spoken to me this way. You never would have stood up to me like this."

"I would have. I *did*."

His eyes creased at the corners, visible pain resting behind his retinas. "You're wrong, Win."

I turned to leave, and he reached out to take my hand one more time. "Sit down. Please?"

My fists clenched and my molars nearly cracked, but I sat down and raised my brows.

"You're right, *now*. You and that fire and everything you do for our daughter."

I gripped the edge of the table to stop myself from doing something ridiculous like throwing my wineglass at his head. "Let's be honest here. She's never been *our* daughter. She is *my* daughter. I have raised her, and I will continue to raise her. I am the one who has provided for her. I have kept her safe and warm. I have loved her with everything I have. And I have always been there for her."

"Exactly. *That's* the fire."

I laughed without humor and closed my eyes. "What in the hell is your point here?"

Goddammit, one more crazy conversation with a man and I was going to scratch my own eyes out.

His perfect teeth shone in the light as he opened his smile wide, teasing, "Maybe I am still in love with you."

"Nick, goddammit."

His fucking cheeky smile grew. "Kidding, Win. But holy hell, I can't wait to be friends."

Friends with the irresponsible, nonexistent father of my child?

God help me.

I crossed my arms over my chest and sank into my seat like a sullen child, and he laughed again.

"Not leaving?" he asked, and I scowled.

Who was he to run me off, anyway? If one of us left, it would be him.

At least... "Not before my soup."

CHAPTER 33

Wes

There came a time in one's life when all the details became no more than bullshit.

Or maybe I'm the one full of shit. But to me, these little tiny nuggets of perceived wisdom feel like truth. So, yeah. Deal with it.

How was I going to make my schedule work? Would I be able to make every single commitment? Were we actually compatible with one another? Yadda, yadda, yadda.

See, I finally realized the ultimate answer, the master key, the solution to all my problems and heartbreak and man angst.

I wanted Winnie, and I wanted to be the best father I could to Lex. I loved them both, and the rest of it…didn't matter.

I'd left the hospital dejected—completely and totally lost and seriously doubting everything about myself. My stupid casual take on life that I'd held on to for so long and the falsehood that Winnie somehow owed me something now that I'd had the great romantic epiphany.

Oh, I'm ready now, Winnie. I'm ready to take you seriously and give you everything I can, but only now that I've been faced with the consequences of my selfish actions.

The more I thought about it as I ambled through Central Park until the sky turned completely midnight, the hour growing too late for even the moon, the more disgusted with myself I became.

Winnie Winslow didn't owe me a goddamn thing.

She'd given me several of the best months of my life, and I'd put more effort in with her than I ever had with anyone before. But what made a man was not the absence of mistakes, but rather, the way he handled them when he made them.

And, apparently, I was complete shit at the whole handling thing.

Change within a person wasn't easy, but I was determined to try. And it was all going to start with the way I looked at things. Instead of skimming the surface, I'd delve deeper. And that wasn't a promise to Winnie or Lexi or some third party, but to myself. I wanted to be the guy who saw things for how they really were. The guy who didn't fly off the handle in a jealous rage and the kind of guy who *listened* when people spoke.

And, as I climbed the last flight of stairs on the way up to my apartment—content to bask in my wandering so much that I'd done fourteen floors the old fashioned way—a hello from the sun now brightening the once dark sky, I knew that included the way I looked at Winnie's time with Nick last night.

From this newly found rational place, the truth was surprisingly clear and all boiled down to one simple statement: Winnie Winslow was no goddamn idiot.

She wouldn't be going out on a date with Nick, the halfway decent guy, but completely absent father to her child just because of what had happened between us. She'd said it best herself—she deserved better.

We all did.

And Nick wasn't better for her or Lex.

But I still could be. I could be better for them and better for me, and I could do all of it whether Winnie wanted to take a chance on me romantically again or not.

This wasn't a world of absolutes, all or nothings.

And in the face of being told I couldn't have it all, I still knew I didn't want nothing.

Nothing in this life was black and white. It was very much gray, and I hoped to God I could find the shade that Winnie would approve.

"It's about fucking time you showed up," Remy greeted, his back to the wall and ass to the floor right beside the door to my apartment and sleep wrinkling even the casual cotton of his clothes.

Jesus Christ. What was he doing here?

"What the fuck?" I asked without mentioning that he'd startled me. Remy Winslow never needed new ammunition to razz anyone. He found enough all on his own.

"I've been here all night." He stood up with a tight smirk covering his lips and brushed his hands down the tops of his thighs on a sigh, as if he was disgusted by the pristine conditions of my apartment building. "Might want to think about letting your landlord know the cleaning service ain't up to snuff here."

See what I mean?

I wasn't one to boast about my style of living, but I sure as shit didn't own an apartment over a fucking deli in Jersey.

"You've been here all night?" I questioned, more than confused by the unexpected visit from the very last person on this planet who wanted to hang out with me.

"Did I fucking stutter? I've been here all night waiting for you."

I couldn't stop the surprise from suffusing my features. *Especially* since he'd been the one to take Lexi home.

"Where's Lexi?"

"At home with Winnie. Some of us don't stay out all night."

Given where she'd gone when she left the hospital, I had to admit, that was a relief.

"And if you were out fucking some other woman, let me just tell you right now, I don't want to know."

I rolled my eyes and ran a hand through my hair. "I was just walking around Central Park."

"Strange place to fuck a woman," Jude offered as he rounded the corner of the hall that ran perpendicular to my door and down to more apartments.

"You're here too?" I asked, as the other two stooges rounded the same corner with smiles of their own.

"I hope you had Mace," Ty remarked, but Flynn just smirked.

"What are all of you doing here?" I asked, pushing past them and unlocking my door. With a splayed hand, I held it open for all of them and watched as they filed inside in front of me.

"Holy shit!" Jude yelled from the front.

Everything happened quickly then, the yelp and the sharp cry of pain followed by Thatch's not-sorry-at-all apology.

"Whoops," he said through a laugh. "Sorry, man."

I shoved through the crowd just as a sleepy Kline sat up on my couch and put his feet to the floor.

"Jesus Christ," I remarked. "Did I not get the invitation to the goddamn party at my own apartment?"

Thatch smiled as Jude climbed slowly to his feet. He looked like he was in pain—and yeah, I smiled a little at that.

"What the fuck?" Remy questioned, glancing back and forth between Kline and Thatch. "You guys have been here all night? Why didn't you answer the goddamn door?"

"Kline had an emergency key," Thatch explained and then looked at Remy with a knowing smirk. "And I don't answer the door when it's not my fucking place."

"A key that will soon be revoked," I replied as I crossed my arms over my chest.

"Hey, all I did was break in and sleep on your couch," Kline said in defense of himself.

The room was completely full of people—for some unknown reason—and yet no one said a word until I prompted them. "Okay, guys. What the hell are you doing here?"

Of course, then they all spoke at once.

This was why we needed smart women like Winnie, Georgia, and Cassie around. Christ, I was sure some men functioned on their own, but they weren't in this group.

"Guys!" I yelled over the white noise. And when that didn't work, one sharp whistle did the trick.

"Everyone shut up." All six of them smirked at me.

"Remy," I said, directing only him to answer. "What are the four of you doing here?"

"We came to make sure you knew Winnie didn't go on a date with Nick."

"Nick?" Thatch bellowed, and then lowered his voice to a dramatic whisper when I glared at him. "Lexi's father, Nick? That Nick?"

"That Nick," Flynn confirmed.

"Good old Nick Raines," Jude said with an evil smile.

"Everyone stop saying Nick," I ordered, rubbing at the tense skin between my eyes.

Kline crossed his arms and put one fist to his chin, smiling at the ground. There was nothing he loved more than bearing witness to a complete shit show, courtesy of his friends.

"I know she didn't go on a date with him."

"You do?" Remy asked.

I nodded and shrugged. "Your sister is not an idiot."

"Damn straight," Ty agreed, and I almost laughed.

"Not that the four of you are a reflection of her," I went on, and they all groaned and chuckled.

"Yeah, yeah," Remy grumbled.

"Look, I'm aware of what's really going on," I admitted.

Remy eyed me with a knowing smile. "What's *really* going on, Wes?"

"Well, I know Winnie wasn't on a date with Nick."

"And?" Thatch chimed in.

I stared out toward the floor-to-ceiling windows of my apartment and noted the pinks and oranges and purples of the sun making its debut. A smile I couldn't deny crested my lips as my gaze moved back to the group of misfits in my living room, and I found myself saying the easiest, most natural words that had ever left my lips. "And, most importantly, I love her."

"Fuckin' right. Cassie owes me fifty bucks and a blow job." Thatch's smile was big enough to light up the whole goddamn city. "Thanks a lot, buddy," he said to me. "I owe you one."

My face scrunched up in incredulity. "Uh…glad my mess of a love life could help get your dick sucked. I honestly couldn't be happier right now," I commented in a voice that was anything but happy.

But Thatch acted oblivious, flashing his signature, annoying as hell wink in my direction. "Me too, Whitney. Me motherfucking too."

Jesus. Once I found a way to get my Win-Win, I sure as fuck needed to be on the lookout for new friends. Preferably ones who didn't enjoy breaking and entering and anteing blow jobs on my love life.

"So…" Kline finally spoke—directly to me. Everyone listened. Well, everyone besides Thatch, who already had his phone pulled out of his pocket and was probably texting his wife to schedule his winning fellatio—and check on the baby.

Christ, I'd almost forgotten. Thatch had just had a baby. What in the fuck was he doing here?

"Wait a second," I told Kline before turning to Thatch. "What are you doing here? You just had a baby!"

Thatch shrugged, but I could tell it was forced. That big fucker didn't want to be here any more than I'd expected him to be. "She kicked me out. Accused me of hogging the baby and mothering her too much or some shit." He looked to his watch. "She said I could come back a couple of hours from now."

"Congratulations and shit," Remy told Thatch, and I almost laughed. "But can we get back to the reason my ass is fucking numb?"

Thatch pretended to look sympathetic. "Hemorrhoids?"

Thankfully, most of us were highly trained in ignoring him.

"What are you going to do about it?" Kline asked me. "What are you going to do to clean up the mess?"

I took a deep breath and smiled. "I have a plan."

Like it was premeditated, all six waiting faces smiled in unison.

Thatch rubbed his hands together and got that familiar prankster look in his eye.

I pointed directly at him. "Not that kind of plan."

He smirked. "Doesn't matter. Whatever it is. Count me in."

And the rest of the group responded with nods and me toos.

It looked like Winnie Winslow had better prepare herself.

"Good. Now get the fuck out."

CHAPTER 34

Winnie

Tonight, my little Lexi would be Betsy Ross in her school's spring performance. We had been practicing her three tiny lines for what felt like the past month, and I honestly had no idea how this was going to go. A child like Lexi wasn't exactly known for doing well in overwhelming social situations, but she had been determined to learn her part with nothing less than the motivation of a Broadway star. And I couldn't deny she looked adorable in her colonial red, white, and blue dress and big, poufy white wig.

No matter what, I was and would be proud of her.

Proud of her for always trying her hardest. Proud of her for trying to overcome her tendencies toward social anxiety. And proud that she was my daughter.

I sat down in one of the metal chairs in the auditorium and thumbed through the program. My mother, brothers, and Nick weren't able to make it, but I'd promised I'd send them a video of her performance.

Yes, I'd even promised Nick I'd send him a video. We were slowly trying to find a comfortable medium where he was more involved in his daughter's life.

Lexi's teacher got on stage and announced that the performance would start in ten minutes and instructed everyone to take their seats.

"Excuse me…excuse me…sorry…" A deep voice filled my ears, and I glanced up to find Thatch attempting to shuffle through the row, his enormous thighs and ass skimming the faces of each person he passed, and heading straight toward me. Literally, a bull in a china shop, his large frame knocked into everyone and everything despite how gingerly he attempted to move. Interestingly enough, the women he bumped didn't look put out at all.

I tilted my head to the side in confusion. *What was Thatch doing here?*

I glanced around the room to see if anyone else was in attendance, but I found that none of the gang was anywhere in sight. He plopped down beside me with a giant, friendly grin, as if it was the most normal thing in the world to just randomly show up at my daughter's school performance, by himself.

"Hey, Win."

"Uh…*hey?*" I responded in confusion. "Not gonna lie, it's a little bit of a surprise to see you here."

He ignored my remark and got his phone out of his pocket, tapping his fingers across the screen. I sighed and returned my focus to the stage until I heard Thatch say, "Whitney? You there? Can you see me?"

My eyes darted back to the giant sitting beside me to find him FaceTiming with Wes.

"All good, T-bag. Mind switching the camera view to the stage? I'd much rather watch Lexi's performance than stare at your ugly mug."

Thatch chuckled and switched the screen view. "Yeah, of course, asshole. You're welcome for this, by the way. It's not like it inconvenienced me. I mean, I only had to reschedule naked dinner with Cass *and* cuddle time with Ace."

Wes laughed. "Thanks, buddy. You're the best. Consider this me cashing in on that IOU you mentioned."

Thatch smirked in response.

Normally, I would've been curious about the details of said IOU, but I'd say it was obvious I was more curious about what in the hell was going on.

Thatch made a show of getting his big frame comfortable in the far too small chair for a man of his size, while he pointed his phone toward the stage and Wes watched from the screen. Had I entered an alternate universe? Was I being pranked? Had I inadvertently become a victim of that show *Candid Camera*, which I wasn't one hundred percent certain was still on air, but that was beside the point.

I mean…What in the ever-loving fuck was going on?

"Excuse me?" I questioned, and Thatch glanced in my direction. "You need to get up, honey?"

"No, I don't need to get up," I spat and pointed toward the phone. "What in the hell are you doing?"

He shrugged and looked at me like I was the crazy one. "I'm getting ready to watch Lexi's school play."

"*With the phone.* What are you doing with the phone? Why are you FaceTiming with Wes?"

"Because his flight was delayed, and he didn't want to miss it," he explained like I was the one missing the point, like I was the strange one in this scenario.

"Hi, Fred." Wes's voice filled my ears.

I leaned forward until my face was in front of the camera and Wes's eyes were locked with mine. A soft smile crested his lips. "You look beautiful tonight, sweetheart."

I was wearing goddamn yoga pants and an NYU T-shirt. I looked like shit.

"Cut the crap, Wes. What are you getting at here?"

My words didn't affect him in the least, and to my irritation, that soft smile stayed glued to his face. "I'm not getting at anything. I didn't want to miss Lexi's school performance. How is she doing? Was she nervous when you dropped her off?"

My brow furrowed in frustration. "I'm not having this conversation with you."

"You're right." He nodded. "We don't want to miss a single second of the performance. How about I'll call you when I get in tonight?"

"No," I responded immediately. "No, no, no. Do not call me tonight."

"Yeah, good thinking," he agreed. "I'm sure Lex will be tuckered out by the time you get her home, and I'd feel like a bastard if I interrupted her much-needed sleep. I'll call you tomorrow."

"No," I refuted. "Do not call me tomorrow, Wes."

Thatch's eyes met mine, and he flashed a rage-inducing wink in my direction.

"Stop. This." I glared at him as I tried to yank the phone from his hands, but he had a serious Hulk-like grip on the damn thing. "Turn it off, Thatch."

He just shrugged in response. "Sorry, Mini Winnie. No can do."

I continued to glare at him for a good minute before I yanked my purse off the back of the chair and abruptly got out of my seat and moved to the row behind Thatch. I refused to be a part of that circus.

But nothing deterred him or Wes. Thatch continued on FaceTiming the performance, and Wes watched animatedly from his phone.

How'd I know this? Well, because I'm pathetic and I kept glancing to the side to see if he was still on the screen.

When Lexi stood on stage and said her three lines with perfect precision, even adding a few extra facts about Betsy Ross and the way the American flag was sewn together, I could hear Wes cheering louder than anyone in the audience.

I hated that my heart enjoyed it so much.

And when I glanced back to see his facial expression, my heart all but melted at the proud smile etched across his handsome face. *Like a father.* He looked like he was Lexi's father, and he couldn't have been more proud of his baby girl.

I mean, what was he trying to do to me?

Seriously? What was the point in all of this?

He was the one who had walked away, not me. He'd said he couldn't do it anymore.

But now, his actions refuted those words. They didn't show a man who simply couldn't do it anymore. They showed a man who wanted to do it. A man who wanted to be a part of mine and my daughter's life.

I honestly didn't know what to make of it.

I had never been more mindfucked than I was in that moment. Ironically, this occurring in the middle of a grade-school auditorium, while a little boy sang "Yankee Doodle Dandy" at the top of his lungs in the most off-key singing I'd ever heard in my life, was about as contradictory as it got.

There was nothing *dandy* about this situation at all.

Goddammit, Wes.

CHAPTER 35

Wes

For the last two weeks, I'd been doing my best to be the kind of guy I wanted to be, showing up to all of Lexi's events and helping out when she stayed with Remy—without pressure.

I didn't want to be in Winnie's face, and sometimes I even sent Thatch or Kline if I thought Winnie would react better to them than me.

If her interaction with Thatch last week had been anything to go by, though…she hadn't. But Thatch had enjoyed it enough for the both of them.

Of course, I hoped that at some point it would lead to reconciliation, but even if it didn't, I wanted to be a part of their lives. I wanted it for them, and I wanted it for me.

Winnie and Lexi Winslow made me happy.

Happier than I'd ever been, happier than when I'd thought I'd been my very happiest.

I liked being *tied down* to them, being someone they could count on and paying witness to every awesome mark they left on the world.

I'd gotten used to it, and whatever the stupid details—like Winnie not wanting to be with me—I didn't want to give it up.

It was selfish. God, so selfish.

But this was the kind of selfish I was okay with being. I wasn't some do-gooder, and I wasn't a perfect guy. I never would be.

I don't want to be.

But I wouldn't mind being the perfect guy for them.

And today, it was finally time they knew where I stood. What they decided to do with it—well, that was up to them.

Thanks to covert operations by not only Remy, but also Jude and Ty, I knew that Winnie and Lexi were planning to go out to the diner on 57th and 6th for an after-school treat. Lex's IEP progress report had just come in, and she was making strides in all the goals they'd set—and then some.

I wanted so badly to be a part of that celebration. Mostly, so Lexi would know that I was proud of her. Proud to know her. So goddamn proud you'd think I'd pushed her out myself.

The bell dinged above the door as I stepped inside and shook the April shower from my hair, and the bright light from outside had my eyes adjusting slowly.

Men are dogs, after all. Am I right?

I could barely see anything, but the vivid coral of Winnie's shirt would have been hard to miss anywhere—if I could have missed her.

Her head was down as she peeled the paper off of her cupcake and laughed at something Lexi said as she chomped away on a donut. It was cut up on her plate, and she was using a fork—something she always did with her donuts—and my knees nearly caved at the sight.

I'd missed the two of them. Even hanging out on the fringes of their life, I missed being on the inside. They had so much to give, and I didn't want to miss any of it.

Winnie's eyes came up right then, as if she'd heard me say the words aloud.

She looked startled.

But not angry.

Giving her the chance to decide if I had the privilege to join them or not, I raised just one hand and showed her the inside of my fist.

All the answer I needed was her small smile.

With one last wipe of my feet on the doormat, I crossed the space until the edge of their table came to my thighs. Lex looked up as my shadow fell across her, and she smiled at the sight of my face.

I might as well have melted right there—because I was done. The two of them smiling at me like they were, welcoming me, was all I needed in the entire world.

Wanting so badly to say how I felt, but knowing blurting it out wasn't the way to go, I folded my hand into the ASL sign for "I love you" and pressed it against my thigh.

Lexi noticed.

"I love you," she said, and my heart flexed.

Choking on words and disbelief and pretty much just being a bumbling buffoon, I only managed to stutter one horrendously eloquent word. "What?"

"Your hand means 'I love you,'" she explained.

"She's started learning sign language now," Winnie added.

I shook my head with a smile and barked the very beginning of a laugh.

"I am so screwed."

Winnie's face changed then, and I realized I *wasn't* screwed. Not yet. But I wanted to be—desperately.

Going with what felt natural, I started with that—with her, with my favorite little girl in the whole wide world. I had two women to tell how I felt, for different, very specific reasons, and that meant I had to start with one.

"You're right, Lex. It does mean 'I love you.'"

Her answering expression said "duh." I laughed again.

I asked Winnie for nonverbal permission to sit down, and she granted it with a nod of her head.

As I scooted into the booth, I pulled Lex's little chin in my direction with one gentle finger.

"I couldn't have fallen for a different kid, Lex."

Her eyes held mine as she tried to make sense of every word I spoke. My voice shook with emotion as I went on. "It's you. You're special, and not just for your brain or the things you won't ever be, but because you took everything I thought I knew—and taught me different."

Not only was a woman with a kid *not* the last thing I needed—it was everything I *did*.

These people—this woman and this child—had taught me to be a man.

"I love you," I told her, but my eyes went over her head and straight to the perfect blue eyes of her mother. "And that's an answer I didn't have to Google."

CHAPTER 36

Winnie

I watched in awe and shock and all-consuming love as Wes told my daughter that he loved her. *My* daughter. A kid who had been through some serious hard knocks in her little life. A kid whose father had been harder to find than Waldo.

Sure, she had my brothers, and they doted on her and loved her dearly.

But she had never had a man choose her like Wes just had.

He'd chosen her. Not out of relation or paternity or obligation, he'd just chosen her because he needed to, because he wanted to, because he loved her.

I couldn't stop the tears from slipping past my lids and down my cheeks as Lexi grinned back at Wes, her wise little eyes all-knowing and understanding of what he just said.

She might not have been able to express it in direct words or a manifestation of emotion, but when she lifted up the rest of the donut on her plate and handed it to Wes, saying, "I love you, too," that was my Lexi's version of handling such a precious, beautiful moment.

Her attention moved across the table to me, and her endearing gaze glanced down at my half-eaten cupcake and then back to my face. "Cupcake, Mommy?"

"You want the rest of my cupcake, sweetie?" I asked while trying not to choke on the poignant emotion lodged in my throat.

She nodded and smiled a sugary sweet smile.

I laughed through my tears and slid my plate across to her. "It's all yours, Lexi Lou."

I had to look in the opposite direction of Wes for a long moment and get myself together. I feared if I met his hazel gaze, I'd truly break into sobs.

But thankfully, he knew me well enough to give me those silent minutes, seemingly content, so very content, with just sitting at the same table as Lex and me.

Three hard swallows and a swipe of my thumbs across my cheeks, I finally looked at him. His eyes searched mine, gentle and tender and oh so filled with love. They truly were. They were just filled with love.

But I wasn't sure if it was because of Lexi or if it was because of me...

"Both," he whispered.

I tilted my head to the side in confusion.

"I love you, and I love Lexi. I love you both."

"What am I supposed to do with that, Wes? You told me you didn't want this, *us*. You told me you couldn't handle it."

"I was an idiot," he answered, not the least bit prideful. "You scared me, Win. You are so strong and so beautiful, and every day I was falling more in love with you. Every day, my feelings for you got stronger, deeper, more intense. Just one glimpse of your soft smile or to hear your rare, girlish giggle was enough to melt my heart. It all happened so fast. One day I'm content with everything in my life, and the next, there you are making it all seem like sh—crap."

He reached his hand out and caressed my cheek. "But I'm not scared anymore. I'm ready. I'm all in. I want you and I want Lex and I want us to be the family we shouldn't have ever stopped being. I want to continue falling more in love with you every day. I need you, Winnie. I need you and I love you and I will do whatever it takes to win you back."

I couldn't help but grin at his choice of words. "*Win* me back?"

"I'm really hoping this is going to end up a Win-Win kind of scenario, sweetheart." He grinned. "I'm hoping you'll forgive me, and I'm hoping you'll let me love you for always. I never want to go a day without you."

My heart couldn't deny that everything he was saying was truth. He was pouring his heart and soul out for me, and I knew with every fiber of my being that this was Wes.

He was handing me his heart. He was giving me *everything*.

"I love you, too, Wes," I whispered, choked up on the sheer volume of how much I meant those words. It was an all-consuming kind of love, an I can't go back from this kind of love.

He pressed a soft kiss to my lips. "Enough to let me be your boyfriend again?"

I giggled and nodded.

"Enough to let me propose to you some day in the very near future?"

I nodded again.

"Enough to let me be your husband?"

My breath got caught in my lungs, but I still managed to nod while my heart was literally staring back at him through my eyes.

"Enough to let me call Melinda to watch Lexi so we can have a little time to ourselves?"

I raised an eyebrow. "A *little* time?"

"A lot of time?" he asked with a sexy smirk.

"How about all night?" I countered.

"All. Night. Long?"

I kissed him softly and whispered against his lips, "You bet your sweet ass you're going to be Lionel Richie-ing me all night long."

He chuckled. "God, I love you, Win."

"Save it for tonight," I whispered and stood up from my seat. "All right, Lexi Lou, we need to leave here in two minutes."

She crinkled her icing-covered nose. "Where, Mommy?"

"You get to hang out with Melinda today."

"Yay!" she squealed and hopped up from her seat a lot quicker than I expected. "Let's go now!" She yanked her little coat off the chair and had it on faster than I could've said, *Okay.* And her little legs were already heading in the direction of the door.

Wes stood directly behind me and held my jacket open so I could easily slip my arms inside. The second I was bundled up in my black pea coat, he wrapped his arms around my waist and pulled my back tight to his chest. *"All night long…"* he started to quietly sing the chorus into my ear. *"All night long…"* He punctuated that statement by softly kissing the sensitive spot behind my ear, before patting my ass and ushering me out the door.

Bossy bastard.

Goddammit, I love him.

EPILOGUE

Wes

"Oh, Jesus," I exclaimed as I rounded the corner from the elevators at Atlantis Resort on Paradise Island, Bahamas and came face-to-nipple with Cassie's obnoxiously large breast. Coral coloring coated the walls, accents of sea life abounding—I knew from the hours we'd already spent here—but right then, I couldn't see any of it.

Thatch hovered over Cassie's shoulder, looking on as his son Ace got ready to feed, but at my shout, his head jerked up and, when he saw the direction of my gaze, his eyes got bubbly with rage. I knew my own had to look nearly schizophrenic.

"Breastfeeding shaming, bro? Not cool."

"What?" I panicked. "No!" I looked to my side to try to enlist Winnie—clad in nothing more than a bikini, cover-up, and my avid affection—in my defense, but she was too busy trying not to choke on her chortle.

Traitor.

"I figured, with you basically being a father and all, this is the kind of thing you'd understand."

I shook my head with a little laugh. "Lexi's six." How was she relevant to my understanding of breastfeeding?

"Did I ask for her age?" Thatch threatened at a near shout. I held up both hands in a peacemaking gesture.

"I'm not shaming anything," I tried to explain. "Breastfeeding is beautiful."

Winnie squeaked, and I flashed hard eyes in her turncoat direction before looking back to a still brooding Thatch.

"I'm just offended by your wife's breasts."

Not good, Wes. Not good.

"Oh shit, baby!" Winnie snapped under her breath. "Are you *trying* to get killed?"

"Excuse me!" Cassie snapped. Thatch stood up abruptly off the wall, all casual anger gone, and I retreated a few steps while attempting to do the same with my words.

"No, no, no! She's got a great rack. Seriously. *Especially* since the baby."

Winnie grabbed me by the forearm and pulled my attention to her. "Should I step away? Dig that hole any goddamn bigger, and I'm going to fall inside!"

With a scoop of my arm, my instincts engaged, I pulled Winnie behind me as a form of protection. "There's nothing wrong with her breastfeeding!" I finally got out. "I'm just saying, for me, as one of your best friends, it feels a little incestuous to get a good view of your wife's..." I nodded in the direction of the evil, tongue-tying, baby-feeders and finished, "That's all."

Winnie gave me a condescending pat on the back just as Thatch's happy face returned.

"Oh. Well, why didn't you just say so?" he asked, and Winnie dissolved into all-out hysteria behind me.

Christ. I'd just woken up, and I already needed a nap. And this was supposed to feel like a *vacation*. A working vacation, anyway.

We'd just turned to leave Thatch and Cassie before I could swallow my foot any goddamn deeper when it hit me.

I turned back so quickly, Winnie tripped as I threw her off balance. "All right," she complained. "Is the whole trip going to be like this?"

I smiled and shook my head before kissing her cheek in apology. "I'm sorry."

She smiled so big, I nearly fell in love all over again. Of course, when I get lost in it, forgetting all about everything else I wanted to say to any other stupid people on the planet, it grew. "Wes," she called in an attempt to break me from my lovesick trance.

Oh. Right.

I turned back toward the place where Thatch and Cassie were... only they were gone.

"What the fuck?" I asked as Winnie started to laugh.

"I didn't imagine that, right?" I asked, afraid hallucinations had set in.

"Nope. They're here. Or they were."

"What are they doing here?" I asked. She shrugged one bare shoulder.

"Crashing the trip?"

"Ah, Christ."

"Hey, guys!" Georgia shouted with a wave as she and Kline stepped off of the elevator.

"Ah, double Christ," I amended, and Winnie laughed again, remarking, "You're funnier than you used to be."

I bobbed my head side to side and mock laughed as she practically skipped over to our friends and pulled Georgia into a hug. For the first time maybe ever, it seemed like Winnie Winslow was completely happy—and I'd had a part in that.

God, it feels good.

I walked toward the group more slowly, but smiling all the same. Kline reached out and took my hand and then slapped my back in one of those manly hugs.

"Did you guys know that Thatch and Cassie are here?" I asked.

"Here?" Kline questioned for confirmation. "At Atlantis?"

I laughed at the look on his face and sank my hands into my pockets. "I'll take that as a no."

"Casshead's here?" Georgia squealed. "Does she have the baby?"

Winnie started laughing so hard that it came out silent. When she finally got herself together, it was she who answered. "Oh, yeah. She's got the baby. Right, Wes?"

I narrowed my eyes in a death stare.

"What am I missing here?" Kline asked, and I waved him off.

"Absolutely nothing," I said at the same time that Winnie spoke, side eyes on me. "I'll tell you all about it later."

Georgia laughed and shoved her way under Kline's in-no-way-resistant arm. "What are you guys up to? We were just about to go eat a little something and then go on some water slides. Where's Lexi? Does she want to come with us?"

"Take a breath, Georgie," I teased.

"She's with Quinn Bailey."

"I'm sorry...what?" Kline asked with a laugh. "Your six-year-old daughter is hanging out with the quarterback of a professional football team?"

Winnie laughed. "Yeah. They actually get along really well. They're on the lazy river with some of the other guys."

"This *work trip* reeks of bogus reasoning," I said to Georgia as I skewered her with suspicious eyes.

She blushed a little but mostly held strong. "I don't know what you're talking about."

"The whole team is on the lazy river!" I said with a laugh.

She swatted a hand through the air. "Don't worry. All the press and photo ops for our joint charity venture with the Miss Teen USA pageant start tomorrow morning."

"It's Miss *Teen* USA?" I shouted.

Georgia tried to look innocent and failed spectacularly. "I told you that."

I was shaking my head before she even stopped speaking. "No, no you didn't." The space between my eyes felt like it might explode. "This is a publicity nightmare."

Then I thought of one of the guys getting a little too comfortable with one of the contestants and nearly had an aneurysm. "This is a nightmare's nightmare."

"Wes," Winnie said in an effort to calm me down. I softened my face before turning to her. "I'm okay."

"I want a team meeting tonight," I told Georgia, and my voice was serious enough, she nodded.

Kline just smiled, the bastard, before wrapping his arm around his wife's waist and pulling her away. "Not to worry, Wes," Georgia called through a giggle as they got farther away.

Not to worry. Yeah, right.

Winnie sighed. "I guess we're not going to eat now, huh?"

Oh, I was going to eat all right.

I jerked a rough finger to the elevator, and her smile came back.

"In need of tension relief?" she asked hopefully, and just like that, all the anger receded. Still, I played the part since she liked it so much.

"Get in the elevator, Win."

The doors pinged just in time. She backed her way in, my hands on her hips, until her back hit the wall and my body hit hers.

"You ready, Lancaster?" she asked teasingly. I smiled and dipped my lips to her ear.

"Always, Winnie Winslow. Always. And do you know why?"

She smiled; I could feel her cheek pull up against mine and her breath hitch right in her throat. "You love me."

"More than your perfect beating heart will ever know."

Winnie

As the elevator doors shut, Wes's eyes changed from playful to predatory. My nipples hardened in anticipation as his thick arms caged me in. We were the only ones in the car, and my ragged breathing sounded damn near obscene in the small space.

He nuzzled his face into my neck, and with the very tip of his tongue, licked a warm path to my ear. "Something has been on my mind all day," he whispered into my ear.

"What?"

I could feel his smile against my skin. "Wicked hotel sex with a woman named Winnie," he answered.

Our name is Winnie! my vagina shouted in excitement.

"Do you want to hear about it?" His hands moved into my hair, caressing the strands and turning my neck to the side so he could suck softly at the base of my neck.

"Yes, please," I answered on a quiet moan.

"It starts with a room covered in white. Duvet, sheets, pillows, everything. *All white*," he said against my skin. "And Winnie is naked, in the center of the big, white bed, on all fours. Waiting. Like a trophy. Prey. Like a pleasure-filled nude. Her skin looks so much darker against everything around her, and the skin between her thighs is already slick with arousal."

Holy fucking shit...

"I take off my clothes slowly, meticulously, with my eyes locked on Winnie, her back arching to stop herself from coming before we even get started," he described with his lips to my ear. "And she's not the only one fighting it off. The sight of her perfect tits bouncing below her with each breath is almost more than I can take."

His hands slid down my arms and then back up again, encouraging goose bumps to pepper my skin. I couldn't fight my moan, and my head fell back against the wall of the elevator. At least, I thought we were in an elevator, but hell, who knew at that point. I couldn't think past anything besides Wes's sexy-as-fuck words and the incessant throbbing between my legs.

"When the anticipation is finally too much, I walk to the bed, to Winnie, taking my time, like a predator savoring his already lost prey. Torturing the little creature by smelling it hungrily and licking its skin. Every fucking inch of her perfect, delicious skin. Dipping my head between her legs, I don't even make an effort to hide that I'm smelling Winnie's perfect cunt."

God. Who knew the whole prey-predator thing was this hot? Who cared if it ended with a praying mantis move. Actually, it's the females who eat the male's head, right? So at least I'm safe.

My hands found their way to his T-shirt, gripping it tightly in a desperate attempt to find some sort of balance. I feared I might melt into a million tiny puddles at his feet.

"I suck her hanging tits, rubbing each nipple with the tip of my tongue until she can't take it anymore, so lost in the numbing sensation that she needs the bite of my teeth. God," he groaned. "We both feel out of control. And we'll stay that way as I whisper into her ear and lean over her from the back, with my hard cock pressed against her cunt.

"Maybe, she doesn't even get my hard cock inside of her. Maybe, I spoil her rotten, and eat her sweet little pussy for hours. The whole time, though, Winnie has no idea what she's in for."

Can you get high from words alone? Because I think I'm high.

High as a motherfucking kite…

The elevator dinged our arrival to the twentieth floor where our suite was located, but at that moment, I wasn't sure if I even knew my name. I just really fucking hoped it was Winnie.

Wes grabbed my hand and led me out of the elevator and down the hall, until we were standing in front of the teal grand entrance. This place cost a fucking lick, but the Billionaire was footing the bill.

Yeah, some things about the money are nice.

He slid the room key into the slot, and our entry was granted with a flash of green. His hand never left mine as he moved through the pristine suite, dragging my willing body toward the master bedroom.

The second we walked inside, I knew everything was about to change.

The golden duvet and matching mahogany pillows were gone.

And in their place, white.

All white.

Everywhere *white*.

"Take off your clothes, Winnie," he demanded. "And get on the bed, on your hands and knees."

I didn't have to think twice, removing my simple sundress, bra, panties, and sandals with the precision of a professional clothes remover. Not that that was an actual job, but I knew if it were, I'd be hired on the spot.

I crawled onto the bed on my hands and knees until I was in the center of the big, white bed, on all fours, with my eyes facing the wall and Wes at my back.

"Beautiful," he whispered and ran a finger down my spine. "So fucking beautiful."

I could hear him removing his clothes, at the exact pace he had described, not rushing, not taking his time, but simply removing with confidence and precision.

The sounds of his shoes slipping off and his boxers softly hitting the carpeted floor only increased the delicious torture, and my spine curved of its own accord, pushing my ass and pussy toward him for some relief.

And then he was on the bed behind me, naked chest pressed to my back. My body trembled in response as I felt his thick, hard cock sliding through my arousal.

"Yes, baby," he whispered into my ear. "Already so wet for me."

"Please, Wes," I begged. "Please, I need to feel you."

He pushed the tip of himself inside of me and then just as quickly pulled back out. I whimpered, and my back arched from the delicious torture.

"Fuuuuuuuuuuck," I whispered, delirious with my need for him. "Please. Please. Please. I need to feel you."

"You beg so prettily, sweetheart." His hand reached forward and pulled my chin back toward him. He licked across my bottom lip and then sucked it into his mouth at the exact same time he pushed himself deep.

My responding guttural moan echoed inside the spacious room.

"Consider this just a taste of what's to come, sweetheart," he whispered against my mouth. "Me and you are going to clock a lot of miles on this bed this week, and you can bet that later tonight, I'm going to feast on that perfect cunt for hours, Win."

I was lost after that.

And he didn't hold back, driving into me with smooth and steady strokes until I felt myself falling into the abyss of my climax.

"Yes," he encouraged, and his hands gripped my breasts, his thumbs sliding across my pebbled nipples. "Let me feel that perfect pussy come all over my cock."

And I did. Just like that. With me on all fours and Wes at my back, the memory of both the actual encounter and the perfect teasing way Wes had painted it preemptively, he thrust inside of me with hard and deep and fast strokes that gave me no choice but to come on a scream that most likely let half the resort know what was happening inside our room.

Holy hell, I have the best life. The best *fucking life. Literally and figuratively.*

About an hour after part one of wicked hotel sex with Wes had come to a close, I was sitting inside a spacious conference room, surrounded by the staff and players of the Mavericks. Wes stood at the front of the room, eyes serious and mouth set in a firm line.

God, he looked so sexy. I knew we were there to discuss important matters—and hopefully, to prevent a publicity nightmare—but I couldn't stop thinking about that white bed. And me on the white bed. And me and Wes on the white bed. And the fact that there would be more of me and Wes on the white bed.

God, if I keep blushing like this, everyone will know what's on my mind. And with these characters, it's bound to turn into a fucking curtain call where Wes and I are forced into alternately bowing and accepting compliments on our performance.

I cleared my throat and tried to gain some perspective. Now was not the time for fantasies, no matter how amazing those fantasies were.

But were they really fantasies?

I mean, I knew they were going to become reality.

Hopefully, part two would begin right after Wes stressed to the group of burly football players dressed in board shorts and flip-flops, that no one would be "crowning" Miss Teen USA unless they wanted their balls FedExed Next Day Air back to their homes from Atlantis.

Yes, good job, Win. Focus on the team. The players.

Anything but the white bed…Goddammit…

"Does anyone have any questions about anything I just explained?" Wes asked the group, glancing around the room as if to dare one of them to ask or say something ridiculous.

I honestly hadn't heard a single word he'd said, too lost in my own pervy daydreams.

"I've got a question," Quinn Bailey announced.

Wes's eyebrows rose, and he nodded toward Quinn. "Yeah?"

"What's wrong with Dr. Double U?"

Within seconds, every person in the room had their eyes on me. I fought the urge to shield my face or crawl under the table. Which was an extremely odd reaction coming from me. I mean, I was generally always composed and could handle anything.

But this was a bed of a different color. *White*, my vagina clarified helpfully.

"Yeah, what's wrong with Dr. Double U?" Sean Phillips chimed in.

"Nothing," I snapped, probably a tad too defensively.

"You look really red right now. Are you sick? Are you not using enough sunscreen?" Bailey continued to harp on my appearance.

I looked toward the front of the room, and my eyes pleaded for Wes to save me from the inquisition. But he just smirked, the devious bastard, and chose only to add fuel to the fire. "Are you okay, Dr. Winslow?"

"I said, I'm fine," I answered through gritted teeth.

"Bailey is right. You're looking a little red? Maybe flushed? Are you running a fever?"

"Nope."

Wes tilted his head to the side, his face smeared with smug. "Are you sure?"

"Yep," I answered and scratched the side of my face with my middle finger.

"OMG," Bailey said in his Southern drawl as he glanced between Wes and me. "How the fuck did I miss that?"

"How the fuck do you get any women saying shit like OMG?" someone in the front row muttered and earned a few laughs.

"Miss what?" Phillips asked, and that led to several other players chiming in with their questions.

All the while, Wes stood at the front of the room, confident and cocky, smiling bigger than the sun, and just being the bossy, sweet bastard I was in love with.

Goddamn him.

Bailey flashed a knowing smirk in my direction, and I chose to act like a child and flip him off too. He just laughed in response. "Well, hot damn. Orgasms look good on Dr. Double U."

I abruptly stood from my seat at those words. "All right, fuck all of you. I'm leaving. Keep your dicks in your pants, and we should all be good to go. If I find out one of you even laid a finger on any chick with a sash and a tiara, I will immediately have to put you on the injured list after I injure you myself."

"I thought they were penises, Doc?" Mitchell asked mock-seriously. "Does this mean you're ready to see them socially."

I skewered him with a glower as all the other sarcastic remarks started to roll in. Mostly, though, at least verbally, I ignored them, too focused on getting the hell out of the room before my horny started to spread like a disease. The last thing Atlantis needed was a team full of horned-up professional football players when teenage pageant queens were striding around in their bikinis.

Unfortunately, the only exit from the room was in the front, which meant I had to pass Wes on my way out. I did my best hair flip and strode on my heels toward the door, but Wes had other plans, grabbing me by the waist as I passed him and pulling me into his arms.

And just like that, in a room full of professional athletes who were actually my patients, Wes dipped me back and kissed me soundly on the mouth.

"I agree with Bailey, you know," he whispered against my lips. "Orgasms look good on you."

I ignored the obnoxious wolf whistles in the room and stared back at my perfect match with a smile on my lips. "Big white bed in twenty minutes?" I asked.

His mouth stretched into an amused grin, and he whispered into my ear, "If you promise to be naked and stretched out waiting for me, I don't give a good goddamn what color the bed is."

"Consider it a deal, Lancaster," I said and silently thanked the universe that Melinda was able to make this trip and keep Lexi occupied with snorkeling this afternoon.

He steadied me on my feet and turned me toward the door. His hand looked ready to pat my ass with a quiet tap, but in the end, he thought better of it. The kiss in front of all the players had been mostly romantic. A smack on the ass bordered on demeaning. Instead, he settled for words and a look so goddamn hot, I started to sweat. "Get that little ass upstairs, Fred, and get ready."

Get ready? Hell, I had been ready.

And more than that, I'd always be ready for anything Wes had to give.

Like I said, I had the best fucking life.

THE END

Love Kline, Thatch, Wes & the Girls?

Stay up to date with them and us by signing up for our newsletter:
www.authormaxmonroe.com/#!contact/c1kcz

You may live to regret much, but we promise it won't be this.
Seriously. We'll make it fun.
If you're already signed up, consider sending us a message to tell us how much you love us. We really like that. ;)

And you really don't want to miss what's next for the
Billionaire Bad Boys.
Say goodbye to the gang in the final novella in the series,
Scoring Her, on November 29th, 2016.

Don't cry, Bad Girls, don't cry.
We say it's the end, and in the traditional sense it is, but we have all sorts of big plans for the future, and you'll be seeing lots of appearances by your favorite Billionaire Bad Boy characters.

Are you kidding? We'll never be able to get rid of Thatch.

Preorder the end of the Billionaire Bad Boys Series here:
www.authormaxmonroe.com/#!books/cnec

CONTACT INFORMATION

Follow us online:

Website: www.authormaxmonroe.com

Facebook: www.facebook.com/authormaxmonroe

Reader Group:www.facebook.com/groups/1561640154166388

Twitter: www.twitter.com/authormaxmonroe

Instagram: www.instagram.com/authormaxmonroe

Goodreads: https://goo.gl/8VUIz2

ACKNOWLEDGEMENTS

First of all, THANK YOU for reading. That goes for anyone who's bought a copy, read an ARC, helped us beta, edited, or found time in their busy schedule just to make sure we didn't completely fuck everything up by missing our deadline. Thank you for supporting us, for talking about our books, and for just being so unbelievably loving and supportive of our characters. You've made this our MOST favorite adventure thus far.

THANK YOU to each other. We're best friends…blah blah blah…you know the drill. Monroe thanks Max. Max thanks Monroe. We do this every book, but it's just our style. We wouldn't trade each other for anything. Writing together is the most fun we've ever had and it feels impossible to go back to the days before we started this journey. So, if it's okay with you guys, we'll just keep on making you laugh via Max Monroe style books. Also, we're thankful that when we lost our souls to serious sleep deprivation and hysteria, we had a comrade in arms, getting the life sucked out of them right along beside us. #bestielove #miserylovescompany #butreallythisisthebest

THANK YOU, our fair Lisa. Don't ever leave us. We love you too much. Good God, we don't know what we ever did to deserve you. Though, we are pretty sure it was more likely a deal with the devil rather than a reward for good behavior from the man upstairs. Will we see any of you down there?

THANK YOU, Kristin and Murphy. Thank you never feels like enough. We don't know what we'd do without you guys. Also, maybe knowing Murphy's angel baby will redeem us for our previously mentioned deal with hell's landlord.

THANK YOU, Amy, for being you. You never fail to be the one person who can always get things done. There is no doubt about it, you are the perfect agent for us. Let's keep doing this. Sound good? ☺

THANK YOU, Sommer, for never giving up on us even though we send you ten emails in the same day asking for exactly one thousand things. You make us laugh. You make us smile. And you've made our Billionaire Bad Boys look so damn good. And here. Here's Wes. You can stop crying now! ;)

THANK YOU to every blogger who has read, reviewed, posted, shared, and supported us. Your enthusiasm, support, and hard work does not go unnoticed. We wish we could send you your very own Billionaire Bad Boy as thanks. We can't. We checked with UPS and they said no. Also, there's no way in hell we could find a box big enough to fit Thatch in. Plus, we'd have to pay extra to keep Wes in climate control, the whiny fucker, and we're not into spending that much money.

THANK YOU to the ladies of Camp Love Yourself for not sending us pictures of you literally loving yourself. Well, not too many anyway. ;) And thanks for being beautiful, amazing, and hilarious enough to let us get away with saying things like you're sending us pictures of yourselves when you're not. You're the cat's meow. Well, every cat but Walter. He doesn't really meow unless your name is Georgia.

THANK YOU to the people who love us. Thank you for all of your patience and understanding and unwavering support. We couldn't do any of this without you. You make life grand and we love you so much.

P.S. We're still going to the Bahamas for the entire month of January. We figured you wouldn't mind at all. You probably won't even notice we're gone.

P.P.S. Kidding!

P.P.P.S. Maybe we're not kidding.

All our love,
Max & Monroe

Printed in Great Britain
by Amazon